CAJUN MOON

a novel

Dwaines Lawless

2nd Tier Publishing

This is a work of fiction. Names, characters, businesses, places, events and incidences are either the products of the author's imagination or used in a fictitious manner. Any resemblance to persons, living or dead is purely coincidental.

Published by:
    2nd Tier Publishing
    13501 Ranch Road 12, Ste 103
    Wimberley, TX 78676

ISBN 978-0-9862290-1-5

Cover design by Bob Cooksey
Book design by Dan Gauthier

For John, My Bienaimée

Acknowledgments

Anna Garza, Barbara Mott, Sandra Collins and Beth Finkle, colleagues and early readers of my first draft who fondly called themselves The Cajun Moon Club, thank you for your encouragement.

Caron Hanes, Lu Ann Howell, Sarah Jackson and Sue Moore, friends who signed a napkin and helped me keep my promise to finish this book, thank you for your faith in me.

Beth Long, Leta Moser, and Jan Steinhour, fellow writers in the WCDW Society who have read, edited and honestly given me their thoughts, feelings and ideas, thank you for your patience.

Lynda Curnyn, my teacher who gave me the confidence I needed to keep writing, thank you for your guiding light.

Dr. Jerry Casebolt and his incredible wife, Pam, mentors through these many years, thank you for keeping the creative fires burning.

Susie Radcliffe, my wise and eagle-eyed editor, who painstakingly and patiently walked me through the necessary changes and became a dear friend in the process, thank you for your wisdom.

Shiila Safer and Dan Gauthier, owners of 2nd Tier Publishing who have mid-wifed me through this long-awaited birth, thank you for taking such good care of me and my baby.

Bob Cooksey, cover artist who has captured the essence of *Cajun Moon* with his artistic hand, thank you for your masterful creativity.

Anne Frugé, PhD candidate, University of Maryland, who shared her wealth of knowledge about The Saint Suaire, thank you for your precious gift.

My brother, Retired Special Agent, Jimmy Thomas (Homeland Security Investigations) who helped me understand Louisiana law, thank you for your criminal justice knowledge.

My mother and Cajun language consultant, Jean Regan Thomas, who lovingly answered ALL my questions and shared her wonderful childhood memories, thank you for the gift of your life.

And of course to my husband, John, who believed in me even when I wanted to quit, thank you for your love.

CHAPTER 1

"The dream always begins the same way, Father Mauvais; a child's voice, a sweet little whisper, singing a song, calling me." Celine stopped. It had taken her weeks to work up just enough courage to confess this. She took a deep breath and kept going. "The voice is there every night as soon as I fall asleep. I can't resist it. So I run after it, I'd be a fool not to! The game is so much fun, like hide-and-seek; running around in the dark, trying to find the little ghost that's calling me. She giggles and plays with me, even taps my shoulder, but I never see her. She's always just out of my reach."

For months Celine tried to pretend that it wasn't so bad. No one knew; no one at work, not any of her friends, certainly not her family. In the end, the secrecy had eaten a hole into what little sanity she had left. Her last shred of hope was right here and right now, in the black box with her parish priest.

"The little ghost teases me like that for a long time but I can't keep up with her. I beg her to stop and let me rest, but she runs ahead. Her laughter just fades away into the darkness. I stand there, waiting in that eternal black, listening, hoping for my little friend to come back. I call out to her. Silence. Then I hear something else, a deep, guttural hissing right behind me. I'm so scared that I can't move. Everything in my gut tells me to get away from it but the hissing isn't just behind me anymore, it's all around me. I can feel hot breath on my neck. I try to run and that's when the attack happens.

"This thing grabs me from behind, pins me down and plunges its teeth into my back. Oh God, it hurts! I try to fight it off but every time I do, it digs in deeper. I want to cry out but I can't. I try to move, I can't do it. I try to turn on my side, to throw off this creature, but I can't! I don't know what has me but whatever it is, I know it's evil, Father, pure evil." Celine stopped, not sure if she could go on.

"Is that all, my child?" He hesitated.

She looked at her tightly folded hands and balanced the weight on her knees. "No, Father. There's more…" She looked up. "…a lot more."

The priest shifted in his seat. "Then let's continue."

"It's all so real, Father, everything about it. Even now, I can still smell it." A cold chill ran through her. She stopped to steady herself. "The beast, this predator, it's so strong that it just breaks through my bones and rips through everything, biting and gorging itself on every part of me. I try to stop it but I'm so weak that I have nothing left in me to fight it off. The pain is forever. But then, I don't know why, it just stops.

"It flips me over like a rag doll and I come face to face with this…" Celine took a deep breath and closed her eyes. Her voice was barely a whisper. "It's…" She stumbled with the words. "…not a man. I can see veins through its yellow, oozing flesh. The face is a hideous skull, no eyes just black sockets. It's got protruding dagger-like teeth, no lips and a huge gaping mouth. But it's the arms, they're not arms, they're sharp bony wings of rotting, stinking skin and it uses them to pin me down while it…" She swallowed hard. "For a long time it just stares at me. I know it's studying me, torturing me with its endless waiting. I know this is the end. I'm actually hoping that it'll finish me off but then it whispers in my ear, 'Wanna play another game?'

"I try with everything left in me to fight it off but it's already clawing at my neck and choking me. I can feel its teeth goring into my skin and the blood is draining away. I'm fainting, but I can hear it laughing. Then it forces my legs open… and the pain, it's so deep…it…it…"

"Rapes you?" Celine winced at the word. The priest's steady voice broke the dream's grip and brought Celine back.

Out of breath, she lowered her head, ashamed. "Yes, Father." There was a long pause. Celine was panting, trying to calm herself, tears streaming down her face. "Father, every night, it rapes me and all the while, that monster hums; it's the same song, the one the child was singing…" She waited for some response from the other side. She looked up. The priest was motionless. The only sign of life was the white collar pulsing back and forth as he breathed. "…and I'm not the only one, Father." She choked back the sobs. "There's a man there and it rapes him, too. It's the most hideous thing I've ever seen, Father, and I know I..."

"Shh, shh now my child. Remember, it's only a dream." The priest cleared his throat and said gently, "You must remember that none of this really happened. I see no sin here. I see how you might feel guilt for having this dream. You've done nothing wrong, but it's possible that this thing has you possessed somehow. Maybe a good old fashioned exorcism is what you need. I know someone who does them. He invites me to all of his little dark gatherings. It's not really my thing, but he could..."

"Oh no, Father Mauvais, please! I don't think I could tell anyone else. I've known you all my life and besides, it gets worse, and that's where I think I..." she whispered "...that's where I KNOW I need your help. You see, I'm sure I could've stopped it. I think this animal thing knew that I wasn't going to fight back. The whole time it was savaging this poor, poor man, I hid in the shadows, like a coward, scared for myself.

"He begged me for help but I just cowered in the corner, covering my ears. The pure terror of what was happening forced a scream from somewhere deep inside my gut and scraped my throat raw. But no matter how loud I screamed, I could still hear his pitiable cries, calling my name. But that sadistic monster tortured him even more, laughing the whole time, singing! When that broken man was finally dead, that thing turned to me and said that I had made him do it; that I killed him."

"But you didn't kill him." The priest's voice was comforting. "The beast in your dream did. Not you."

She sighed. "But Father, isn't a dream a reflection of what's really going on inside my soul? Why didn't I do something? What kind of person watches such a brutal murder and does nothing to stop it, even if it is just a dream? And I keep having it over and over, every night. It's gotten to where I'm afraid to even close my eyes anymore."

"...Every night?"

"Yes, Father."

"Well, there's no doubt that your conscience is being tortured by something." The priest's calm voice wafted through the screen. "So, how do you think you could have stopped any part of this? You were asleep. We have no control over dreams, Celine, they just happen."

Her voice was trembling. "I don't know how, but it seems like I could've. I know I should've at least tried." Tears dripped onto her hands. "It took a bite out of his heart, Father, and then offered it to me. I even thought about eating it just to save myself."

"Did you?"

"Did I what?"

"Did you eat it?"

"No, I..."

"...and why not?"

"Why not? I was scared; scared that if I joined in its wicked feast I would belong to that thing and then become completely evil!" Tears burned her eyes as she sobbed. The faint rustling of the priest's robe was the only sound coming from behind the wooden lattice grate.

"Is that the end of the dream?"

Beads of sweat trickled down her back. "No Father. Just one more part." Celine closed her eyes. "When I didn't eat the heart, the beast started screeching at me that he would be back, that he would be back every night until I ate with it! And then he disappeared. After I was sure that hideous thing was gone, I crept out and sat next to the dead man. He had a huge jagged hole in his chest and his neck had been ripped open. There was blood everywhere, on him, on me.

"But there was something about his face; there was a kindness about it. That beautiful, beautiful man didn't deserve any of the torture and it was completely my fault! I don't know how long I sat there, staring at him, but then he moved. His eyelids twitched and he took a short breath. I couldn't believe that he was still alive, so I..."

She glanced up and saw the priest pulling off his collar and unbuttoning the top of his robe. "... I held him and rocked him. I was looking at him closely, trying to remember where I'd seen him before and then he opened his eyes..."

She squinted, straining to see what the priest was doing. "I couldn't believe that he was still alive. He was breathing and I was so happy. I started to remember him; we'd been together somewhere before but my memory of him was so vague that I..."

The priest stood up. His purple sash fell to the floor.

"Father, Father? Oh my God! You're not Father Mauvais ..."

"Yes, Celine?" A low growling voice came through the screen. "Yes, Celine? What do you want, Celine?"

Celine jerked herself up, crashing into the back of the confessional. She smelled the beast's decaying flesh and heard the slow, stalking laughter again. She cowered back, trying to hide inside the darkness of the confessional closet.

Clawed hands splintered the screen and in one swift thrust, grabbed her throat. The beast's hot breath spit into her face as it pinned her up against the wall. "Welcome back, Celine." Its voice, like hot metal, scorched into her, laughing. "Dreaming again, I see. Want to wake up? Oh, what a pity. You know I can't let you do that." It snarled into her ear as it ripped its way into her, tearing her flesh, ravaging her core, humming.

"And what's all this about needing forgiveness, hmm? Silly girl, of course you murdered him. You watched and you enjoyed it! I saw you! And here's a little secret. He saw you, too!" Hot tears burned her face as the specter pounded into her, scorching its brand deep.

"Did you think a visit to the black booth would clean you? Not so easy! Forget the Hail Mary's and Our Fathers." A punishing whip of pain snapped inside her, its burning tip brought fresh agony. "Forget him. Forget everything. Just give me what I want. I know you want me." The monster cackled. "Don't worry. I'll forgive you when I'm done."

CHAPTER 2

Celine sucked for breath as she burst out of the dream. A violent fit of coughing seized her as she lurched forward. Panic crushed her. She could still feel the monster's claws around her throat. Terrified, she jerked her head back. The sudden snap of her neck sent a searing burn straight into her gut. She clutched her stomach; the pain was unbearable. A gush of hot, black blood oozed between her legs and down her thighs. The putrid stench of the monster was all over her.

Her gut wrenched and she leapt for a trash can nearby. She heaved over and over again. The memory of the hideous beast pounding into her brought a tidal wave of nausea. Every inch of her body broke into a cold sweat as she vomited until she was finally empty, body and soul.

She had nothing left. She curled up on the cool floor, exhausted. Celine's tears made a small pool on the cold tile. *Will it ever stop? God, please make it stop! I don't understand any of it. A priest? Confession? In the dream I know him but I don't ever remember a Father Mauvais! And why does it always end with...* She stopped herself. This was all part of the mad cycle when she woke up; questioning what happened over and over, struggling, trying to remember where she was. A soft rain pattered a calm soothing sound. For a while she thought she heard children laughing but soon there was only silence.

Celine sat up slowly, searching through blurry eyes, hoping to find anything that looked familiar. A sharp cutting pain sliced through her head, making everything around her look chopped and surreal. Her throat felt like sandpaper. Her chest burned with every breath. She looked down at her shaking hands, trying not to think.

And then she remembered the dying man from her dream; holding him in her arms, his beautiful, sad face. Her hands could still feel the softness of his thick, night-black hair. His smooth dark eyebrows carving deep arches into his creamy white porcelain face, an angel's face. But it was his eyes, steel blue-gray, like liquid mercury that burned into her mind.

Her fingertips tingled with the stubbled brush of his lightly-bearded cheek. His long, muscled legs and his strong graceful hands gave her a strange comfort. The hands. What was it about his hands that she remembered? Gentle hands pulling her to him, a hug and a vague, distant memory of a kiss, but no, not in the dream, but when, where? The chill inside her was melting and her breath grew even again. The pain was leaving, but with each softer breath, he was leaving, too. She could feel the tears welling up and all she could think was, *Please, don't go!* But he was gone and the emptiness left her feeling used, like crumpled paper.

Slowly, she looked around. She was surrounded in a gray hazy light, except for a sliver of white peeking through the drapes in the room. The clock on the desk said 4:10 p.m. Pictures of unknown people were perched next to it, staring at her. Confusion gripped her as she struggled to put the puzzle together. Then she saw the nameplate, **Celine B. Dupré, MFA, M.Ed., Louisiana School for the Blind, Assistant Principal**. Her fragmented thoughts latched onto it like a drowning cat. *Oh God, I've got to get up. 4:10. Jesus, I'm probably the last one here.*

The air in the office was stifling. She pulled herself up and stood, leaning on the desk, waiting, testing her strength. Then a wave of dread washed over her. She looked down expecting to see her legs and skirt covered in blood. But there was nothing. She reached down slowly, her hands trembling as she touched the fabric. *Dry?* She looked in the trash can. *Empty?*

She fought back the tears angrily. *I've got to stop this. It's the dream again. Only the dream again, but...* She looked around. *How did I end up on the floor over here?* The last thing she remembered was lying down on the sofa, hoping that the splitting migraine she had would stop hammering her head. She gripped the edge of the desk. She shook her head in disbelief. *And now I can add sleepwalking to the list. It's getting worse. I have got to get out of here. Thank God for summer break.*

She forced herself to move in slow, short steps to the window behind her desk. She drew back the drapes and squinted as the glare of gray light exploded into the room. She looked out; pouring rain against dark clouds. She was only able to pry the window open just a slit, but that was enough to get a steady breeze on her face and cool her sweat-drenched body. She collapsed into the black, faux-leather chair, holding back tears and trying to think only of what she had to do next.

She opened her purse and pulled out a small hand mirror. Her face was flushed and swollen and the whites of her eyes were bloodshot, like she'd been on a drunken spree for days. She pressed her fingertips against her crimson cheek, then slowly across her feverish, rosebud lips. Her fingers dropped to her dimpled chin and traced an imaginary line back to her cheek. *Where's Miss Azalea Queen now? What had that judge said? Perfect example of a Cajun girl; porcelain skin, delicate nose, full raven-black hair. Yeah well, a lot has happened since those college days. If they could see me now.*

She tried to finger comb the tangles out of the damp strands of her shoulder length hair but just that small effort exhausted her. She took a deep breath and wiped the sweat from her forehead. It was unbearably hot. She took a closer look at her eyes; the light emerald green that her grandmother loved so much. There'd be no way that anyone could love them now. She looked like a hunted animal.

She put the mirror back in her purse and rummaged around looking for her pill box. Generalized Anxiety Disorder, that's what the doctor called it. At first he prescribed antidepressants but she flushed those down the toilet. All they did was make her sleepy and the last thing she wanted was more sleep!

She pulled out the tiny silver case and opened it; Xanax and Zipsor, the magic pills. That's all she needed, and just a few more minutes. The teachers had all surely left by now, but there might be a secretary or two. Probably the custodian was around. Yeah, the pills would help her hurdle any happy, smiling faces as she got to her car and off to a well-deserved summer vacation.

She placed the pills on her tongue and let them melt. She had gotten used to the bitter taste long ago and had become an expert at taking them without water. It was easier to hide taking pills during a school day if you could swallow them without the telltale water chaser; better that no one knew that she had to take them at all. She dropped the pillbox into her purse and let herself curve into the chair.

At first, she thought the sound was only the rain tapping against the window pane but when the tapping became a whisper, she gripped the chair and froze. The room grew quiet. The sound had gone. She took a deep, nervous breath. Just a few minutes more so the Xanax could take over and then she could...

"Celine?"

She jumped as she spun her chair around. A man's voice. *Oh God, didn't I lock the door to my office before I lay down?* She let out a rush of air when she realized who it was. "Dave! I didn't hear you come in!" Her fifty-something boss walked towards her, clutching a Coca-Cola in each hand and a flashlight under his arm. *What the hell? Why does he have a flashlight?* His forehead was beaded with sweat. His always perfect, slightly-graying hair was frizzled. Even his pristine, charcoal-colored, Perry Ellis suit couldn't hide how miserable he was.

Quickly she wiped her face, hoping that any traces of smudged mascara were erased. A trickle of sweat rolled down her back. She nervously ran her fingers through her hair once more as she scrambled awkwardly to stand. She reached for her suit jacket hanging on the back of her chair.

Dave's mood could shift without warning; easy-going, southern boy one minute, calculating politician the next. That made him nearly impossible to predict and Celine was always on edge around him. One thing was certain, he held everyone to a strict dress code and right now she was too sweaty and disheveled to fit his definition of professional.

She was pushing her arm into the sleeve when he gave her one of his dazzling charismatic smiles. "Hey, forget the coat. Electricity's gone out again and it's just too damn hot to worry about that. Besides, the kids are already gone; the teachers, too." Relieved that for now, he was one of the good old southern boys, she gave him as much of a smile as she could, draped her jacket on the back of the chair and sat back down. He put both cans on the desk, popped one can open and held it up for her. She took it from him, certain he'd seen her hands shaking. He frowned. "You feelin' okay?"

"Oh yeah," she lied. "I finished all the Braille packets for summer school but those end-of-the-year reports are so tedious. They gave me a little headache so I thought I'd come back to my office and rest for a few minutes." She looked away, pretending to organize some loose papers on her desk. *If he knew what was really going on...*

Dave looked out the window, pulled the flashlight out from under his arm and turned it off. He shook his head when thunder rumbled. "Man, when is this storm gonna let up?" He reached into his back pocket and wiped his face with an already damp handkerchief. "'Hope it's soon. At least you've got a little light in here from the window. The rest of the place is in pitch dark. Maybe someday they'll fix the wiring in this old dump, but then I guess they think the School for the Blind doesn't need lights? I mean what do blind kids need with light, right?"

He smiled at his own little joke as he stuffed the crumpled cloth into his back pocket. He pulled off his coat and plopped down into a nearby chair. He raised his can in the air. "To the end of another school year." He took a long swig from the Coke can and looked back at Celine. "Hey, drink up. I grabbed these outta the machine in the teacher's lounge. They're a little warm but who cares?"

Celine reached for the can, relieved that the lights were out. At least he wouldn't see her bloodshot eyes. The fizz of the Coke tasted cool, washing the last of the pill taste away. Even though her neck still felt very stiff and sore at least her throat was back to normal. She started to relax and managed a little smile as she looked back at Dave. "So, did everybody get off okay?"

He shifted in his seat, trying to find a cooler position. "Yeah, good thing they left when they did, though. The last bus left just as the lights started to flicker. A couple of the kids asked about you." He took off his red silk tie and tossed it to the sofa, but missed. It made a snaky crimson ess as it landed on the rug. "Leah wanted to tell you 'bye'."

Celine looked down, sad that she'd forgotten the promise of a good-bye hug to the little first grader. Her thoughts filled up with the child's happy little smile. "I'm sorry I missed her. She's one awesome kid."

Dave leaned forward in his chair. "She sure is, but I still don't get it. How does a blind child survive for six years in that rat hole of a house in the French Quarter with a meth-addict mother?" He shook his head and leaned back in his chair. He finished off his Coke and tossed the can across the room into the wastebasket. It landed with a hollow *thunk*. "Didn't you have to testify in Leah's removal hearing?"

Celine took a sip of her Coke. It seemed years since she'd been called by Orleans Parish for her 'expert testimony' on blind kids. *Was that really only seven months ago?* "Yeah, Child Protection called us in right away. The DA's office arrested the mom on child abuse and lots of drug charges; possession, intent to sell. She's still in jail. I think the case is still open though. Leah's adopted mom told me that they're still trying to break up that drug gang down there."

Dave's eyes grew wide. "Wow! Are they having any luck with that?"

Celine shook her head. "I don't know and I'd rather not know. Those people sound dangerous. You remember Leah when she first came, right?"

Dave nodded. "Yeah, poor kid. Pretty messed-up. Isn't she a shaken baby?"

"Shaken baby, crack-addicted from birth. What kinds of people do that to a child? I'm just glad she's responded to the art therapy so well. Her adopted mom and dad have made the biggest difference, though. Now she can at least have a fighting chance for a normal life."

Dave added, smiling, "...and she's the best thing that could've ever happened for us, too. All that newspaper coverage really helped us out."

Celine frowned. "Yeah, well, that was a big mistake. The Times Picayune should've never published that picture of her and me after the hearing. I mean, sure, it might've been great publicity for the school, but they completely forgot about student confidentiality laws. They could've totally blown it if they would've revealed her adoption family."

"Hey, but the article about you and the school was terrific. It totally shamed those tight-fisted jerks on the school board into increasing our funding. I've seen more increase in revenue over the last seven months than I have over the last seven years! Only one more committee review and they should approve my budget plan for next year. We just have to get through tonight and then..."Dave's voice rambled on. She could feel a dark cloud hovering. *What have I forgotten?*

"Tonight...?"

"Yeah, don't you remember? I'm presenting next year's budget proposal while you're meeting with..." Dave's voice trailed off.

She looked at her watch. How much time had passed? How long had she been out? Her heart raced as she leaned forward, grabbing her appointment book. She thumbed quickly to June 13: *A. Arnaud. 5:30. Good, about another hour.* She looked back at Dave still talking.

"…fill me in. What's wrong? You didn't double book yourself again, did you? Celine, you're gonna burn out for sure if you keep doing this."

"No, no…" she stuttered. "I-I just couldn't remember exactly what time I had to be there, but it's okay. I don't have to leave for a little while yet. What's his name again?"

Dave dried his sweaty palms on his pants leg. "Arnaud, Alexandre Arnaud. You'll like him." Dave shifted again in the chair.

She jotted the name down, wiping the fresh sheen of sweat from her face while Dave rambled on. "Yeah, after Alex saw all those articles and pictures of you and Leah in the paper, he called me and said he wanted to donate some of his big bucks to the school. It's pretty much a done deal. All you have to do is show up, talk art and convince him we really need a big check. You can do that, right?"

"Me?" She looked up quickly. "You know I'm no good at that kind of thing. That's your department. I thought I was just supposed to pick up his proposal for how he wants us to spend the money."

Dave gave her a placating smile. "Really, Celine, this'll be a no-brainer." His smile broadened. "Alex would much rather deal with you about his ideas. Hell, he even asked for you specifically. Anyway, this'll be good practice." He looked at her with a crooked little grin. "Don't worry; you'll make it home tonight. You and your mother will have plenty of time to get those last minute plans done for the wedding. When is it? Three weeks?" He stopped. From across the room she could see his grin melt into a quizzical frown. "Hey, just look at it this way; it's your last professional act under the name Dupré."

She shook her head and tried to shrug it off, but he'd opened an old wound. "No." She hesitated. "No, there's not going to be a wedding."

Dave's eyes softened. "Oh. I'm sorry, Celine. I didn't know." He glanced down at her hand obviously searching for the diamond ring that was no longer there.

She squirmed and managed a weak smile. "That's okay. I thought everyone knew by now. We broke it off right after Christmas. It's all turned out for the best, anyway. I don't know what I was thinking.

A fiancé, a wedding and writing a dissertation all at the same time don't mix."

Dave added. "Add a full time job to that? Besides, you're too young to get married anyway. How old are you? Twenty-eight?"

Celine gave out a short laugh. "An old maid by the Cajun standard. I should be celebrating a tenth anniversary by now and have at least three, maybe four kids, too."

Dave grunted. "Yeah well, you just get that Dr. in front of your name. There'll be plenty of time for the Mrs. later."

Celine could feel herself relaxing, relieved that the pills were finally kicking in. The sharp, brittle edge that had been cutting through her had finally eased up, but letting her defenses down with Dave could lead to too many probing questions. He was first and foremost a political animal with an eye for human weakness. And right now he had his focus aimed right at her. She knew it was time to change the subject.

She gave Dave a half smile and stood up. "I'm just glad this school year is finally over and I get to go home for summer break." She walked over to the window and tried to force it open a little wider. "And since my vacation won't start until after I meet with this…" She stumbled with the name, "…Alexandre Arnaud, right?" Dave nodded. Celine kept tugging as she continued to talk. "Then you better tell me everything I need to know. How do you know such rich people, anyway?"

"We met at Tulane. Alex, his twin brother, Robert, and I all pledged Sigma Nu our freshman year." Dave stood up to help her with the stubborn window. "They came from beaucoup money, so Robert and Alex never wanted for anything." Dave jerked hard as the window popped open.

Celine closed her eyes as the cool air rushed in. "So then Alex is just a rich man investing in art?" She stood there letting the breeze wash over her.

"No." Dave let out a little laugh. "No, Alex's an artist and always has been. He's sort of the family outcast. All the rest of the Arnauds are macho oilmen, but not Alex, he's gay."

Celine walked back to her desk and sat down. "Oh brother, their family get-togethers must be a riot."

Dave shook his head, chuckling. "Yeah, I bet they don't have too many of those. They don't want to have anything to do with him, especially now that he's so sick."

Celine looked at Dave. "Sick? What do you mean?"

"HIV. He was diagnosed way back in the early '90s but he was one of those rare few that got the good drugs. Lots of money helps. But just lately, he's gone downhill. Real weak. When I talked to him last night, his voice was so hoarse, I could barely understand him. He's convinced he doesn't have much longer, but I'm not sure if that's true or not."

Celine frowned. "I can't tell you how many artists I've known that have wasted away from AIDS. In the end, most of them lose it all; friends, family, and of course all their money. They die alone. It's so sad."

Dave shook his head. "Try not to feel too sorry for him. He's got tons of money and his nephew, Michael, is taking care of him, so he's not alone. He's lived on the edge his whole life. Truly, I don't think Alex regrets anything he's ever done, no matter how outrageous. He'd do it all again if he could." He stood up. "But enough of the gossip. When you're done meeting with Alex, shoot me a text, okay? Oh yeah, I think Matt's gonna be there tonight, too."

"Who's Matt? What have you gotten me into?" She started gathering her things and reached into her purse for her keys.

Dave smirked, "Oh, Dr. Matt Sonnier." He laughed, clutching his heart and acting surprised. "What? You haven't heard of the great Dr. Matthew Sonnier, Chief of Staff at LSU Medical Center? Believe me, he's no big deal, but he thinks he is. Another frat brother. He's weaseled his way into Alex's life, pretending to be his medical advisor." Dave made air quotations around medical advisor. "It's pretty obvious that he wants whatever part of the money he can get his hands on. Man, I'm glad I don't have to see that creep."

She glanced at her watch and scooted forward in her chair "...I really should get going. The bridge traffic's gonna be backed up, so..." A flash of lightning and a crash of thunder stopped her mid-sentence. She jumped up and stood frozen, waiting for the building to stop rumbling. Just then the lamp on her desk flickered once, then flickered again before fading.

Dave frowned. "Hey, what's that?" He walked closer to her.

She cocked her head, looking back at Dave. He wasn't looking at her face. She took a small step back. "What's what?"

He stepped closer, reaching out with his hand, pushing her hair back. The brush of his hand made her wince. "My God, Celine. What happened to your neck?"

She turned reaching quickly for the mirror in her purse. "What are you talking about?" She pulled her collar down and saw three deep-purplish-red claw marks scraping from her ear down into a black bruise at the base of her throat.

CHAPTER 3

The windshield wipers beat madly against the blinding rain as Celine inched her car slowly up the Mississippi River Bridge. She could see her exit just a few yards ahead and prayed for an opening in the endless line of cars. The driver behind her honked his horn angrily as she tapped her brake and maneuvered behind an eighteen wheeler. She felt safer with the big rig in front of her. It was like an iron wall against the whipping wind.

It wasn't until then that she realized how tightly she was gripping the steering wheel. Her knuckles had turned white. Her hands ached as she lifted each finger slowly and flexed the joints. The tension, like needles, crept up her arms. She sat back and tried to relax, but each breath only increased the pain in her shoulders.

For a moment the traffic stopped. She rubbed the back of her neck and a stinging pain made her wince. In an instant, it all came back; the frown on Dave's face when he saw the ugly purple gashes, his endless questions as she tried to hide her neck. She knew there was no way he believed any of her lame excuses; 'cut myself working in the yard…it's just a scratch really…' but she didn't give him a chance to ask any more as she rushed out the door.

She leaned over and turned the rearview mirror toward herself. Pulling her collar to the side she saw the deep, evenly spaced stripes, bruised and red. She reached up and gently touched the wounds. *Did I do this myself? Yes, I must've, but how?* She glanced at her fingernails, short, unpolished, hardly a dangerous threat. She drew a tired breath. So many questions but never any answers.

She glanced up at the traffic. Gridlocked at the top of the bridge.

Great! I am gonna' be so late. Celine looked at the car clock; 5:56. *Damnit! I was supposed to be meeting with this guy 30 minutes ago. Sup-*

per's out. I better call home. Just as Celine reached for her phone, it rang. She jumped. The caller ID registered 'Mama'. Her mother's timing was right on target as usual.

"Hi, Mama. I was just about to call you."

"Celine, chere'. Where you at? You Mo-maw and I, we been trying to call you all day. I tried your cell but it always went straight to voice mail."

"Sorry, Mama. My phone's been acting weird. Probably has something to do with this storm."

"What? Your voice is fading. I can't hear you. Talk louder."

Celine raised her voice looking out over the treacherous currents of the river. "Listen, I still have a couple of things to take care of and then I'll be on my way home. I can't be there for supper but I'll probably be there by about nine."

Luisah's voice faded. "Nine? …but….storm…bad. Don't come home now."

"Mama? What? Don't come home?"

Luisah's voice was interrupted by crackling static. "Mo-Maw said…"

The call cut off. Celine tried the speed dial but the digital screen glared back, 'lost signal'. Frustrated, she tossed the phone back into her purse. Her thoughts raced home as she worried over her mother's words. *Don't come home? Surely that wasn't what she meant. Maybe they're leaving? But that can't be it. The only time they leave the house together is for Mass or funerals, maybe the occasional wedding. Even then, it's only for an hour or two. That's their rule. God forbid, they'd ever break it. Wait. Could the storm be so bad that they have to evacuate? Oh God!*

Just as she was reaching for the phone again, the giant truck in front of her lunged forward, its brake lights flashing. She gripped the steering wheel and stayed close behind. Like floats in a parade, the traffic crawled along until finally Celine descended the exit ramp, her six-year-old Honda Civic struggling against the wind and rain.

The Old River Road was eerily empty. She had always hated driving on the plantation route. Snaking its way along the Mississippi all the way past New Orleans, it was once the main highway for exporting cotton.

Now it was reduced to deep pot holes where the asphalt had given way to the original gravel and mud. Celine turned on her radio hoping to get a weather report, anything that would tell her what to expect.

She caught the weatherman mid sentence. "...flood watch is in effect for the Port Allen/I-10 area 'till 9:00. Folks, if you're out there on the road, be careful in the North West section of town. We've got wind gusts reported up to 45 miles an hour. "

Celine looked out her window. Levee to her left, Port Allen to the right. *Jesus, this is insane. What am I doing? I should just head home now!* Celine pulled up alongside the road and stopped the car. Her heart was pounding and her head had started a sharp staccato drumbeat. *But if I head for home now, I'd have to get back on I-10.* She looked behind her at the bridge traffic. Bumper to bumper. She looked back into the dark road ahead, a stream of rainwater pooling under her car.

Maybe if I meet with this Arnaud person, I can cut it short and then get the hell out of there! Maybe the storm will calm down by then. She decided to look at the sketchy directions Dave had given her. She looked out. No street lights. She realized that between the pouring rain and the darkness, trying to find street signs was going to be impossible.

She looked at her car clock again, *6:15, forty-five minutes late. Oh, this is crazy. I'm just gonna call him and reschedule.* She reached in the back seat and grabbed her appointment book flipping through the pages, searching for Arnaud's number. *Okay, I know I wrote it down.* She muttered the emergency prayer to St. Anthony that she always used in school.

Tony, Tony, please come 'round...

Where did I put that number? Okay, one more place. She thumbed through her notes.

...something's lost and must be found.

No luck. *Maybe I can google his number.* Just as she reached for her phone, the screen went blank. Fluorescent green letters glared back, "recharge battery."

What? No, you can't be dead! She opened the glove compartment and rummaged around for her car charger. Nothing. The floor? Under the seat? Nothing. Even before she had finished pulling everything out of the console, she knew she'd been defeated. She slumped back into the seat and stared at the ceiling. The rain was pounding a constant roar on the roof of her car.

Okay. Now, what am I gonna do? Her short breaths made the windshield start to fog. The entire left side of her head was throbbing, so she dug around once more in the bottom of her purse and pulled out her little pillbox; the last Xanax, last Zipsor. She placed the pills on her tongue and forced herself to take a deep breath, hoping that the migraine would begin to fade. She watched the rain pour down the windshield. A flash of lightning pierced through the black night and immediately the crack of thunder rumbled through her car.

Celine gripped the steering wheel, trying to hold off the panic attack that she knew was coming if the Xanax didn't kick in quick. *I need to get out of here. I'll figure out some excuse later.* She turned the key.

Click. She turned the key again. Click, click, click. *Oh God, please, no. Not again, not now!*

Tears welled in her eyes. She screamed into the car. "I'm done, I'm so done! I give up!" She leaned back, tears streaked her cheeks. She closed her eyes and drew a sobbing breath. *Why didn't I listen to Mama? Maybe her weird herbs really would work for my headaches. God knows, the doctors and the therapy, even these stupid meds have all been useless; like Band-Aids on bullet wounds!*

Celine took a deep breath, her whole body was throbbing. *Okay, okay, the car's done this before. I just need to wait a little while. It'll start. I just need to be still for a minute. Relax. Then I'll try the car. I'll try, yeah, I'll try...* Celine sat quietly for a moment remembering her mother's words. "...the tea I sent you? Celine, chère, it's the best thing for those headaches. Have you tried it yet?" Celine hadn't. Instead she'd thrown it away. Only ignorant people tried folk remedies, right?

The rumble of thunder sounded a little further away and the rain turned into slower drips onto her windshield. She opened her eyes and placed her hand on the key. She took a deep breath and turned. Click. *Okay, okay. I just tried it too soon.* She leaned back again and took a deep breath. Her body was relaxing and the headache pounding in her head was reduced to a dull slow tempo. The magic pills had done the job once again. She watched as raindrops raced down her windshield, some fat and slow, others thin and in a rush but one tiny raindrop just stayed put.

No matter what the others did, it just stayed. *Stay, stay, one of us always stays...* Celine heard her mother's voice again. "...at home, Celine, because we have to. It's what we do, chère. If we didn't, many people would suffer."

Someone was always home because the phone rang day and night; a sick baby, a woman in labor, a farmer or maybe an oil rig worker badly injured or one of the old folks dying; the constant job of the *traiteuse*, the Cajun healer.

She remembered her mother and grandmother in the kitchen, packing nasty, stinking salves or that God-awful-tasting, rust-colored liquid. They unpacked and repacked that old bag each time they received a call, but three items were always in there; holy water, holy oil and that little black prayer book. *What did they call it; the St. Suaire?* Once everything was prepared, one of them would leave while the other one would stay behind, lighting incense and candles, muttering prayers and thumbing rosary beads.

When the townspeople tried to pay them, they'd refuse and say that they were only doing God's work. Still, the pantry was always full of fresh vegetables from private gardens and they never had to worry about any kind of car repairs. If the roof needed fixing or a pipe broke, there was always someone who would fix it, free of charge, of course.

When Celine had been a little girl, she had always been proud of the work that her mother and grandmother did. It was even a little prestigious to be the daughter and granddaughter to Mama Luisah and Mo-maw B. All around town, she was known as Little Ceecee, but as a teenager, the cute name wasn't so cute anymore.

When her friends started to tease her, and that included potential boyfriends, she began to resist everything her mother and grandmother did. Inside, she boiled with resentment, and sometimes that resentment would spill over into defiance, "Why can't we be a normal family instead of always taking care of everyone else? Don't you realize how embarrassing all that superstitious, mumbo-jumbo drivel is?" With each year in High School, the arguments grew, ending with Celine slamming doors, followed by disapproving sighs from her mother and grandmother. She always felt horrible for hurting the two most important women in her life but, couldn't wait for her chance to break away.

By the time she left for college she vowed to herself that she was leaving all of it behind. No more weird medicines or talk of herbs and stupid prayers, no more playing the part of obedient little girl. Apart from visits home, she'd decided that there was no way she'd ever live there again. There was more to life than this stupid little backward town.

Celine watched the dripping rain. "And right now," she whispered into the car, "I'd give anything to be back in the middle of their warm, lovable, crazy lives."

Headlights shining into her face snapped her back to reality. She sat up and quickly tried to start the car again. Click…click, click. *Oh terrific! What if he doesn't see me?* The black Mercedes came closer and closer. He flashed his lights. *Thank god!* He pulled up alongside her and stopped, the driver's tinted window lowered. Celine's gut tensed. *Please, God, let this guy be okay.* She rolled down her window, blinking as the rain spatters hit her face.

"Celine Dupré?" The man was frowning but his voice sounded friendly.

She called back. "Yes, I'm Celine."

"I'm Dr. Sonnier. Alex sent me to look for you. He thought you might be lost or maybe stuck in the mud somewhere. Looks like he was right."

She nodded. "I thought I'd taken a wrong turn. I would've called but my phone is dead and so is my car."

The doctor smiled. "Try starting it?"

Celine grabbed the key and turned it. The engine purred like a satisfied kitten. "What?"

The man in the Mercedes said, "Happens a lot on these ridiculous roads when it rains. Let me turn around. You can follow me. It's just the next road over. Don't worry. If you stall out, I can help."

She rolled her window back up, feeling embarrassed and miserable. She followed the Mercedes onto an unmarked and muddy one-lane road. Celine sighed with relief when she saw porch lights twinkling through moss-covered tree limbs. She followed the doctor into the curved driveway and stopped the car nervously.

She sat quietly, waiting for a break in the rain but the doctor wasted no time hopping out of his car, umbrella in hand striding toward her. With those long legs she knew it was only a matter of seconds before he reached the car door. She quickly looked at herself in the mirror, ran fingers through her hair and rearranged her blouse, making sure to pull her collar up high.

Just as she turned to look back out the window, the doctor was pulling her car door open. She hooked her purse onto her shoulder and stepped out underneath his umbrella. He spoke above the thunderous rain. "Let's get to the house before we get swept away." She nodded as they hurried to the porch and into the house.

The doctor pushed the door shut behind them, replacing the towel at the base to keep the water out. He handed her a dry towel that had been hanging on a coat rack nearby and took another to wipe his face. "This is some really wicked stuff. To tell you the truth, I'm really surprised to see you came out in this. I told Alex he should call Dave and tell him that this could wait."

"No it couldn't, Matt." The feeble voice came from behind the doctor. She turned and saw a sickly, thin man in a wheelchair slowly moving toward them. He offered a long graceful hand to her, his shirt looking two sizes too large. The teal blue silk scarf he wore around his neck brought a flash of color to his lifeless gray skin but his hair was a gorgeous mop of curly white hair.

"Hello, Celine. I'm Alex. Thanks so much for doing this. My health is so unpredictable, if we didn't meet tonight, I don't know when we'd have this opportunity again."

Instantly, Celine's heart melted as she saw the frail man smile. "Sure, I just think it's wonderful that you're willing to help the kids out at LSB."

Alex nodded. "Matt, take her towel there and let's get settled in the den. Can I offer you a drink, maybe some wine or even something a little stronger?"

She smiled, "Oh, just coffee or tea. Driving home in this rain might be a little tricky if I drink anything stronger than that, well, if my car decides to start."

The doctor gave her a reassuring smile. "Don't worry. We can get you up and running, but no hurry, right? You'll need to wait out this storm."

Alex, said, "A little café au lait will warm you right up. Matt, could you go tell Dora to bring us two cups and get whatever you want. Tell her to put the Bushmills on the side." Dr. Sonnier left the room as Alex slowly struggled to turn his wheelchair toward the den. "I'm very glad you're here. I've wanted to meet you ever since I read that article in the paper about the little blind girl you've been working with."

They entered a large room and Celine sat down in a red leather easy chair. "Yes. Dave told me you were very interested in our little Leah. She really is a walking miracle."

"And how is Dave?" The doctor's booming voice bellowed as he entered the room. "Tell us the truth. Is he still a pit bull or has he mellowed?"

Celine gave a short laugh and looked back at Alex. "Well, the pit bull is very happy to finally have the chance to present all his charts and spreadsheets to the board tonight. He truly is amazing with financial plans and budgets." She let out a little laugh. "I'm doing great just to be able to balance my checkbook, so I hope you don't mind working with me on this."

Alex laughed. "Mind?" He stopped and watched Dr. Sonnier settle on the matching red leather sofa nearby. Alex took a raspy breath and then continued, "I'm thrilled that you're here. Dave wouldn't know the first thing about designing an art department, much less what we're trying to research."

Celine cocked her head, confused. "I'm not sure I understand what you mean. He said you wanted to make a donation, but…"

Alex frowned. "That's all he said? Celine nodded. Alex took a deep, rattling breath and smiled. "Well, he left out the best part. I'm donating the money for a brand new art building at LSB."

She sat back, eyes wide. *How could Dave have left this little tidbit of information out?* "A new art building! That's wonderful and very generous, Mr. Arnaud. Thank you!"

Alex shook his head. "First of all, you've got to call me Alex. You make me feel old calling me Mr. Arnaud and second, you need to know up front that this isn't generous at all. I'm doing this for completely selfish reasons. I want to leave a legacy to this world. Unfortunately, I'm running out of time pretty quickly. I want you to help me plan every detail of this project, the building, the research, everything and that way, if I die before it's finished, then I know it's all been left in good hands."

The doctor shook his head. "Now Alex, I've already told you. When we start the new drug regimen tomorrow, you'll start feeling like your old self in no time. There's no need to start your doomsday…"

Alex waved his hand dismissively and looked at Celine, his crystal blue eyes pleading with her through his pained, ashen face. "Will you help me?"

She hesitated. This was such a wonderful opportunity for the kids, but all of her internal alarms were screaming. It would certainly mean working throughout the summer. And what if this poor man died before they finished? What then? "Well, I do have some research I'm supposed to complete for my doctoral thesis. My supervising professor is a stickler for prompt submissions so I really don't think I can…"

Alex smiled and interrupted her. "Don't you worry about Jimmy Turner. I've already talked to him. He's promised an extension on your due date. Believe me, when I told him that the new art building would be used for research, and that a nice donation for his pet projects just might come his way, well, let me just say, he's a man who can easily see reason."

Dr. Sonnier cleared his throat. "Yeah, I read your thesis. It really made me stop and think. I mean how do blind kinds understand what color really is? Fascinating stuff you've presented."

Alex smiled. "You've got a wonderfully creative and probing mind, Celine. Your ideas are exactly what I'm looking for. I want everything that we design to be state-of-the-art. We'll hire research assistants and study every facet of what motivates blind children when they paint; is it the feel of the paint, the smell, or is it something far reaching inside of themselves? Do they 'see' something that we don't?" He nodded. "Yes, I'm certain that you're just the right person for the job. Besides…" He let out a little cough. "…I don't want anyone else."

Celine's face was fixed with a smile but her gut was churning. *Already talked to Dr. Turner? Jimmy? He called him by his first name? Nobody does that! And he doesn't want anyone else for the job? What the hell does all this mean? There are lots of other people who could do this, lots of people better than me, I'm sure.* "It sounds like you've spent a lot of time thinking about this."

Alex turned his face suddenly very serious. "My dear, about all I have left is time for thinking. If I can make some child's world a little brighter, then now's the time to be doing something about it. Will you help me?"

Celine squirmed a little. His voice was weak and shaky but his determination to get what he wanted was unwavering. She knew that somehow he'd figure a way around all the excuses she'd come up with. But wasn't he offering a wonderful opportunity for the children and an extended break from the brain drain that her doctorate was sucking out of her?

He reached up and scratched the side of his head and in that moment Celine realized that his gorgeous profusion of white curls was a wig. Her heart sank. There was no way she could say no to this poor, suffering man.

She gave him a slight nod. "I'd be happy to work with you."

Alex sat back. "Then that's a yes?" Celine nodded, trying to ignore that sinking feeling in the pit of her stomach. *Oh well, there's no turning back now.*

Alex clapped his hands together, his eyes wide with excitement. "Perfect! Tonight we'll take a look at a rough draft. I've put together some basic ideas, just as a kind of outline. Then, as soon as I'm done with these new drugs that Matt wants me to try, I want you to come meet me in New Orleans. We can finalize the plans and have it ready for construction before the new school year starts."

"Well…" Celine interrupted, her thoughts racing. "…do you have any idea how soon that might be? I'm expected at home for the next few days. Actually, I was hoping for maybe, well, a week?"

Alex looked at Matt, waiting. Matt crossed his arms. "I've told you. You'll be out of the hospital and ready by the weekend."

Alex smiled, a brightness filling his pained eyes. "Well, that's wonderful! After you've spent some time with your family you can come meet me in New Orleans. Is next Saturday all right?" He didn't wait for her to answer. "You won't need to worry about anything, of course. Your hotel and an expense account will be taken care of. The Hotel Ste. Jeanne has an apartment that's quite nice and it's just a block away from the gallery. Would that work?"

Matt laughed, "Whoa. Slow down, Alex. You're overwhelming her!" Alex started to laugh but then buckled over, coughing. Matt stood up and quickly reached for his medical bag next to the sofa. He opened it as he squatted next to the wheelchair. "Alex?"

Alex waved his hand and nodded his head. The coughing lessened as he sat up. He looked back at Celine. "I'm so sorry. I'm just so happy that you and I will be doing this…" He panted. "I got too excited, I guess."

A clinking sound from the corner of the room made all of them turn around. Alex gave a weak smile, his voice slowly regaining volume, "Dora, you're just in time." A petite black woman entered the room carrying a tray. Alex turned to her as she strode toward the coffee table in front of them. "My nephew should be here shortly. He went to pick up the blueprints, but I'm afraid the traffic and the storm slowed him down. He called just before you got here." Alex looked at the tray. "Matt, add the Bushmills to mine, would you?" He turned to Celine and smiled, his eyes still red from the coughing. "Sure you're not up for a little shot of whiskey, just as a celebration?"

She smiled back finding herself amazed at his determination to forge ahead in spite of how badly he was feeling. "Oh no, I really can't. I've had a headache all day. If I drink anything, it'll come back with a vengeance."

"Headache?" He gulped down the coffee in one swallow. "This is the only thing that keeps my headaches under control. Maybe you should try it?"

The doctor looked at Alex, snapping his bag and shook his head. "You know, you might feel better if you lay off this stuff!" The doctor turned to her and said, smiling, "He's on his best behavior for you. He's well-known for downing a whole bottle of Bushmills 21 back there in his studio while he works on his paintings."

Alex gave a sheepish grin, "Oh, stop it, Matt. She won't want to work with me if you tell her that. Besides, you already took my cigars away. I won't let you take all of my delicious vices."

Alex turned and looked at Celine. "I hope you understand that Matt's being a bore. He's just a doctor. What do doctors know about beimg an artist?" He turned and looked at Matt mockingly. "We artists tiptoe on that razor's edge of life and death, testing the soul and dancing on the face of God every day." He winked at Celine. "I'm sure you know what I'm talking about."

Celine smiled nervously and tugged at her collar self-consciously. She tried to shift the conversation. "So you have a studio here? I thought it was in New Orleans."

"Yes, a small one. I have a studio in all my houses." His hands shook as he poured another shot of whiskey into his coffee cup. "I can't go a day without painting. It's like breathing for me." She watched him as he downed the warm amber-colored whiskey. Sadly, she tried to remember that wonderful feeling when painting was like breathing for her. It seemed like ages since she'd let everything inside her flow into color onto a canvas.

The cup shook as Alex placed it back on the tray. "But my main working studio is alongside my gallery. I keep my best work and my latest collections there. I've been very lucky to have purchased several Renoirs and..."

The doctor interrupted Alex, reaching for the coffee pot. "Why don't you give her a peek at some of those portraits you've been working on?" He turned to Celine smiling, "Lately, he's been turning out some of the most incredible paintings I've ever seen. He told me they're portraits of death."

Alex flashed an angry look at the doctor. "Matt, those paintings are for my private collection only. After I'm dead, I'm going to let you do whatever you want with them, but for now..."

Matt never took his eyes off Celine. "Just ignore him. This is the reaction I get when I try to convince him that there are lots of people out there who'd love to see them..." He turned back to Alex, "...while you're alive! They could make a lot of money for a certain hospital that you're about to get some first-rate treatment from, too. Of course they would only be shown to select patrons of the hospital—you know, those that could appreciate them. But the buyers would rather meet the artist while he's still on this side of Heaven!"

Alex gave a snort, "You mean only for those with big checks to go along with them. You're as bad as Dave, Matt."

Matt retorted, "What could it hurt? Look, isn't Celine a professional artist? Let her be the judge of whether she thinks they're public-worthy. What do you think, Celine? Would you help us settle this little disagreement once and for all?"

Celine sipped her coffee nervously. She had walked into an ongoing argument and was being forced to take sides. "I really would love to see them, but honestly, some works are meant to stay strictly private. When you paint your lifeblood and hang it up on a wall for everyone to see; well, only the artist can decide if he's willing to bare everything and risk being crucified."

Alex smiled at Celine, his angry expression melted. "You are such a jewel." He looked at his watch. "Michael should be here any minute..." He looked back at Celine, "My dear, I'd be honored to get your opinion on my paintings. Only another artist could understand how I feel about them, but..." He reached across and patted her hand, "...they are pretty gruesome, so if you want to stop, please, just say the word. I'll understand."

Celine smiled back, her heart warmed by his compassion. She stood up and pushed his wheelchair down the hallway and into a large room. "Matt, turn on the lights, would you?" When the lights clicked on, she saw several easels, each draped with a white sheet-like cloth.

Matt reached to pull one of the covers off when Alex called out, "Wait..." He pointed to the one nearest to him. "...this one first."

When the drape fell away, the painting looked like a broken mirror. Hundreds of silver shards filled every inch of the canvas, capturing a fractured piece of someone's face; an eye, half a mouth, an ear. She stepped closer trying to get a clearer look.

She turned to face Alex. "Is it you?"

Alex nodded as he wheeled his chair closer to her. "You know, the night that I painted this was very long and very hard. I had just been told that I had graduated." He let out a sarcastic cackle. "No longer HIV. Now full-blown AIDS. I call it, 'Shattered'."

She looked back at the slashing savage strokes of paint on the canvas. "This one piece would take hours to completely examine; all these parts of your face, and your hands. My God, Alex, what you must've gone through! "

Matt moved to the next one. "Then look at this one." Before Alex could say anything, Matt had pulled the drape and dropped it to the floor.

Celine turned and slowly walked to the next easel, drawn like a magnet to the bold, almost violent colors that outlined the back of a nude, haggard man. His body had been degraded to flesh stretched over protruding bone. His bald head hung, disjointed from the neck while his arms reached up into the darkness.

It took her breath away. Something about this one made her head start pounding again. She looked at Alex. "This is hauntingly beautiful. I'm drawn inside it and at the same time want to pull away from it. He's both the prisoner and the prison." Alex just nodded, and began to roll forward to the next easel.

From a distance down the hall, she heard a voice, "Uncle Alex?"

Alex turned to Matt. "It's Michael. Would you go tell him we're in the studio?" Matt nodded and left the room. Alex looked back at Celine. "We have time for one more." He nodded toward the canvas in front of him.

She stepped closer and pulled the drape down and came face to face with an eyeless skull. She took a quick step back and instantly became frozen. Her legs felt like blocks of cement and a cold sweat poured over her body.

From somewhere behind her, she heard Alex's voice. "Yes, this one's, well, I call it, 'The Dream'. Would you excuse me?"

She took another step back, stumbling. The thing's transparent skin ran taught against the skull. Black ice sockets stared directly at her, its long knife-like teeth dripped with traces of blood from its lipless mouth. Its veined arms pulsed as it straddled a lifeless body. The victim's neck was slashed. Purple gouges lay the skin open. She grabbed at her throat, unable to breathe.

"Yes, Celine. Come!" She could hear the hoarse voice coming from the canvas. Crushed between its silver talons was a still-beating heart held inside a bony palm. She could feel it sucking at her chest, laughing. It snarled into her ear as it ripped its way into her. She screamed as someone grabbed her by the shoulders, pulling her away from the painting. Panic-stricken, Celine turned around, flailing wildly at the air, but strong arms wrapped around her.

"Miss Dupré! Celine!" Celine blinked, trying desperately to focus on the face in front of her. She could feel the strength of his hands; warm, loving, kind hands, holding her close. She looked up; *night-black hair?* She shook her head in disbelief. "No, no!" She tried to step back but the steel blue-gray eyes, angel eyes, the dead man's eyes reached into her as she slipped through his hands and fell to the floor.

CHAPTER 4

The Cajuns of St. Maryville slept while the red sun of daybreak crept over the land. The morning light was edging its way up the porch and found Mo-maw gently rocking in the new day. This is where she was every morning, a part of her own ritual, her own religion. The still, humid air had not yet awakened the mosquitoes, but the old woman knew that with the sunrise, her peaceful time would soon be over.

The mourning doves cooed, urging Mo-maw out of her chair. *S'occuper aujourd hui, Lots to do today. Celine's coming home tonight.* She smiled as she imagined her granddaughter on this last day of the school year, saying good-bye to all those sweet little blind children and helping the teachers pack up for a well-deserved summer break. She hadn't seen Celine since Christmas and had missed her deeply. Of course she'd talked to her briefly over the phone, but Mo-maw never felt comfortable holding that thing up to her ear. Besides, her hearing wasn't so good anymore. No, she left the phone calls up to Luisah. *Chère 'tit fille, it'll be so good to finally see her. Yes, lots to do today.* But Mo-maw didn't move. Instead, the old woman sat still, thinking. Something was not right.

She could feel it, taste it; every pore on her skin vibrated with it, but what? What was this thing just out of her reach?

A storm was approaching, of that she was certain. All the signs were there, the smell on the air, the strange behavior of the animals as they moved to higher ground. Even this morning, the dew was thicker than usual, its moisture sitting on her chest, making it difficult to breathe; she had seen and felt all this for several weeks, almost three months, now. Yes, the storm would be a bad one.

It wasn't a hurricane. She'd felt them before, Audrey in 1957, Betsy in '65, even Katrina and Rita she'd felt long before the weatherman had seen their demonic whorls on his radar screen. The old woman let her head rest on the back of the sun-bleached chair and closed her eyes. A rush of water surged toward her, the Bayou Teche flooded and people scattered in muddy darkness. She saw men panicked inside a vicious wind as they tried in vain to save their crops. Mo-maw opened her eyes. It looked like a hurricane all right, only it wasn't. She wished she was sure of the rest.

Mo-maw felt the heavy hand of age press her down. Her fingers ran swiftly through the pearl rosary beads, the soft clicking giving her a breath of peace. A deep sigh escaped her wrinkled lips. She pushed the aged rocking chair with short, stout legs. Her black, lace-up shoes shuffled on the wooden planks of the porch. She gripped the arms of the chair with time-worn hands and stared at the ceiling, her gold-rimmed glasses slightly askew.

Mixed in with the coming storm had been dreams, dreams she had tried to block out, dreams she hoped meant nothing. But this morning she forced herself to face them, to face the fact that her granddaughter was in trouble. She watched the sun's rays dancing around her feet and knew another storm was brewing inside the young woman's heart. One Mo-maw could feel but not see.

"Celine, *mon cœur*", the old woman whispered. "My heart, my heart." She smiled as she let her thoughts drift back to the summer of 1946; to the eve of her wedding and the wonderful fête that came after the rehearsal. That warm evening, when everything was quiet, and the sweet smell of honeysuckle was on the breeze, Mo-maw's grandmother invited her into the altar room for a special blessing. That was when she learned her family history and the secret that came with it. But there was a price to pay—a vow of silence.

No words of the secret could ever be spoken to anyone except her mother and grandmother. Mo-maw could still see the old woman's wrinkled face, stern and unbending on this rule. And someday, if the vow had not been broken, she would be granted the right to share the secret with her own granddaughter on the eve of her wedding. Mo-maw remembered feeling confused and scared. How did her grandmother know she would ever have a granddaughter? But her fears were shattered when her grandmother laughed louder than she'd ever heard her laugh before, "You will have a daughter and a granddaughter and someday your arms will overflow with great-grandchildren."

Mo-maw's smile faded. Things were different now. Somehow, time had slipped past and Celine was still not married. None of the young men had been right for her. At first, Mo-mow thought that Greg might have been the one, but in the end, he was just like all the rest, *Z'Américaine*; too influenced by all the trappings of American life; always hungry for bigger, better, more! Besides that, he was just another impatient young man. Mo-maw had sensed more than once that he had a low opinion of the Cajun way of life, but then he was one of those Baton Rouge boys; high aspirations for a lawyer's life, his arm draped with a trophy wife.

Mo-maw sighed. She was glad that the wedding was off but what of the great-grandchildren that would overflow in her arms someday? Oh sure, there was still plenty of time. Gone were the days when girls got married at sixteen. Nowadays they married as late as even thirty. Celine was only twenty-eight, so there was still time for her to get married and have kids. Mo-maw shook her head. That wasn't the problem.

Mo-maw wasn't getting any younger; eighty-seven at her next birthday. Suppose she passed away before Celine married? Then what? Of course, Luisah would reveal the secret to Celine but Mo-maw grew sad at the thought. *I've looked forward to sharing that special moment with Celine from the minute I saw that child born. Will I live long enough? Bon Dieu, please don't let me pass before then.*

In the distance Mo-maw heard the whine of a crop duster as it sprayed the sugar cane fields with pesticide. It reminded her of modern things and how the earth around her had changed so much. She looked around. The bayou filled everything with a vibrant, fresh smell. No, it wasn't the earth that was changing so much; it was the people, always in such a hurry. Her granddaughter was caught up in that hurried, busy world; work, school and then there was the broken engagement. Celine was riddled with lots of worries laced with sadness. Could this be the trouble that was churning inside her?

Mo-maw sat still, listening; waiting for the sounds of the bayou to tell her what was inside Celine's heart. She never really knew where the voices came from, but they whispered among the sounds of life; the sudden call of the blue heron flying overhead, the playful splash of the Mallard ducks during their morning bath, the throaty croak of a lone bullfrog looking for its mate. Mo-maw listened and heard her old friends, their voices speaking in an ancient but familiar tongue.

Mo-maw closed her eyes. Images danced behind her lids; burning candles, the faces of saints, a box, a doll. The voices grew clearer, stronger. Swirls of gray haze separated Mo-maw from the present world and without warning, an image of Celine appeared, her face streaked with tears, sobbing, kneeling, surrounded in darkness. *Where is she?* Mo-maw looked closer. *The confessional?* Mo-maw could hear Celine's voice. *What is she saying?* Mo-maw strained to hear and then she heard something else, a guttural grinding voice. *Something's in there with her, something evil!* Celine screamed. Mo-maw called to her granddaughter with the voice of her soul, but Celine couldn't hear her. Instead, she faded slowly away, her screams echoing in the emptiness.

Mo-maw jerked herself back, drawing in a deep breath and fighting back tears of her own. The vision was disturbing, different from the visions she had received before. Celine's image still flickered in front of her opened eyes, a bad sign. Then, in an instant, it was gone. Breathless, Mo-maw sat, regaining her calm, clicking her beads.

Mo-maw had spent nearly all her life healing people. Some called it a black art. Others called it a blessing. No matter. Mo-maw knew it was simply something she had to do, a gift given to her by God and taught to her by her mother and grandmother. But the key to it all was waiting for the right moment. It was more than wanting to be healed. The patient had to take responsibility for their part in the illness; anger, fear, jealousy, hate. All these had to be faced, or a healing would never happen.

Something was tormenting Celine. This was something more than just the stresses of her daily life. No, this was something horrible and Mo-maw was ready to protect her. The question now was with Celine. Mo-maw rested her head on the back of her chair as she prayed. *Si le bon Dieu veut, God willing, is she ready? I won't know 'til I see her, touch her, talk to her face-to-face. Tonight.*

The sun warmed her face and Mo-maw knew her solitude was over. She eased out of the old rocking chair and gave her thoughts to the earth, thanking the old friends for the gift and asking them to keep Celine safe. She could already hear her daughter, Luisah, in the kitchen, cooking breakfast. She could smell the aroma of bacon frying and hear the grease sizzling as she entered the house. While the porch door slammed behind her, Mo-maw called to her daughter, "Don' f'get to save da grease! Those babies will be needin' it today."

"Yes, Mama." Luisah knew better than to question her mother about these things. She carefully strained the grease from the bacon and stored it in a bell jar to cool. As she set the breakfast table, Luisah thought about the twins that she had midwifed only a week ago. Poor Irma's labor had been hard and long, longer than usual. But as of yesterday, mama and babies were just fine. Luisah smiled. If her mother said the babies needed the grease, then that was that. She had learned long ago to trust the old Cajun healer, the *traiteuse* of St. Maryville.

Luisah was happy that for now she was still the apprentice. The easier part of healing was nothing more than remembering what herb helped a badly sprained ankle or what to prescribe for the flu. The formulas for healing were easy and Luisah knew how to do that. Someday she knew she'd take her mother's place, but Mo-maw's job as the Guardian of the People required the 'sight'. Every once in a while, Luisah would have short glimmers of things to come, but the 'sight' just wasn't her gift. Besides, the 'sight' demanded a clear conscience, free of the burden of guilt. And this was where Luisah knew she fell short.

Her husband had died too soon. He was only forty, leaving Luisah alone with three-year-old Celine; no life insurance and a heavily-mortgaged hardware store. There wasn't any time for grieving. The gulf of debt she faced forced her back to work one week after the funeral, but for all her hard work and careful budgeting, there was never enough money. Every night after supper, Luisah retreated into a bottle of wine. It was the only thing that could turn her exhaustion and worry into a dreamless sleep. Celine was such a good little girl through it all. She would play alone in her room and somehow manage to put herself to bed, but on one of those nights, Celine went missing.

Luisah never knew what woke her up that horrible night. She looked for Celine everywhere. She found the front door open and Celine's favorite doll, the one she always slept with, at the end of the driveway. Luisah ran to her mother's, hoping beyond hope, that somehow Celine was there. It was nearly dawn when they found the child, floating face-down in the bayou, covered in mud, her body cold and lifeless.

Had it not been for Mo-maw, Celine would've died. What kind of mother neglects her child like that? What kind of mother would put her child in such danger? If Celine had died, it would've been Luisah's fault. It didn't matter how many times Luisah went to confession or recited the holiest of healing prayers, The Saint Suaire; it could never erase the deep guilt she felt for what happened to Celine that night.

After Celine recovered from the near-drowning, Mo-maw took them in. Luisah sold her house and the store and followed the family tradition to be her mother's apprentice. Luisah smiled, deeply grateful for her mother. Mo-maw's love had saved them; Luisah from depression and Celine from death.

Luisah looked up as her mother walked into the kitchen, the red floral pattern of Mo-maw's house dress swaying gently as she shuffled slowly to the table. "Mama, there's no need for you to be up. Why don't you go back to bed?"

The old woman ignored the words, waving her hand at her daughter as she sat at the kitchen table and buttered her toast. Luisah sighed. It seemed no matter how hard she tried to slow her mother down, Mo-maw would just do more. She reached into the cupboard to get the coffee cups and started to ask her about the twins when her thoughts were interrupted, "Lala," her mother fondly called her, "Dere's something wrong."

Luisah stared into the black coffee as she poured it into the blue willow cups. Silently she walked over to the table and stood, her face wrinkled with questions. She noticed how her mother looked more bent than usual; tired, old. "What's wrong, Mama? You feelin' all right?"

Mo-maw shook her head. "I don' mean me, chère." Luisah placed the two coffee cups on the table and sat down, waiting for her mother to say what was bothering her. Mo-maw peered over her glasses. "Haven't you sensed it?"

Luisah sipped her coffee, thinking, "Well, something has the chickens spooked. When I went to get the eggs this mornin', all of them were huddled out there along the fence. Even old Rooster was curled up under the coop. I thought maybe a rat had gotten inside, but Rooster's tangled with those before and always managed to chase them off."

Mo-maw looked down at the toast and bacon on her plate, suddenly not hungry. She whispered ominous words to her daughter, "*Maudit Temps*, the Wicked Storm. You never know what it's gonna do. I saw one once, when I wuz a little girl. I hid under the bed, I wuz so scared. The wind whipped an' screamed like I'd never heard before. The lightning, it jumped sideways. Den it jus' stopped. No one ever knows how long it'll last or where it'll go next but one thing's for sure, it changes everything and everyone that stands in its way."

Luisah sipped her coffee and nibbled a piece of bacon, wondering if the weatherman had a name for this.

Mo-maw stared out the bay window overlooking the yard, "What side of the pasture wuz the horses on?"

Luisah frowned as she thought back to the morning chores. "They were over by T-Joe's yard. Come to think of it, they were very jumpy this morning and pushing up against the fence."

"Yeah, chère, they gettin' as far away from dis t'ing as dey can get. It's coming out of da east." The old woman took a sip of her coffee. "As for when? I say supper time. We've got just enough time to get everyone ready. Call T-Joe, chère, and ask him if we can put the horses in his barn tonight. They'll kick ours down trying to get away."

Luisah didn't move. Her brow wrinkled, her widow's peak digging deeper into her forehead. "How far east, Mama? I mean what about Celine?"

Mo-maw waited a moment before she answered. "It's hard to say, chère, but..." Mo-maw looked straight into Luisah's face. "...Celine's in some kind of trouble, Lala."

Luisah put her coffee cup down. "Trouble? How do you mean, Mama?"

Mo-maw sat back. "I'm not sure, but dere's something she's not telling us."

Luisah looked down and nodded thoughtfully, "The last few times I've talked to her, I wondered if somethin' was wrong. At first I thought it had something to do with her and Greg breakin' up, but I don't know anymore. Every time I ask her if she's okay, she just gives me these short answers. We never talk very long. She's always so busy."

Mo-maw patted her daughter's hand. "When did you talk to her last?"

Luisah stared off into space, her eyes fixed on some faraway place. "Day before yesterday. I tried to call her this morning but all I got was her machine. Mama, I don't know. She said she was just tired and ready for the end of school. She's looking forward to coming home." Luisah wiped her hands on her apron, "She said she hadn't been sleepin' very good. I asked her if she'd tried the snake tea I sent her, but..."

Mo-maw's body grew tense. "Not sleeping good? I thought all that had passed. What'd she say?"

Luisah looked at her mother. "She keeps waking up from some bad dreams but when I asked her what they're about all she says is that it starts out in church."

Mo-maw sat up straight in her chair. "Church?"

Luisah nodded. "Yeah, but that's all she says. I think it has something to do with the wedding. Don't you?"

Mo-maw shook her head. "Pas sur, Luisah. Mais, I'm not sure." Mo-maw got up from the table and walked over to the salt shaker. She opened it and poured some into a small bowl as she spoke. "Chère, we got lots to do! Call Celine and tell her to get home as soon as she can. She needs to be here before dat storm hits. If she can't do dat, then tell her to stay put until it passes over. I mean it, chère, tell her to stay put! If she gets stuck in dat storm..." Mo-maw stopped when she saw the look of worry on Luisah's face. "Just keep calling 'til you talk to her. And call T-Joe, too."

Mo-maw put the bowl of salt on the counter and opened a small tin canister. The sweet smell of crushed iris leaves and lavender filled the room. She reached in and pinched out a small bit of the purple mixture, added it to the salt and stirred it with her finger. "Oh, and stop by Irma's with da grease, her nipples are sore from da *bébés*. Tell her to go to her mama's tonight. She'll need extra help." She looked in the refrigerator. "Where'd you put Old Midnight's egg?"

Luisah pointed to the small plastic bowl as she reached for her cell phone in her apron pocket. "Right there. Can you believe it? That black guinea hen laid two today. Who's the Black Iris for?"

Mo-maw's hand stopped mid-air as she turned slowly around. "Two?" Luisah nodded. Mo-maw reached into the bowl and took the brown speckled eggs out.

Luisah saw the look of determination in her mother's age-worn face as she cracked both eggs, careful not to break the yolks. As her mother shuffled past her, Luisah called out. "But Mama, who's it for?"

Mo-maw stopped. Should she tell her now? Luisah would surely worry and worry might only make Celine more vulnerable. But then again, Luisah needed to know. Mo-maw turned and looked at her daughter, her voice clear and sure. "It's for Celine, chère."

Luisah sat back, stunned. "Mama?"

Mo-maw walked back to the table and sat next to Luisah taking her hands in hers. "Lala, come on now, chère, Celine will be all right. She's strong; we jus' have to help her through this and before we help, we jus' have to be sure of what's causing it."

Luisah looked up, "Help her through what, Mama? What do we need to be sure of? Please tell me."

Mo-maw sighed. "This dream she's having, I have a sense of it, but I can't see it all, yet. We've got to get her home first. Right now, she's not telling you much of anything. That's not like her. She's hiding something."

Luisah let out a nervous laugh. "But, Mama, she's gone through such a hard time these last few months; working with those blind babies, and going to LSU at night and even weekends. Well, with all that and Greg in the picture, too? It's no wonder they broke up. You know, ever since she was a little girl, she thought she could handle everything on her own; president of this, leader of that. Maybe now, she's finally realizing that it's okay to need help sometime. All she needs is to come home and let us to take care of her for a change. Once she's rested, she'll tell us. She just needs some time."

Mo-maw looked pensively at Luisah. "We have no more time, chère. Something's found her and it's chasing her in her dreams. Something bad, Luisah."

Luisah wrinkled her brow. She looked at the purple salt circling the eggs in the bowl. "So you've seen it then, this something that's chasing her? Otherwise you wouldn't have used the Black Iris."

Mo-maw patted her hand. "Luisah, now, you listen to me. We've known from the very beginning that Celine is special. Because of that, we've done everything that we can to keep her protected for all these years. We've done everything but the one thing that might protect her the most, and that is to tell her the whole truth. We've got to tell her. It can't wait any longer. Now I know..."

Luisah shook her head vigorously. "What are you saying, Mama? Nobody's ever broken the rule. If you do that, couldn't it make things much worse for her? And what about you? It could hurt you, too."

Mo-maw nodded her head. "You're right, chère. We don't know what will happen after we tell her, but dere's one t'ing I do know for sure. This t'ing in her dream, it's broken through all the protection we've given her. If she knows the truth, she'll be protected in ways that we never can. Now, I know that I'm asking you to break the rule with me, and if you don't want to, I'll understand, chère. I'll just have to do dis on my own. I know that there's a big price I'll have to pay, but Luisah, when I face God at my end, I'll be able to say, '*Mon Dieu*, I did all that I could.'" Mo-maw patted Luisah's hand. "So, what do you say, eh?"

Luisah forced a smile and nodded. "Okay, Mama. I mean, I'm still not sure about it, but well, when it comes to Celine these days I'm not sure about anything. I'll call her right now and then T-Joe."

Mo-maw gave out a short laugh. "Whatever dis t'ing is, it'll have a hard time gettin' past you and me, yeah?" She stood, picked up the bowl and shuffled toward the door. "Now you start the gumbo. Celine will be so happy you made it. You know it's her favorite."

As Mo-maw walked out of the room, Luisah picked up the phone and hit the automatic dial for Celine. She held her breath as the phone rang. *Pick up, Celine, pick up.*

"You've reached Celine Dupré. Please leave a message and I'll call you back."

Luisah waited for the beep. "Celine, chère, call me as soon as you can, okay? It's..." Luisah looked at the clock on the stove. "...8:30. I know you're busy with the kids or maybe you're in a faculty meeting. Just call me as soon as you get this. It's very important. Love you." Luisah hung up. *Please God, please, have her call me soon.*

Luisah dialed the number for T-Joe. No answering machine here. Instead a bright, happy voice boomed over the phone. "*Comment ça va*, Miz Luisah?"

Luisah smiled as she heard his voice, always so friendly and helpful. They fell into a fluid Cajun French banter as she explained the threat of the coming storm. His promises of help lightened her mood a bit as she hung up the phone.

Luisah cleared the breakfast dishes, trying hard not to let her fears for Celine creep back in. She grabbed a dishtowel and began to wipe the counter top, then the stove, the table and around the sink. Over and over again she cleaned, wiping out the thoughts. Her hands flew from one job to another.

She moved swiftly around the kitchen as she gathered ingredients for the gumbo. She pulled out the old black pot and mixed the flour and oil for the roux. The heat from the burner sizzled the mixture. The dull thud of the wooden spoon against the pot brought back memories for Lala. She could still hear her mother's voice during an early lesson. "Be slow and steady, never in a hurry. If someone comes to da door or if da phone rings, don't answer while you stir da roux. Wait for da right color and only use a wooden spoon, never metal. T'ink only good thoughts az you stir. What you t'ink will become part of those who eat dis food. A good gumbo iz filled with love and, like real love, cannot be rushed."

Luisah stirred the roux, waiting, watching carefully as the deep chocolate brown color began to appear. As she poured the bouillon into the gumbo pot and watched the steam rise to the ceiling, she said a silent prayer: *Holy Mary, Mother of all mothers, please take care of my daughter as she walks through this trouble. And please, please, watch over my mother. She's so good, but what if…*Luisah paused…*just take care of them both, please Mary. I give you my heart. Please, give it to your Son.*

Luisah put the lid on the pot. As she untied her apron, she thought of all she had to do. First, she'd try calling Celine again. It would be hard to catch her at work, but she'd call all day if she had to. She'd drop in on Irma with the jar of bacon grease and then drive over to the church, too. Fr. Dubois could make some calls and some visits too; such a good priest and always so willing to help especially with the old folks. She set the pot to simmer and left the kitchen making sure not to disturb her mother.

Mo-maw never heard Luisah leave. She was busy in the altar room, rearranging the candles and softly humming prayers to the saints. She placed Celine's picture in the center of the linen-draped table and set three white votive candles on both sides of it. As she lit each one, she prayed for protection against all storms, especially those inside Celine. She ran her fingers over the photograph and draped her rosary beads around it, kissing the crucifix.

Mo-maw sat back, looking over the altar. For now, everything looked right. Throughout the day, she would place other things on the altar, a lock of Celine's hair and photos of her childhood. Slowly, the altar would become an offering of Celine's life as proof of her goodness, but for now, she needed to dedicate the offering to St. Ezilie, the family saint. Mo-maw eased herself onto her knees to the wood floor.

She placed the Black Iris on the floor in front of her and with both her hands on the altar, lowered her head. "Ezilie, Ezilie, hear my heart of hearts." She dipped her fingers in the egg, breaking the yolks and made the sign of the cross. "A new beginning I ask for my sweet Celine." Then she dipped her fingers lightly into the salt and held them up in offering. "Cleanse her, my Ezilie, virgin and saint." Please cleanse her of all that makes her life bitter and protect her from the darkness that chases her." She brought her fingers to her tongue and tasted. "Only you can make her life sweet again." She sat back on her feet, raising her head and looking into the eyes of Celine's photograph. "…Talk to me and tell me what to do."

Mo-maw stared for a long time. Warmth came over her. She could smell the gumbo, cooking, simmering, and waiting for Celine. Mo-maw smiled. She reached below the altar and pulled out a large black trunk. She opened it and sorted through newspapers and old photographs. "Yes, of course I need this…" She pulled out a smaller wooden chest with deeply engraved markings burnt into the cover. Soon she would show it to Celine. She smiled as she placed it on the altar next to Celine's picture. Everything was nearly ready.

She rummaged through the trunk, searching with her hands. "Where are you, little one?" Then she felt it, the soft satin of Celine's favorite doll. Mo-maw nearly laughed out loud as she picked up the doll. "Here you are!" Its little dress was slightly rumpled and its black hair needed combing. In spite of the mud stains, she was perfect. "Oh, you just need a little help, dat's all." She straightened the dress and patted down the hair. She looked into the light emerald green eyes and said, "Oh chère, 'tit fille, you went through a lot but now you look better."

Mo-maw stood up and cradled the doll like a newborn. She carefully carried it to Celine's room. The old woman walked over, gently pulled the lace mosquito net back and placed the doll on the bed. Deep from within, a lullaby from childhood came to her. She smiled and hummed the tune her grandmother had sung. Mo-maw whispered to the doll, "Call her, little one. Call her."

CHAPTER 5

Celine tried not to remember, but no matter how fast she drove down I-10, the haunting memories chased close behind. Nothing made sense anymore. A cold chill ran through her as she remembered seeing the painting, the monster exactly as her dream, right down to the very last blood-dripping talon. She took a deep breath and gripped the steering wheel tighter. She could still hear Alex's shrill voice screaming at Dr. Sonnier, "Help her, Matt! Do something!" *Poor Alex, he's already sick enough. I'm sure my little fainting act didn't help him any. God, I feel like such a fool!*

Celine let out a deep sigh. Remembering what happened next was nearly unbearable, but she couldn't stop the thoughts from rushing in.

From the moment she opened her eyes, there he was, the man from her dream, but now he had a name. *Michael. His name is Michael.* He carried her to the sofa, cradling her gently to his chest. As he laid her down, a few curls of his jet-black hair fell into his face. He looked directly at her and smiled. *Those beautiful blue-gray eyes.* Her first reaction was to try to sit up, but the room was spinning. He whispered in a soft, low voice "Easy now, don't move too fast." *Could it be him? Could Michael really be…*She sucked in a quick breath. *No, that's impossible.* She drove faster, turned up the radio, rolled down the car window and let the last fragments of the rain slap her in the face; anything to escape.

She couldn't remember how long she sat in the driveway at her mother's. She couldn't even remember how she had gotten there, really. She stopped the car and dropped her hands into her lap. It was dark and everything was quiet. She watched the pine trees swaying, the green needle hair waving to her in the gentle, after-storm breeze. She closed her eyes and let the cool air wash over her. The smell of rich black mud, the kind that squished through her toes when she was a kid made her smile. *I'm home.*

She sat there staring at the old Acadian-style house with its sloping tin roof and deep, wrap-around porch. Lights twinkled from the windows, inviting her inside. Her mother and grandmother greeted her half-way across the porch with hugs and kisses and before she knew it she was sitting at the dining room table, a huge bowl of gumbo in front of her. At first, she didn't think she could eat. The tension had her stomach in knots but after the first bite, she realized how hungry she was.

Mama and Mo-maw talked about the storm while she ate. Celine was grateful that she really didn't have to say much. A nod of her head and an occasional 'really?' was all that was needed. When the bowl was empty, her mother ladled more into it, "Here. Have some more, chère. Dere's plenty."

She pushed the bowl away, "No, Mama. Really, I've had enough."

Mo-maw frowned. "Oh, chère. You got to eat you mama's gumbo. You'll feel better. You're off the road and home safe now. So, you eat." Mo-maw wouldn't take no for an answer as she broke off another piece of crisp French bread and plopped another dollop of potato salad into her bowl. Celine looked at the two of them staring back at her. She already knew what was coming. She sat up and mustered the best smile she could find, but the ploy didn't work.

Mama, as usual, was the first to say something. "You're looking so pale, chère. Are you feeling alright?" She reached over and felt Celine's cheek with the back of her hand. "Your face is so warm!"

Celine shook her head just a little too quickly, "Really, I'm fine." She squirmed a little in her chair. "It's just the gumbo. It's hot, but it's delicious, just like I like it. Thanks for making it." She sipped her iced tea.

Mo-maw squinted through her glasses. "Fine? *Mais*, chère, Look at you. You done got skinny. Why you think that is, huh?"

Celine pushed the glass away. She drew a deep breath. She'd forgotten how they always worked as a tag team. How could she explain any of this to them? She hadn't even been able to explain it to herself. Tomorrow. She'd tell them tomorrow; figure out some way to explain everything that had happened. But for now, she just had to get past their questions. "I know I look pretty bad. Driving in that storm was horrible. I would've been home earlier, but I had a meeting and found out that we're getting a new art building. Did I tell you about that? The kids are gonna love it and…"

The clock down the hall chimed 10:00 and Mo-maw struggled to stand up. She gave Celine a small frown that told her she hadn't fooled her at all. "…and we wanna hear all about it, but right now I got a surprise for you. You mama and I, we been workin' on it for a little while now."

Celine sat back, relieved that she had averted the grand inquisition for now. "Is it really 10:00? Oh geeze, I'm sorry it's so late. You shouldn't have waited up for me. You two must be exhausted."

Mo-maw smiled. "Oh yeah, chère, it's late, but not time for sleep yet, *non*. Help this old Mo-maw to your bedroom." Celine walked around the table as Mo-maw stood up. Mo-maw turned to Luisah. "Come on, Luisah, you too, chère." Celine slipped her arm through her grand-mother's and together the three women shuffled down the hall.

As they reached the bedroom door, Celine laughed. "Okay, what have you two been up to?"

Luisah giggled, "You'll see, chère, you'll see."

Mo-maw opened the door and smiled. "It's all ready for you." When she turned on the light, trinkets of Celine's past bounced to life. All her favorite childhood mementoes had been reborn, pinned neatly or framed. Even the dirty toe-shoes had been stored in a glass case along with medals for all those art competitions.

Celine looked at the newly-framed paintings that had won her the awards. "Mama, Mo-maw, this is wonderful!" They laughed as Celine stepped further into the room. She felt like she had entered a time cap-sule and couldn't help marveling at everything they had dragged out from who-knows-where.

Luisah turned the ceiling fan on and the old thing from some era long-gone churned to a slow spin. It still had that hypnotizing, muted *whump* that had always lulled her to sleep as a child. The gentle breeze stirred the floor-length lace netting of the canopy bed into a lazy dance.

"So, you like it then, chère?" Mo-maw asked, a little grin on her face.

Celine hugged her. "Of course, I do! But why did you do this?"

Luisah shrugged her shoulders. "Just seemed like the right time. The idea started after you got…" Luisah struggled with the word. "…

engaged. We thought maybe it would be a good idea to fix some of these things special, you know, keep them from going bad. We were thinking that Greg's family might like to see…" Luisah hesitated.

Mo-maw picked up where Luisah stopped. "…like to see all the wonderful talents our wonderful Celine has. But then we decided, after the break-up, Greg and his family, they're not so important." Mo-maw flicked her hand in the air, like she was brushing away a fly. "What is important is for our Celine to remember that she's wonderful and special. Always was, always will be. So here it is, our little present for you."

Celine hugged Mo-maw and then Luisah as she fought back tears. She held on a little longer as she said "Thank you both. I love it and I love you!"

Luisah smiled and glanced over at Mo-maw. Mo-maw smiled back and gave Luisah a slow nod. Luisah gently stepped back, fighting tears of her own. "Oh, my Celine, we love you, too, chère. She turned to Mo-maw. "Show her the rest of it while I go clean the kitchen. I'll be back in a minute."

Mo-maw nodded. "Make the coffee, okay?"

As the two women chatted for a moment, Celine crossed the room, pulled open the French doors and unlatched the huge shutters that guarded them. She stepped onto the back porch listening to the sounds of bullfrogs and crickets coming from the bayou. The moon was full and silver light draped across the yard, peeking through the trees, but the magic moment was broken when she heard Mo-maw's voice "O-o-o, chère. Pull dem doors! You gonna let the *loup garou* in!"

Celine laughed as she stepped back inside, pulling the shutter doors behind her. "Come on, Mo-maw. You know I don't believe in the bayou werewolf anymore!"

Mo-maw gently pushed her aside and reached for the French doors. She locked them with a snap. "Maybe not, chère, but everyone knows dere's more bad t'ings on the bayou at this hour than the *loup garou*. Besides, jus' because you don' believe don' mean it's not for real!"

"Well, the *loup garou* and Madame Grand Doigts went out of style years ago, Mo-maw, and besides it's just so nice to…"

Mo-maw pulled Celine to her, hugging her tightly. Her voice came out in a half-pant, "Okay, so you don' believe in the closet witch either, 'cause she went out of style, too, huh? Well, my shoes went out of style years ago, but that don' mean my shoes aren't for real now, does it, chère?"

She let herself melt into the old woman's chubby arms, "No, ma'am." Celine stepped back and looked at Mo-maw's old-fashioned lace-up pumps. "Besides, I like your shoes. You know they really are coming back into fashion." They both laughed.

Mo-maw playfully shook her finger in Celine's face. "Now, I know you tellin' you Mo-maw a fib." She walked over to the bedside lamp and clicked it on. She pulled the canopy to one side, smiling impishly. "I found someone I think you might like to see. Do you remember her?"

When Celine saw the doll sitting on the bed, she knew she was looking at a long-lost friend. "Mo-maw, where did you find..." She walked over, picked up the doll and cradled her in her arms. "I mean, all this stuff..." She looked into Mo-maw's face and saw her sweet, tender smile. It was too much. The tears fell. She sat down on the bed and couldn't stop crying. She held the doll and listened to Mo-maw sing a song she hadn't heard since she was a little girl.

♫ *"Gue-gue Solingai; Dreamland opens here.*
Balliez chimin-la; Sweep the dream path clear.
Ma dis li, oui, ma di li; My child, now listen well.
Calbasse, il connain parle; What tortoise has to tell.

"Gue-gue Solingaie; Dreamland opens here.
Balliez chimin-la; Sweep the dream path clear.
Ma dis li, oui, ma di li; My child, now listen well.
Cocodril, li connain chanter; To the Song of crocodile.

"Sail, Sail, pretty babe, while the moon is low,
Through bright bayou night the dreamboats drifting slow." ♫

When everything was quiet, Mo-maw whispered into her ear. "Celine, look at me, chère." Celine looked at her grandmother sitting next to her. "What's wrong, Celine. You need to tell me. Your heart is full and if you don't tell me now, it will only hurt more when you do."

She sighed and wiped away the last few tears. "I don't even know where to start, Mo-maw."

Mo-maw nodded. "Just start, chère. We'll figure it out as we go."

Celine laid the doll on her lap and reached for her grandmother's hand. Mo-maw gave it a little squeeze for encouragement.

Celine took a deep breath. "About three months ago, I started having these dreams, but not like any dreams I've ever had before. It was like I had stepped into a night world that really existed; it was all so real. Even after I'd wake up, it was with me all the time. I'd be going through my day, but then I'd find myself daydreaming about it. I just couldn't shake it. I can't tell you how many times someone would ask me if I was alright, because I'd be staring off into space.

"At first I thought I was having them because I'd been under so much pressure from work and school and wedding plans, so I just tried to ignore it, but that only made it worse. It went from once or twice a week to three and even four times and I'd wake up screaming and shaking. That's when Greg and I started having problems. He just had no patience with me, always telling me that I'd better do something about them because he couldn't marry someone who was..." Celine stopped and squeezed Mo-maw's hand a little tighter.

Mo-maw sat patiently. "Who was what, chère?"

Celine whispered the word. "Crazy. He even went so far as to tell me I might need to be hospitalized; 'committed for medication evaluation' were his words. He sounded like such a lawyer when he said it to me, but he scared me so badly, I went to my Dr. and he gave me some pills; told me I was having migraines and had developed an anxiety disorder because of all the pressure I was under."

Mo-maw let out a little huff, "*Ça c'est couillon!* But dat boy, he's the crazy one! Committed? Well those pills, they must've made Greg happy, *non?*" Celine looked down. The pills killed their sex life so, no, they didn't make Greg happy, not at all. That was the last nail in the coffin for the future Mrs. Gregory Conrad Drescher III, but how could she tell her grandmother this? Mo-maw stroked her granddaughter's hand and took a deep breath. "It's okay, chère. I know now. I know."

Celine looked at her grandmother. "At first, the pills did take the edge off and I was able to get my work done, but the minute I'd fall asleep, the dream was there like it had been waiting for me all day. I don't know what to do anymore. I'm scared, Mo-maw, really scared." Celine stopped, afraid to go any further.

Mo-maw sat quietly. "The dream, chère, tell me the dream."

Celine struggled with the right words. "In the beginning of it, I'm always so happy. I'm like a little girl again, but…"

Mo-maw nodded. "That's good, chère. Keep going."

"…but then I'm attacked by a kind of animal, a monster. It tortures me and it's not just me that it tortures. There's a man there, but what it does to him is far more terrible than what it does to me. I could've stopped that poor man's suffering, but instead I hide. He's dying and it's all my fault!" Celine's tears were free falling now. "He's so innocent in all of this. I'm a coward—a selfish coward!"

Celine shook her head, trying to erase the images out of her thoughts. "Greg's right! I must be crazy! I keep trying to tell myself, 'it's just a dream. It didn't happen. Get over it!' but after tonight, I'm not so sure anymore." Celine's hands were trembling now. Mo-maw put her hands over hers and waited, silently.

Celine took a deep breath. "You remember me telling you and Mama about the meeting I went to tonight? The man I met with, he had a painting of the monster from my dream. That hideous thing was right there in his studio! He painted it, Mo-maw, right down to its last vein! When I saw it, the dream started all over, but I was awake! How is that possible?" Celine started to pant and gasp for breath.

Mo-maw patted her hand. "Shhh, Shh. Chère, it's okay."

Celine felt flushed. Her hands were beginning to shake. "When I saw it, I just panicked and all I remember is backing up, trying to get away from the painting, but I bumped into someone and when I turned around, it was that poor tortured man from my dream, Mo-maw. It was him! I know it was him! When I saw his face, everything went black. It was horrible, Mo-maw. I don't know what to think anymore. I must be going crazy!"

Mo-maw pulled Celine to her and held her while she sobbed. She stroked her hair. "Chère, it's okay. We'll figure this out." As Celine sat back up, Mo-maw's eyes grew wide. She looked closer at Celine's neck. "Chère, where did you get this?" She pushed Celine's hair away from her collar. She frowned as she saw the purple gouges. Celine began to shiver. Mo-maw felt her forehead.

"Luisah!" Mo-maw laid Celine on the bed. Luisah came running into the room. "She's burnin' up with da fever. Bring me the Black

Iris. Crush the bay leaf in rum. Hurry!" In what seemed like seconds, Mo-maw was rubbing liquid sandpaper on Celine's neck.

Mo-maw took the rum from Luisah and together they helped Celine sit up. Mo-maw brought the amber liquid to Celine's lips. "Here, chère. Down your throat. All of it." Celine took a sip but the moment it touched her tongue, she gasped and sputtered. Celine turned and pushed it away. Mo-maw pushed it to her lips again. "No, chère, all of it." Mo-maw forced it to her lips and then turned back to Luisah. "It's *cochemère*. Lala, go get some gauze and..." she sighed, "burn some basil. We need the incense in here."

Luisah stood up. "Do you want *Le Monguilier*, too? I could boil the leaves down. It'll only take a few minutes."

Mo-maw cut her off. "That'll take too long, chère. We need to break this fever now. It's worse than I thought!" Luisah hurried out of the room, a pinched look of worry on her face. The stuff on Celine's neck began to itch so she reached up, trying to rub it with her fingertips. Just as Celine touched it, Mo-maw pulled her hand away. "Chère, leave it alone. It needs to work into those cuts."

Celine stared at the black tar on her fingertips. "It's starting to itch and, oh God it smells like..."

"Shh..." Mo-maw rubbed Celine's back. "It's best to just sit still for now. You won't feel the itching much longer."

Celine was beginning to feel warm inside. Everything felt muted, numb, like she was floating. The only thing that she could feel was the heat from Mo-maw's hand. "What is that word, Mo-maw? Kosh what?" She knew her words were slurring, but she had to know what was happening.

Mo-maw helped Celine to sit up. "*Cochemère*. It's a living nightmare, but now you must tell me. This is very important, Celine. How did you get those gashes? The nasty stuff I've just given you will help you remember, but you won't be afraid anymore. So, think back, chère, how did it happen?"

"...it happen..." was all she heard when she found herself back into the dream, but Mo-maw was right, she wasn't afraid this time. *What's that sweet fragrance I smell, so calming, so relaxing. Oleander?* Celine looked back at Mo-maw's face. There she was, but younger somehow. *No wrinkles?* She reached up and gently touched Mo-maw's face. "I'm at confession…with a priest, someone I don't know, um, his name is Fr. Mauvais. And it's him who becomes that monster. It chokes me with its claws while it…rapes me." Celine closed her eyes and was kneeling in the black box.

"Celine? Celine! Stay here with me now. Open your eyes. Look at me, chère." Celine looked at Mo-maw.

"This is very important, Celine. This priest, this Father Mauvais, he becomes the monster?"

Celine nodded. The dream began to fade.

A rush of air burst from Mo-maw's lips, "Oh *Mon Dieu*! Celine, listen to me, chère. Don't try to remember anymore."

Celine sat slumped on the bed while Mama and Mo-maw wrapped her neck with gauze. The wrapping was warm and left her feeling calm and safe. When they were finished, Mo-maw cupped Celine's face with her hands and asked, "How you feel, eh? Better?"

Celine nodded. "Just sleepy, though."

"Well, dat's a good sign, chère. But no sleeping yet. You'll perk up in a minute or two. We have to wait 'til the Black Iris is done with its work."

Mo-maw stood up and with Luisah's help, gently pulled Celine to her. The three women walked slowly down the hall to the altar room. As soon as they stepped through the doorway, Celine could smell the old familiar scent of melting candle wax. The odor was so refreshing that she took a deep breath and realized that, for the first time in a long time, she could breathe deeply again.

Mo-maw smiled. "You're looking much better now, chère. Here, sit in this chair." Mo-maw helped her get settled into the middle of three chairs that were in front of the altar. Mo-maw and Luisah went back into the hallway and whispered urgent words between them. If she would've tried, Celine could've heard everything they said, but suddenly it just wasn't important. She sat there, feeling calm and looking at the massive three-tiered altar in front of her.

There were statues of saints on each level, some she recognized and some she didn't. Some had been made out of clay and had been dressed in handmade clothes. But at the very top, Celine saw the one she knew all too well, St. Ezilie, the Black Virgin. To the Catholic world, she was known as the Black Madonna of Montserrat, but Celine had always known her as Ezilie and she still looked magnificent.

The candlelight danced against her ebony skin, her cheeks streaked with tears. The piercing black eyes were softened by the faintest wisp of a smile on her pink lips. Her crown glittered in a rainbow of colorful hearts and her long black hair draped down the golden robe. In her arms was the dark-skinned child, his little face peeking from the swaddling.

Celine sighed and said softly, "St. Ezilie, please, help me."

The room was quiet. Celine looked over at the doorway and saw her mother and grandmother frozen, staring at her. Mo-maw said, "Well, there's your answer, Lala. There's no reason for us to wait any longer. Celine wants it, too."

Luisah nodded, smiling. "Then let's get started." Together, the two women sat down next to Celine.

Mo-maw crossed herself and mumbled a quiet prayer. The sleepiness that Celine had felt was melting away and suddenly she was strangely alert. Her five senses jumped to life. Everything around her became crisp and focused. Her hands tingled and she could hear her heartbeat. The room was filled with the scent of rose petals. Finished with her prayer, Mo-maw turned to Celine. "You feelin' better now?"

Celine reached out and touched their hands. "Thank you, both. Whatever you two did, I feel so calm now. My head doesn't hurt anymore…" She took another deep breath. "…and I can breathe, too!"

"Good, chère. That means you're ready." Mo-maw reached for the wooden box that had been sitting on the altar. She put it in her lap and turned to Celine. "But before I go any further, there's something you need to know, chère. You have never known any priest named Father Mauvais because no priest would ever call himself that."

Celine cocked her head. "I seem to know him in the dream, though."

Mo-maw wearily nodded her head. "Oh yes, he wants you to know him, chère. Do you know what the word *mauvais* means in Cajun French?" Celine shook her head slowly. Mo-maw looked straight ahead at the altar. "Evil, chère. The word means evil. And evil nearly had you. But not anymore." Mo-maw patted the box in her lap." This will keep Father Evil away. He don' like the truth." Mo-maw looked back at Celine with a tiny smile.

Celine looked at the top of the box. A large heart design had been intricately carved into the surface. A grid of squares had been drawn inside the heart with dots inside each square. Wispy curves had been etched around the outside of the heart. "The truth?"

Mo-maw smiled. "Well, it's time for you to learn the whole truth anyway, chère. Up to now you've known only bits and pieces and dat was because, well, you were too young to understand the whole story; like the story of why we all share the same middle name. What'd we always tell you?"

Celine shrugged her shoulders. "You said that Bienaimée was French for 'beloved' and well, the first born girl of our family is always given that name out of affection, but you're telling me there's more?"

Mo-maw smiled and gently put two fingers over Celine's lips. "No more talking, now." Mo-maw gently stroked the top of the box and Celine realized how her hands, wrinkled and worn, matched the old wood. Mo-maw took a deep breath and then began. "A long time ago when I was about to get married, my Mo-maw gave me this box. And now, it's my turn to give it to you." She sighed. "You mama and I, we've looked forward to this day for a long time, chère. I wasn't even sure if I'd live long enough to be able to do this, but here we are. My prayers have been answered." She smiled.

"This box has been in our family for a very long time, ever since the earliest days when they came to Louisiana, maybe even before that, but well, I don't know. It's been handed down to all the firstborn girls in our family on the eve of her wedding. So tonight, I..."

Celine straightened in the chair. "But Mo-maw, you know that..."

Mo-maw held up her hand. "Now, Celine, I'm not senile, chère. I know you're not getting married. Well, not to Greg, anyway, but there's a reason for this; a good one." Mo-maw peered over the top of her glasses. "The cochemère is serious, chère. It's a sign that something is very out of balance in your life. I don't know what's making this evil come after you, but I do know that I need to give you all the tools you need to fight it and I need to give it to you now. We can't wait for you to marry. That's what's in this box, Celine."

The old woman drew in a long breath. "And there's something else. What you're about to find out is something that must remain a secret for the rest of your life. You can only tell one person about this, your firstborn daughter. Just like we're doing with you tonight, you and Luisah will show her everything in here, but until then, it stays only amongst the three of us. Do you promise?"

Celine was confused. She looked at her mother and then her grandmother. "Yes, but what if I never marry or ever have any children? The way my life is going now, I doubt if I'll ever…"

Mo-maw cut her short, her voice honed to a cutting edge. "Right now, none of that is important but what is important is this: you must promise me right now, Celine, or we have to stop. If we stop, we can't keep you safe."

Celine sat back. Mo-maw rarely used such a harsh tone of voice with her. Celine answered quietly. "I promise."

Mo-maw's stern face softened. "Now, Celine, Luisah, give me your hands." She placed Celine's hand over the heart, then Luisah's then her own as she prayed.

> *"Mari se pou ou Kontan,*
> *ou menm ki plen faré*
> *Granmet la avèk ou*
> *Li beni ou pase tout fi*
> *E, li bemi Jezu pitit ou féa*
> *Maiu ou sen, ou se manmam BonDye*
> *Nou se péche*
> *La priyé pou nou jodya*
> *Allé nou prët pou mouri. Amen."*

Celine smiled as she heard her mother and grandmother recite the prayer. She never knew what it meant. It sounded French, but not like the Cajun French she was used to hearing. All she knew was that it was a version of the Hail Mary. There was always something soothing about hearing the deep-throated words. By the time they recited the end of the prayer, Celine had joined them "…*Allé nou prët pou mouri, Amen."*

Luisah laughed. "Mama, she does remember it!"

Mo-maw clapped her hands together. "Oh yes, it's time, chère!" Celine could see the excited twinkle in her grandmother's eyes. "Celine Bienaimée Dupré, you are the next Bienaimée to learn the secrets. St.

Ezilie, she is ready for you to learn. You asked her for her help and she is ready to give it."

The old woman opened the box and removed a dark brown, leather book that was very old. She placed it in Celine's lap and opened it, careful not to tear the delicate pages. Celine soon realized it was a family Bible, written in French. "Oh! This is beautiful!"

Mo-maw and Luisah sat quietly watching Celine's face. Mo-maw turned the pages to the back of the book and there, written in different handwritings, were the names of all the Bienaimée women who had seen this book. Celine read each one carefully and noticed the dates of birth, going back to 1784. With a loud and clear voice, Mo-maw carefully read each woman's name, starting with Celine's mother, Luisah.

> "Luisah Bienaimée Dupré, born-1946
> Blanche Bienaimée Guidry, born-1928
> Aurelia Bienaimée Cazanoux, born-1900, died 1980
> Adrienne Bienaimée Trahan, born-1874, died 1953
> Fremanse Bienaimée Devereaux, born-1831, died 1928
> Celeste Bienaimée Beauvoir, born-1812, died 1899
> Adele Bienaimée Beauvoir, born 1797, died 1855
>   , born-1784, died 1848."

Celine looked closely at the fading ink print. When she noticed that there was no name written beside the date 1784, she asked, "Why is this line empty?"

Mo-maw stared at the altar, her eyes fixed on St. Ezilie. "Some say she was an angel. Others say she was a demon, but I can tell you that she saved many, many people and became quite famous. She made some bad choices in her life, bad choices that probably led to her death. But there was one person who never let all the bad overshadow the good. That person, her daughter, Adele Bienaimée Beauvoir, took the secrets and hid them away in this box so that they could only be used to do God's work. Every woman's name you see on this page has been chosen by firstborn blood to inherit her gift."

Mo-maw paused and faced Celine, smiling. "Chère, my sweet Celine, you are the next in line to inherit. You are the seventh generation granddaughter of the great healer, Marie LaVeau."

CHAPTER 6

A reverent hush settled over the room. Celine sat stunned, staring at her grandmother. A slight shiver ran through her as she spoke, "Mo-maw, did you say Marie LaVeau?" The old woman nodded slowly. Celine leaned back in her chair and looked at Luisah. "But how can that be? Wasn't Marie LaVeau a…" She lowered her voice. "…a *voodoo-ienne?*" She looked back at Mo-maw. "All the history books say she was an evil woman, but you called her a healer. And we're related to her? I really don't understand."

Mo-maw smiled and put her arm around Celine's shoulder. "Oh chère, I know it's hard to hear this. The first time I was told and I heard the name Marie LaVeau, it scared me to death. You're right. She wasn't a very nice woman. Dat's one of the reasons her name isn't written in the bible but there's always two sides to every story. When I heard the other side, I was able to understand her a little better. I think you will, too." Mo-maw gave her a little squeeze. "Now let's get started".

Mo-maw put her hands in her lap and stared into the candlelight. She gently stroked the age-worn box and took several deep breaths, each one longer and deeper than the one before it. Her hands slowed and then stopped. Celine looked at Mo-maw's chest, barely moving up and down. She turned to her mother but her eyes were closed and her head was bowed in prayer. Celine took a deep breath, soaking in the silence. She could feel herself being drawn to someplace far away, a holy ground that held all the answers to her questions.

Mo-maw's voice was low but clear. "I want you to try to see in your mind, chère, old New Orleans. It's the year 1780 and New Orleans is called Ville La Nouvelle Orleans. There is no French Quarter, *non*, chère; the Vieux Carré is the only settlement at the mouth of the Mississippi River. And every day, every hour, the bells of St. Louis Cathedral toll out the city's heartbeat.

"It's alive with French émigrés, Royalists from the court of Louis and Republicans from the French Revolution. Royal or rebel, it don' matter. One thing makes them all the same; they're all on the run from the guillotine. Rich plantation owners, French and Spanish, walk down Rue Rampart, arm-in-arm with their laced and jeweled, café-au-lait mistresses, while dere lily-white wives languish in the countryside. Sprinkled among dem are pirates and priests, slave traders and da sad shiploads of slaves, shackled in cattle pens for the next day's auction. And dat is where our story begins.

"Charles LaVeau, a rich and childless widower, was at the slave auction dat day, hoping to buy a cook when he saw Marguerite on da slave block. She was a beautiful African woman of twenty, newly-arrived from the D'Arcantel Plantation in Haiti. She had been jus' a young girl of about ten when her tribe, the Efik of West Africa, had been invaded by white slavers. Her father, a tribal chieftain, had been brutally killed during da invasion but her mother, a well-known and honored priestess of the ancient Vodou, realized that if she fought, she would be killed, leaving Marguerite all alone to face the slavers. She grabbed Marguerite and surrendered.

"Together dey made the horrible and agonizing journey to Haiti. They landed dere, half-starved but alive and together at D'Arcantel. But, chère, it was a miracle that they were both chosen as kitchen maids to serve the family. Over da next ten years, Marguerite learned everything from her mother about the sacred healing arts and mysteries of Vodou, right dere in that kitchen. But when her mother died, Marguerite wuz sold again, this time to a slave auction company in New Orleans.

"Marguerite stood all alone that day, da tall and proud daughter of a chieftain and a priestess, defiant and beautiful. One look at the ebony-skinned beauty and Charles LaVeau outbid every man in dat room. Oh, it wasn't long before he fell deeply in love with her, but of course he couldn't marry her. Marrying anyone with Negro blood was *pas consacre*, unholy, but he taught her how to read and write and he even gave her a small salary.

"He brought her with him to Mass everyday, too. It was there at St. Louis Cathedral, that LaVeau introduced her to his priest, Père

Charlevoix. When the old man greeted her in Haitian French sprinkled with a few words of Efik, a great bond grew between them and over time, Marguerite began to see that the old Latin Catholicism and Vodou were not that different; Holy Communion, Jesus on the Cross, even St. Ezilie all just went by different names. It was their friendship that made Catholicism an important part of the work that Marguerite did.

"The union between Charles LaVeau and Marguerite soon became *placage*, the closest thing to marriage outside of the law and when Marguerite became pregnant, LaVeau wuz overjoyed. But there wuz a problem. Children born of slave women were born into slavery even if da father was free. The good-hearted LaVeau wanted no child of his to have to endure dat fate so he paid the enormous sums to buy da baby's freedom. On September 10, 1784, Marie Catherine LaVeau wuz born a free, mulatto child.

"Little Marie never really knew her daddy. He died three years later, leaving Marguerite some money and a house on St. Ann Street on da northwest boundary of the Vieux Carré. From there, Marguerite was finally able to fulfill da true calling of her West African roots, Healer and Guardian of the People.

"Over the years, the house on St. Ann became well known as a healing house with Marguerite, the doctor and Marie the assistant. By the time Marie wuz twelve years old, Marguerite wuz letting her make house calls to take care of minor illnesses." Mo-maw shook her head. "But it wuz along da way to one of those early morning calls dat tragedy struck and changed Marie's life forever.

"By now, La Nouvelle Orleans of 1796 had become a horrible place to live. After the American Revolution, the *Z'Américaines* were settling the boundary of the Vieux Carré by the hundreds, boxing in the Orleanians. Even though the Vieux Carré wuz protected under French and Spanish Law, violent riots broke out over slave rights. These lawless men hated the French Code Noir, the law that allowed the free people of color nearly equal rights of the whites. They believed that all blacks, no matter how white they looked, should be forced to live as slaves and that the Vieux Carré should be run like the rest of the slave south. Day after day, these horrible men sat in wait for any opportunity to make life miserable for da people of the Vieux Carre.

"On dat fateful morning, Marie decided to take a short cut. No-one knows why she did it. Her mama had warned her many times, but dat day, she went dangerously close to the Vieux Carré boundary. As she wuz walking by, one of these *Z'Américaines* just took her right off the street, threw her in a carriage and hid her in a house far away from the Vieux Carré; a place called the Garden District, but it was no garden then, chère, non.

"When Marguerite found out what happened, she wuz sick with grief. It took her days to find out where Marie wuz and even longer to get anyone in the Garden District to accept da child's free papers. Many weeks and lots of money later, Marie wuz brought home, but dat poor little thing had been beaten, raped and wuz nearly dead.

"Marguerite nursed dat child, day and night. Several months passed and finally Marie wuz over the worst but it turned out the poor child wuz pregnant. Marguerite begged her to get rid of it, telling her it wuz an evil white creature and would only bring her deep sadness for the rest of her life, but Marie kept saying no! The child needed to be born. Marie wuz certain the baby wuz a girl and dat it was calling to her. Finally Marguerite gave in and helped Marie. Her labor lasted two days and nearly killed poor Marie. Weak and weighing barely four pounds, her sweet little baby, Adele, came into da world."

Mo-maw stopped for a moment, looked down and closed her eyes. The silence in the room swallowed the echo of the old woman's words. Celine was in awe of all that she was hearing. She had endless questions, but something kept her from asking anything. She glanced over at her mother, her head still bent and eyes still closed. Celine felt surrounded by a mystic presence and was afraid that if she spoke, the spell would be broken.

Mo-maw looked at Celine. Tears filled the dark brown eyes, but a wrinkled smile was etched across her face. Mo-maw looked back into the candlelight and with a soft, hoarse voice, continued the tale.

"Adele learned everything from Marie, following her around as time went on. When Marguerite died, Marie took over as Healer and Guardian of the People, but chère, by then things had changed. There wuz no more La Nouvelle Orleans. It was now New Orleans and the Vieux Carré was renamed the French Quarter. With American statehood looming closer wit' each passing day, da people of the Quarter needed Marie now more than ever.

"Marie, wit' Adele at her side, continued her daily home visits, treating and helping anyone in the Quarter who needed it. She never let them pay her, even though many of them tried. Even after the day's work, Marie and Adele would spend many late hours working hand-in-hand and treating the untouchables, the slaves dat had been brutally abused by their masters. When cholera and yellow fever swept through the city, killing hundreds, Marie and Adele never abandoned da sick and dying of the Quarter. In the end, the people all loved Marie, even worshipped her as a queen and Adele as their sweet angel.

"She did treat whites, but she had a different set of rules for dem. Oh, she healed them just as she healed her own people, but being in and out of the homes of those wealthy families gave her a doorway into all their family secrets; the pregnancies that she helped get rid of, the secret love affairs of husbands, the alcoholic wife. The list went on and on. She always told them that her cures were free but her silence would cost them. Big! If they didn't agree, her cure would turn into a curse.

"News traveled far and wide dat there was a magic woman in the Quarter. It was the whites that first called her a *voodooienne*, and they claimed that she could cure any sickness. Rumors even had her raising the dead, but of course dat was never true.

"Still, people talk and the talk made Marie and Adele more popular than ever, so it was really no surprise when late one night, a beautiful carriage bearing the Royal Fleur-de-Lys of King Louis, drove up to the St. Ann house. A frantic young man pounded on the door, yelling for Marie LaVeau. He explained dat his cousin, Etienne, had been badly wounded in a sword fight and he begged dat Marie come quickly to his father's plantation outside of New Orleans.

"Marie hesitated. She recognized the young man, or at least his family name, Beauvoir. His father was one of the richest sugar cane producers in New Orleans. She asked him if his cousin was also a Beauvoir. When he said yes, Marie told him non! She wouldn't come. The cousin's father, the owner of a riverboat shipping business in the Quarter, had a horrible reputation for being brutal and merciless to his slaves. He wasn't the only one, either. His wife was free with the whip, too. The fine house that they lived in near the Place d'Arms was the site of much cruelty. They even kept some of their slaves chained and gagged in the attic.

"The Beauvoirs were *sauvage* and Marie hated them with every inch of her soul. She had secretly treated those poor dying slaves many, many times, but to treat their son was something that repulsed her. Marie told the young man to go to the royal doctor. Surely the royal doctor would be a better choice. Instead of an answer, the young man handed her several hundred newly minted gold Francs from his purse with a promise of more, much, much, more.

"Marie and Adele raced in the carriage wit' the young man past New Orleans and up the old Mississippi river road to the plantation. They entered the grounds through a back gate and stopped at a *garçon-nière*, the private quarters reserved only for the unmarried sons of the family. The two women were hurried inside and found Etienne alone, bleeding profusely from his chest, his fine white linen-and-lace shirt covered wit' blood. He had been gored very deeply near his heart.

"The wound had been a mistake, horseplay really, between the two cousins, but it wuz a game turned deadly. Neither of the young men wanted their fathers to know what happened. It wuz clear that they feared them just as much, if not more, than the slaves did. Marie told them her usual fee for whites; the treatment wuz free, but the secrecy would cost them. The two women worked on him all night and by the morning, Etienne wuz pale and weak but sleeping peacefully. Marie returned to the Quarter just before daybreak with another payment of Francs tucked away in her bosom.

"She let Adele stay on for several weeks after dat, making sure dat Etienne was healing properly. One thing Marie didn't want to have happen; if Etienne died, Marie and Adele both would suffer a long, drawn-out and torturous death as revenge from the Beauvoirs. Still, there was the money and Marie decided dat the risk was worth it. Dat poor cousin paid Marie huge sums every week and made sure dat Adele had all the supplies she needed. He lied to Etienne's parents by weaving some story about his absence. I don't know what story he told to hide the truth from them, but whatever he said, it must've worked because they never found out.

"A powerful and forbidden magic was at work, chère, because over the course of the time that passed, Adele and Etienne fell deeply in love.

Adele knew that her mother would be furious with her, but day after day, night after night, away from prying eyes and listening ears, Adele came to see a good and kind-hearted man; nothing like her mother had told her of the Beauvoir family. As Adele heard the long and sad stories of Etienne's abuse at the hands of his father, their love deepened. They were so young and so in love, she fourteen, he barely twenty-one; so blinded by their innocence, to them, no one else mattered and their love would last forever and a night.

"Under Adele's skillful care, Etienne healed and eventually needed to return to his family home in the Quarter. The magical excuses were wearing thin, as well as the cousin's money. Adele had prolonged the healing as long as she could. She knew that Marie would grow suspicious and demand to know why Etienne wasn't completely healed. It was a sad day when they said good-bye. Their Garden of Eden was gone but before they parted, Etienne asked Adele to marry him. The 'yes' that Adele gave Etienne was easy, but they both knew that facing their families would be *difficile*. Still, they parted in hope.

"When Etienne told his parents of his plans to marry Adele, they laughed, believing that this was just a young man's folly. To them she was just another woman of color, a quadroon, probably beautiful and of course necessary for a virile young Frenchman to have in his bed. They encouraged him to buy Adele an apartment on Rue Rampart and care for her as his mistress. Of course, they would have children, but they would simply become part of the *gens de couleur libre*, the free people of color that were so much a part of New Orleans.

"They reminded him of the royal edict, *Noblesse Oblige*; with royalty come responsibilities. He, of course, would be required to marry a royal French woman to match his bloodline, have sons and oversee his father's shipping business for the rest of his life. As the only son, he would inherit the entire fortune, provided he lived by their rules. This enraged Etienne and he told them that with or without their consent, he would marry Adele. When his mother and father realized that he would not change his mind, they did something wicked.

"Behind his back, they bought a consignment for him in Napoleon's Grand Army and then made arrangements to have him returned to France, against his will if necessary, as a soldier to the Russian Front. Of course, if he gave up his fantasy of marrying Adele, after a short stint in the army, he could return to New Orleans, provided he brought back a proper French bride with him. By the time he learned of what they had done, it was too late. He had no choice in the matter; consignment to the French Army was irreversible.

"Adele and Etienne became desperate. They met secretly and as often as they could, but the trysts were very short-lived. Finally, with only one week left before Etienne was to set sail for France, Etienne appealed to his Aunt, his father's only sister, the Lady Beauvoir. She was very kind, so different from her two brothers. Etienne had always been her favorite and so she made secret arrangements for the two young lovers to have one last tête-à-tête at one of her lush apartments on the plantation.

"That night Etienne promised Adele that he would return and marry her one day. He gave her a ring as he told her of his plan; when he served his time on the Russian Front, the honor of being a successful soldier in Napoleon's Army would earn him high rank and quite a lot of money. With that status, his parents would be powerless to stand in the way of their marriage. It was then that he called her his *Bienaimée*, his eternal beloved."

Celine let out a little gasp. "That's where our middle name comes from?" Mo-maw nodded as she opened the box on her lap. "Shh, shh, quiet now, I have something for you to see." She removed a beautiful diamond-and-sapphire-studded ring wrapped in a royal blue cloth and handed it to Celine. The gems formed a triple Fleur-de-Lys, the bases touching, forming a flower. The single fire opal that was set in the center glistened in the candlelight. Celine turned it over and over, gazing at its beauty.

Luisah smiled as she looked at the ring. "Adele wore it faithfully, hoping and praying to St. Ezilie for Etienne's safety, but he never returned. Adele never heard from him again. She wrote Etienne many, many letters but they were never answered. Maybe his parents got their wish after all; maybe he fell in love with another. Whatever happened to him, I guess we'll never know. One thing we do know, though; she never stopped praying to St. Ezilie for his return."

Celine stared at the ring, the proof that the story wasn't just some fairy tale. The three women sat in respectful silence for the love that still lived in the ring. Celine turned to her grandmother and hugged her and then turned to her mother and hugged her as well. "This is such a sad, sad story. It's hard to understand why they just couldn't be together."

Mo-maw gave her a tired smile. "Chère, we will never understand, eh? Just let Adele and Etienne live in your heart, where they belong. You will make them happy to be there together again, non?" Mo-maw stopped and looked down. Her shoulders slumped as she let out a sorrowful sigh.

Celine looked at her grandmother, worried. The hall clock was striking 11:00 p.m. It was late, too late for her grandmother. Telling the story was taking its toll on Mo-maw. Celine placed the ring carefully back into the box then reached over and took her grandmother's hand. "Mo-maw, you need to go to bed. Can't we finish this tomorrow? Let me help you."

Celine inched herself forward in her chair when Mo-maw stopped her. "No, chère, no. We can't stop. The story, it must be told now. We are at the last part."

Celine hesitated and turned to her mother. "Mama, don't you think we should…"

Luisah shook her head slowly. "No, Celine. Sit back now. You Mo-maw's right."

Mo-maw smiled as she patted Celine's knee. "Anyway, it's you mama's turn. Let her tell the rest of the story."

Celine sat back and turned to her mother. Luisah stared into the candlelight just as Mo-maw had and, with a clear steady voice, continued the tale.

"The whole time that Adele was with Etienne in the *garçonnière*, a romance of another kind was happening back at the St. Ann house. Marie took up with a man, a freed slave, Touro Ozinee. He was black and not just black. He was Mandingo, the most feared of all the tribes of Africa. Strong and good-looking, he was the unchallenged leader of the freed slaves of the Quarter.

"There were dark secrets about how he gained his freedom, but very few men, whites included, ever dared cross Ozinee. He hated whites almost as much, maybe even more, than Marie did. The whip stripes on his back were his testimony to that hatred. They were probably joined in hatred more than they were in love. I guess I would have to add greed to their unholy attraction. They both had ways of making money that will always remain a mystery.

"Oh, there's no doubt that Marie felt safer with him at her side; no white man would ever harm her again; no white man would ever dare. And who knows, maybe Ozinee, after all those years of abuse at the hands of whites, wanted Marie's healing touch. No matter, together they were a powerful and formidable team, the likes of which the French Quarter had never seen before.

"When Adele returned to the house, she was surprised to find Ozinee living there. Immediately, bad blood grew between them. Here stood Adele, a beautiful, cream-colored quadroon, the product of everything that Ozinee wanted destroyed. When Adele told Marie of her plans to marry Etienne, she found herself in a horn-locked battle with her mother and this black stranger. Ozinee screamed at her horror stories of the *sauvage* treatment that the slaves had received at the hands of the Beauvoirs and Marie finished those stories with detailed descriptions of the painful deaths many of those slaves had endured. The house on St. Ann became a battleground with Adele on one side; Marie and Ozinee on the other. Adele was dumb-founded. Why would her mother side with this man over her? Poor Adele, she just kept trying. Many times she tried talking to Marie in private, but Marie would never change her mind. It would always end badly.

"Adele's morning sickness began after Etienne left. Adele didn't have to tell her mother she was pregnant. Of course, she already knew. Adele was scared to death that Marie would put her out; a white child in the house? What would Ozinee do to the baby? Would the child be safe? Then something very strange happened. In spite of Ozinee's threats, the two women fell into a silent acceptance of the other. Maybe it was because the sick people of the Quarter needed them; maybe they realized that they needed each other, now more than ever. You see, Celine, Adele wasn't the only one pregnant. Marie was now carrying Ozinee's child.

"Oh, but two newborn babies could never have looked so different! Celeste, Etienne's little white dove, was blonde and blue-eyed and by the legal standard, was the highest rank in the *gens de couleur libre*, only ⅛th black, an octoroon. By all legal rights, this child had more freedom than anyone else in the LaVeau family. But Eve, Ozinee's little black panther, was a *griffe*, ¾ black with black eyes and coarse midnight hair. Although she was born free, there was little else that this poor child would ever be allowed to claim. They were both so sweet, but you might as well say that these two baby girls were from different planets. Just by the color of their skin and the content of their blood, they were marked for very different lives.

"Many years passed, and both children, Celeste and Eve, apprenticed under Adele with an aging Marie looking on. As these two developed into young women, Adele always kept a watchful eye over Eve. More than once, Adele caught Eve making poisonous potions and selling them. She made them for Ozinee, too. Who knows what he was using them for? Adele would tell her mother and the old resentments and arguments would rise again. Celeste would always side with Adele and Ozinee would always side with Eve, but as Marie approached her fifty-sixth birthday, she just got too tired to fight anymore.

"Life had taken its toll on Marie. Her eyes had gone bad and she could barely hear. Adele was now the Guardian of the People while her old mama sat in her rocking chair, mumbling prayers all day. And that's when Ozinee got worried. With Marie dying, he knew that Adele would inherit everything and that included the St. Ann house. Adele planned to put him out after her mother died and continue the work. But Ozinee, he had another plan.

"It was at Marie's funeral when Ozinee gave Adele the document that said he was now the owner of the St. Ann house. At first, Adele just laughed, but then she read something that horrified her: the original house deed of Marguerite LaVeau was null and void! All property deals that were made under French Law were supposed to have been renewed under American Law when the United States bought Louisiana. No one had ever done that and now it was too late. Ozinee, that wicked snake, had gotten old blind Marie to sign the house over to him and then he renewed the deed in his name.

"And then, he did something even more evil. Just as Adele was reading Ozinee's name on the new deed, he went to the pulpit and pulled out another document, one he claimed was Marie's verified last will and testament. On that day, at St. Louis Cathedral, in front of hundreds of her devotees, flanked by his henchmen, Ozinee announced that it had been Marie's dying wish that Eve be the new Queen and Guardian of the People!

"Of course, Adele flew into a rage, screaming that Ozinee was lying. She threw herself into the group of men and attacked him, flailing at his face, scratching and clawin' like a wildcat. There was a mad scramble of people as they tried to pull her off him. She pleaded to the people that Ozinee had forged her mother's signature, but no one would listen. In that moment, she realized that she had been duped. He had won and there was nothing she could do about it. Sad, oh chère, so sad, Adele just left the funeral, broken, never the same again."

Luisah turned to Celine and touched her hand. "That lying daughter, Eve, and that even bigger liar, Ozinee, changed the healing into something wicked. They had long been turning the healing herbs into poisons. Who knows? They might've even been using them to make people sick so they could turn around and cure them or, God forbid, they were killing off all their enemies. Maybe they were even slowly poisoning old Marie." Luisah shook her head. "I can hardly believe how evil they were. Eve changed her name to Marie LaVeau and then she and Ozinee started living together as man and wife! Can you believe that? They even turned the St. Ann house into a whore house! They called it Maison Blanche, The White House, for all their rich white customers! I can't even think about it, it's so evil!"

Celine squeezed her mother's hand. "But Mama, what became of Adele and Celeste? Where did they go?"

Luisah gave Celine a sad half smile. "They went to live with the Lady Beauvoir on the plantation. By this time, both of her brothers had died and their wives had long since moved back to Paris. The one son, Etienne's cousin, was now the owner of the plantation so he welcomed them with open arms. He had married and had several sons of his own by that time, so Adele and Celeste found a new home, a new family. Adele never called herself LaVeau again. For the rest of her life, she was known as Madame Bienaimée and it was then that she gave Celeste the legal name Celeste Bienaimée. That's when the tradition of our middle name began; a sort of sign that we all still honor the love between Etienne and Adele."

Celine sat back in her chair, tears streaking her cheeks. "Madame Bienaimée. She must've loved him with all her heart. Poor Adele. What a sad life."

Mo-maw nodded her head and patted Celine's knee. "Sad yes, chère, but you know something? We have so much to be thankful to Adele for." Mo-maw patted the box. "In spite of all her losses and all her pain, somehow she managed to gather the important things, put dem in this box and escape with Celeste. Somehow, over all dem generations, the Bible, the box, the ring, they're still with us, here tonight." Mo-maw stroked the box, smiling. "It's because of Adele that we don't use herbs to hurt people. It's because of Adele that we don't charge money for what we do. If Adele hadn't left the French Quarter, who knows where we'd be; still in the Quarter selling Voodoo dolls on the streets?" Celine laughed. "You think dat's funny, chère, but it could be. It could be."

Mo-maw looked up at the statue of Ezilie and smiled. "She gave us St. Ezilie, too. 'Made her our family saint. Adele prayed to St. Ezilie, day after day, year after year, and never gave up hope that Etienne would return. Even though he never did, she told Celeste to keep praying to St. Ezilie for all things, especially those that even seemed impossible. She told her that sometimes prayers aren't answered in our lifetime. Sometimes, it takes years, even generations for our prayers to be answered. They might not be exactly as we asked for them, but over time, the prayers would be transformed into something much, much better than we ever dared hope for.

"Adele never married, but she didn't die sad and lonely. Every day she had a reminder of Etienne's love for her in Celeste. As little Celeste grew, Adele had the joy of watching Etienne grow in her as well. And there was Lady Beauvoir, too. She had memories of him as a young boy. I'm sure she told Adele and Celeste many of those tales. And when the day came for Adele to hold her granddaughter in her arms, I can tell you, chère, I know the joy she felt. Having you mama and you here with me has been a joy indeed!" Mo-maw looked down and took a deep breath, then looked back at Celine, tears in her big brown eyes. "Adele made it through all the ugly things in her life because Ezilie was right by her side, walking with her, talking to her. Now, I don't mean just watching over her like most everyone else believes, but with her, like

I'm here with you. Tonight, right here, right now, St. Ezilie is with us and she wants me to tell you something.

"Celine, on the night that I was told our family story, my Mo-maw told me that St. Ezilie would bless me with a wonderful daughter someday and that my daughter would give me a granddaughter that would be special. That special one is you. She told me that you would be gifted in many ways, but dreams would be your greatest gift, dreams dat would bless others and heal others, dreams that would help yourself and your family. She said dat this gift was straight from St. Ezilie, herself."

Mo-maw stopped and crossed herself. "And now it's my turn to tell you dat St. Ezilie will bless you wit' a daughter someday by a man that you will love with all your heart and all your soul!" Mo-maw took Celine's hand in hers and gently slipped the ring on Celine's left hand. "His love for you is eternal. He will have no other. Even now he waits for you. You are his Bienaimée."

Celine shook her head. "Mo-maw, what are you doing?"

Luisah smiled. "It's okay, chère. We've decided that we want you to have it."

Celine shook her head. "What? No, no. This is too precious. I don't want to take the chance of losing it. It should stay in the box where it's safe."

Mo-maw put both her hands over Celine's. "No, chère. This is where it belongs and this is where it needs to stay. It will protect you." Mo-maw paused. "Celine, chère, everything you've been going through, the nightmares, the wounds on your neck, and even seeing dat painting of the monster; all of it, chère, are clear signs that you're going in the wrong direction. You've got a wonderful life ahead of you. Do you want that life?"

Celine looked down and nodded. Mo-maw lifted Celine's chin. "Then this is what you need to do. Everyday, I want you to say a little prayer to St. Ezilie on this ring. Ask her to show you what it is she's trying to tell you. Where does she want you to go? Who does she want you to meet? Ask her for true love, the kind of love that's inside this ring. Wearing it every day shows St. Ezilie that you mean it, that your prayers are sincere. When you do, I promise that your life will start to fall into place. The nightmares will melt into messages, healing messages for you and everyone around you and you'll start on the road to the life you deserve. Can you do that?"

Celine looked at the ring. *Mo-maw's right. I'm not happy with anything in my life right now; work, school, love. I've never known the kind of love that Adele and Etienne had for each other. Will I ever find that kind of love? Is it even possible? Is there really someone out there waiting for me?* For just a fleeting moment, she remembered the long horrible months of being plagued by the nightmares made worse by Greg's judgments, the inexplicable scratches on her neck, Alex and his monster, Michael's face as he laid her on the sofa. Celine looked back at her grandmother. "I promise you, Mo-maw, with all my heart."

Mo-maw patted Celine's hand. "*Si le Bon Dieu Veut!* Follow the dreams Ezilie sends you, chère. They know the way and pray that God is willing because there are children yet to be born, children, children."

Luisah laughed. Celine turned to her mother. "Children? What are you talking…?"

Mo-maw laughed and let go of her hand. She opened the Bible and said, "*Non, non.* Not yet, chère. This is enough for one night."

Mo-maw wrote Celine's name in the Bible, closed it and carefully placed it back in the box. "Someday chère, you and you mama will do this for your daughter." She kissed Celine on the forehead.

"Thank you Mo-maw. Thank you, Mama. Celine kissed both of them. "I love you."

Mo-maw hugged her tightly. "Oh chère, *'tit fille*, I love you, too. Now off to bed with you. She watched as Celine and Luisah walked out the door. When she was alone, the old woman slowly knelt on the bare wooden floor, sliding the wooden box under the altar. She hesitated for a moment, saying a special prayer of thanks to Adele. She blew the candles out, one at a time, smelling the melted wax, rose petals and smoke. She hobbled down the hall to her room.

The moonlight lay across the bed as Mo-maw dressed in the dark. She let out a deep sigh. Now she could wait without fear or thinking. She lay in bed, staring at the tall cypress tree just outside her window, its roots digging deep in the mud. A gentle breeze combed the long, gray moss hair, braiding and twisting it against the wrinkled red trunk.

"Thank you" she said as she fell asleep.

CHAPTER 7

Celine stood at the edge of the bayou, her bare feet sinking deep into the cool, black mud. The silver light of the full moon rippled across the murky waters, painting the water hyacinths with iridescent streaks of purple and pink. In the stillness of the sultry night, she heard a chorus of tree frogs while the deep raspy bellow of an alligator called out. The throaty grawk of a bull frog was answered with the *hoohoo haoo* of a watching owl. Just to her right, she watched a snow-white egret tread silently around a cypress knee, his long neck straining to see what cold, wet creatures he could slither down his throat. That's when Celine saw her, a magnificent, tall African woman, standing on the bank, hidden amongst the reeds. Her gown, a translucent gold, sparkled brightly against her ebony skin. Her long black braids were covered in cowrie shells that clicked like rain falling as she walked toward Celine.

"You've finally returned, I see." Her voice was low, like the bass-pitched rumble of a djembe drum. Celine held her breath. She glanced nervously around her. She tried to move backward, but her feet were held in the mud. The woman's laugh was a clatter of *tiktiks* as her hair swayed. "Scared? You don't need to be afraid, unless you have something to hide?" Celine shook her head nervously. "Hmm, we'll see.

"I heard what you told that old one. What were your words?" The woman mocked her with a high pitched baby's voice "...I promith you, Mo-maw, wif all my heart." With black eyes fixed on Celine, the woman looked at her and said, "That old one believes you. Of course she does. You're still her little baby, her little chère. Last time you were here, I saw you and yes, you were a little baby, a sweet innocent little girl. Hmphh. Not anymore. No. Before I let you go one step further, you have to pass my test."

From under her robes, the woman pulled out a clay cup and offered it to Celine, a red liquid spilling over the sides. "Drink. All of it. Show me that you're telling the truth. If you are, well, you'll be just fine and I can let you continue your journey with my blessing. If you're not..." The woman stepped closer to Celine, her voice, a low purr. "...it'll be over before you know it." She shoved the cup into Celine's face. Celine took the cup and looked at the thick red liquid. It smelled pungent, like blood. She gagged, but brought the cup to her lips and let the warm, sour acid pour down her throat. Celine threw the empty cup down, her throat burning. She fell to her knees and looked up. She saw the woman through blurry eyes. The woman's face melted into a smile and then into uproarious laughter. The deep sound of drums boomed through Celine's chest; a high-pitched *katkat* rang in her ears. The woman put her hand on Celine's head and eased her onto her lap. "Oh, you've done well. Sleep now. Just sleep. You won't remember a thing."

Celine opened her eyes, lost in the space between sleeping and waking. She could hear drums faintly and then she realized it was the beat of music from a radio. She could smell coffee. The sunlight's golden rays streaked through the window and lazed across the white lace coverlet.

She smiled. *Home.*

Celine got up from her bed and slipped on jeans and her favorite red-turned-pink Saturday T-shirt, happy that she didn't have to put on a suit and rush off to work. The smell of coffee drew her, like a magnet. She knew her mother and grandmother were in the kitchen preparing a scrumptious breakfast, something Celine rarely made time to enjoy.

She walked barefoot down the hall and found the two women going about their usual routine. The clicking sounds of a Cajun accordion and a zydeco washboard snapped and pinged from the radio, while the King of the Bayou Boogie, Clifton Chenier, belted out, *'Te Te, Fé'*.

"Good Morning!" Celine walked over to her mother and gave her a kiss on the cheek.

Mo-maw looked up. "Bonjour, chère. You must've slept good, since you got up so late." Mo-maw looked at the clock on the stove and gave Celine a teasing smile.

Celine laughed and gave her grandmother a kiss on the forehead. "I did, Mo-maw! For the first time since I don't know when!"

Mo-maw smiled. "Any dreams?"

Celine shook her head. "None. I sort of remember something about drums beating but that's all. I think I was hearing the radio as I woke up."

Mo-maw nodded. "No monsters? Father Mauvais?"

Celine let out a sigh of relief. "No. Thank God and you and Mama for that!"

Mo-maw smiled. "But dis is good, chère, dis is good! Let me see you neck." Celine obediently lifted her chin and pushed her hair aside. Mo-maw reached up and pressed her thumb gently over her neck. "Oh, c'est bon! Almost healed. There's hardly a trace there. It'll be gone by tonight." She turned Celine's face to hers and smiled. "And what about the rest of it? Any thoughts about last night?"

Celine shook her head. "I just feel really calm about it all. I mean, I don't think I've had much time to process everything. Everything the two of you told me… Wow. Lots to take in."

Mo-maw laughed. "That word you young people use nowadays, process. Don't think about it too much, chère. You can think yourself right into plenty of doubts. That's why the story is usually told the eve of your wedding, so you don't have too much time to think. You sure look better than you did last night. What ya think, Luisah, eh?"

Luisah turned from the stove. "Oh yeah, Mama. She looks rested. More like my Celine."

"Mmm. Something smells good." Celine walked behind her mother and peeked into the frying pan.

"Celine! Get your face outta there! You don't want it to pop on you!" Luisah waved her away. "Go get some coffee."

Celine poured herself a cup of coffee. She had forgotten how dark her mother and grandmother liked it. Since being away, she had gotten used to the flavored coffee-house brands that had become so much a part of her generation. There was no replacement for strong black coffee with chicory. The taste of it filled her with the long-needed feeling of being taken care of by the people who loved her.

Luisah put the fried eggs and bacon out while Celine helped her grandmother set the table. Homemade mayhaw jelly and fresh butter were placed next to the warm biscuits Luisah had made earlier. Celine sipped her coffee. "So what are you two doing today?"

Luisah turned to Mo-maw. "I have to go see Miz Gautreaux this morning. Mr. Bobby called. She's not getting any better."

Mo-maw frowned. "Hmm, so the snake tea didn't work?"

Luisah buttered another biscuit. "No. He said she was real pale this morning and very weak."

Celine sat back in her chair. "Snake tea? Sounds awful."

Luisah smiled. "It's not made out of snakes, if that's what you're thinking. It's a tea made out of a swamp plant. It's just as good as penicillin, but better. It works on viruses too. You've had it. You just didn't know what it was called."

Celine raised her eyebrows, surprised. "I'm glad I didn't know. I probably wouldn't have had anything to do with something named snake tea. So what's wrong with Miss Gautreaux?"

Mo-maw wiped her mouth on her napkin. "We're not sure, chère." She started off with what seemed like a cold. We treated her, she got better, then she got worse. She's been doing this off and on now for three weeks." She turned to Luisah. "Probably time to do a walk, check if it's a conjo. Take Celine with you." Luisah nodded.

Celine's eyes grew wide as she looked at both women. "What can I do? Shouldn't she go to the hospital if she's been sick that long?"

Mo-maw smiled and patted Celine's hand. "You just watch you mama and do everything she tells you to do. Hospital?" Mo-maw brushed the words away like an annoying fly, "Dat's where you go to die. Miz Hazel's no where close to dat yet."

Luisah reassured Celine. "Don't worry. If she's not better after today, we'll make sure she gets to the hospital. There are some illnesses that are past our skills."

Mo-maw stood up, smiling. "Yeah, but not many!" She winked at Celine. "I have to go feed the chickens. We've been wasting too much time. Don't forget to save the grease, Lala." The old woman shuffled out the back door.

"Yes, Mama." Her daughter dutifully called back. Celine helped clear the breakfast dishes while Luisah placed the large black case on the table. Celine had seen this old-fashioned doctor bag a thousand times, but never asked what was in it. Luisah opened it and Celine could see several little bottles labeled with the names of different herbs and spices, candles of different colors, vials filled with oil and grease, a bottle of Holy water, a black prayer book, a rosary, a flask of whiskey, a bag of small fragments of colorful cloths and a carefully wound up roll of knotted string. Celine knew there was a lot more packed away in hidden pockets.

The clock chimed, calling out nine a.m. "Oh Celine. We gotta go. Mr. Gautreaux is waiting!" Luisah grabbed a box of salt from the pantry, put it in the bag and snapped it shut.

Celine ran to her room, put her shoes on, brushed her hair and grabbed her purse and keys. "I'll drive!"

Luisah called back. "We're going in my car. Your car is too little." The two women hurried out the door.

Celine slid into the driver's side of her mother's Mercury Marquis and snapped the seatbelt on. While she drove, Luisah coached her on how to assist with the elderly woman. "The best thing for you to do, Celine, is just watch me. If I need anything, I'll ask you for it."

Celine answered nervously. "Now Mama, you know I don't know all those things in that bag of yours."

Luisah smiled. "Don't worry, chère. Everything's going to turn out okay."

Celine took a deep breath and remembered the times as a little girl watching her mother and grandmother treating people who were sick. She hadn't paid much attention and now she was wishing she had. She glanced down at the ring on her hand. Not so very long ago, she called it superstition, 'the old people's way'. Not anymore.

Mr. Gautreaux was sitting on the front steps of his old wooden frame house as Celine and Luisah drove up. Luisah called out to the elderly gentleman as she stepped from the car, "*Comment ça va*, Mr. Bobby?" Celine smiled as she heard the Cajun greeting.

The old man stood up shaking his head. "Oh Miz Luisah, *de mal en pire*, chère. It done gone from bad to worse."

Luisah frowned. "Is Miz Hazel worse than when we talked this morning?" Don't tell me she ate those figs!"

Mr. Gautreaux looked down still shaking his head. "No, no but well, she done got it in her head dat someone done fixed her."

Celine knew that to be 'fixed' was bad news. She wondered who could've wished to hurt poor old Mrs. Gautreaux by placing a hex on her. While Bobby and Luisah chatted on in French, Celine looked around the steps for a conjure ball, a wax ball with matches or feathers melted inside. She knew they were usually left during the night on the front steps or under the porch. She didn't notice anything unusual and waited while Mr. Gautreaux finished talking.

"No, chère. Me, I already looked. I can't find nuthin', but Hazel still sure that someone done fixed her." The old man just kept shaking his head.

Luisah patted Mr. Gautreaux on the shoulder. "Well, let's go in and see her, eh, Mr. Bobby?"

The three of them entered the sick woman's bedroom. The heavy, dark curtains were drawn and all the windows were shut. The air was stifling in the summer heat. The quilt was thrown back and the woman was covered in a mist of sweat that soaked her gown. From the moment the elderly woman saw Luisah, tears and words flowed from her. The two spoke in fluent Cajun French while Celine looked around the room.

It was the 'old way' to keep the bad spirits out by shutting the windows and covering them up with dark curtains. It was the 'old way' to 'sweat out' the fevered spirits from the body, and poor Mrs. Gautreaux was drenched. It was the 'old way' not to 'catch a chill', so the room had to stay as hot as the sick person could stand it.

Luisah opened the bag and started to take a few items out. She turned to her daughter, "Celine, I need you to do some things for me. First, you and Mr. Bobby go to the kitchen and warm these bottles under hot water. Have him bring them back to me and then you go do a walk."

Celine whispered back. "I heard Mo-maw say that this morning. What do you mean?"

Luisah nodded. "Walk around outside. Go look for that conjure ball. It's probably black or a reddish color. If you find it just tell me. Don't touch it."

"I already looked, Mama. I didn't see anything."

Luisah whispered quietly to her daughter. "Mr. Bobby's eyes aren't so good anymore and just, well, look again. Miss Hazel thinks Nina Gaudet put one out on her. She was here for coffee yesterday afternoon. Make sure you look in all the flower pots on the porch." Luisah turned and was reaching back into the bag as Celine left the room.

Mr. Gautreaux slowly led Celine into the kitchen, his steps short and crippled. She ran hot water over the two bottles. When they seemed to be the right temperature, Celine started to walk back to the bedroom, thinking she was doing the old man a favor by hurrying the bottles to her mother, but Mr. Gautreaux stopped her. His dark eyes pleaded as he said, "You know, chère, me, I don' see too good no more. Dat conjo ball, if it in da yard, Miz Hazel, she won't git no better. Please, go look for me, eh?"

Celine smiled and touched him on the arm. "Sure, Mr. Bobby." She handed him the bottles. "I'll go look."

The old man smiled back. "You know, you look jus' like you Go-Maw Aurelia. I remember her. I always taut she wuz a pretty woman. She had a great big heart jus' like you Mo-maw and you mama. Dey iz all good women." He took the bottles from her and toddled slowly to the bedroom.

Celine walked up and down the porch, half-heartedly searching for the wax ball. She checked the flower-pots like her mother told her. Nothing. She went down the front steps and around the corner. Overgrown honeysuckle and azalea bushes skirted the base of the house.

As she walked in front of Mrs. Gautreaux's bedroom window, she paused and tried to look through, pushing a honeysuckle vine aside. *That poor woman is probably going to suffocate if she stays in that hot room much longer.* She turned to continue the search when she noticed one of her furry friends from childhood perched in the corner of the window frame, a wooly bear caterpillar. She laughed when she recalled all the times she would catch the soft, fuzzy little worms and put them in a jar, waiting for a glorious butterfly to emerge, which of course never happened.

Celine looked at it more closely and reached out to run her finger over the soft fur, but then she saw what looked like oil oozing from it. When she saw the tip of a chicken claw coming out of it, she pulled her hand away quickly and jumped back.

Celine had ignored lots of details about her mother and grand-mother's work, but she'd been told more than once, 'if you don't know what it is, don't touch it!' Sometimes even innocent-looking objects were laced with poison like snake venom or something worse that could easily penetrate the skin. This thing looked downright evil. Celine carefully reached around it and knocked on the window.

Her mother pulled the drapes back, her face wrinkled with concern.

Celine pointed to the ugly ball. She raised her voice so her mother could hear her. "I think I found it!"

Luisah opened the window a crack, leaned forward and looked closely. She looked at her daughter. "You didn't touch it, did you?"

"Absolutely not!"

"Okay." Luisah never took her eyes off the ominous black ball. "Come on in. I'll get it."

By the time Celine reentered the bedroom, Luisah was carefully removing the conjure ball from the window sill. With plastic gloves on, she lifted the oozing thing and put it in a plastic bag. Celine thought she looked like a surgeon as she skillfully packed it away.

Luisah spoke softly to Mrs. Gautreaux. "We found it, Miz Hazel. It's going to be okay now." The old woman showered thank-yous to both Luisah and Celine.

Luisah didn't stop the work. She took the box of salt and sprinkled the window sill, then outlined the area around her bed. She sprinkled Holy water in all four corners of the room and promised that she would sprinkle it throughout the house before she left. Luisah anointed the old woman with the oil and recited prayers to Mary and Ezilie. Then she made an herb tea out of Carencro Root and Palmetto leaves to calm the old woman's nerves and help her sleep. Only one more thing remained.

While Luisah pulled out her black prayer book, she motioned to Celine and Mr. Bobby to stand beside her. "In the name of the Father and the Son and the Holy Ghost. Amen." Luisah opened the book to the first page and read aloud. "Saint Suaire De Notre Seigneur Jesus Christ…"

When Luisah was done she gave instructions to Mr. Gautreaux. "She's going to be fine now, Mr. Bobby. You need to scrub the window sill, but don't forget to wear rubber gloves and throw them away when you're done." Luisah patted him on the arm. "It's okay, Mr. Bobby. By tonight, she'll look better. She just needs to sleep right now. When she wakes up, have her sip some more of the tea. It'll help her relax. I'll call you later this afternoon to check on her, okay? Have you got those penny nails?" He nodded. "Sign of the cross in the ground, twelve front door, twelve back door, remember? For now, you just rest, too. No need for the nails 'til sunset. Don't worry. Nina's not coming back." Mr. Gautreaux gave her a tired smile.

Celine could see his face was ashen and his shoulders were slumped. "Mr. Bobby, are you alright?"

He turned to Celine. "Me, I be alright. It jus' good to have dis t'ing over." He sighed with relief.

Luisah and Celine walked through the house, sprinkling Holy water in each room, saying St. Michael's prayer of protection. When they were done the mother-daughter team left. Celine started the car. "Where to now, Mama?" Celine was flush with excitement, ready to see her mother at work all over again.

Luisah looked straight ahead. "Nina Gaudet's house."

Celine was stunned. "What? You mean the lady that made the conjure ball? Why are we going there?"

Luisah had already opened the black bag and was reaching for her plastic gloves. "Don't go yet, chère, I need to be steady here." Luisah carefully took the ball and placed it in the palm of her gloved hand, cupping it like a tiny captured animal. Luisah turned to Celine. "Okay. Let's go."

Celine looked at her mother in disbelief, the car idling, "But, Mama..."

Luisah cut her short. "Listen, Celine, Nina's been tormenting poor Miz Gautreaux and a few others for a long time. Look, let me show you what I'm talking about." Luisah carefully peeled the black wax away from the claw tip. As she dug deeper, she found hair, gray hair, wrapped in what looked like greenish, crushed up leaves. "Hmph! I thought so!"

Luisah showed the contents to Celine. "Nina's serious about hurting Miz Hazel. She must've gotten this hair yesterday from the old lady's hairbrush when she went for a visit." Celine nodded her head, listening carefully. "She went back last night and put it on her window." Celine looked at the thing more closely. Luisah jumped back. "Not so close, chère!"

Celine jumped back, too. "But why is it sweating like that?"

Luisah said one word. "Oleander."

Celine frowned. "What, the flower?"

Luisah looked at her again. "No, the leaves. If they're fresh leaves and they're crushed up, the oil sweats and oozes. If they're dried and crushed, any food you sprinkle it in could kill you. Either way, it's bad. Oh yeah, one more thing." Celine looked at her mother. "Don't ever call that woman a lady. She's no lady! Now go."

Celine drove and was ready to do everything her mother said, but she was worried. "But why would she do that to poor old Mrs. Gautreaux? Mama, what are you going to do?"

Luisah smiled, "I don't know why. Does evil ever need a reason? Now don't worry, chère. It won't take me long. You just stay in the car. I'm not going inside."

Celine drove into the woman's driveway. Luisah got out of the car, still cupping the conjure ball in her gloved hand. As she approached the door, Celine noticed someone pull the curtains back and peer out. Luisah rang the doorbell with her elbow. After what seemed like forever, Nina Gaudet opened the door. With lightning speed, Luisah grabbed Nina's hand and pressed the ball into her palm. Luisah turned and walked back to the car, dropping her plastic gloves on the front porch.

Luisah didn't turn around to watch Nina screaming and trying to throw the ball from her hand. It was no use. It was stuck and she had to use the other hand to peel it off. The woman was yelling something in French that Celine couldn't understand. By now, Luisah was back in the car, a mischievous little smile curling at the sides of her mouth.

Celine drove the get-away car out of the driveway, laughing. "Mama, I can't believe you did that! What's going to happen now?"

Luisah closed the black bag and put it in the back seat. "Well, if I'm right, Nina's going to get real sick. She's not going to call Mama or me. Not at first anyway. Instead, she's going to try her own home remedies. When that doesn't work, she'll try that old quack, Doc Billeaud, in town.

When that doesn't work, she'll call us."

"Will you go?" Celine couldn't believe what she was hearing.

Luisah looked at her daughter, surprised. "Of course, chère. Me and your Mo-maw, we always go when we're called." Luisah let out a little laugh. "Of course, you Mo-maw will go instead of me. I don't think Nina's gonna want to see me anytime too soon."

"But Mama, what if you're wrong? What if that wasn't Nina's fix?" Luisah looked straight ahead. "It's hers. I've seen it before, a long, long time ago." Luisah turned her body in the seat, facing her daughter, a girlish smile on her face. "But come on, now. Let's not worry about Nina right now. Let's go eat."

Celine smiled. There was so much to learn.

CHAPTER 8

Celine sat in the restaurant waiting for her mother to return to the table. She looked around the room taking in all the renovations that had been made to the place. What had once been the administration building of her old Alma Mater, Our Lady of Mt. Carmel All Girls High School, was now transformed and renamed 'Sister Cajun'. The restaurant became an instant hit for the local lunchtime crowd and tourists always gave it five stars. Still, the place just wasn't the same without Sister Jean's nervous fidgets and red face when one of the girls used the 'S' word—Sex! Then there was Sister Claire's fast *clip-clip* walk with her head always bowed and her hands tucked away in the folds of her habit. If she hadn't been a nun, she might've made a good football player. Of course, she would've played for the Saints.

Celine smiled as she ran her hand over the tablecloth; chocolate-brown and ballet-pink plaid, just like the uniforms they once had to wear. Even the windows were draped in the trademark brown and pink. The walls were covered with old photos and awards, now forgotten like the tarnish that slowly clouded the silver and brass trophies. She could almost hear the voices and laughter as she saw her senior class portrait.

Classmates from years ago looked back at her with young smiles and naïve hopes. In the midst of all of her girlfriends, there she was innocently looking back. Celine got up from the table and stepped closer to the glass case, squinting as she read *"Celine Bienaimée Dupré —Follow Your Dreams. They Know the Way."* Celine took a quick breath. In her senior year, when the girls had been given the assignment of choosing a favorite quote for the yearbook, Celine hadn't put much thought into it, until now. The quote stunned her. *What had Mo-maw said? 'Follow the dreams Ezilie sends you. They know the way.'*

"Bring back any memories?" Luisah's voice jolted Celine out of her reverie.

Celine turned to face her mother. "Lots. I can't believe they've used all these old photos, but it's nice to see them again. When good old Carmel High closed down, where did all the sisters go; back to the Mother House in New Orleans?"

Luisah and Celine sat down at their table. "Yeah, but after Hurricane Katrina hit, they were all evacuated to San Antonio. I think they're still there." Luisah scanned the restaurant looking for the waitress. "Did you order for us?"

Celine nodded as she sipped her iced tea. "The crab cakes sounded yummy so I ordered that."

Luisah smiled as she tore open a sugar packet for her iced tea. "Mmmmm, the remoulade sauce that comes with it is the best I've ever had. Good choice."

Celine spread butter on a warm roll. "A young woman named Gail took the order. She's the one who suggested it."

Luisah smiled sadly as she put her teaspoon down. "Poor thing. Her husband got blood poisoning when he was baiting his crawfish traps; cut himself with that nasty knife he uses. He's okay now, but he got very sick. Put him out of work for nearly three weeks and boy, they sure can't afford that."

Celine smiled. "Mama, I have to say, I am amazed at you."

Luisah cocked her head. "Amazed? What are you talkin' about?"

Celine smiled. "Well, maybe I should say amazed and proud. Watching you in action with Miss Hazel and Mr. Bobby was really wonderful and then what you did to Nina, well I…"

Luisah looked over her shoulder, a smile on her face. "Shhh. Let's not broadcast it, okay? It'll be all over town soon enough."

Celine whispered. "What I'm trying to say, Mama, is that I think I finally understand. The two of you help so many people. It's wonderful. I'd never be able to do what you do; all those herbs and treatments? How do you remember it all? You never even consult a book or anything, well except for that black prayer book, but you really don't even read it. You practically know it by heart. When did you learn all this stuff?"

Luisah smiled and patted her daughter's hand. "Oh, I used to be just like you, Celine. I had absolutely no desire to learn until after you…" Luisah hesitated. "…until after your accident. That was the turning point for me."

Celine nodded her head. "You mean the night I almost drowned?" Luisah sighed. "Yeah."

Celine shrugged her shoulders. "It's really kind of weird, you know. I have an almost-memory of it, but I'm not sure if what I remember is real or just what you and Mo-maw have told me what happened."

Luisah looked down, her fingers absently tracing the lines of the plaid tablecloth. "Well, there's a blessing in not fully remembering some things. I know I'll never forget it. That night, when I saw you lying there, I didn't have the first clue of what to do. It's sad, you know…" Luisah looked up. "…how it takes something so tragic to wake us up to what's really important. I sat there stunned, scared to death, but then Mo-maw handed me the black prayer book, the Saint Suaire, and told me to read it out loud. So I did. Over and over and over until Mo-maw told me that you were gonna be okay."

Luisah gave Celine a little smile. "After it was all over, I made a promise. I'd learn everything I could of the old ways. If I could help save someone else's life, then that would be my thanks to God for saving my Celine."

Celine looked at her mother. "I think you've saved quite a lot of people's lives by now, don't you, Mama?"

Luisah shrugged. "Oh, I don't know. No time to stop and count."

Celine asked. "How long did it take you to learn it all?"

Luisah let out a little laugh. "I'm still learning. I'll never learn it all, I'm afraid, and I'll never match Mo-maw's level, I can tell you that! I came to it a little too late, but Mo-maw, she learned it all practically at birth from her mama Aurelia. You want to talk about someone amazing? Now that old lady was something!"

Celine nodded as she sipped her tea. "You know, Mr. Bobby said he remembered her, said I reminded him of her."

"You do look like her," Luisah said nodding. "But I bet you don't like wrestling?"

"What?" Celine's eyes grew wide as she laughed. "Wrestling? She was a WWF fan?"

Luisah smiled. "Yeah, but it was WWF 'Cajun style'. These guys were local and she loved watching them every Saturday afternoon on TV. Can you believe it?"

At that moment, the young waitress brought the crab cakes, the remoulade sauce drizzled artfully over them, forming a heart and ending with a sprig of parsley. Celine sat quietly as Luisah chatted with the young waitress. When she walked away, Celine picked up her fork. The food looked and smelled delicious. "I would never have guessed that a healer would choose wrestling as a favorite TV show."

Luisah smiled as she cut into the crab cake. "Well, she sure was an interesting character and always had a story to tell. She told me the story about Adele when I was a little girl. I feel really blessed to have had her as my Mo-maw."

Celine looked at her mother, surprised. "So she told you about Adele and Etienne when you were a child?"

Luisah nodded as she ate. "Well, not all the details, of course. It was my favorite bedtime story though, so by the time she showed me the Bible, I already knew the story backwards and forwards. You can imagine how surprised I was when I found out about..." she lowered her voice, "... all the parts that were secret."

Celine was fascinated. "So when you were a little girl, you got the '...and they all lived happily ever after' version?"

Luisah laughed. "Not quite! Aurelia was quite the storyteller. You know, castles in Paris, masked balls. 'Loved those tales. None of them true."

Celine leaned back in her chair. "Did you ever get the true stories? I mean like what happened to Adele and Celeste, after they went to live on the plantation?"

Luisah looked at Celine's plate of food. "You better eat before it gets cold."

Celine took a bite. "Wow, this is delicious!"

Luisah laughed. "I told you! Okay, so what happened to Adele and Celeste? Well, Adele lived out the rest of her life on the plantation. They buried her in the Beauvoir family graveyard, but I've never seen it. I tried to, a long time ago; I took a drive hoping to get a look at it but the old place was closed up. From what I could see from the road, it was pretty run down, but just the other day I heard that someone's renovated it. They've been working on it for about five years."

Celine smiled. "Really? I'd love to see it when it's ready. Where is it?"

Luisah nodded her head. "It's about an hour north of New Orleans off the old river road. The new owners kept the original name of the place, it's Belle something. Wait now; I can't remember, oh yeah, Belle Ange, Beautiful Angel."

Celine took another bite. "So, Celeste grew up at Belle Ange. What happened to her?"

Luisah smiled. "You might say she's the only one who came the closest to 'happily ever after'. She married one of her cousins, Jacques Beauvoir."

Celine wrinkled her nose. "A bit of incest in the family, right?"

Luisah let out a little laugh. "No, not really. He was like her fourth cousin or something. That's what they did in those days. He was quite a bit older than her and died right after their daughter, Fremanse, was born. Celeste raised Fremanse there on the old plantation along with all her Beauvoir family. For many years it was a safe place. Celeste believed that no one from the Quarter knew where they were until something strange happened."

Celine frowned. "Strange?"

Luisah shrugged her shoulders. "You're not the only one in the family who almost died when she was a little girl."

Celine leaned forward. "What?"

Luisah sipped her tea as she explained. "Well, Fremanse was only three years old when it happened. She'd been playing outside in a playhouse that her uncle had built for her near the kitchen outside. She played there with her dolls nearly every day for hours and hours. So, it wasn't unusual when it grew dark and Fremanse didn't come for supper when she was called. But after many calls and no Fremanse, the whole place went into a search. They found her tied up on the levee of the Mississippi, unconscious and nearly dead from snake bites."

"After a long recovery, Fremanse did get better, but she suffered with nightmares about a wicked woman with red eyes and snakes in her hair, coming to get her. It plagued Fremanse for years. Even on her death bed, she was warning everyone that the red-eyed witch was coming. She always had a horrible fear of snakes, too."

Celine put her fork down. "Nightmares, huh? I guess it runs in the family. 'Sure hope I don't end up screaming about monsters in confessionals when my time comes."

Luisah frowned. "You'll be all right, Celine. Mo-maw grew up hearing all about those dreams from her mother, Aurelia. You remember, Aurelia was Fremanse's granddaughter. Believe me, you're in good hands. Mo-maw knows how to treat nightmares, especially the truly scary ones. The methods were drilled into her and have been improved as the years have passed."

Celine sighed. "Well, I feel terrific today, better than I have in a long time. I'm just going to keep doing what you two tell me to do. God knows everything I tried before didn't work." Celine smiled at her mother. "So, what happened to Fremanse?"

Luisah nodded. "Well, after that Celeste was convinced that whoever had tried to kill Fremanse surely had to be someone from the Quarter. She didn't trust anyone. She was a young widow and she didn't have too many options, but she knew that she had to get Fremanse away from the plantation and far away from New Orleans."

Celine shook her head. "So where did Celeste go? France?"

"No, no chance of that. Etienne's mother and father had disowned her. Hardly a safe place for her there." Luisah smiled. "Celeste was one tough cookie, though. She traveled with little Fremanse by riverboat up the Mississippi, then up the Bayou Teche. She had heard of the little town called 'Le Petit Paris'. It was hardly more than a little village then. The Cajuns had settled it but there were lots of wealthy French who had left New Orleans for reasons unknown, probably wanted to keep it that way, too."

Celine nodded her head. "Le Petit Paris, the old name for St. Maryville, right?"

"Yep, right here. She had papers from the Lady Beauvoir that claimed her royal connection to France and with that, and with the help of a few of the families who knew the good Lady, she started working with the church, helping the people, just like Adele had done. But…" Luisah looked over her shoulder, lowering her voice to a whisper. "…she never told anyone about her mama or her grandmother. She always just claimed the Beauvoirs as her family."

Celine leaned into her mother. "Was she still afraid for Fremanse? I know I would be if she were my child."

Luisah gave her daughter an almost stern look. "Yes, of course, but there were other reasons, too."

Celine cocked her head inquisitively. "What other reasons, Mama?

"She didn't want anyone to know that she had anything to do with what was happening in the French Quarter. Everything good that Marguerite, Marie and Adele had done had been corrupted. Believe me, Eve-turned-Marie and Ozinee had made it all into a very profitable black market business; prostitution, blackmail, extortion, even murder. If the people here found out that she was connected to them in any way, she'd become an outcast overnight, maybe even considered a criminal. Then where would she go? No, she just kept it all to herself."

Celine leaned back. "That was a smart move on her part. She kept her and her daughter safe. But why do we have to keep all of this such a secret? Our family's been here how many generations now? I don't think we have to worry about anyone from the Quarter coming to get us any-more. And Voodoo in New Orleans doesn't mean much of anything these days, just fun stuff for the tourists. I mean, it's the 21st century for God's sake. I think it's cool that we're related to Marie LaVeau. Weird, yeah, but really Voodoo is…"

Luisah looked at her daughter panic stricken. "Celine!" Luisah looked around the restaurant. One man, eating alone, looked up and turned his head in their direction and then quietly went back to eating. Luisah turned back to Celine. "You're lucky this place isn't as full as it usually is, but keep your voice down." She whispered, "It might be the 21st century, but if anyone here were to find out that we're connected to Voodoo in any way…" Luisah took a deep breath and looked down "… it would ruin everything."

Celine frowned. "Ruin everything? But how? I mean…"

"All the work we do, Celine, and I mean ALL, depends on one thing: these good people believe that we are trusted servants of God's healing work. They also believe that Voodoo is more than just 'fun stuff' like you call it. Way more. They look at it as pure evil. What do you think they would do if they found out we were blood related to that evil? I can tell you right now, in their eyes we'd stop being trusted servants of God! Overnight we'd be labeled as evil fakers."

"But why? I don't understand. You and Mo-maw, and every woman in our family for that matter, have done nothing but heal them, take care of them. All those years, all the healing, doesn't that count for something?"

Luisah gave a little shrug. "It wouldn't matter how much good we've done. Oh sure, a few of those good people would stand by us, but most of them? By the time the rumors got finished flying around, believe me our work would stop. A hundred-fifty years of good healing work, the way it was meant to be done, would be finished. Forever. And all because we couldn't keep our mouths shut."

Celine let out a little sigh. "These people, this little town, I guess some things won't ever change."

Luisah closed her eyes and took a deep breath. She opened them and stared hard at Celine. "Try not to judge them so harshly, Celine. You'd most likely do the same thing if suddenly you heard something about someone that made you distrust them."

Celine sat back shaking her head. "Mama, I'd never ..."

Luisah interrupted her. "Would you keep going to a doctor if you'd heard rumors that his license was fake? That he learned his skills from a well-known quack? Would it matter whether the rumors were true or not? How would you feel? Confused? Angry? Of course you would! And just to be safe, wouldn't you find another doctor to go to? In their own way, the people of St. Maryville are not so different from the modern world."

Celine reached over and took her mother's hand. "Mama, I'm sorry. You're right. Really. I wasn't thinking."

Luisah looked up. "Didn't you promise last night not to talk to anyone but me, Mo-maw and your granddaughter about this?"

Celine nodded. "Yes, I did."

Luisah leaned back. "That also means you can't tell anyone by accident, you know, like someone overhearing you? I think you've forgotten that this little town has very big ears."

Celine laughed nervously as she turned to look over her shoulder. She let out a little sigh of relief. No one was seated near them. The lone man had left. She looked back at Luisah. "I think we're okay."

Luisah took the last bite of her crab cake. A little smile curled her lips. "I think so, too. We're lucky. Let's just keep our voices down, okay?"

Celine leaned in closer to her mother. "Okay." Celine made sure her voice was low. "So Fremanse grew up here?"

Luisah sipped her tea. "Yes and Celeste lived out a full life, watching Fremanse raise her daughter, Adrienne, your great grandmother. Oh yes, St. Maryville's been home to us all; Adrienne's daughter Aurelia, Mo-maw, me and you, all born and raised here. Someday, I guess Mo-maw and I will take our place next to them and be buried at the church cemetery."

Celine was surprised. "So Celeste is buried at the church?"

Luisah nodded. "Yeah, in the old section, in the family crypt; Celeste on the bottom, Fremanse in the middle and Adrienne on the top. You can't miss it."

Celine was puzzled. "Family crypt? I don't think I've ever seen it."

Luisah smiled. "Oh, sure you have. If you go down there, you'll remember. The name 'Bienaimée' is carved across the top. At the foot of Celeste's grave is a very old statue of St. Ezilie."

Celine finished the last of her tea. "St. Ezilie. After last night, I realize how very little I really know about her."

Luisah wiped the corners of her mouth with her napkin. "Okay, so what do you want to know?"

"Well, if Marguerite brought St. Ezilie with her from Africa as part of her religion, she's not really a Catholic saint, right?"

Luisah shook her head, smiling. "Whether St. Ezilie came to us from Africa or Haiti, or wherever else, doesn't really make much difference, though. She's always been part of the work that we do. That won't ever change."

Celine was fascinated. "In the prayers, right?"

Luisah nodded. "The prayers, mainly. Of course first we call on Jesus and the Virgin Mary, but then we always call on Ezilie. When we read the Saint Suaire, first we call on Jesus and Mary for their help and protection, but it's Ezilie that we ask to take the sting of death away. The dying person has to ask for it, too. When they do, she offers the cup of truth to drink.

"If they have a good soul, and they still have work to do on this Earth, she postpones their death and they get well. If the good person has finished their time on Earth, she blesses them with three more days to say good-bye to all their loved ones, then death comes peacefully.

But if she finds that the person has an evil soul, well, they die in tremendous pain and torment and go straight to Hell."

Celine sat back, amazed. "So, this cup of truth; what is that?"

Luisah raised her eyebrows. "I don't know. We're just the instruments of passage." Luisah joked, "I've only read the Saint Suaire. I've never had it read to me...yet." Celine sat silently and stared at her mother. Luisah let out a little laugh, "Okay, you're quiet. That means the wheels in that brain of yours are coming up with something."

Celine said quietly, "Well, I was wondering..." she hesitated. "...when I almost died, when you read the Saint Suaire to me that night, do you think St. Ezilie offered the cup to me?"

Luisah leaned forward, her smile melting into concern. "Of course she did and found your sweet little soul to be good and you came back to us."

Celine nodded. There was a flicker of an image in her memory; a woman offering her a cup, but then it faded. Celine leaned back in her chair, still thoughtful. "So if you only read it for the dying, why did you read it for Miss Hazel this morning? She wasn't really dying, was she?"

Luisah smiled. "No, but she believed she was. Once you get that thought in your head, it can start a downward spiral that can cause death. I've seen it happen. Hearing the Saint Suaire gives people strength and a new hunger for life. Poor Miss Hazel just needed to be reminded that she's not ready to die yet. Speaking of which..." Luisah looked at her watch. "...you ready to go?" I need to get back to the house and call Mr. Bobby."

Celine grabbed her purse. "Sure. Do you mind if I drop you off while I go to the library? I want to research a few things."

As Celine drove, Luisah chatted on about someone getting married, then about someone who recently died, but Celine wasn't fully listening. She was already mentally creating the list of things she wanted to Google. Celine pulled up to the house and Luisah opened the car door. As she got out she turned to Celine. "You'll be home in time for supper?"

Celine nodded. "Oh yeah, I don't plan on staying that long." But as she booted up the old IBM computer at the St. Maryville public library, the groans and clicks told her it was going to take longer than she thought.

Finally she was able to type St. Ezilie in the search bar. Each search brought her back to the same place, the history of the Efik tribe in West Africa.

"The reclusive tribe called the Efik (now extinct) was located on the coast of Nigeria along the Niger Delta. It is believed that they were part of the larger Dahome' Tribe, but functioned as a secret society, living away from the main tribe and dedicated to preserving the healing arts of the people. Ancient texts suggest that these healing arts stem as far back as Ancient Egypt and the cult of the Black Virgin. (See Isis, Black Madonna)

"Masters at herbalism and the use of animal parts for healing, they protected the healing practices and secrets to the death. Considered a branch of Voudoun, they con-sulted the Black Virgin, or Ezilie as she was known, for the secret formulas used. Their animistic and secret societal prac-tices required them to poison or sell into slavery anyone they suspected of giving away the secret formulas.

"Fed, clothed and treated like royalty by the Dahome', every member of the Efik was trained to be a healer and when the member came of age, was tested through a variety of rituals. Those who passed the rigorous and sometimes life-threatening tests were sent back to the Dahome' as peacekeepers. Though they were known for their diplomacy and healing ability, they were quite versed in the making and distribution of poisons.

Many of their drug formulas are used today in
the making of common drugs and anesthetics.
"One herb, Datura Stramonium, more commonly
known as Zombi's Cucumber, (see photo) has
recently been researched and tested to aid
in anesthesia-free surgeries. The nature of
the herb is to completely paralyze specific
regions of the body without affecting the
consciousness of the patient. The herb is
administered orally. Practitioners who have
used the herb for surgeries report faster,
more complete recovery and no side effects.
However, the FDA is quite a few years from
approving it for the U.S.

"Though a large majority of patients who
have used the drug have reported no short or
long-term after effects, some tests outside
the U.S. have resulted in coma and death.
Datura Stramonium has only been found in the
rich delta swamps of the Niger. Expeditions
are taking place in Africa for new sources
of the herb."

Celine scrolled to the photograph of the herb. The innocent-looking,
purplish-white flower was so dainty; Celine could hardly believe how
dangerous it was. She read the caption: *The deadly Datura Stramonium, also known as Zombi's Cucumber or Angel's Trumpet*. She looked
back at the picture. It certainly did look like a kind of trumpet.

When the librarian gave the fifteen-minute warning to closing time,
Celine couldn't believe she'd been online all afternoon. She looked at her
watch and quickly checked her email. She groaned as she scrolled down
the long list; school, work, work, school. The list dragged on until she saw
one from Dave and one from Dr. Sonnier. She clicked on the one from
Dr. Sonnier first.

"Dear Celine, Alex is responding well to
the new treatments. All he talks about is

> meeting with you. Can I tell him you're still
> on? Matt"

Then she opened the one from Dave.

> "C. All good news from Alex about the
> meeting. Don't worry about getting in touch
> with me. Thx to u we're in the $$! Enjoy your
> vacation. D."

When the librarian started flicking the lights, Celine quickly typed back "yes" to Dr. Sonnier then picked up her notes and hurried to her car. She left with every intention of going home but something pulled her to St. Joseph's Catholic cemetery instead. She sat in the car for a moment, looking at the above-ground tombs; miniature stone houses rising over the landscape like solemn white cement guards, watching stoically as they held their dusty dead occupants high above the threatening floodwaters of the Bayou Teche.

Celine got out of the car and walked first up one row of tombs and down the other looking for the crypt that her mother had told her about. She smiled as she recalled the All Saint's Day picnics that she, her mother and grandmother used to have here in this City of the Dead. The day after Halloween, everyone in the town would gather at the graves of their loved ones and clean the above-ground tombs.

Celine remembered cleaning the Dupré family tombstone, planting flowers and then spreading a tablecloth on her father's grave and having a picnic, but that was in the newer section of the graveyard. She had a vague recollection of the crypt, but where was it?

She turned toward an older section of the cemetery. Gnarly roots of live oak trees branched their way dangerously close to the tombs, threatening to crack the graves. She walked carefully amongst them. For most of the crypts, the names and dates had faded with time but as she turned the corner, she found it, *Bienaimée*.

Celine carefully made her way to the white-washed tomb. The breeze under the trees was wonderful, almost cool. Dragonflies darted and the cicadas' symphony burst, swelled, then tapered into silence once again. A large, white flowering bush was blooming on one side of the crypt, a sweet-scented backdrop for the St. Ezilie statue that stood there. Celine read each name engraved on the front, running her fingers gently over and around the letters: Celeste Bienaimée Beauvoir, Fremanse Bienaimée Devereaux, Adrienne Bienaimée Trahan.

Celine reached over and picked one of the dainty little white flowers—no, not white, a purplish-white, really. She smelled it, so sweet, then turned the trumpet-shaped little beauty over in her hand.

CHAPTER 9

Supper was over. The table had been cleared. Luisah stood wiping the stovetop, her thoughts drifting. Her hands slowly stopped. The sun had set almost an hour ago and still there was no sign of Celine. *Where is she?* Luisah turned and stared out the kitchen window.

There's no end to motherhood. She may move away from home, but never from my heart. Off in the distance, Luisah heard the crunch of gravel followed by the slam of a car door in the driveway. She sighed with relief and grabbed the dishrag to wipe her hands.

"I'm home." Celine called into the house. Luisah met her daughter halfway into the living room.

"Celine, where have you been? I tried to call but your phone kept going to voice mail!" Luisah scolded.

"Oh Mama, I'm sorry." Celine looked at her mother, realizing how much she had caused her to worry. "My phone's dead. I'll recharge it tonight." She put her purse and notes down on the hall table. "I have so much to ask you and Mo-maw about. I found out a lot at the library, but oh man, they need to do something about those computers and when I finished there I went to…"

Luisah's brow relaxed and she let out a little laugh. "Whoa. Slow down. Why don't you sit down and relax first. Have you eaten anything?"

Celine shook her head as she let out a deep breath. "I'm really not hungry. I'll fix myself a sandwich or something later."

Mo-maw called from the kitchen. "I'll fix it. You two sit down in the living room and I'll bring it to you. I wanna hear everything, so don't start without me."

Celine called back to her grandmother. "Thanks, Mo-maw, but you really don't have to do that. Why don't you come sit down with us, okay?"

Celine heard a muffled "be dere in a minit" from the kitchen. She looked at Luisah. "Really, Mama, she doesn't have to do that."

Luisah shrugged her shoulders. "Don't try to stop her. She'll just shoo you away."

Celine picked up her notes from the hall table and knelt down on the floor. She spread all of the papers down like a white fan and then sat down on the rug in front of them, crisscrossing her legs. She felt like a kindergartener waiting for the teacher as she faced her mother's and grandmother's favorite chairs. "So, how's Miss Hazel? Is she doing any better?"

Luisah nodded as she sat down in her easy chair. "Much. I talked to Mr. Bobby and he said she was actually out of bed and sitting in a chair. He even put her on the phone and she was laughing just like her old self."

Mo-maw smiled a proud smile as she walked into the room. She set the sandwich and glass of milk on the coffee table next to Celine. "Sounds like da two of you made a great team dis morning, well, except for the part about going to Nina's house."

Celine met her mother's eyes from across the room then turned to her grandmother. "Mama told you about that?"

Mo-maw shook her head as she settled into her rocking chair. "Oh no, chère. I heard all abo't it from Miz Annie down at the post office. She called me before you mama even got home." Mo-maw picked up her knitting needles as she spoke.

Celine looked back at Luisah. "Uh oh. I guess it's all over town."

Luisah gave her daughter a crooked smile. "I told you it would be and by now everyone knows that it's Nina who's been doing all that evil work."

Mo-maw laughed. "And now you'll have to go to confession for it, too, chère."

Luisah nodded. "Oh, I know, but first I have to be sorry for it and I'm not the least bit sorry right now."

Celine shook her head in disbelief. "I don't think you have to be sorry for anything, much less confess it. Really, Mo-maw, what Nina did was an evil thing and Mama stopped her. What's wrong with that?"

Mo-maw glanced at Luisah then looked at Celine. "Nothing's wrong with helping Miz Hazel, chère, but getting revenge, well that's another thing."

"Revenge?" Celine looked at her mother. Luisah sighed.

Mo-maw explained, her eyes twinkling. "It was when you mama and daddy got engaged. Nina was jealous of you mama. She was sweet on your daddy so she tried to fix you mama by getting her sick for her wedding day."

Celine laughed, reaching for her sandwich. "What? Mama!"

Luisah turned up a brow. "I wasn't sick for long and I sure didn't miss my wedding. Your Mo-maw found that fix and figured out that it was Nina's. Every time one of her black balls show up, we always know it's hers. Today was the first time I did anything about it, though."

Celine took a bite of the sandwich. "Well, I bet that crazy woman will think twice before she tries hurting anybody again."

Mo-maw's smile disappeared. "She'll think twice about it, alright, and make sure she's twice as sneaky next time; 'might even make those black balls of hers more potent. That's the way of evil, chère."

Celine sipped the milk. "More potent? You mean with something other than oleander?"

Mo-maw put her knitting needles down and stared at her granddaughter. "She'll probably try mixing her nasty oleander leaves with some of those black berries she grows in her yard." She turned to Luisah. "What's it called again?"

Luisah looked over at her mother. "Black Beauty."

"Yeah, that's it. Black Beauty. That's not something we use. It gives you a fake fever. All it does is brighten your eyes and make your cheeks flush. Women used to use it in the old days 'cause they thought it made them pretty." Mo-maw sighed. "That's okay, we'll just keep a close watch for Nina's new tricks."

Celine reached for her notebook. "That reminds me." She shuffled through the pages. "There was a special herb mentioned in all of the stuff I found this afternoon and I want to know if the two of you have ever heard of it. Oh, here it is." Celine read from her handwritten notes.

"Datura Stramonium. Zombi's Cucumber. It works like an anesthetic that..." Celine looked at both her mother and grandmother. Their faces were expressionless, almost cold. "What's wrong? What did I say?"

Luisah stared at her daughter. "Where did you find out about that?"

"I found it online. I started out trying to find out anything I could on St. Ezilie. As it turned out I found out quite a lot about the Efik. Isn't that the African tribe that you said Marguerite came from?" Luisah nodded as Celine kept talking. "Hmmm, let me see if I can find that article..." Celine leaned forward and pulled out the Xeroxed copy. "Yeah, here it is, the Efik and they use this herb called Zombi's Cucumber. So it made me wonder, since Marguerite was an Efik healer, she must've used this stuff, but do you know anything about it?"

Luisah said quietly. "Zombi's Cucumber is part of our healing, Celine. We rarely use it but it's very important."

Celine was astounded. She uncrossed her legs and sat back on her heels, staring at her mother and grandmother. "So where do you get it? I mean you must grow it yourselves, right? The article said it could only be found in West Africa, but..." Celine grabbed her notebook and thumbed through the pages. "Is this it?" She pulled the flattened purplish-white bloom from between the pages and placed it carefully in the palm of her hand.

Mo-maw squinted her eyes trying to see the tiny flower as Celine got up and showed it to her. Mo-maw took it from her looking at it closely. She peered over her glasses at Celine. "Where did you find this, chère? I know you didn't get it at the library."

Celine squatted next to her grandmother. "The graveyard."

Mo-maw leaned back her shoulders melted into the back of the rocking chair. She looked like she'd been stung. "The graveyard? You found this at the old crypt?"

"Yeah, I went down there after I was done at the library. That's why I was late getting home."

Mo-maw looked at Luisah. "Did you tell her about this?"

Luisah shook her head. "No. I told her that Celeste was buried in the old section but I didn't say anything about that."

Mo-maw looked back at Celine, smiling. "Well, chère, you found where we keep our Cucumber. There's other bushes of it all back in there. They've been there for as long as I can remember, but Celine, nobody knows what it is. Nobody ever asked about it, until today. Until you. You are really something, chère."

"But, Mo-maw…" Celine sat back and hugged her knees. "I don't understand. That stuff can kill you. The article said it paralyzes, not to mention can cause coma and death. Why would you give something so poisonous to anyone so sick?"

"Chère, chère," Mo-maw was shaking her head. "For us to use da Cucumber, the sickness has to be very bad. By dat time, we've tried everything else. The worst thing is the pain for those poor people and da Cucumber, well, dere's no pain after dey take it. It slows everything down, gives the body time to choose life or death. I've seen real miracles happen wit' the Cucumber, things I can't explain."

Celine shook her head in disbelief. "You mean, like cancer?"

Luisah took a deep breath. "Cancer might be one reason we use it, but there are other sicknesses like a mental illness that no medicine helps or chronic pain, even female problems, anything that has reached a dead end; the kind of dead end doctors have given up on."

Mo-maw added. "But it's only used as a last try. If the Cucumber doesn't cure it, then nothing will. You can only take it once so before we give it to anyone, we have to be very sure that we've done everything we can."

Celine hugged her knees tighter. Her voice was almost a whisper. "But how do you know that giving them this poison…" she hesitated "…won't accidentally kill them?"

The question hung on the air. Mo-maw stood up. "Dere's some t'ing I need to show you. I'll be right back."

As she left the room, Luisah answered. "First of all, the amount given is very, very small, less than a pinch, and it's diluted with water and a little whiskey, but that's only to make it go down better. It's very bitter and it burns."

Just then, Mo-maw re-entered the room with the box in her hands. The old woman opened it and pulled out a tiny clear glass vial half-full of a purplish-white powder. "This is Cocombre Zombi, Zombi's Cucumber. This is the oldest and strongest of our stock, probably mixed by Adele, maybe even older. We don't know. The Cucumber you found in the graveyard was planted by Celeste. We use that most of the time. Those blooms are newer. They're still very potent but don't have as much after effect. We've never used dis…" She shook the vial. "…It's very, very potent."

Celine gently took the bottle from her grandmother's hand and looked at it. "How do you know it tastes bitter, Mama?"

Luisah glanced nervously at Mo-maw. The old woman nodded her head. "Go ahead, chère, tell her."

Luisah looked back at her daughter. "Because I took it once."

Celine was shocked. "What? You took this? Mo-maw, did you know about this?"

Luisah let out a nervous laugh. "She's the one who made me drink it."

Celine sat back, looking at the two women in complete surprise. "But why? This is crazy!"

Mo-maw just smiled, "Maybe so, chère, but you're here because of it."

Celine put the vial down on the coffee table, leaned forward, closer to her grandmother. "Okay, what on earth do you mean by that?"

Luisah sighed heavily. "I don't know if it's a good idea for you to know all of this…"

Mo-maw interrupted. "No, Lala, you know she needs to know." Mo-maw drew a huge breath. "It was when you mama couldn't get pregnant. You know, they tried and tried, but no baby. After you mama and daddy went to New Orleans and those doctors told them that it was Luisah's fault and that they should adopt, I had a long talk with you mama. I told her that if she wanted, we could try da Cucumber. Well, by that time, you mama wanted a baby so bad that she was willing to try anything, so we took a trip to the Atchafalaya Swamp to the old deer camp."

Luisah smiled. "I remember the moon that night. It almost filled the sky with its huge silver face. We could see everything out there."

Mo-maw smiled back. "Yeah, dat old Cajun Moon watched everything we did dat night."

Celine rested her chin in her hands. "So what did you do, Mo-maw?"

Mo-maw smiled. "Oh, dere's lots of parts to it all, but da main part wuz da mud bath and da swim."

Celine let out a little laugh trying to imagine her mother bathing in mud. "Mud Bath?"

Mo-maw laughed. "You mama wasn't the only one who got muddy. First I made you mama strip naked and then we walked into the swamp a little ways. I had already mixed the Cucumber with the whiskey, so I made her drink it. While she was coughing and sputtering, I dug up some of that black sticky mud from the bottom and I covered her, head to toe in that thick stuff. Boy she hated that, but I just kept praying."

Luisah couldn't keep quiet any longer. "Yeah, and that's how I know it's bitter and burns." Celine let out a little laugh, but quickly looked back at her grandmother.

"The last part was the swim and I tell you, chère, now that was a hard thing for me to do." Mo-maw sighed. "As soon as I finished smearing dat mud all over her, the Cucumber had started its work so I pushed her into the water as hard as I could. She went down. The current just sucked her down in that black water and I thought, Oh dear God, I done killed my daughter! I groped around for her but I couldn't find her but then, all of a sudden, pop! She just came right up!"

Luisah laughed sarcastically. "Oh yeah, sure, Mama, I just popped right up. There's a little more to it than that." Luisah turned to Celine. "I don't remember much, but I do remember after drinking that nasty stuff I just collapsed. When I came to, I was surrounded by long strands of swamp grass. I could see that yellow moon glow through the surface of the water so I tried to swim toward it, but the grass had wrapped itself around me and pinned me.

"I tried to fight it, but the more I fought, the more tangled I got. It coiled around me and pulled me deep into the black water. The reeds were sucking me so deep that I felt like my lungs were going to burst. Then a horrible cramp, like nothing I'd ever felt before, grabbed my gut and blood gushed out between my legs. As soon as that happened, the swamp grass let go and I rushed to the surface."

Mo-maw nodded her head. "Yeah, chère, when I helped her out of the water, she had blood all down her legs. It was hard walking her back to the cabin, but we made it." Mo-maw smiled. "We stayed at the camp 'til the bleeding stopped a week later. Then you mama came home with me until she healed completely. After fourteen days, I sent you mama home and told you daddy they should try now. Well, I tell you, you daddy was real happy about that!"

"Mama!" Luisah blushed.

"There's no shame, Luisah. All that work and all that love, well, here she is, living proof." Mo-maw reached over and squeezed Celine's hand.

Celine shook her head in disbelief. Mo-maw patted Celine's hand. "Oh, I know, chère. You've found out a lot since you've been home, but now you know the whole story."

Celine crossed her arms and pretended to be angry. "Are you sure? I mean, I'm not gonna find out my real daddy was a fish or a gator or something…"

Luisah laughed. "Oh no, kiddo. You are really a Dupré inside and out."

Mo-maw smiled. "Not too many people can claim that it was the Cucumber that opened the way for them to be conceived. That brings special blessings, you know. And after today, well I know now that it's not just your dreams that make you special."

Celine leaned back. "What do you mean, Mo-maw?"

Mo-maw glanced over at Luisah and then looked back at Celine. "When you were a little girl, you always wanted to know why to everything. Why this, why that? You were never satisfied with any answer until you found it out for you'self. You never changed, you know. You're still like that."

Celine gave her grandmother a little smirk. "That doesn't make me special, Mo-maw. Just makes me stubborn. I mean, look at all the trouble I caused myself with the nightmare I was having. Instead of calling you guys about it all, I had to do it my way. If I would've just called you when it all started, I wouldn't have taken all those pills and caused myself a near-nervous breakdown."

Mo-maw leaned forward. "And you wouldn't know everything you know today, either."

Celine shook her head, confused." I don't understand."

Mo-maw smiled. "If you would've called us right away, the nightmare would've stopped sooner, right?" Celine nodded her head. Mo-maw continued. "And you'd maybe still be planning a wedding? To the wrong man? You wouldn't know about Adele and Etienne and you sure wouldn't be wearing that ring right now."

Celine looked down at her hand and let out a little groan. She looked back up at her mother and then her grandmother. "But now, I think I'm more confused than ever before. I feel like I've been caught up in a kind of hurricane with all that you both have told me. It's just swirling around in my head, making me ask more and more questions."

Mo-maw nodded. "Well, chère, you mama and I, we have an idea that might help you."

Celine looked over at her mother. "Yeah?"

Luisah answered. "Well, what do you think about going down to the Atchafalaya and staying at the old deer camp for a few days? It's really a special place for you. It's where Ezilie opened the door for you to be conceived. We think she'll open the doors to all your questions there."

Celine sat back, staring at the two women. *The deer camp where it all started. I haven't been there in years.* Celine frowned. "I thought you'd sold it after Daddy died, Mama."

Luisah shook her head. "I would've, but your Mo-maw wouldn't let me. It's still there, just waiting for you. We were thinking that maybe you could go down there for the weekend; spend some time alone, sort of like a little retreat. No one will bother you there; no phone, no neighbors. We're not that far away. Maybe Ezilie will tell you what we can't."

Celine smiled a tired smile. She had fond memories of the old place, a prehistoric land, trapped in time. "Well, I was going to go to New Orleans on Saturday, remember? I'm supposed to help plan the new art department."

Luisah nodded. "You just take some time and think about it. You've got the whole week with us yet. It's just an idea we had."

Celine nodded. She'd always loved the old deer camp. Going back there felt right somehow. *Maybe I should go, but what about New Orleans, what about Alex and...* Celine's shoulders shuddered when she remembered Michael's face. "I like the idea, but I'm way too tired right now to decide. I just need to get some sleep."

Mo-maw stood up, the box in her hands. "That's a good idea for all of us. It's been a very long day." As Mo-maw turned to walk out the room, she stopped and looked back at Celine. "Dere is one more thing, though, chère."

Celine was scooping up her papers. "What's that, Mo-maw?"

Mo-maw glanced at Luisah then looked back at Celine. "Don't ever take the Cucumber."

Celine laughed and went back to shuffling pages. "Oh, don't worry, Mo-maw. I have no plan to..."

"No, chère, I mean you can never take it, no matter how sick you get. I mean you'll die if you do."

Celine froze and slowly looked up at her grandmother. "Die?"

Mo-maw took a deep breath. "You can only take it once and you already did, the night you drowned; the night you died. I gave it to you that night." Mo-maw patted the box. "St. Ezilie and the Cucumber, they brought you back." Mo-maw turned and walked down the hall, muttering, "St. Ezilie and the Cucumber. Yep, St. Ezilie and the Cucumber."

Celine stared at her mother. "Did you know?"

Luisah shook her head. "Not until it was all over. You were gone, Celine. There was no other choice."

Fatigue swept through Celine's body. "I've got to go to bed. I'm exhausted. Can we talk about all this tomorrow?"

Luisah wiped away the tears. "Of course. Go on."

Celine stood up and padded her way to her bedroom, pulled back the netting and dropped onto the bed. The quilt was soft and smelled like freshly-cut lavender.

There was a voice whispering quiet words, chanting over and over; words that Celine couldn't quite make out. Celine was curled in a woman's lap. The woman was rocking, stroking Celine's hair gently. The sun was coming up. No! Celine resisted the unfolding of the night into day. She nestled closer, drawing her body deeper into the woman's arms as she listened. "I am Ezilie, your spirit mother. I live in the shadow of the moon. I have given you life and you belong to me." Celine opened her eyes, turned and saw the beautiful African woman in gold. She cupped Celine's face and kissed her softly on the cheek.

CHAPTER **10**

The sleek, black limousine moved down Interstate 10 like a cat; stealthy, quiet and fast. The passengers of the other cars looked for a famous face through darkened windows, curious who the celebrity might be. Maybe it was a famous singer or actor, maybe a politician or even a capo for the Mafia. Whoever it was, they were protected, private and headed for the Crescent City.

Julien had grown used to the stares. He usually smiled back from under his navy blue chauffeur's cap and gave a casual wave to the passers-by, especially the children. His thoughts were focused on getting into New Orleans without running into Saturday afternoon traffic when his employer tapped gently on the dark window behind him. Julien pressed the button to lower it. A waft of cigar smoke floated into the driver's compartment. "Yes sir?"

"How much longer, Julien?"

"About an hour-and-a-half, sir. It's opening day for the Saints training camp but I know a shortcut to get past the tourists."

"Good man. Let me know when we arrive." Alexandre Arnaud leaned back in his seat as the shaded window enclosed him again in his private mobile world. "Disgusting sport, football. Well,…" He let out a little laugh. "…except for those tight pants they wear." Alex turned to his nephew Michael.

Michael looked up from his computer, his silver blue eyes twinkling as he smiled. "Well, I'm glad to see you're feeling better, though I don't think smoking that nasty cigar is helping you any."

"Nasty Cigar?" Alex looked at Michael, feigning surprise. "But it's a Churchill Sumatra. The old British Bulldog never smoked anything else and he lived until he was ninety."

Michael ignored Alex's comment as he typed the last words of his email and hit 'send'. "There, okay, that's the last of your death paintings. They now officially belong to the LSU Medical Center. I'm sure that'll make good old Dr. Matt happy." He turned to Alex as he closed up his laptop and put it away. "You might slow down with that Bushmills, too. You've only been out of the hospital, what, an hour?"

Alex laughed shaking his head. "Oh, but my boy, I feel wonderful; perfect in fact. As soon as my hair grows back and I gain a little weight, I'll be handsome again, too." Alex tugged gently at his curly white wig. "I have to give all the credit to Matt. Glad to be giving all those horrible paintings to him. Good riddance to them!" Alex raised his glass of whiskey in a mock toast. "'Hope they bring lots of money for the hospital because he was right. I feel just like my old self!'"

Michael reached for a highball glass at the bar and filled it with ice. "And that's what scares me." He carefully poured a shot of Jameson. "It won't be long before you'll be back to your old tricks again, too."

Alex gave his nephew a little laugh as he watched Michael cap the Jameson and return it to the liquor cabinet. "Don't put that away yet. Pour yourself a double. You need to relax."

Michael smiled at his uncle. "No, thanks. One of us has to stay sober."

Alex unbuttoned his suit coat and settled more comfortably into the seat, a sly grin on his face. "You're just so fussy. You're more fussy than an old queen. I'm going to have to get you a wig, a boa and a sequin dress. Then you can fuss all you like. What color do you want? I mean, anything's better than what you have on. Didn't the cuffed-up blue oxford shirt and jeans go out in the '80s? Boring." Alex raised his eyebrows playfully, waiting for what was sure to be a retort from his nephew.

Michael shook his head as he leaned back into the plush ivory leather seat. "Nope. Not this time. I won't spar with you. I see what you're trying to do. You do it every time; distracting me with something else so I stop reminding you to take better care of yourself." Michael sipped his drink. "Besides," he added smiling. "You're the only old queen in this family. You can have your sequin dresses. I'll be sitting over here, comfortable in my boring blue oxford shirt and jeans in my boring blue, very straight world, thank you very much."

Alex laughed. "Well, sequins aren't for everyone. I don't really think you could pull it off. You're much too serious. You'd be no fun in a gay bar."

Michael raised an eyebrow at his uncle. "Glad to hear it. You just made my day."

Alex gently tapped his cigar. "Oh, you know I'm just kidding with you. I'm very happy for you that you're straight, believe me. The gay world is a tough place to be even now with gay rights and all that. I mean, I'm happy for these young guys that find their 'Mr. Perfect'. But they're fooling themselves if they think that's gonna fix everything, as if marriage will wipe out AIDS or some other hideous disease that comes along." Alex shrugged his shoulders. "Oh well, I have no regrets. I was never very good at the one-partner thing. Maybe I was addicted to the excitement of one-night-stands in my favorite high heels. Apart from catching AIDS, I'd do it all over again, but in better clothes." He looked back at Michael, rearranging his turquoise ascot and matching pocket handkerchief.

Michael teased. "Are you sure there's nothing you regret?"

"Not a thing."

Michael gave his uncle a playful smirk. "Oh come on. Are you completely sure about that? We've all got things we regret."

Alex gave his nephew a little push on the shoulder. "Okay, so I did go over the top a few times, but there's nothing I really regret. When I was a young man, things were different. I lived two lives, the 'family-approved-straight-have-a-job-pretend-to-be-looking-for-a-wife' life and my real life, my gay life. It was pretty hard trying to keep those two worlds separate in 1970s New Orleans, believe me. And my good old dad, your grandfather Warren, God rest his sweet, hard-ass soul, was a card-carrying member of the Church of Homophobia. A gay son? Now, that was something he wouldn't hear of. I did try to tell him several times but he'd just never listen. A person can only lead a double life just so long before something snaps, so when I'd had enough, I gave him a little preview of the real me."

Michael laughed. "Oh, I heard all about that preview. Like showing up at his Mardi Gras Krewe meeting dressed in drag? I'd say that's more like the whole movie."

Alex beamed with pride. "It was the best coming out ever! I should've gotten an Oscar for it, too. If I have any regrets, it's that I didn't do it sooner. I admit it was quite tacky of me to do that in front of all his friends. Warren had daggers coming out of his eyes and then he erupted into a rage. He even called the NOPD, but I managed to get out of there before those fine boys in blue showed up. Had it not been for dear old Aunt Chloe, I don't know where I would've ended up. Thank God for her."

Michael leaned toward Alex tilting his head. "Aunt Chloe. Wasn't she Grandpa Warren's sister?"

Alex nodded and then sipped his drink. "Yeah, Warren and Chloe, brother and sister. I'll never understand how two people so different could come from the same family. He was an absolute demon and she was an angel." Alex smiled as a shadow of memory fell across his face.

"When I was a little boy, the whole family would get together at her house about once a month. That's when she'd pull out all those old trunks of hers. They were like treasure chests overflowing with dresses and jewelry and hats and shoes. Aunt Chloe and I would put them all on. We'd laugh and sing all the old show tunes, pretending we were on Broadway…" Alex's smile faded. "…until Warren would yell at her for dressing me like a girl and shuffle us all home. But through all of his temper tantrums, Aunt Chloe never raised her voice. She'd just shake her head and say, 'Someday you'll see it, Warren. Someday, you'll see it.'" Alex turned back to Michael, his smile returned. "She knew I was gay before I did!"

Michael frowned. "But where was Father when all this was happening?"

"Robert?" Alex sighed. "Ah yes, Robert my good brother. Good old Robert was never very far away from Warren most of the time, just like a well-heeled puppy with a nasty little sneer on his face; always the good one, the obedient one. 'Yes, Father. What was that you wanted, Father'?" Alex shook his head. "After the yelling episodes at Aunt Chloe's were done and we were home, Robert would wait until after we were alone and then he'd tease me and call me a queer and lots of other choice things. Of course, I'd deny it and a fist fight would always follow. One of us would end up bloody, which always made Warren happy, and once again, male supremacy would be restored in the Arnaud household. Oh yes, those were the good old days."

Michael leaned back, his brow wrinkled. "Yeah, I remember visiting Aunt Chloe, not very often, though. It was always me and Mother. Father was never with us. While Mother and Aunt Chloe had coffee, I would just wander around that huge three-story house of hers. It was something. But about the time I went into first grade, all the visits just stopped. I'm not sure why. I remember asking Mother one day if we could go visit Aunt Chloe and she whispered something like 'we can't go visit her anymore. She's gone crazy again.'"

Alex shifted in his seat and stared at his drink. He swished the Bushmills into a golden swirl, the ice clinking against the side of the glass. "I'm sure they certainly wanted you to think she was crazy, but…" Alex downed the drink, swallowing hard. "You weren't allowed to go visit her anymore because of me."

Michael looked at his uncle, a curious frown on his face. "Because of you? What do you mean?"

Alex drew a deep sigh. "It was after I'd made my grand announcement at Warren's Krewe meeting. I really thought he might kill me so I ran to the only place I knew might be safe, Aunt Chloe's house. I knew that she'd at least let me stay there until Warren got over his mad."

Alex reached over to the bar and poured himself another drink. "That was the longest night of my life, I tell you. Talk about family drama! Warren and your father showed up at her house screaming at her, telling her this was none of her business, but Aunt Chloe stood on that front porch and defended me like a champ. I can still hear her yelling at him, 'He's just a homosexual, Warren, not a criminal! If it was a crime, half the Louisiana legislature would be in jail! Now get off my G—D'd property!'

"When she said the word 'homosexual', it was like she hit him with a bullet. His face went ashen and his knees actually buckled. Robert had to help him back into the car." Alex looked sadly at Michael. "So, that's why you never visited her again. Robert wasn't about to let his little boy, his precious only son, spend time with anyone who had so severely wounded the Royal Ass-Holiness, King Daddy Warren."

Michael shook his head. "You do know that I heard a totally different story, right?"

Alex shrugged his shoulders. "I'm not surprised. Aside from the fact that the whole Garden District must've heard the screaming match that went on, I'm sure that Warren and Robert came up with a real juicy lie or two to cover up everything that happened."

Michael gave a sarcastic little laugh. "You're forgetting Mother. She's the real mastermind behind every story that gets told to the public." His lips tightened as he spoke. "I overheard her on the phone, talking with one of her friends." Michael rolled his eyes. "God, her friends. Anyway, she said you inherited the 'crazies' from Grandma BB; that it had been a real problem for "that" side of the family. She even said that Aunt Chloe had certainly inherited the trait and had to be put in an insane asylum once. Is that a juicy enough lie for you?" Michael let out a little laugh as he sipped his drink. When he realized Alex was unusually quiet, he turned. "What's wrong?"

Alex sat in silence while he clenched his jaw. "Yeah, that's what the Arnaud's are really good at; weaving big lies around a small truth so no one can ever find out what really happened."

Michael frowned. "Wait. What are you saying? None of this is true, right?"

Alex's shoulders slumped. "It's all true and it's all a lie, but I think you need to hear the whole story." Michael stared hard at Alex, waiting. Alex looked over at Michael and took a deep breath. "It was the 1940s. Aunt Chloe was only sixteen when she fell in love with a man her old papa Arnaud didn't approve of. The love of her life was Jewish or something. But anyway, when he asked for her hand in marriage, old man Arnaud threw him out of the house and told him never to come back. One night, not long after that, Aunt Chloe ran away and married the young man. The only one she told was her brother, Warren, and that was her biggest mistake."

Alex locked eyes with his nephew. "We come from a long line of cruel bastards, Michael, and poor Aunt Chloe was surrounded by them. Only a few hours after she left, Warren, the little rat, told his old papa what she had done. Well, when that hateful bastard found out, he tracked them down, had her new husband arrested and charged with rape. As if that weren't bad enough, he had her declared insane and thrown into a mental hospital. His own daughter, can you imagine? And here's the worst part, he told her that she would stay there and her husband would hang unless she signed the annulment papers."

"What? Did she sign?"

"Of course she did, but that mean S.O.B. made her sit in the asylum for close to a month before he had her released. He even had her go through shock treatments. Now, that would mess anybody up, but insane? Aunt Chloe was probably the sanest person in our entire family."

"But where was Grandma BB in all this? Didn't she try to get Chloe out of the asylum?"

"No woman in 1940s Louisiana had that kind of power over her husband. I'm sure she begged, but it got her nowhere. So, she was forced to sit there and wait while her daughter endured God-knows-what in that place. I don't think either Grandma BB or Aunt Chloe were ever the same after that."

"Shock treatments? In the '40s?" Michael shuddered. "I can't even imagine."

Alex sipped his drink. "Aunt Chloe made the best of her life, though. Oh, she was certainly eccentric. Her house was a mountain of junk. She was a hoarder par excellence. I swear she never threw anything away. All those old trunks? Filled with family stuff from I don't know how long ago. She just refused to get rid of any of it. Anytime I'd ask her if we could clean them out, she'd always say, 'Alex, these are the only things I have left of my sweet mama, your good old Grandma BB. Besides, I don't want her to haunt me 'til the day I die, so why don't we just let her rest in peace.' So they just sat there year after year while those damn smelly cats took over her house…" Alex stopped and pressed his fingers under his wrinkled nose. "…but she had the kindest heart of anyone I have ever known and I'll always be grateful to her."

Michael shook his head. "Poor Aunt Chloe. Thank God you had her."

"Yeah, she was my hero." Alex looked at his empty glass, then reached over to the bar and poured himself another shot of whiskey. "After she hit Warren with the 'H' word, she and I sat in her kitchen all night and polished off a few bottles of Bushmills." He held his glass up in the air. "Now you know why it's my favorite drink." He took a sip. "She told me that I could move in with her and stay there as long as I wanted, which I did, for several months."

"Did Grandpa Warren ever cool down and try to get you to come back?"

"Cool down?" Alex let out a cynical laugh as he eased back into the seat. "As far as he was concerned I was dead. Within a month I got the official papers that I was fired from Arnaud Oil and Robert got pro-moted to Vice President. I was never so relieved in my life. Of course, I was able to hold onto all the trust fund money. If I couldn't have done that, well, that would've changed things drastically. I would've had to go crawling back, but thanks to all those delightfully-antiquated Napo-leonic Blue Laws that are still on the books, Warren couldn't touch my money. I was free and an official member of the Arnaud Family Out-cast Club, membership of two; Aunt Chloe and me."

Michael gave a disgruntled laugh and sipped his drink. "Make that three. You can add my name to your roster."

Alex's face softened as he watched his nephew's face set into chiseled anger. "Come on, now. It's not as bad as all that, is it?"

Michael stared at the melting ice in his glass and then turned to Alex. "Yeah, it's as bad as all that."

Alex reached over and gently touched Michael's shoulder. "Robert can be a hard-ass, I know. He's my twin, remember? He's a lot like Warren, but no one could ever be as mean as him, not even Robert. He'll come around. I could even go to him and take the blame."

Michael put his hand up, shaking his head. "Take the blame for what? You had nothing to do with what happened. No. No way! Father would just paint you into another crazy corner with Aunt Chloe and the rest of Grandma BB's family. You don't deserve that."

Alex gently pulled his hand back. "What difference would it make? There's nothing he can say or do that could hurt me."

"But it would make a lot of difference to me. I wouldn't be able to stand listening to him criticize you and berate you behind your back. And he would, you know. Besides, you're fooling yourself." Michael glanced out the window. "He IS a hard-ass. Anyway, he sort of did me a favor. He showed me just how evil he really can be." He looked back at Alex. "Now I know everything about Robert Edgar Arnaud and I don't want to know anymore. I'm done."

Alex frowned sadly. "You don't mean that. Just give it some time..."

Michael downed what was left of his drink. "I do mean it. Listen, the man went power mad! After the oil spill disaster, he was firing everyone at the company and none of them had anything to do with it. All he kept saying was that I didn't understand. This wasn't personal. It was 'business'." Michael stared at the empty glass. "He was covering his ass is what he was doing. He fired everyone who knew the whole thing traced back to him." He looked back at Alex. "Then, when you got so sick, I asked him to take me off the payroll for a few months while I took care of you and then maybe that way he could keep a couple of people on instead of firing them. He simply said no. Not why. Not how long. Just no, and then turned his back on me. Even after I explained the whole situation, how badly you needed me and that my absence at work would help everyone, all he said was no. He dismissed me, like I was back in grade school. That's when things got ugly.

"Everything that I'd been feeling for years just came spewing out of me; all his rejection of my success as an artist, all of his rejection of everything I've ever done that's made me happy. Oh man, I blasted him. I told him I was done. That's when Mother came out of her bottle of wine and started crying. She was running from Father to me, begging us to stop fighting. Do you know what he said to her? Nothing. Do you know what he said to me? Nothing. The man has no heart."

Michael looked hard at Alex, the blue of his eyes darkened by the furrow of his brow. "Arnaud Oil is not for me. It's never been for me. I only got my business degree because that's what he wanted me to do. I think I'm the only person in Tulane's history who's ever gotten an MBA and a Masters in Fine Arts at the same time. All these years, I've given him everything he's ever wanted from of me; always let him have the last word. Well, not anymore."

Alex reached over and touched Michael's arm. "Oh Michael, I didn't know. I'm so sorry for all of this."

Michael's shoulders slumped. "It's not your fault." He took a deep breath. "Uncle Alex, you've given me the greatest gift in the world. Taking care of you has made me feel again. God, I was turning into a robot and I didn't even know it. Painting again in the studio, buying and selling for the gallery, I..." His voice grew very quiet. "...I know your illness has been hell for you, but in a weird way, it's given me freedom that I never even knew I could have. I'll always be grateful to you for that. You've been for me what Aunt Chloe was for you. You've shown me that there's a different way to live life and now I want to live it and if it's crazy, then so be it! I'm in the best of company."

Alex stared at Michael, his face wrinkled with a strange mix of pride and sorrow. "Please, promise me one thing. Don't close the door completely on your father. The day might come when you'll have to go back to him and patch things up. He and I, we're not getting any younger, you know. You don't want him to die with all the hurt between you still there. It's the one thing that I wish could've been different between King Warren and me. When the old bastard died, he took every chance of reconciliation between us straight to Hell with him, but there is a chance for you and Robert. If there's an opportunity somewhere down the line, take it, okay?"

"I'll try, but I can't promise you anything." Michael tightened his grip on the empty glass then placed it in the cup holder.

Julien's voice came over the intercom. "Mr. Arnaud?"

Alex looked out the window as he answered. "Yes, Julien?"

"Sir, we're on Canal Street. We should be at the gallery in about twenty minutes."

"Thank you, Julien."

As the intercom clicked off, Alex turned and faced Michael, his brow wrinkled in thought. "Did you remember to move your paintings from the main gallery? Miss Dupré is meeting me, so…"

Michael nodded. "Yeah, I told René to move them to storage. Two of them are locked away in my studio."

"Have you given any more thought about what you're going to do with them?"

Michael shook his head as he rubbed both his palms on his jeans. "I haven't decided yet. I mean, I certainly won't be selling them. I probably should just burn them. I know that's probably the smartest thing to do. But, I just can't. Not yet, anyway."

Alex took a puff on his cigar. "I do wish there was some other alternative. Maybe we could keep them. Let Miss Dupré get to know us a little better then maybe over time, we could show them to her. You know, she is an artist. She might really appreciate the…"

Michael let out a little laugh. "Oh yeah, right." Michael looked past Alex's shoulder pretending to talk to someone. "These paintings that I've done, Miss Dupré, might look just like you, but they're not really paintings of you. Oh no, they're paintings of a woman I created after I read a bunch of old letters that my sweet eccentric aunt had hidden in a trunk. I had no idea, Miss Dupré, that my imaginary woman would turn out looking exactly like you." Michael looked back at Alex.

"Really? You really think she'd believe that, especially after the fiasco with your death paintings? You're right. She's an artist, an extremely sensitive one. If she fainted when she saw your paintings, I don't want to even imagine what she'd do if she saw mine."

Alex tapped his fingers on his knee. "But suppose you changed the woman's face, made her a blonde. You could do that, couldn't you? That way we could still sell them and Miss Dupré would never know."

Michael ran his fingers through his hair, a loose black curl falling into his eye. "I couldn't do that. The woman that wrote those letters looks exactly as I painted her, exactly like Celine Dupré. To change any part of her would be a lie. No, I can't change them, so they'll just have to stay a secret between you and me."

Alex shrugged his shoulders. "It's sad that the world will never know that your Lady ever existed. We could've published the letters and sold that as part of the collection." Alex brushed his hand in the air as if reading a theater marquis, "Lady of the Letters." He sighed. His voice was laced with disappointment. "I know they would've gotten incredible reviews, especially the first one; the one of her seated at the desk, crying while she's writing the letter. It's so powerful. Her face is so sad and so full of love."

Michael nodded. "Yeah. It was like I was sitting right next to her, watching her cry; writing that sad, sad letter to me. I could even hear the scratching of her quill on the paper. I just wanted to reach across all those years and hold her, hug her, tell her I was sorry; take all her pain away. I know it sounds crazy, but I fell more in love with her with each letter I read."

"Her words haunted me day and night, but the dreams … oh man, that was the worst. She was always whispering to me, but I could never quite make out what she was saying. I would wake up covered in sweat, I'd been trying so hard to hear what she was saying. The only thing that brought me any relief was painting her, over and over. As soon as I finished one, I was on to the next one until…" Michael stopped and looked at Alex. "…until you saw Celine Dupré in the newspaper."

"I know, Michael." Alex nodded. "This whole thing just doesn't make any sense. How many résumés did I read before I finally found Miss Dupré? I was so excited when I finally found the right person to help me with the project—her credentials, experience. I couldn't believe how lucky it was that Dave was her boss. Who would've ever thought that Dave, the party animal in college, turned into Dave, the Principal of the School for the Blind! When he said she was the absolute best, I knew I'd hit the jackpot! I really thought I'd covered all the bases. So why hadn't I ever bothered to find a photo of her?"

Michael shook his head. "You were on a lot of pain meds then and buried deep in your own paintings of death and hideous monsters. Maybe you saw a photograph of her and didn't remember seeing it. I don't know. Somewhere between all the doctors and therapies, I never thought to ask you about it. At the end of the day, all I wanted to do was hide in my studio and paint."

Alex pulled at the cuff of his shirt. "Well, I'll never forget that morning, that crazy morning, when I saw her picture in the paper alongside that little blind girl. I was completely stunned!"

Michael's eyes widened. "You were stunned? How do you think I felt? Beautiful woman like that? I thought she only existed in my mind. Then I find out she's real? Believe me, that night that she came to see the blueprints, the night I actually saw her..." Michael looked down. His normally strong, smooth voice was lowered to a whisper. "...I knew I was standing face to face with my muse. Not many artists ever get that chance."

"Speaking of which..." Alex looked at his Rolex watch. "She'll be at the gallery at 7:00." He looked out the window. "Good, we're already on Royal Street. I still have plenty of time to get myself ready. Will you be joining us?"

Michael shook his head. "No. I need to clear my head. This has been one helluva ride. Besides, I don't know if seeing her right now is such a good idea. I'm still trying to get used to the idea that she's really human, you know? I think I'll take a long walk around the Quarter, maybe go by Café du Monde, I don't know."

CHAPTER 11

Celine sat back on the wood-and-iron park bench in the French Quarter, settling herself into the shadow of St. Louis Cathedral. She smiled when the softest of breezes rustled the banana trees near her. *This is a great little spot. I can watch all the tourists from here and get some shade, too.* A soft little *drroo-drroo* sound came from above. She looked up at a fat, overfed pigeon looking back at her. *Stinky birds! They mess up everything!*

Celine looked around at the tourists milling around; one or two stopping to watch an artist at work busy with a caricature, another anxiously pulling out her wallet, waiting for her fortune to be told. *I wonder if I should get my cards read.* She watched the psychic, a woman dressed in a white dress with a white head scarf and large gold hooped earrings, pull out a deck of cards and begin to shuffle. *Hmmm, probably a scam. Pretending to be Marie LaVeau!* Celine laughed to herself. Visiting New Orleans again felt so different after hearing the stories from her mother and grandmother. *I wonder what it was like to live here during that time. Maybe I'll have time to explore all the places Etienne and Adele walked and lived. I wonder if the St. Ann house is still there? Probably torn down a long time ago.*

As the sun peeked between the spires of the cathedral, a beam of golden sunlight shown into Celine's face. She reached for her purse and searched for her sunglasses. *Great! Where are they?* She pulled out an old fashioned bronze key and placed it on her lap as she rummaged around in her purse. *Oh, here they are.* She put on the sunglasses and picked up the key, turning it in her hand, admiring it, reading the engraving on it, *Hotel Ste. Jeanne, Room 733.* She smiled, remembering the unique hotel room that Alex had reserved for her. It was like walking into late 1800s Paris; French provincial furniture, black lacy ironwork. *The suite is bigger than my entire apartment; king size bed, my own balcony over-looking Royal Street. What a place!* She put the key in her purse and settled back into the bench again. *This is going to be so wonderful! Alex is just such a nice man. He sounds so different than he did last week. So energetic! It's amazing what just one week of the right kind of healing has done for us both.*

"Hey lady, want your shoes shined?" Celine looked over at the young teenager standing just few feet away from her.

She smiled. "I don't think I need my sandals shined, do you?"

The young man looked down at her blue sandals then back up at Celine. He shrugged his shoulders, looked at her purse sitting on the bench next to her and walked away. Celine laughed and shook her head.

Shining sandals? Really? She put her purse up on her lap and took her sunglasses off. The sun had set behind the spires and suddenly, the square took on a dingy gray hue. She dropped her sunglasses back in her purse as she watched one of the shop owners come out of his store and lock the door, calling it a day. She watched him from behind — tall, slender, dark haired. *Could that be Michael?* She sat up looking at him a little more closely. *I think it is. Does he have a shop in the Square?*

When he turned around, she raised her hand to wave but then realized too late that she had been mistaken. She was embarrassed when the young man smiled and waved back but walked on. *Oh, what am I doing? What is it about Michael that makes me so anxious and nervous? I have to try to separate the real person from my horrible nightmare. Saying that little prayer to Ezilie has worked so far; that and wearing the ring. All I have to do is look at it and I feel stronger somehow.*

Celine watched as several more shop owners came out of their stores from around the Square, clearly disappointed at the unusually light crowd for a Saturday. Even the artists were counting their change and calling it quits. *Boy, I wish my job was like that. No such thing as leaving when I'd like to; always way too much to do. I'm glad that Mama and Mo-maw convinced me to go to the deer camp when I'm done here. I'll just take a few days; rest and explore all those things in the box. I still can't believe they let me bring it here with me.*

St. Louis Cathedral pealed out the hour. Even though sunset was still a few hours away, the narrow, cobblestone streets and closely-knit, French colonial stucco buildings were already being cast into long sepia-colored shadows. The black, wrought iron balconies that looked so quaint by day now looked like interlaced fingers hiding some sinful secret from the people walking the maze of thin sidewalks below.

Celine turned as the bells of St. Louis sounded its second level of chimes, announcing a call to evening prayer. *Wow! 6:00 already? I should probably go and grab a bite to eat before I meet with Alex.* She stood up, straightening her peacock blue sundress and hooking her matching canvas purse on her shoulder. She looked over at the old Cathedral. *How many years have you done your job, old man? I bet you've gotten tired of it, too, from time to time. I'm sure Adele did. What kept her going? Was it her love for Etienne? Don't worry, Adele. I'll take care of the box. I'm keeping it in the trunk of my car. It's safer there than in that dinky little safe in my room. I don't trust the hotel safe. I don't want a maid going through it or, God forbid, something goes missing!*

As the last of the chimes sounded, Celine heard a man's voice calling out from the street behind her. "You're in luck, folks. We're passing right in front of St. Louis Cathedral just as he's calling out the hour. It's good luck to pass by when that happens, so make a wish or say a prayer or, if you're like me, you'll do a little of both. Keep your bases covered, you know?" Celine watched as a bright blue, mule-drawn carriage tee-tered down Decatur Street. The driver called back to his passengers, "Wave hello to General Andrew Jackson! He's waving to you! Now, we have a special place in our hearts for Jackson because back in 1814, he led the troops to victory in the Battle of New Orleans. We even have a song about it. I'll give a free ride to anyone who can sing it with me."

Celine smiled as she listened to the well-rehearsed spiel of the car-riage driver. Without waiting for any one of his passengers to even try, he belted out the song in a booming bass voice:

♫ *"In 1814 we took a little trip, along with Colonel Jackson down the mighty Mississip'. We took a little bacon and we took a little beans and we fought the bloody British in a town called New Or'leeens..."* ♫

The last of his melody was swallowed by the clip clop of the old nag plodding along, her left rump quivering as a car sidled around the yellow-wheeled rig. *Hmmm, a few minutes after six. Still too soon to get to the gallery. I'm not really hungry, but...* The smell of café au lait wafted on the breeze. The bustling, open-aired Café du Monde was just across the street from Jackson Square... not as crowded as it had been earlier. Now would be a perfect time to enjoy a cup of chicory-laced coffee, maybe even a plate of beignets—those light fluffy pillows of fried dough drowning in powdered sugar. Decadence! Celine stepped in rhythm with a small crowd of pedestrians as they crossed the street.

"Au lait or black?" The waitress asked Celine as she settled into the only empty table facing busy Decatur Street.

Celine sat down, glancing at the menu that was pasted onto the side of the chrome napkin holder. "I'll take au lait and..."

"Beignets?" The words came rushing from the woman's lips.

Celine looked at the waitress. She was a pretty Vietnamese woman, but her face was covered in a sheen of light sweat. Her black skirt was sprinkled with powdered sugar like a connect-the-dots kids' game. The green-and-white paper hat perched on her head had lost its cute tilt hours ago. She looked tired, no doubt a result of waiting on indecisive tourists all afternoon and the heat from the sizzling, round-the-clock, fry kitchen from which she had just come.

Celine smiled at her, hoping to get a tiny smile in return, but that's when she saw him. Michael was standing at the cash register just a few feet behind this poor tired woman. Celine peeked around the waitress' elbow, watching Michael as he paid his tab. He must've known the cashier. They were laughing together like old friends as Michael handed him the money. *He has such a beautiful smile. Tall, handsome, just like the man in my dream.*

"Lady, 'you want beignets?"

Celine looked back at the waitress, embarrassed just a little. The unexpected surprise at seeing Michael had erased the impatient waitress for just that moment. "Umm, no I..."

As Michael stepped out of the café and onto the sidewalk, Celine couldn't help but watch him stride by and then stand at the intersection of Decatur and Dumaine. *I wonder where he's going? Probably to the gallery.* Celine glanced down at her watch. 6:20. *I should head there too. I might be a little early, but...* Her eyes drifted to the ring. *St. Ezilie? What do you think? Should I follow him back to the gallery?* The waitress blew an impatient little huff. "Okay, beignets or no beignets?"

Celine watched as Michael stepped out into the street. He drew her like a magnet. In one flowing movement, she stood up and grabbed her purse from the back of the chair. "Sorry. I changed my mind." Celine skittered down Decatur Street and up Dumaine.

She ran along at a quick pace and could still see Michael's back as he walked in long unhurried strides. Celine paused to catch her breath and watched Michael cross Chartres Street up ahead. *It's better if I hang back, let him get to the gallery before me. When he turns on Royal Street, I'll start walking again.* Celine watched but when he didn't turn down Royal, her curiosity was piqued. *He's going to Bourbon? Why's he going there? Maybe he's not going to meet with Alex and I.* Intrigued, Celine started walking again, her pace quickened to catch up with him.

Just as she crossed Royal, she saw Michael disappear into a crowd of Bourbon Street tourists, folding in behind him like a school of laughing, drunken fish. Celine stopped at the corner. *God, I hate Bourbon Street.* She could see the back of Michael's head over the revelers as he passed Bourbon and walked on, the image of him melting into the shadows.

Good thing he's so tall. I can still see him, but... She looked at her watch again. *6:30. Yeah, he's obviously not headed to the gallery. I should, though. I'll just turn around and...*

Before she could finish her thought she was lifted off her feet by a set of very strong arms. "Hey, pretty lady! Let's parrrr deeeee!" Before Celine could stop him, the drunken overweight man twirled her around, laughing and sputtering to all his friends "Hey, Lookit! I got me a date!" Celine pushed against his chest trying to gain some distance between her and his beer-soaked breath. Staring into a pair of too-much-to-drink eyes, she said, "Put me down!" She pushed harder. "I said, put me down!" His grip was broken but as he let her go, she landed in the middle of a mock Mardi Gras parade, filled with bead-wearing, hurricane-drinking convention goers.

Celine tried to steady herself as she dodged around the swaying, laughing mob. "Where'd she go?" Celine could hear the drunk's voice. She stepped up to the sidewalk on the other side of Bourbon Street, crouching low so he wouldn't see her, but one of his friends spotted her. He yelled, pointing at Celine. "Here she is!" He turned to Celine. "Hey, Tommy's okay. He's only been divorced twice. If you just give him a chance, he'll..." Celine turned and ran up Dumaine Street as fast as she could, leaving Bourbon Street behind and drunk Tommy yelling, "Hey, come back!"

Celine stopped running when the din of Bourbon Street faded into silence. She turned. No one was behind her and no one was ahead. In fact, she was all alone. Relieved, she shook her head. *What was I thinking? I'm not going back that way.* She looked at her watch. 6:40, almost 6:45. *Oh, terrific! That's what I get for following Michael. Who the hell knows where he went? Now, I've only got fifteen minutes to get to the gallery!* She looked ahead and saw a street sign illuminated by an old fashioned coach lamp, Rue Dauphine. *If I take Dauphine I'm sure I'll find one of those back streets that'll get me there. I don't want to go back to Bourbon, but I'm not sure which way to go.*

Celine walked briskly to the corner and stopped, looking up one way and down the other. *Hmm, either way should at least get me back to Decatur. I can start over from there.* She turned left onto a very quiet Dauphine Street. At first the silence was a welcome change from the partying crowd she'd just escaped, but it wasn't long before the lonely echo of her heels on the sidewalk made her uneasy. The disjointed strains of a saxophone wafted in on the humid breeze carrying with it the smell of stale beer and whiskey. A clinking of utensils from a kitchen somewhere and a man's laughter made Celine look behind her. No one. There were no restaurants or bars on this street. Only shop fronts, dark and closed. She clutched her purse a little tighter, stepped out into the street away from parked cars and quickened her pace. She could see the intersection ahead, but the coach light had burned out, making it impossible to read the street sign in the hazy twilight. She'd have to get closer to read it.

As she approached the next corner, she slowed down just a bit and looked at the lamp post. No sign. *Great. Some idiot took it, probably as a souvenir!* She looked further down Dauphine Street but it looked even eerier than the way that she had come. She stepped onto the unnamed street and saw a sign about midway down the block illuminated by a single light bulb. *If this is St. Peter, then I'm in luck. If it's not, I'll stop and call Alex.* She hurried on.

As Celine got closer to the wooden, hand-painted sign, she realized it was a business front of some kind. Lights shining from shaded windows told her it looked open. *Good. I can ask someone what street this is.* But just as Celine approached the front step, she stopped suddenly, 'The Marie LaVeau Apartments, Rue St. Ann'. She took a quick breath, looking at the disheveled house in front of her. It was old, very old and parts of the front steps were rotting. It was a worn out shoebox shape, one story, flat roof that had been painted, peeled and painted again. It looked like an old whore that might've still had street appeal. To the left, a bent wrought iron gate stood slightly ajar, the only thing that separated a small, wildly overgrown yard from the street. Celine stared at the place, stunned.

Could this be it? St. Ann Street. Could this really be Marie LaVeau's house? Celine reached out and touched the damp stucco wall.

Marguerite, Marie, Adele… She stopped and turned the ring around her finger with her thumb. *And Etienne. Oh God…* Celine was deep in thought when she realized someone was standing close to her, too close.

She turned sharply and faced an old black woman wearing a white scarf wrapped tightly around her hair. Her large gold hoop earrings bobbed up and down. Her filthy, once-blue dress was torn at the sleeve and smelled of days-old sweat and urine. She wore stained, once-white house slippers and her heels were cracked and dirty. The old street woman smiled a near-toothless smile. "You lookin' for Marie LaVeau?"

Celine answered cautiously and took a step back. The old woman's breath had a sickeningly sweet metallic odor. "No, no, um, I thought I was on St. Peter. I'll just…"

Her smile made Celine uneasy. "Now what you be wantin' on St. Peter? Young thing like you lookin' for Marie, lookin' for her to help you with your man. I gots just the right thing for you."

Celine took another small step back. "No, that's okay. I'm meeting someone in a few minutes so…"

"Oh chile, it won't take long. I'll even lets ya talk to Old Marie. She talks to me, ya knows. She talks to my daughta, too. She reads the cowrie shells and the cards. You wants a readin'? It'll only cos' you about ten dollars. You got ten dollars, don' you? Well, sure you does." The old woman reached out and took Celine's arm.

Celine pulled back. "No, really. Maybe another time."

Celine tried to step around the woman, but she was faster than Celine had anticipated. "Now chile, you don't want to goes back over there. The square gots nothin'. Those readers pretendin' to be Madame

Marie's children—fakes, all of 'em!" The old woman spit at Celine's feet. "Whatcha wants with them? Look, I can show you the real thing. Dis here is Marie LaVeau's house, and Bayou St. John where she done did all her hoodoo is jus' across Rampart up there, and, hey, I bets you ain't seen Congo Square, neither. Her grave is right up next to that. That'll only cos' you twenty-five bucks. You looks like you got that much."

The old lady was fast. She grabbed at Celine's purse and managed to get the strap down her arm before Celine pulled back. The old woman lunged, pulled a long hatpin from her scarf and held it to Celine's throat. "You white bitch! Give me that!" Celine stood as still as she could. The old woman pressed the hatpin deeper into her throat. Celine felt the prick of the point break through her skin. "Yeah, that's it, girlie. Now hand it to me, nice and slow." Celine held her arm out, the strap hanging from her wrist. When the old woman grabbed at the purse, Celine jerked back and stumbled hard on the jagged pavement. As she crumbled to the ground, the purse fell open. Her wallet, phone, hairbrush and hotel key spilled onto the sidewalk. Celine grabbed for the wallet as she tried to scramble back to her feet.

The old woman was on her, grabbling at her legs like a starving buzzard. She clawed at Celine's things, pecking at them, grabbed her watch off her wrist in a flash and stuffed everything into her bosom. The black woman's jagged smile widened as she looked past Celine and up at the man's voice behind her. "Whatcha got, Mama?"

"Nate, baby!" The young man towered over Celine. The glare from the light bulb behind him shaded his face. "I gots another one fer ya, honey, but I bet this one's gots money."

Who's that you callin' Mama? That's not my name, remember?"

The old woman grinned. "Rooster, baby. You my struttin' Rooster."

"Yeah, that's right and I'm sure if you just ask this nice lady here, she'll let you see what's in her wallet." The young man turned to Celine, sneering. Celine still couldn't see his face, but she caught a glimpse of his unnaturally thin chest and long bony fingers. His faded threadbare T-shirt hung from his shoulders like a sack. She could smell a hint of burnt plastic on him. "Isn't that right, miss?" Celine scooted back, but the old woman snatched the wallet from her hand. Celine pulled back, still trying to move away.

The old woman reached up and gave the wallet to her son. He unsnapped the clasp and pulled out the license. "Hmmmm, let's see here. What's a nice white gal doin' here, huh? Baton Rouge. Celine Dupré, pretty name. Pretty girl. Got any money, Celine?" He tossed the license at the old woman. She caught it and with a magician's hands; the license disappeared down her dress. He unzipped the side pouch of the wallet and peered inside. "Hundred? That's all you got?" He pulled the cash from the wallet and slid it into his pocket.

"Credit cards." The old woman barked. "Get her cards! Bet she's gots lots of 'em!"

Rooster barked back at his mother. "Old woman, that's how they caught us the last time! No cards. Just cash, unless she's got something else we want."

"We could sell 'em!" The old woman screeched.

"Shut up, you ol' fool. It's me goin' to jail if she talks, not you." The young man unzipped another compartment of the wallet. "But you're not gonna tell the cops nuthin' are you, Celine Dupré?" Celine shook her head and inched her way out of the glare of the light, hoping to get a clearer view of his face. "Let's see what else you got in here." He pulled out a few photos. "These your kids?" He rifled through the few pictures but then stopped at one. "What you doin' with a little black girl's picture in here?"

Celine took a short breath. He'd found the photographs she kept of her students. Her voice cracked as she said nervously, "She's one of my students. I'm a teacher."

Rooster looked more closely at the picture, his eyes growing wide as he studied it. He looked back at Celine. "One of your students, huh? Hey Mama, take a look at this."

The old woman squinted as she looked at the photo. Suddenly her eyes went wild. "Rooster, this here is Leah!" She turned to Celine, yelling. "How come you got a picture of my grandbaby? I knows you! You stole her! Where'd you take her?!"

Rooster never took his eyes off Celine. "You know where Leah is?" Celine didn't answer. He reached down and jerked Celine up from the sidewalk, clenching her arm like a vise grip and pulling her into his chest. "I asked you a question, bitch!" Celine tried to pull away but Rooster held her tight, both his arms pinning her. "Where is she?"

Celine's thoughts were racing. *Oh God, is this Leah's family? But that's impossible! I've got to lie.* "I don't know any Leah. That little girl in my wallet, her name's Bonny. I…"

The old woman screeched. "She's lying! I remember her from the Picky'oon. She had her picture took with Leah and the picture in her wallet, that's Leah! This bitch is the one who helped put Trish in jail and she's got Leah hid somewhere! Somewhere close! I know she do!"

Rooster yelled at his mother. "Shut up, Mama!" He shook Celine. "Is this true?"

The old woman grabbed her son's arm. "It's true! I gots the picture. I kep' it. You remember me showing you, don't you? I gots the paper back at the house. I can show you!"

Rooster shook his mother away. "Get off me! Yes, I remember. Now, shut up while I take care of this!"

Rooster glared coldly at Celine. "You know where she is?" Celine didn't answer. "He shook her. "Tell me where and I'll let you go."

Celine thought fast. *What can I tell them so Leah will be safe?* "They moved her out of state. She was only with me for a short time." Celine hoped that they'd believe her lie. They could never find out that Leah was still living in New Orleans with her adopted parents.

"Moved her!" The old woman flew at Celine, scratching at her face. Celine crossed her arms trying to defend herself. "You took my baby. You took my Leah!" The old woman flailed at Celine. "I wants her back, now!

Give her back!" Celine covered her face while the old woman clawed at her arms. "You stole our best sneak thief. I trained her from a baby! Everyone believed she was blind! You bitch! I'll kill you! And then I'll find Leah and get her back!"

Suddenly Rooster started laughing. "Stop it, Mama. I see something that'll make up for it." The old woman kept hitting at Celine. Rooster pushed the old woman back. "Stop it and look at her hand!" He held Celine's left hand up, the ring shining brightly in the glare of the garish light bulb.

The old lady's face melted into a crooked grin as she reached up roughly and grabbed Celine's hand. Celine was wedged between them while the old woman pulled hard at the ring, twisting her finger. "How much this worth?" Celine clenched her fist and turned her hand, trying desperately to wrench free. The old woman squeezed her hand tighter as Rooster held her. "Let go, you little…"

Rooster grabbed a handful of Celine's hair and jerked her head back. Pain shot through her as he shook her head like a dog with a toy in its mouth. When he stopped, Celine dared not move. He put his face down into hers. His chocolate brown eyes were bloodshot and dilated. His cheeks were pockmarked. His gnarled dread locks hung in her face. His rancid breath crawled into Celine's pores as he growled through rotten teeth. "Listen, bitch. You don't know my mama. She will hurt you, hurt you bad, if she doesn't get what she wants. She knows things. Things that nice white folk like you would never know about. So, if you want to get out of this, you'll just give us this sweet little ring. You owe it to us. You put my sister in jail and stole Leah, right? Now you pay us and it'll all be over and we can let you go." He shook her head once more. "Now stay the fuck still!"

Celine fought back the rising panic and tried to stay calm. The old woman dug her hand down into a pocket of the dirty dress she wore. "I bet you likes baby powder, right?" Celine didn't move. The old woman pulled her hand out of the pocket, hiding whatever she had in her fist. "Mmmm, yeah. I bet you like lots of baby powder all over that pretty white skin." The old woman opened her palm, showing a small mound of white powder. "Isn't it pretty? Want some?"

Celine pulled back. "No, get away. Just let me go…" Before Celine could finish the words the old woman blew the powder in Celine's face. Celine sputtered. Her nose and eyes burned. She coughed, but the bitter-tasting powder trickled down her throat. She was getting dizzy. The words came out chopped. "What…did…you do?" Celine took a deep breath. Just as she did, the old woman blew again. Celine coughed and sputtered, her breath was shallow and her head was swimming. She fought the urge to collapse even though her legs felt heavy.

"That's enough, Mama!" Rooster yelled.

"It'll keep her quiet, 'sides, there's not enough there to hurt her, just slow her down." The old woman spit on Celine's knuckle as she twisted it round and round. Celine could feel the warm spittle dripping into her hand. She heard the old woman screaming with delight. "Ohh, it's coming, baby, look!" Rooster turned his head and grinned as he watched his mother try to pry the ring off, but it was stubbornly holding on to Celine's hand. "Here, Mama. Let me." Celine felt Rooster let go of her hair as he reached for the ring. She felt his rough hand twisting the ring as it started to slide over her knuckle.

Celine shook her head. She blinked her eyes and willed her legs to standing. *No! NO!* In one big push against the two of them, she pulled her hand back and screamed "NO!" Her sudden move forced Rooster backward. The old woman looked up at Celine, confused. With just a few inches between her and the old woman, Celine stepped back and kicked her with everything she had. The old woman groaned as she buckled over, falling backward, pulling her son with her. As Celine wrenched her arms free, she scratched Rooster's face. He fell on top of the old woman as he yelled, "You fuckin'…!" The rest of his words smashed into a bloody gurgle as his mouth hit the pavement. From a tangled mass of arms and legs, the old woman screamed, "You white cunt! I'm gonna kill you! Kill you dead. I knows where you're stayin'. I gots the key right here!"

Celine didn't waste a second. She spun around and ran as fast as she could down St. Ann. *People…up ahead….Got to get…back to square.* She thought she could hear someone running behind her. *Faster.* She was panting now, but her face felt numb. Every breath burned. *Oh God, please…* She looked back for a split second. Then something hard hit her square in the chest. She tried to scream but the air rushed out of her lungs. *No breath. No breath.* She clawed at the air. She backed up as fast as she could, but she tripped and fell backward onto the brick street. A sharp pain jolted through her body as her shoulder hit the brick pavement. She tried to scream but her voice was frozen inside her head.

Someone was standing over her. A man. *How did he catch me so fast?* Terrified, she fought; hit, scratched, but her hands were losing strength. She could hear the man's voice, feel his breath and the power of his iron hands.

"Someone help!"

This voice, it's not the robber's voice. She could feel her legs growing weaker. The man lifted her up from the waist, keeping her from falling. Everything moved in slow motion. Celine looked up, trying to focus on the man's face. *He's talking to me, saying something. What?*

"Hold on to me, okay?"

Michael?

CHAPTER 12

Celine could hear the buzz of people talking, some even yelling, just outside the exam room door. The urgent care center had been a crowded madhouse when she checked in; tourists, mostly drunk, all of them confused and hurt in some way. *I still can't believe Michael was there. Thank God he called the police. I was so panicked. I wasn't making any sense at all.* She took short raspy breaths. Her face felt tingly, almost numb. Worse was the headache that was thundering through her head.

Pain spiraled from behind her neck and coiled tightly around her forehead, exploding at her temples. She closed her eyes, trying to escape from the fluorescent overhead lights that blazed brightly against the bare white walls.

She reached up and ran trembling fingers through her hair. She could smell the faint odor of baby powder on her hands. The memory came surging back; the old woman blowing the white cloud into her face. She rubbed her eyes and nose trying to get the smell off her skin. *What the hell is in that stuff? It must be bad if the police insisted a doctor check me out before they even finished questioning me. Suppose it's mixed with…* She stopped herself. *No, no. I can't think about it. I'll wait to see what the doctor says.*

She heard the door knob squeak and opened her eyes. She blinked, trying to focus. "Hello, Miss Dupré. My name is Sarah. I'm your nurse." Celine turned toward the voice and saw a young blonde woman closing the door, dressed in sea-green surgical scrubs. "Are you sleepy?"

Celine squinted her eyes open. "No, but my head is killing me." She pointed to the overhead lights. "They're so bright."

The nurse stepped to Celine's side and took the blood pressure cuff from the hook on the wall. "Sorry. Is your head the only thing that hurts?" She wrapped the gray cuff on Celine's arm. Celine gave the nurse a little nod. She didn't want to talk. Words only made the pain worse.

The nurse squeezed the bulb. "The doctor's gonna take a look at you in a few minutes. I just need to get your vitals first." The slow whoosh sound made Celine's head throb. She squirmed with every pump of air. When the valve began to hiss, she closed her eyes, retreating to that dark place behind her eyelids.

The nurse unrolled the cuff from Celine's arm. "Just a little elevated, but I think that's to be expected. The police said you were robbed?"

Celine whispered with her eyes still closed. "Yeah."

Sarah nodded as she hooked the cuff back into the slot on the wall. "Open your eyes. I need to take your temp now." Celine opened her eyes slowly and saw the waiting thermometer at her lips. "Did they get everything?"

Just as Celine opened her mouth to answer, the nurse placed the cold, wet thermometer under her tongue. "Yesh," was all she said as she tried to keep the alcohol-tasting stick from slipping out of her mouth.

Sarah frowned. "I hope this doesn't scare you away from New Orleans. It really is a nice place, you know." Celine nodded her head as the nurse curled cool fingertips around her wrist, felt for a pulse and watched the clock on the wall. Celine closed her eyes again, relieved with the minute of dark silence that followed. "Good. Let's see now…" The nurse took the thermometer out, read it and then shook it back down. "Normal. We've got a full house tonight. It's a little crazier than usual. So sit tight and …"

Before Sarah could finish the sentence, the doctor opened the door, letting the sounds from the waiting room burst their way in. "Miss Dupré, is it?" The doctor walked over to the sink and washed his hands.

Celine managed a weak, "Yes". She opened her eyes just enough to see that he was a young man, possibly fresh out of med school. His starched white lab coat in the fluorescent lights made her head pound even more.

"I'm Dr. Bergeron. Sounds like you've been through a rough time. Someone blew some powder in your face?" He pulled a paper towel out of the dispenser and dried his hands.

Celine shifted, making the tissue paper on the exam table crackle. "Yeah." She blinked, trying to fight back the fireworks of light dancing in her eyes. "I've got a raging headache, too."

The doctor snapped on a pair of latex gloves and walked over to the side of the table. "Baby powder mixed with over-the-counter antihistamines. That's all it is. The latest thing in robbery down here. They want to scare you; make you think they've blown some street drugs into your lungs but it's harmless, really. 'Might make you a little sleepy, blurry vision, dry mouth; all that passes pretty quickly, but that headache will be with you for a while. Let's just check you over, okay?" The doctor pulled out a penlight from his coat pocket.

Celine tried to sit up a little straighter. "So, it's not mixed with street drugs like heroin or anything like that?"

The doctor let out a little laugh. "You kiddin'? These people wouldn't share their heroin with you. Besides, all that stuff, crack, heroin, it gives you a sense of euphoria. You don't look like you're feeling very euphoric to me. Now, let's look at your throat." Obediently, she opened her mouth. "Yeah, a little irritation there. He reached out and slowly felt the glands on her neck. As his palm touched her throat, she jumped.

"That hurt?"

"Yeah, just under my neck"

"Lift up your head for me? Celine looked up. "Looks like you have a small red spot right there; 'looks a little inflamed." He turned to the nurse.

"Let me have an alcohol swab." The nurse opened a sealed package and handed him a white gauze square. "Any idea how that got there?"

Celine looked at the ceiling, fighting back tears. "The old woman held a needle to my throat."

The doctor gently rubbed the swab over the prick site. "A needle? What kind of needle?"

"It was long, like a hatpin. She pulled it out of her headscarf."

"It was probably filthy. Not very deep but…" He looked at Celine. "…are you current on your tetanus?" The doctor stepped back and threw the swab away.

Celine nodded. "I work with kids. We get updates on our shots every year."

The doctor nodded as he placed his hands gently on her neck. "HepB, too?

"Yeah."

"Okay. Well, your glands aren't swollen. Now, try to open your eyes as wide as you can."

Celine blinked trying to open her eyes enough for the doctor to look. The tiny light cut like knives through her head. Tears filled her eyes to the brim as she fought to keep them open. "Your pupils look okay but your whites are a little bloodshot." He gave her a little smile. "Have you been drinking?" Celine shook her head no, pulling away. Explosions of light flashed behind her closed lids. She reached up and wiped the tears from her cheeks. "Drinking with antihistamines would make all the symptoms worse. Just lift your head slightly and let me look in your nose." Celine raised her chin looking at the ceiling. "Yeah, just a bit of redness there. Any stinging sensations?"

"No, but it feels like I want to sneeze."

The doctor pressed her cheekbones gently. "Yeah, that's the baby powder. Does that hurt?"

Celine let out a sigh of relief. "No, it actually makes the headache feel a little better."

"What about numbing?" He kept pressing gently on her cheekbones all the way up to her temples.

"When I first got here, my face felt a little tingly, but that's better now."

The doctor stepped back, looking at her arms. "Let me take a look at the rest of you. Bruise here." He tapped her bare shoulder. Celine grimaced as he touched the dark spot just past her sundress strap. He looked down both arms and then at her forearms. He let out a short whistle when he saw the long claw marks left by the old woman. He turned to the nurse. "This needs to be cleaned." He looked more closely. The doctor stepped back and looked at her legs and feet. "A couple of cuts here, too, Sarah."

Celine looked down, noticing for the first time her scraped knees and scratched legs. "I fell."

"Did you hit your head?"

"No."

He placed his hands gently behind her neck and slowly turned her head from side to side. "What about migraines. Have you ever had them?"

Celine closed her eyes and let her head move with the flow of the doctor's hands. "Yes." She could smell the biting odor of alcohol and then felt a sharp sting as the nurse cleaned her cuts.

"Well, what you just went through could trigger a migraine, especially if you have a history of them." He placed his hands on the crown of her head and gently worked his way around her scalp. "No lumps. Do you take anything for your migraines?"

Celine winced as the nurse ran the alcohol swab over the wounds on her legs. "I used to but I haven't had to take anything in a while."

The doctor walked over to a desk in the corner of the room. "You're gonna need something for the next twenty-four, maybe forty-eight hours." He pulled a prescription pad out of this lab coat pocket and started to write. "You could've been hurt a lot worse. Robbery happens to the tourists all the time down here. They never realize just how dangerous it is, especially at the six o'clock hour; the Quarter drains like a bathtub at that time. Only thing left is the dirt and the scum." As he handed the prescription to Celine, he looked down at her hand. "Wow, you're lucky they didn't take that."

Celine's head started pounding again as she remembered the old woman grabbing her wrist and spitting on her hand. She turned the sapphire ring around on her finger but it felt slimy and damp. "Can I wash my hands?"

"Sure, sure, in just a minute. You're probably gonna feel a little weak for the rest of today and that headache's gonna be with you until tomorrow. The 'script is for the headache, but it's pretty powerful stuff. I've given you two days'-worth, but just take it as needed. Don't take any other pain meds with it. 'Could cause you some problems if you do. 'Probably make you a little sleepy. Are you feeling up to talking with the police?"

Celine answered weakly. "I think so."

The doctor smiled and closed the folder. "I'll send him in. Just take it easy for the next couple of days and you'll be fine." The doctor didn't wait for an answer. He left the room just as Sarah placed a light blanket on Celine's shoulders. She let out a little moan of comfort as the warm blanket cocooned around her. "That feels good, I bet." Celine nodded, her shoulders sagging. The nurse looked down at the doctor's notes then looked back up at Celine. "Would you like for me to fill the prescription for you? We have a pharmacy on site."

"That would help. I don't know where the pharmacies are around here, anyway."

Sarah took the prescription from Celine. "You just stay here. When I get back, I'll help you to the sink over there and you can wash up a little." As the nurse left the room, Celine pulled the white blanket tighter around her shoulders. The warmth helped her headache dull to a slow throb. She took a deep breath and looked down at the ring. In spite of everything it had been through, it glistened in the bright, cold room.

Memories of the two thieves crept back in. She looked down at her blue sundress. The hem was torn and the embroidery threads had been ripped and frayed. *He held me down, pulled my hair. She attacked me, spit on me.* Tears dripped down Celine's cheeks. She shook her head, fighting to push the memories away. *I've got to wash them off me.*

Celine edged her way to the side of the table, gingerly stepping down hoping that the headache wouldn't come storming back. She steadied herself and crept in little steps, the blanket trailing from one shoulder. In slow, calculated movements, she walked to the sink and turned the water on. Almost out of breath, she put her hands under the cool water and let out a deep sigh of relief. She looked at the soap dispenser. She pumped once, twice, three times and scrubbed her hands, front, back, up to her elbows. She lowered her face and began to scrub. That's when the tears came. She steadied herself on the side of the sink and like the tide, the sobs rushed over her.

When the door opened and the nurse walked back in, Celine leaned down and splashed more water onto her hot cheeks. "What are you doing over here?" She placed gentle but firm hands around Celine's shoulders and turned her toward the chair. "Now, take it easy, okay? You've gone through a terrible ordeal and you'll need to take it slowly." Sarah sat Celine down in the chair and then pulled several paper towels from the dispenser and handed them to her. "Are you feeling a little light-headed?"

"No, washing my hands and face really helped."

"What about the headache? Scale of 1-10, 10 being the worst?"

Celine thought for a moment. "Probably about a 7..." She paused, "...and-a-half."

Sarah let out a little laugh. "Well, I have your pills here. If you'd like, you could take one now. It might help you feel better."

Celine gave her a little frown. "I think I need to talk to the police first. The doctor said the pills might make me sleepy. I need to stay awake enough to answer their questions and when they're done, I still have to get back to the hotel. I don't know how I'm going to do that."

Sarah smiled. "Not to worry, the police will get you there. Your Guardian Angel's watching over you, too."

Celine turned slowly to the nurse, confused. "Guardian Angel?"

Sarah stood up and pulled a paper cup from the dispenser next to the sink. "The guy that came in with you."

Celine gave her a little smile. "Oh, you mean Michael. Yeah, I guess he is my Guardian Angel, even though I hardly know him at all."

Sarah gave Celine a little shrug as she poured water into the cup. "Well, he's pretty nice if you ask me. The policeman that's covering your case thinks so, too."

"The policeman, what's his name again? I remember him introducing himself and then asking me some questions, but I was in such a fog."

"Officer Vincent Cabrini. He's not one to joke around much, but right now, he's out there drinking coffee and visiting with your Guardian Angel like they've known each other for years. Maybe they have. I don't know." Sarah handed the cup to Celine. "What about the headache? Wanna take one, or no?"

"No, I'm actually feeling a little better. I mean my head still hurts but not as bad as it did."

"Well, you can drink the water, anyway. Keep hydrated. That'll help flush those antihistamines out of your system."

Celine drank the water like a dutiful child. As she dropped the cup in the wastepaper basket, she pulled the blanket from around her shoulders and handed it to Sarah. "What about the bill?" She let out a resigned sigh. "I don't have any cash or credit cards. They took everything. I could give you my insurance information but all that's back home, so I hope..."

The nurse laid the blanket on Celine's lap. "Hang on to this for now. You might want it later." She handed Celine the amber-colored medicine bottle as she stood up. "And don't worry about the bill. That's why I called that guy your Guardian Angel. He took care of it."

"He did what?" Celine heard a soft knock on the door.

Sarah smiled as she nodded and walked over to the door. Celine heard a man's voice. "Hey, Sarah. Dr. Bergeron gave the OK."

Sarah stepped aside as Michael and Officer Cabrini walked through the door. "She's doing much better, Vince. I think she's ready for you. I checked with the front desk. It looks like the zoo out there has calmed down a bit so you've got the room for a little while."

The police officer nodded as Sarah looked down at Celine. "If you need anything, I'm not far away." Celine nodded as Sarah disappeared behind the door.

Michael sat down next to her. "You look better. How are you feeling?"

Celine gave him a small smile. "Much better. Thank you so much for all your help, I can pay you back for..."

Michael reached over and put his hand over hers. "Let's not worry about that right now. I think Vince wants to talk to both of us."

Officer Cabrini sat down across from her, doing his best to find a comfortable position for his broad-shouldered, muscular frame in the hard plastic chair. "Hi, Miss Dupré. Ready to finish up?" Celine took a deep breath and nodded. The policeman shifted in his seat. "Michael's already given me his statement but I need him to verify a few things while we talk, okay?"

Celine turned and looked at Michael. "Sure."

The officer flipped open his notepad. "Now, you said earlier that you were on St. Ann Street at about 6:00 when two people robbed you, is that right?"

Celine gripped the blanket in her lap, dredging back the memory. "Yes, yes, that's right."

Cabrini looked back at his notes. "You gave me a description of the black woman, but what about the black man. Can you tell me anything about him?"

Celine thought back. The dull throb started to sound in her ears. "He was taller than the woman, probably about six feet. Real skinny. His skin was very, very dark." Celine shivered as she recalled the man's face. "I remember the old woman said his name." Cabrini clicked his ball point pen and leaned forward, ready to write. Celine closed her eyes, trying to recall what the old woman said, but no matter how hard she tried, the name was gone.

When Celine didn't answer, Cabrini turned to Michael. "Did you see him? Miss Dupré told me earlier that she thought he chased her from St. Ann Street into Jackson Square."

Michael shook his head. "All I saw was Celine running toward me. That's when I reached out and caught her. She was scared to death. I think at first she thought I was the thief because she kept trying to push me away but when she finally did recognize me she was screaming that this guy was chasing her. I looked around but I never saw anyone that might've been running after her."

"Does that sound right, Miss Dupré?" Celine nodded sadly. "Do you think you could identify the thief if you saw him again?"

Celine's hands trembled. "I think I could. I can see his face very clearly in my mind but…" She hesitated. Her whole body began to ache as she imagined seeing the man again. "…would I have to?"

"We don't have to worry about that now. We have to catch him first. Now, they took your purse. You said it was…" He looked back at his notes "blue-green?" Celine nodded as he read on. "And your wallet, right?"

Celine's voice lowered to a whisper. "That's right." The dull throb in her head had grown sharper. She closed her eyes as she forced herself to remember. "He went through my wallet and…wait!" Celine opened her eyes with a slight jerk. "Rooster, that was his name. And the old lady was his mother. He kept calling her Mama! She called him something else, but I can't remember what it was."

Officer Cabrini jotted the name down. "Rooster. You're sure?"

"Yes, yes."

"You said he went through your wallet? What was in there?"

"All the cash I had. A hundred dollars. He gave all the other stuff, my license and credit cards, over to his mother."

"Did he ever use the mother's name?"

"I don't think so. No."

"Okay, can you think of anything else they took?"

Celine thought back. Her heart sank as she remembered the photographs. "Leah."

Officer Cabrini looked up. "Is that the mother's name?"

Celine shook her head. "No, no. Oh God!" Tears began to sting her eyes as she remembered the old woman's rage when she found the child's picture.

Officer Cabrini put his pen down. "Okay, who's Leah? Was that someone who was with you?" He turned to Michael. "Are you sure she was alone when you saw her running?" Michael nodded and then looked at Celine.

Celine rubbed her sweaty palms on the blanket. "No, no! Leah's one of my students. I'm the Assistant Principal at the School for the Blind and I carry some of the kids' school pictures in my wallet. It was her picture that they took."

He straddled the notepad on his knee and began to write. "Oh, okay, so besides the picture, anything else?"

"No, no, I don't think you understand..." Celine's head was drumming in short, hard raps. Officer Cabrini looked up, frowning. Celine took a shallow breath. "Look, I know this sounds crazy, but when the old woman saw Leah's picture, she recognized her."

He leaned back. "She recognized her? You mean she thought she recognized her, right?"

Celine tried to take a deep breath, but the air in the room felt hot and stale. "No, I mean she really did recognize her. Oh, why did I keep Leah's picture in my wallet? I should've never done that."

Cabrini was silent, his face expressionless. When he finally spoke, his voice was laced with doubt. "So you know the people who robbed you?"

Celine's voice began to break. "No, I don't know them. Not directly, anyway. I only know Leah." *Why is he staring at me like that? He doesn't believe me! How am I going to explain this?* Her words came out in a rush. "I know it all sounds unbelievable but really, I don't know them; 'never seen them before. I'm worried that they're gonna try and kidnap Leah; try to get her back. I..."

Officer Cabrini cocked his head, an intense frown stretched across his forehead. "Kidnap? Okay, okay. Let's slow down. Why don't you just start from the beginning? Tell me about this child, um..." He looked back down at his notes. "...Leah?"

Celine nervously pushed a strand of hair from her face, trying to calm herself. "Leah was removed from her home here in the Quarter by Child Protective Services about seven months ago. Her mother lost custody of Leah because of a string of drug offenses that landed her in jail for a very long time. Because Leah's blind, she was placed with us at the School for the Blind and the judge appointed me as temporary guardian until CPS could locate another family member to take Leah in."

Cabrini scribbled notes. "Okay, so she lived at the School for the Blind over in Baton Rouge with you as temporary guardian?" Celine nodded. "And the mother lost all rights to the child?" Celine nodded again. "And did they ever find another family member to take the child?"

"No. The CPS caseworker told me that they interviewed the grandmother, but that wasn't an appropriate placement. I never asked why and they never explained."

Cabrini wrote feverishly. "And you never met the grandmother. She never met you?"

Celine could feel her heartbeat in her ears. "No, and I didn't meet any other of Leah's family, either. Really, there just wasn't anyone there for her, so when a very nice couple applied to adopt, the judge had no problem with it. I'm sure you could look up the case records in family court. It's all there."

Cabrini shook his head. "Then how did she recognize you and why are you afraid they'll kidnap her?"

Celine took short breaths, trying to hold back the pain. "The Times Picayune published an article on Leah. She and I were featured in the Life and Arts section back in January; 'huge picture of us sitting together, right there on the front page." Celine shook her head. "The old woman must've seen it. When she saw Leah's picture in my wallet, she went completely berserk. She screamed at her son that she recognized me from the paper, the Pickyoon, she called it. She even said she still had the newspaper clipping. It has to be the same article."

Officer Cabrini leaned forward. "A newspaper article; she recognized you from that?" He shrugged his shoulders. "I gotta tell you, this makes the top ten. So why do you think they're going to try to kidnap her?"

Celine leaned forward and looked down at her feet. The shift of her body stopped the pain a little. "After she saw Leah's picture and she figured out who I was, she started hitting me; screaming that it was my fault her daughter was arrested and that I'd stolen Leah. She said she was gonna steal Leah back. The only thing that made her stop was when her son saw my ring." Celine rolled the ring around her finger nervously. "He told me that if I gave them my ring, it would be payback for Leah."

Michael looked at the ring then gently reached out and pulled her hand towards him. "It looks old, very valuable." He frowned as he looked at it more closely. "A triple Fleur-de-Lys…an opal?"

Celine slowly looked up at Michael. "It's a family heirloom. Irreplaceable. God, if it would have been stolen, I don't know what I…" Tears welled in her eyes. Michael stood up to get a tissue from the desk behind him.

Cabrini nodded. "But, obviously they didn't get it."

"They almost did." Celine took another short breath. The pain in her head was dulling again. Michael handed her the tissue and sat down. "That's when the old woman blew that powder in my face. I really thought I was gonna pass out but when I felt the old woman pulling on the ring, I fought back and got away. That's when I started to run."

Cabrini smiled as he jotted down a few more notes. "Good for you. You must've put up one hell of a fight."

Celine gave him a weak smile as she wiped a few tears from her eyes. "I did, but I paid a price for it." She lifted up her forearms and showed him the long scratch marks.

"The doc saw these, right?" Celine nodded sadly. Cabrini made a quick note. "We'll need his records for assault charges."

Michael stared at her arms, his face horror-stricken. "What kind of people would do such a thing?"

Cabrini said matter-of-factly, "Cockroaches. These people are cockroaches! This disgusting filth comes crawling out of their slime holes to steal what they can get their hands on, but if you show a little force, POW! They scurry back to their slime holes to hide. Unfortunately, it's nearly impossible to get rid of 'em!" He turned back to Celine. "Was there a weapon? Did they use a gun?"

"A needle; the old woman held a needle up to my throat."

Cabrini put his pen down for a moment. "A needle? Like a syringe?"

Celine shook her head, trying not to let herself relive the memory. She took a deep breath. "No, a long hat pin. I was afraid to move. I…" Celine stopped and brushed away a tear.

"The doctor saw that too, I suppose." Celine looked down, nodding her head yes, fighting back the tidal wave of tears that were crashing into her.

Michael squeezed Celine's hand. "I didn't realize you'd been hurt so badly. I'm just glad you're okay."

"Okay, one last thing." Cabrini turned to Michael. "About how much time passed from the time you saw Miss Dupré running toward you to the time you called 911."

Michael frowned trying to remember. "I'm not sure. She was really scared. It took me a little while to help her realize that I wasn't that creep. I don't know, maybe ten minutes?"

Cabrini finished jotting his notes and clicked his ball point pen. "Ten minutes is long enough for the thief to see you helping her and then escape, but someone in the square might've seen him. It's a long shot, but we'll check it out. I wish I could say that we'll recover everything that was stolen but honestly, that probably won't happen unless they use your credit cards. They've certainly already spent the cash and probably dumped everything else. What I can say is that we're sure gonna follow up on this grandmother. We might even get lucky and get the son, too."

Celine gave him a little frown as she took another short breath. "But what about Leah? Do you think she's safe? I mean I'd like to call her adopted mom and make sure she's all right."

He looked up at Celine. "Did you have the child's address or phone number anywhere in your wallet? On the back of the picture maybe?"

Celine thought back. "No."

"And you didn't tell them anything about the child, where she lives, anything?"

"No, of course not, but I'll feel better if I can just call her mother and check to see if Leah's okay."

"Do you have the number?"

"Oh yes, yes!" She sat up straight. "I do. It's on my cell…" Celine's shoulders slumped when she remembered. "They got my phone, too."

"Okay, what's the child's full name?"

Celine's voice began to break. "Leah Dawn Medearis." Michael reached over and took her hand.

Officer Cabrini wrote the name down as he asked, "Her new parents must've given her their last name, right?"

"Yes, yes they did."

"Well, I think your little Leah is safe. We'll have the records of the removal and the adoption so we can call the family. It'll be better if we do it. We don't want to panic the parents." Celine nodded, suddenly feeling very tired. "I think this'll just about wrap it up unless you can think of anything else."

"No, nothing..." Her words hung on the air as Celine sat stunned, her mouth open. "Oh no, they got my hotel key, too. She said she knew where I was staying and that..." She let out a little groan. "I've got to get back to the hotel and get my things out of that room." Suddenly she sat upright. "My car keys! Did they get my car keys? Wait... no, I left them with the valet. Did I? I can't remember. I've got to get back to the hotel."

Officer Cabrini inched forward in his seat. "Where are you staying?"

Celine closed her eyes, using every fiber of her will to hold back the fear that was trying to strangle her. *The box. Oh please God, Please Ezilie, keep it safe!* "Hotel St. Jeanne."

Cabrini grunted. "Great. The Old Joan. The key had your room number on it, right?" Celine nodded. "We've told them over and over to change those f—" Cabrini stopped and stood up. "Don't worry, I'll call that in right away. Do you remember what room you're in?"

Celine thought for a moment trying hard to remember the number but her thoughts just kept focusing on the box. "Seven-hundred-something. I don't remember."

Cabrini nodded. "Don't worry. We'll get it." He stepped away, speaking into his shoulder radio.

Celine watched as Cabrini snapped the notepad shut and walked out of the exam room. She put her face in her hands. "Oh, God. What am I gonna do?"

Michael leaned forward and gently pulled a few strands of hair away from Celine's face. "Don't worry. I know Vince. He'll take care of it. Please, don't worry about anything. Alex told me to..."

Celine sat up clenching her hands in her lap. "I never called him, I never called Alex. I..."

"I did and everything's fine. He told me to tell you that we're here to help you in any way that you need us." He lowered his voice and placed his hand gently over hers. "We're here, Celine."

She dropped her head to her chest. "This is just a mess. I feel awful. Thank you so much for helping me. I don't know what I would've done if you hadn't been there. Did I hurt you when I ran into you? I was so scared, I…" Celine looked at his hand over hers and noticed a speck of blood oozing from a small scratch. Her eyes followed the scratch, like a line on a map and saw claw marks on his muscled arm and another one across his jaw. "Oh dear God, did I do that?"

Michael squeezed her hand. "It's okay."

"But…" Celine's face flushed, embarrassed. "I'm so sorry. I didn't even realize…How could I have done that to you?"

"Really. They already cleaned it. I'm fine." He said playfully, "You don't have rabies do you?"

A smile crept over Celine's face. It felt brittle but comforting at the same time. She gave his hand a little squeeze. "No, well, not that I know of anyway." Like lightning, a surge of pain raced through her head. She closed her eyes and leaned forward.

Michael moved with her, whispering urgently. "Are you okay? Do you want me to get the nurse again?"

The warmth of his hand steadied her. She turned and looked at him. "I think I should probably take one of these pills after all. Could you get me some water? There's a paper cup over by the sink."

Michael stood up, pulled a cup from the dispenser and poured her some water. Celine's hands trembled as she fumbled with the pill bottle cap. As Michael sat back down, she tapped one of the white pills into her palm and swallowed it down. She sipped the water and then closed her eyes again.

"When Vince gets back we can get you to the hotel."

Celine nodded, opening her eyes and looking back at Michael. "I'm feeling cold again. I need to put this blanket around me."

Without a second's hesitation, Michael stood up and draped the blanket around Celine's shoulders. When he sat down next to her, he rubbed his hands up and down her arms. "There, 'that better?"

The chills began to fade. In that moment, she realized that Michael had curled his arm around her shoulder. The warmth of his body was so comforting. She leaned into him. Celine nodded with a trace of a smile. "Much. Thank you." She looked into his eyes. *Such a kind smile. Such a kind man.*

Just then Officer Cabrini returned. "Okay, I've gotten in touch with the St. Jeanne security and they're moving your things to the hotel office until you get back there. They'll put you in another room on another floor. As for your car keys and your car, they're still safe and sound with the valet."

Michael nodded. "Thanks, Vince."

A quick tap-tap sounded on the door as the nurse stepped into the exam room. "'Sorry, Vince. We need the room. It's getting crazy out here again."

Officer Cabrini smiled at Sarah. "We're done." He turned back to Celine. "If we need anything else, I'll be in touch and don't worry about that old lady. She has no way to get to either you or Leah. Now, I'll get you back to your hotel so you can get some rest."

Sarah walked over to Celine and helped her unwrap the blanket from around her shoulders, patting her arm compassionately. "Did you take one of your pills?" Celine nodded. "Good." She looked over at Michael. "Can you make sure she gets to her hotel room? I think she's gonna need a little help."

Michael nodded then looked at Celine. "Of course I can."

Sarah smiled at Celine. "Okay, so your Guardian Angel here is gonna get you to your room. After a nice hot bath and a good night's sleep, you'll feel much better."

Celine eased herself out of the chair. "You have no idea how great that sounds."

Michael stood up next to Celine. "Here, you can lean on me." He put his arm around her shoulder as they walked down the hallway and made their way through the waiting room menagerie of bewildered tourists. As the three of them walked outside and approached the blue and white police car, Michael helped Celine into the back seat. The pill had eased the pain in her head and now a wave of exhaustion washed through her. She turned to Michael as he sat next to her and shut the door. "Are you sure you don't mind helping me? I'm getting so sleepy, I don't know how I'll manage."

Michael smiled, his blue eyes dancing. "Of course I can help. I'm sure they've already got your room ready and waiting…"

His voice faded as Celine watched him talking. *Blue on blue eyes. How many shades, I wonder?* Her eyelids began to droop.

Michael's smile quickly disappeared. "You look so tired. Would you like to put your head down?"

Celine opened her eyes and gave him a small smile. "I think she's right, you know."

Michael gave her a questioning look. "What? Who's right?"

"Sarah, the nurse. She said you're my Guardian Angel. I'm pretty lucky. It's not everyday you get to meet your Guardian Angel face-to-face." Celine took a long deep breath as she let herself curl into Michael's shoulder.

Michael watched as she closed her eyes and fell into long steady breaths. He reached over and gently rubbed his thumb over the ring. "I'm pretty lucky, too. It's not everyday you get to meet your muse face-to-face, either."

Celine drew a deep sigh. *A hot bath and bed. Get this day behind me. Yes. How many shades, I wonder?* They rode in sweet silence back to the hotel.

CHAPTER 13

Blue upon blue danced together, swirling, twirling. Celine laughed as she floated along with it, gently tossed from color to color. Morning sky blue melted into sea lagoon blue, then trickled into peacock teal blue and deepened into midnight. A thin sliver of moonlight pierced the still night, just enough for Celine to see satin shoes peeking out from under her cobalt blue taffeta dress. Her long tapered sleeves ended with a touch of lace at the cuff, brushing gracefully against the sapphire ring she wore.

Celine looked up. An empty street. She was alone. All was quiet except for the soft pad her shoes made on the wooden boardwalk and the *whish, whish* of her petticoats as she walked.

She looked at each of the little whitewashed houses along the way, a warm glow shining from inside. She knew the people that lived here, knew them well; talked to them, ate with them and laughed with them. She remembered walking this sidewalk before. No, not a sidewalk. *We called it a banquette and I remember when there was no banquette, just a horribly-muddy street. But why do I remember it? Where is this place?*

The wrought iron gate was open, making a gentle creaking noise as it swayed in the summer breeze. Celine stopped. She knew where she was now even though there was no sign hanging over the doorway; nothing that said The Marie LaVeau Apartments. The lush garden that grew alongside the house was overgrown with hibiscus, banana trees and azalea. The wood dwelling had been painted white. Its French windows were open and looked like two bright eyes inviting her inside, welcoming her home. She stepped onto the deep, rough-hewn, cypress porch ready to walk through the ornately-carved double doors when a voice from behind called her. "Careful, my child. Careful."

Surprised, Celine turned and saw the beautiful tall woman from her dreams. "Ezilie! You look so different!" A stiff white tignon covered her hair, the knotted turban with its carefully-tied knots holding back thick folds of shiny black tresses. Her arms were covered in thin gold and silver bracelets that reminded Celine of tiny bells, all clinking at the same time. Her long white gossamer robe was cinched at the waist with a single golden braid. She smiled at Celine, the soft curve of her lip causing only a slight wrinkle on her smooth café-au-lait complexion. "This is how I am known to all my Creole children. I have many faces and this is just one." She pointed to the house. "This was once your home, but not anymore. Now, you must knock."

Celine turned back and looked at the doors but they were gone, replaced by a thin sheet of plywood. The cheerful white house had disappeared and what was left was a shabby, peeling shack. The windows were cracked, their shutters sagging on rusted hinges. The deep porch had been replaced by broken wooden steps. The house smelled of age and old earth, like a crypt grown-over, forgotten by its family. When Celine reached out to knock, she realized that the blue taffeta sleeve of her dress had vanished. She looked down. *What am I doing back in my sundress? She ran her fingers over the ripped embroidery. No, no! I can't be here!*

Celine turned to run, but Ezilie whispered. "No. Do as I say. Knock." Celine stopped. *This is St. Ezilie, Saint of my family. The one I've prayed to. The one Mama and Mo-maw pray to.* She took a deep breath and nervously reached up. She knocked on the door but no one came. She knocked again, but still there was no answer. She looked back at Ezilie but she stood like stone, watching the door, waiting.

Slowly the door opened and Celine heard a small, frail, crackle of a voice. "Ezilie, is that you?" Celine backed away but Ezilie grabbed her by the arm. She leaned into Celine's ear and whispered. "She doesn't see us. Say nothing."

Celine whispered back. "But this is the woman that robbed..."

Ezilie tightened her grip. "Nothing!"

Celine stayed perfectly still as the old woman walked out onto the step. She was inches away from Celine's face as she sniffed the air. "Ezilie?" Celine fought back a choking, suffocating fear. "I know you're there. I'm glad you've come."

The old street woman walked back into the house, leaving the door open behind her. Ezilie nudged Celine inside as the old woman spoke. "I guess you heard about what happened today." The old woman walked into the room, kicking away the leftover food boxes and dirty clothes that littered the floor in her path. "Little white bitch," she muttered. "She's gonna be sorry for what she done."

Celine looked around the room. To her left was a scorched fireplace, remnants of the original red brick peeking through ash and soot. On the parched wooden mantle was a beat-up old alarm clock. Next to it, a corncob pipe sat in a small bowl of tobacco. Behind the mantle hung a cracked mirror, dotted with the black flecks of time. A straight-back wooden rocking chair sat in front of the hearth with a newspaper open in the seat.

Celine looked at it. On the front page was a picture, but not just any picture—the photo of Celine and Leah sitting together after the custody hearing. *No wonder she thinks I took Leah.* Ezilie tugged at Celine's arm and pulled her along, following the old woman as she walked around a huge wooden table covered with a plastic tablecloth. Celine's once brightly-colored summer purse sat deflated and dirty in one corner, its contents spilled out. The old woman picked up a few guinea peppers from a bowl and tucked them into her cheek.

With a deep, angry breath, the old woman growled. "She gonna wish she never done that to me. See if she ever kicks me again or hurts my sweet Nate, either. I needs your help, Ezilie. She took our Leah. I gots proof over there in the paper." The old woman looked back into the room, her eyes looking deeply into the mirror directly across from her. She sucked hard on the peppers making an evil kissing sound. "My sweet Leah, the one that you done blessed, Ezilie. Your special one!" She scooped out a handful of black clay and mud that sat in a bowl and looked at it closely. With weathered and leathery hands, she began to mold and shape the figure of a doll. "This here is hard stuff to come by these days. It was bad enough when they cut up Bayou St. John to make Louis Armstrong Park. But now, since Katrina, the old Bayou ain't the same at all. Don't you worry none, though. I found 'nuf of it to do what I gotta do. She took our Leah, the one I trained! And now she gonna pay!"

The old woman looked down at the purse contents on the table in front of her. She picked up the driver's license and put it close to her rheumy eyes. "Oh yes, so pretty, but not for long." The old lady laughed as she carefully cut out Celine's face and pushed it into the head of the clay doll. She reached down and picked up the hairbrush, pulled out some of the long, black, silky hair and stuffed it around the head of the doll. She carefully cut out the name on the license, Celine Dupré, spit on it and then smiled as she plunged it into the belly of the doll. "Won't be long now." The old woman looked over the table once again. Her eyes lit up when she saw Celine's school ID card and read the words slowly, "School for the Blind". She cut out the word, 'Blind' and pressed it into the heart of the doll. Then she cut out Celine's school picture and set it aside. "I can use this later."

The old woman picked up the black clay doll and laughed. She turned it toward the mirror. "What d'ya think, Ezilie? Good enough?" As if she'd heard an answer, the old woman shook her head. "Oh no, I didn't think so. But that's okay. Wait 'til you see. Wait 'til you see!" She grabbed the butcher knife and shuffled outside onto the back porch.

Celine felt a small push from behind. She turned and Ezilie coaxed her toward the table. Just as they stepped closer, the old woman came back clutching the butcher knife in one hand and a huge, moccasin snake gripped tightly in the other. The snake curled its ebony body around the old woman's arm, past her elbow, nearly touching her shoulder. "See what I caught? Isn't he beautiful? That old Bayou still gives me all what I need. And I knows I would'nt've caught him if you didn't want me to. He's quiet now. I've had him hanging out there for a few hours."

With her grip firmly around the snake's neck, she turned its vicious face within inches of her own. Its eyes and mouth were shut. Even the great tail had grown somewhat limp. She eyed the snake suspiciously and prodded the sagging creature with the edge of the knife. "You faker, you ain't dead!" She tapped the tip of the blade on the water moccasin's mouth. Instantly, the yellow eyes raged with revenge and its mouth flew open, revealing fangs glistening with fresh poison. The old woman jumped back, but held on tightly as the snake writhed, trying to get away. She slammed the snake down onto the table, maneuvering the butcher knife through the coils and chopped off its head, crushing bone and spewing blood. Celine closed her eyes and turned away as the old woman plunged the knife into the work table, the tip digging deep enough into the wood to make the handle stand straight up.

Ezilie shook Celine's arm. "Open your eyes. You must see. You need to know!" Celine reluctantly opened her eyes and saw the old woman holding the headless snake from its tail high over her head. With her other hand, she squeezed the still-twitching body, draining the blood into a bowl. As the last drops fell, the old woman chanted:

> *"Eh, ye, ye, Mamzelle Marie,*
> *Ya', ye, ye, li konin tou, gris-gris,*
> *Li ti kouri lekal, aver vieux*
> *kokodril, Oj ouai, ye Mamzelle Marie.*

> *"Ge Rouge, Marie, Ge rouge, Ezilie*
> *Maman Marie, from my enemies, free me.*
> *Red eyed one, eat her heart, eat her soul.*
> *I give her to you, buried deep in a hole."*

Celine looked down at the table in horror. The blood-soaked snake head lay next to a rooster's head and claw. Small bowls filled with dried herbs and powders were sitting next to several needles threaded with long lines of fishing string. Her stomach began to churn as she saw the faceless, nameless driver's license, her school picture, her hairbrush and her hotel key right next to the demonic clay doll.

The old woman grabbed the snake head and pried the jaws open. The poison, still deadly, dripped from its fangs. Its once-golden eyes were now glazed over in death. She picked up the clay doll and stuffed it, legs first, into the deadly white mouth. She pressed the fangs into the soft clay breast and repeated the prayer, "red-eyed one, eat her heart, eat her soul." Then she pulled out the long hatpin she had hidden in her head scarf.

Celine drew in a quick breath when she saw it. That same treacherous needle had been at her throat just a few hours ago. "No! I should leave!"

Ezilie tightened her grip around Celine's arm. "I told you. Quiet!"

The old woman stopped and looked up. "Ezilie?" She looked around the room, her eyes squinting as she searched. "There's someone with you, isn't there?" A wrinkled smile slowly crept across the old woman's face as she returned to her work. Carefully, inch by inch, she plunged the pin through the top of the snake's head, piercing through the doll's heart until the pin reached the lower jaw of the snake. She set it aside and whispered, "I give her to you, buried deep in a hole."

The old woman stood up straight, arching her crooked back, a long sigh rushing from her lips. She was getting tired but the work was not quite done. Her shoulders slumped again as she stretched the snake's body down the length of the table. She pulled the butcher knife out of the wood and carefully sliced the scaly body down its center. Blood oozed out onto the tablecloth but the old woman didn't stop until she had cut a long slit to the tail.

Bloody knife in hand, she walked to the kitchen and threw it into the sink. She wiped her hands on an oily rag and then pulled her scarf from around her hair. Scraggly tufts of wiry gray hair dotted the balding scalp as she tied the scarf around her face and put rubber gloves on to finish her work. From an old black bag that she kept under the sink, she pulled out a vial of purplish-white powder and walked back to the table. She sprinkled the powder down the length of the snake's body.

Even though it smelled like baby powder, it fizzed when it hit the wet blood. The old woman moved her face away, laughing. "Oh Zombi, Zombi, just enough to give the smell. Too much and you could kill her too soon. Not yet. No, we don' want that yet. I blew just enough of you into her face to start your work. I made sure she breathed you in. It got all up in her nose and mouth and best of all, her eyes. She wants blind? Yeah, a few hours is all you need, my Zombi." Celine turned and looked at Ezilie, hoping she would hear the words that were screaming through her mind. *She's trying to kill me! That stuff she blew in my face, is it Zombi's Cucumber?* Ezilie didn't answer. She stood, silently staring at the old woman's handiwork.

When the powder began to clot on the inner flesh of the snake, the old woman reached for the hairbrush and pulled the rest of the jet-black strands out of the bristles. She rolled it into a tight ball in the palm of her hand and sprinkled a bit of the purplish-white powder over it. She took a glob of black clay and worked it into the hair, rolling it into a smooth sphere.

She looked over at the rooster's claw. "Now, it's your turn." She picked up the hooked spur claw and embedded it into the clay ball.

Then she picked up Celine's school ID picture, placed it in the clay ball with the claw and rolled it in her palm once again. She looked over at the rooster head. "Oh yes, my Rooster gonna get his revenge through you!" She took the rooster head and opened the beak, shoving the black conjure ball into its mouth. "Open wide. You gets to eat her, too!"

Carefully, she picked up one of the sewing needles and began to sew. She wired the rooster's jaw shut so the beak held the conjure ball firmly. Then she took the snake head and looked at it closely. "Yeah, you're dry." Slowly, she pulled the long hatpin out of the snake head and put it on the table. She took the snake head and pushed it into the belly of the snake. "You're in a hole, alright. The deepest, darkest hole I can put you—the gut of Mr. Snake." She laughed as she sewed the snake's body shut all the way to the tail. When she finished, she picked up the rooster's head. "...and this here is my sweet boy, Rooster. Watch out he don't peck you!" She fit the rooster head onto the snake body and sewed the neck, rooster skin to scales.

When she was finished, she carefully placed the deformed creature into a plastic trash bag and eased it into a large backpack. She picked up the hotel key and placed it in the front zipper pouch, patting it and smiling. After she cleared the table of the dried herbs and powders, she grabbed the purse and stuffed the brush and the last few scraps of plastic pieces into it. She peeled back the gloves, untied her scarf and threw them onto the bloody plastic tablecloth, folding it over into a sack. She straightened up, stretching her back and with a grunt, pulled the plastic sack onto the floor. She toddled over to the fireplace, dragging the sack. With one final "humpf", she threw it into the hearth. The old woman squatted down and reached for the newspaper in the rocking chair. She took one last look at the photograph. "I don't know if we can get you back, baby, but we sure as hell gonna get that woman that took you." She stuffed the newspaper around the sack, soaked the fireplace in lighter fluid and lit a match, laughing as the tablecloth exploded into flames. "That's it. Burn!"

Slowly she stood up and looked at the clock. "Hmm, two a.m. They'll be here soon." She reached for the pipe and with long, dirty fingernails, pinched out a bit of the tobacco from the bowl on the mantle, tamping it down with her thumb. She turned and gazed into the mirror. "And you." She said with a toothless grin as she lit the lighter and sucked hard on the pipe, "Did you see?" She sucked again, a swirl of smoke pouring out of her mouth as she spoke. "I hope you did because I see you. Oh, I see you so good!" The old woman took a deep draw of the pipe, the tobacco embers burning into an orange glow. She blew the smoke into the mirror. "You'll be dead soon and you'll never wake up ever again…Celine Dupré."

Celine stood frozen facing the mirror, possessed by the image of the old woman's grin. She coughed, choking on the smell of the pipe smoke. Celine screamed as she reached for Ezilie. "She sees me! I've got to get out of here!" Celine whipped around, searching the room for Ezilie but she had gone.

The old woman laughed. "She left you, you little fool! She left you here with me!" She started to sing in a scratchy voice. "…and you'll never wake up, wake up, WAKE UP!"

The image of the old woman's face slowly disappeared in the swirl of a white cloud, an echo of her laughter trailing behind. A cold chill raced up Celine's back. She blinked her eyes. Where did she go? She looked around the room. Wait, this isn't the same… she turned, looking back into the mirror. Oh God! Horrified, she realized that she was standing in front of the dresser mirror in her hotel room. She looked down. Sleep shirt. Bare feet. She looked back into the mirror and saw only herself staring back. A dream but no, not a dream! Her head pounded as she stumbled her way to the side of the bed and sat down. *Okay. Okay. This is my new room. Michael got me in here last night and then left. After I took a bath, I went straight to bed.* She looked at the clock. *four a.m. Too early, but I've got to call now.* She groped around in the dark for the lamp switch and picked up the phone on the night table. She blinked her eyes, trying to focus as she dialed the number as fast as she could. When it began to ring, she held her breath. *Pick up. Pick up. Please!"*

A soft voice answered, "Hello?"

"Mama! Oh, thank God, you're up!"

"Celine, Celine! We've been up for hours! Mo-maw and me, we tried to call you but you didn't answer. Mo-maw had the worst dream abo't you. Tell me you're okay!"

"No, Mama. No." Celine burst into tears. "I'm not okay."

"But Mo-maw, why? Why would Ezilie send me a dream like that? Why would she want me to watch that insane woman do all those horrible things?" The phone hummed with silence while Celine waited for her grandmother to answer.

"I don't know, chère. Me, I can't explain everything Ezilie does. I do know that she wanted you to see it. She's like dat. Sometimes she'll show you terrible things, things that make no sense but there's a reason, Celine, always a reason. Ezilie was in my dream, too, chère. She wuz tellin' me that I had no choice but to wait. I kept asking her, wait for what? But she wouldn't answer. She just kept sayin', be patient. Wait. Not long now."

"Not long now?" Celine tucked her knees under her sleep shirt. "Mo-maw, when the old woman robbed me, she blew that horrible white powder in my face. In the dream she called the powder 'Zombi'. Do you think she…" Celine's voice started to break. "Do you think she used Zombi's Cucumber on me? Do you think Ezilie was telling you 'not long now' because the old woman's found a way to kill me?"

"Celine, Celine…" Mo-maw's voice was calm but stern. "Chère, you listen to me right now. NO! That old woman is just some old street woman tryin' to scare you. She couldn't possibly know anything about it. Where could she get it? It can't grow in da city. Dere are plenty of other herbs dat are called Zombi, all of them really harmless. Besides, I don't think Ezilie meant dat at all. I think it was more like you're very close to finding the answer to somet'ing and it won't be long now 'til you do."

"The answer to something…" Celine echoed. "…but the answer to what?"

"That's between you and Ezilie, chère. But Celine, you've got to remember, it wasn't but jus' a week ago that you were suffering with *cochemère*, remember?"

Celine nodded. "*Cochemère*, the nightmares."

"Well, you haven't completely healed from dat. Even with the right kinds of herbs and treatments, it sometimes takes months for *cochemère* to completely go away and any kind of bad luck can bring it back. You wuz robbed, chère. I'd say dat's bad luck enough to bring back the *cochemère* in full force.

Celine sighed. "You think that's why I had the dream?"

"Of course, but dere's one thing you've forgotten. Ezilie was with you in the dream, right?"

"Well, she was, but then she left."

"Why did she leave, chère?"

"I don't know, except…" Celine thought back to the dream. She could still hear the old woman taunting her in that scratchy voice. "…I just remember turning around and she was gone. I was so scared, I…"

"Celine, chère, you're letting dat old woman take hold of you. Now, push dat woman outta your mind. Think back. Ezilie must've had a reason for leaving. Now think, chère, think."

Celine took a deep breath. "I said something to her. It was…it was…I wanted to leave. I told Ezilie I wanted to leave. She got angry then. She had already told me not to talk and I did." The phone hummed in silence. "Mo-maw? Are you there?"

Mo-maw's voice was barely a whisper. "Ezilie can be a hard teacher, chère. Dat's why she left you."

Celine lowered her voice. "You mean because I didn't listen to her?"

"Yeah. You need to listen to her always. Always, Celine. Not jus' some of da time. This wuz Ezilie's way of getting your attention. If she says don't say anything, she means it, or there's a big price to pay. I bet you listen next time, huh?"

Celine let out a cynical laugh. "Absolutely! She got my attention, all right! But in your dream, did she tell you anything else? Did she give you any clue about what this answer is I'm supposed to be looking for?"

Mo-maw blew a tired sigh. "No. All she said was I have to leave you with her now; that I need to step back and wait. I've never been very good at waiting, chère, 'specially when it comes to protecting you.

You're not the only one who has problems with keeping her mouth shut. I told Ezilie that I didn't want to do dat. You're my chère, *'tit fille*, my Bienaimée. I told her I didn't t'ink you were ready, but..."

Celine could hear the tearful waver in her grandmother's voice. "Ready for what, Mo-maw?"

Mo-maw hesitated. "I will tell you dis, Celine, and den I can't say no more. You mama and I, we have different ways of healing. You mama, she knows all the herbs much better than me; knows everyt'ing like a book. Me, I can see t'ings. They come to me in dreams and visions and dat's what I t'ink you've been chosen for, too. You're a seer, a dreamer, Celine, and dat's something I can't teach you. Only Ezilie can and right now, she wants you all to herself, away from me, away from my protection. Dat's hard, chère, dat's hard for you old Mo-maw, but Eziie's with you now and I need to step back. It's part of your training." Mo-maw's voice grew strong again. "And I will, Celine. I'll listen to Ezilie and you will, too, right chère? Promise me you will."

"I will, Mo-maw. I promise but what if I have another dream, what if..."

Mo-maw laughed softly. "Don't you worry. Just because I have to step back, dat don't mean that you mama can't help you out. Ezilie didn't say nuthin' about dat." Celine heard Luisah say something in the background.

"What did Mama say?" Celine heard a few more muffled words as Luisah took the phone from Mo-maw.

"I said I can sure help you out with prayers and herbs and if you have another dream, you just call me and we'll work it out, okay?"

Celine took a deep breath. "Okay."

"Now, do you need anything? After the robbery I mean?"

Celine shifted the phone to her other ear and unfolded her legs from under her shirt. "No, I mean other than canceling my credit cards, getting a new license and oh, a new cell phone, too."

"Of course you'll have to do all that, but how are you feeling?"

"I still have a bit of a headache. Nothing like last night though. My body aches and my stomach's a little off, but I haven't eaten, so..."

"Look in the side pouch of your suitcase. I put some different teas in there. The one you want right now is the snake tea. It'll help with the headache and the body aches, too. Mix it up good and strong. One cup, maybe two and you'll start feeling better again, okay? In fact, if you drink some right now, you'll probably be able to relax. You said you went to the doctor last night, yeah?"

Celine stood up and walked over to her suitcase. "Yes, and he gave me some pills for the headache. I took one and it helped, but it really made me sleepy."

Luisah grunted. "That could've been part of the reason you've had *cochemère* again, too. Don't take more pills. Just drink the snake tea."

Celine unzipped the side pouch and found a large plastic bag. She pulled it out. "Wow! There's definitely more than snake tea in here, but how did you know? I mean, did you have some kind of premonition that I might need all this?" She looked at the bag carefully. There was a collection of teas and herbs in smaller plastic bags, all carefully labeled in her mother's handwriting.

"I don't get premonitions or visions or dreams, Celine. My job is just to try to think of everything you might need. So I put in Mayhaw, Elderberry, Black Iris and a few others, too." While her mother talked, Celine walked over to the in-room coffee maker, poured water into the carafe and clicked it on. "I wrote down all the instructions for each one and what you use them for. For the snake tea, two teaspoons in one cup of boiling water. Just drink it straight. No cream or sugar. I know how you like it sweet, but no sugar, okay?"

"Thank you, Mama. I'm already feeling better just knowing I've got all this." Celine pulled out one of the mugs and spooned out two teaspoons. "I just wish this stuff wasn't called snake tea. Right now, I'd rather not have anything to do with snakes."

Luisah laughed. "It's called snake tea because when you put it in boiling water, those little crooked sticks look like snakes. Pour the water on it and see what they do." Celine picked up the carafe of hot water and poured it onto the tea leaves. She watched as the leaves wriggled and danced like little snakes, turning the clear liquid into an amber hue. The vanilla aroma brought an instant calm to Celine's nerves. "Do you see it?"

Celine was amazed. "Yeah, tiny snakes."

"And don't drink it until they stop moving. You do need to remember, Celine, Ezilie can't keep you protected if you don't do what she says. Follow her ways and you'll be healed. Drinking her teas is one way to follow her."

Celine closed her eyes, blowing on the hot steam. "Ummm, I love this smell, brings back so many memories."

"Now, you drink it all and then drink one more cup. Everything from last night will look very different, I promise. But I put something else in your suitcase. They're in the box. I put two vials of bath powders in there. The dark blue one is for protection and the bright red one is for courage. They're very helpful in healing *cochemère*. Open up the box. Do you see them?"

Celine stammered, afraid to tell her mother the box wasn't there. "I left the box in my…" She looked at the dresser and saw the box mysteriously sitting there. *Wait, I left it in my car. How did it get in here?* "Uh, just a minute." She walked over to the dresser and opened up the box. There were the two clear vials, each filled with a blue and red powder. "Here they are." *Did Michael go and get the box from the trunk of my car? I vaguely remember asking him to go and get it, but I'll have to ask him.* She picked up the blue vial and held it up to the light and then carefully placed it back into the box. "How do I use them?" Celine sat back down on the edge of the bed, watching as the last of the little snakes stopped moving.

"It's not so new to you really. You've taken the baths before but that was a long time ago. Using herbs isn't always about drinking them. With both of these, you just sprinkle a little in your bath water and take a nice long hot soak."

"That's it?"

"That's it."

"But what's in it?"

Celine heard her mother's tell-tale short, breathy laughter. She could almost see her shaking her head. "Oh, my Celine, you're always worried about what's in everything. The blue one is crushed lavender and muscadine vine and the red is wild rose and Tabasco peppers."

Celine laughed. "Tabasco peppers. Won't that sting?"

Luisah sighed ever so lightly. "A little, but the peppers give you the energy to move forward, the roses keep your nerves calm and steady. Courage needs both. Now the lavender opens the pores and the muscadine penetrates into your bloodstream. So you're protected inside and out."

Celine let out a deep sigh. "A nice long soak sounds wonderful but which one of these should I use?"

"Well, which one do you think you need more of, protection or courage?"

Celine took a sip of the snake tea. "I'm not sure. Protection of course, but I could sure use a lot more courage right now. I guess I need both, really. What would happen if I mix the two together?"

Luisah let out a chuckle of delight. "Now you're thinking like a healer, Celine! If you mix them together, you strengthen the power of each. After yesterday, I'd say you could use a double dose, right?"

"Yeah. When I think about that old woman I still get the creeps."

"Try to remember what Mo-maw said, okay? That old woman really is just an old street woman. She robbed you. Yes, that's serious, and the part about your little student, yes, that's serious too, but as for the rest of it? She was just trying to scare you. Yeah, sure, she might have loads of ways to scare tourists, but Celine, you're a lot stronger than that. Remember who you are: the seventh generation granddaughter to Marie LaVeau. You have to fight back. You might not be able to actually do anything to them, but you can stay strong inside yourself. It's gonna take a lot more than a little baby powder to hurt you, right? Besides, everything they took can be replaced. Other than a few bumps and bruises, what harm did that street woman do, really?"

Celine laughed. "Yeah, I know. It all looks a little foolish in the light of day, but yesterday and last night, especially last night's dream, well, it certainly felt very different then. I know I'm safe now. I just hope Michael and Alex don't think I'm some sort of weakling. This is the second time they've seen me lose it."

"Oh, Celine. You're far from that! You fought back and it sounds to me like you left the robbers with a few bumps and bruises of their own. I'm just so glad Michael was there for you. He sounds so nice, so understanding. And Alex, too, he was helpful just by offering to make sure you had everything you needed. After all that poor man's been through, AIDS and all, he knows what it's like to need help. I don't think either of them would think you were weak. Just makes you human, okay? Besides, today, you're going to be fine, right?"

Celine sipped the tea. "Right!"

"Now, are you going to get a new cell phone? I want to be able to be in touch with you, just in case you need anything."

"I can at least report my credit card and cell phone stolen online. I'll stop the phone service. For now just call me here at the hotel or at the gallery. They can get a message to me."

Celine could hear her mother shuffling papers over the phone. "I have the gallery and hotel phone numbers, but what room are you in?"

Celine picked up the room key and looked at the number. "970. They moved me last night." While she talked, she unpacked her laptop and plugged it in.

Luisah jotted the room number down. "What about cash? Do you need us to send you some money?"

"No, no. I didn't have it all in my purse. I hid extra in my suitcase. I have enough for a few days, anyway." Celine sat down in front of her computer, holding the coffee mug in one hand and the phone in the other. She turned and looked at the bedside clock. "Six a.m.? We've been on the phone for two hours? Oh Mama, I'm so sorry! You and Mo-maw should've gotten to bed hours ago!"

"Now, you should know better than that. There's no way we could've slept until we knew for sure that you were okay."

"Is Mo-maw okay? I mean, the dream she had sounds like it really upset her."

"It did. She woke me up somewhere about three in the morning and told me we needed to call you. The way she was acting scared me to death. She was kind of talking out of her head. Then when we couldn't reach you, she…" Luisah stopped and took a deep breath. "Well, I've never seen her like that."

"Is she okay now?"

"As soon as she heard your voice, she was fine."

"You're sure? I mean you're not just saying that to make me feel better?"

Luisah laughed. "I wish you could see her right now. She's already outside, feeding the chickens. I'm sitting here at the kitchen window, watching her. You'd never know by looking at her that anything even happened last night." Luisah sighed. "She's on her way back in. I guess I'll be fixing breakfast soon."

Celine laughed. "Business as usual?"

"Looks that way. So, you just drink the tea and relax in a nice hot bath, hot as you can stand it, and you'll feel much, much better. Do your best to just get on with your day."

"So you're saying I should get back to business as usual, too?"

"Yep." Luisah's voice was even and calm. "You went through something terrible but you don't have to let it ruin your time over there in New Orleans. Enjoy planning the art department with Alex and Michael. Once you get into it, you'll forget any of this ever happened."

"Thank you, Mama. And please, tell Mo-maw thank you. I don't know what I'd do without the two of you."

"I will and I love you. Hugs."

"Love you, too." Celine hung up the phone and grasped the hot mug of tea in both hands, blowing the steam and sipping the warm vanilla-flavored elixir. She stared at the computer screen. *God, I wish I didn't have to do all this. Maybe I should take that bath now.* The icons popped up one at a time and the happy little computer song called. *Oh okay, I might as well get this over with. Then I won't have to worry if they're using my credit cards. All right.* She put the mug down. *Here goes.*

Two mugs of snake tea later, she was breathing easier. *Cell phone cancelled, check. Credit Cards cancelled, check. Bank Account, debit card protected, check. Let's see, what else? Oh, yeah. I've gotta ask Officer Cabrini about that temporary driver's license. I wonder if Google is right about New Orleans offering an emergency driver's license for tourists?*

Celine sat back in the chair and stretched. *Time for that bath.* She stood up and walked over to the dresser, opened the box and took out both vials of bath powder. She smiled. *I wonder if you mix the red and the blue, will it make purple?* She walked into the bathroom and turned on the bathtub faucet. *Hot as I can stand it.* She sat on the side of the Jacuzzi tub and plugged the drain. Almost immediately, steam began to rise.

Celine stood up and walked over to the bathroom counter and put the vials down. Her arms ached as she pulled off her sleep shirt. When she looked back into the mirror, the bruise on her right shoulder had grown to the size of a hand. She shivered. Suddenly, she felt naked. She picked the shirt back up, covering her breasts. She inched her way closer to the mirror and touched the bruise carefully. She lifted her arm and looked at the long scratch marks that ran from her wrist to her elbow. *Those horrible, horrible people!* She stepped back looking at herself in the mirror, searching her body for any other bruises or marks that were left from the struggle.

As she pushed her hair away from her face, she saw a red and angry-looking rash across her neck. *Oh my God, that's in the same place that the claw mark was!* She looked closer. The claw mark had healed, but the rash had clearly taken its place. She looked at herself in the mirror. *Okay, it's nothing. I've gotten rashes like this before, especially when I'm stressed. It'll go away. These rashes always do.* She ran her fingertips tenderly over the rash. *Yeah, yeah, it'll go away.*

Celine stepped back, picked up the blue vial, opened it and tapped a tiny bit into her palm. She took a deep breath. *Lavender. What a nice smell.* She carefully opened the red vial, and immediately, the soft scent of roses filled the steaming bathroom. *Oh, this is wonderful.* She tapped the vial of roses over the lavender and mixed the fine powders together. She leaned down and looked at the mixture carefully. *Purple, just as I thought.* She looked at the mirror. It was almost completely fogged over now. She took her sleep shirt and rubbed a circle through the haze. At first, she made the circle just big enough for her face to show, but then she wiped the mirror until the circle exposed her entire chest. She dropped the shirt, remembering the old woman from her dream staring at her from the other side of the mirror but this time, she wasn't afraid. This time, she felt strong. *Yeah, you might've hurt me yesterday, even last night, but not anymore. You have no power over me, you crazy old bitch! Come closer. Let me show you just who I am.*

CHAPTER 15

Vincent Cabrini stood in the middle of Room 733 shaking his head. He'd never seen anything like this before, never heard about anything like it before, either. He looked over at the sobbing house-keeper—another of the many eastern European immigrants working at a French Quarter hotel, trying to eke out a living. His longtime buddy, Jack, was questioning her, but he was having a hard time. If she wasn't crying, she was blabbering on in Russian or Romanian or some other language. All she kept saying was, "I do my job. I not do this!" His buddy flashed him a sidelong glance and mouthed the words 'inter-preter'. Cabrini nodded.

He turned to look at the rest of the yellow-taped room. It was a bee-hive of activity. Standing over the bed, gloved, masked and tense, were the forensic guys. *What's up with them? Dead bodies never give them a moment of thought. Guts of steel, usually, but a dead snake? With a roost-er's head? Yeah, they're spooked. No wonder they're sweating so much. I bet they're wondering what's inside that thing. It bulges at the belly. Do snakes even have bellies? And that rooster's head? What's sticking out of its beak? Weird.*

And what the hell is that thing drawn on the mirror in the bathroom? Looks like a heart, but why is the inside of it marked off with squares with a red dot inside each square. All those little curly-ques sketched on the sides of it look like something a teenager would draw on a notebook with an 'I love you' written in bubble letters scrawled on it somewhere. 'Sure isn't puppy love though, not with a sword sketched like it's stabbing into the center. Is it a sword? Looks more like a knife or maybe even a machete.

Cameras flashed from different angles. The photographers were having a hard time getting a good shot with a mirror in the back-ground. The chemical guys picked away carefully at the design, placing tiny flecks of it into small plastic bags. The whole thing was painted in red. *Blood? Snake blood maybe? Chicken? At least it's not a homicide. The blood guys already said negative for human. But what is that woman's picture doing glued right at the tip point of that knife? The captain's right. She has to be interviewed again, no doubt.*

Cabrini watched as the guy pried the photograph off the mirror and tweezed it into a plastic bag. *Jesus. Had they glued that on the mirror in blood? Yeah, there'll be stories told and lots of beer-drinking over this one.*

Stories. Vincent Cabrini had grown up with tons of them. The son of an ex-Marine-turned-cop, there was no better time than when Vince's dad lit up one of his camel cigarettes and told true crime tales straight from the streets of the French Quarter. Vince loved all those stories, but his favorites had always been the unsolved ones, the mysteries that stumped even the old timers. He missed his dad. In the end, those damn cigarettes got him, but at times like these, Vince could hear the old man's voice loud and clear: 'Talk to that woman again. She knows more than she's telling.' *On it, Pop, on it.*

Jack walked over to Vince, a look of 'I give up' written all over his face. "That maid won't stop crying, man. All she keeps saying is 'no send me back.' She's gotta be an illegal. 'Girl's more scared of me than that damn snake in the bed!"

"Want me to try?"

"Nah. We need to get an interpreter in here. She might relax if she's questioned in her own language. I just wish I could figure out what-the-hell language it is." Cabrini nodded as Jack rambled on, looking around the room. "Be glad you're a beat cop, man. This kind of shit gives me the creeps."

Cabrini laughed. "Hey, you're the one who decided to make detective. I told you to stay with us grunts. No, you decided to upgrade, right? Well, enjoy your upgrade."

Jack fake-punched Vince in the shoulder. "Hey, this is your chance to join us hot dawgs, pal. If you play your cards right, you just might hit the big time and get to move to headquarters with me instead of being stuck at a sub station like District 8."

Cabrini shook his head. "No thanks, man. Give me the street any day. Captain only wants me here to follow up on that robbery last night. When I'm done, I'm outta here."

"You check on the girl? The perp that did this was probably targeting her. Did you see her picture on the mirror? Creepy shit, man. Hell, that could be her blood in there for all we know." He looked over at the blood-soaked sheets on the bed. "Could be her blood in here, too."

Cabrini frowned. "Nope. The blood guys already left. Animal. The captain told me to talk to her again, but I have to wait until these guys are done."

"Again? I thought I read in your report that there were a couple of suspects. Shouldn't you be out there beatin' the streets for those scumbags?"

Vince cocked his head and gave his friend a half-smile. "Look around, you hot dawg. Don't you think this is over the top? I mean, I could understand vandalism, but this? Even the print guys are stumped. Whoever did this was neat and nasty. Not likely to be your normal thieves."

Jack looked around. The fingerprint team had already covered most of the room with their brushes and black dust. None of them looked very happy. Jack shook his head. "Nah, I'm not buying it. It's probably all just a sick joke. I'll bet you some good money that all you're gonna find is a coupla junkies strung out on Horse with some weird zoo fetish tryin' to mess with that girl."

Vince shrugged his shoulders. "You're probably right."

"Yeah, yeah." Jack nodded eagerly. "The most you're gonna get on these guys is a good old fashioned "breaking and entering"; maybe a low-grade vandalism. Nothing's gone missing, no dead bodies, human that is. I don't know why the captain is puttin' up such a fuss over it. Anyway, when you're done, gimme a call. Some of the boys are going to Boon's to watch the game tonight, drink a few brews…" Cabrini watched Jack's face transform from his usual eat-shit grin to a scowl. "Oh, crap." Jack nodded toward the door. "Who let the freaks in?" Cabrini turned and watched as a tall, slender woman dressed in a pale peach-colored suit, followed by three nerdy-looking men walked into the room. "The H-Squad? Are you shittin' me? They can't be serious."

Vince had never worked with the H-Squad, but he'd heard about them. Officially they were the S.I.U, Special Investigations Unit, but to the boys in blue, they were called the Hoodoo Squad, H-Squad for short. Tons of stories always followed this crowd. Everyone laughed behind their backs. This bunch had been the brunt of a thousand jokes, but never in front of the beautiful Dr. Simone DaQuin; café-au-lait skin; bright, ice-blue eyes; Creole to the core.

Beautiful all right, but those eyes cut like razor blades when she'd been challenged. Her tongue cut, too, only deeper. The other three guys were just her flunkies. They never crossed her. Jack tensed as Dr. DaQuin walked towards them. He leaned into Vince, whispering, "Here comes the Voodoo witch. Trust me, you don't want to work with that one!"

"Officer Vincent Cabrini?" Dr. DaQuin read his badge quickly and looked up into Vince's eyes. "Captain Brady said you're the man I'm supposed to see. I don't think we've ever met. I'm Dr. Simone DaQuin." She reached out to shake his hand. "The captain called and wants my team in on this. 'Looks like we've got an interesting case here."

Vince smiled as he shook her hand, hoping that she didn't overhear Jack's 'Voodoo witch' comment. "Yes, ma'am."

Jack interrupted, not even trying to mask his condescending tone. "Dr. DaQuin, 'sure don't know why you'd want to get your pretty hands dirty with this one; 'probably just junkies messing around. I'd say some of the maid's friends." Jack motioned over to the maid who had finally stopped crying and was sitting in the chair like an alabaster statue, staring off into space.

Simone looked over at the maid and then back at Jack. "Have you finished questioning her?"

Jack shook his head. "Foreign. 'Need an interpreter."

Then Vince saw it, the famous stare. "I'm sure Captain Brady would like to hear all about your theories, Detective Moynahan. I suggest you give him a call right now, while Officer Cabrini and I get on with more important things."

Vince watched Jack storm away. It was clear she had pissed him off and he was certain he'd hear about it later. "So, Officer Cabrini, the captain gave me the basics, but I want to hear your take on what's happened."

Vince watched as her team moved into the room like ants at a picnic. If he didn't know better, he'd swear that they looked giddy with excitement as they opened up case after case of very expensive equipment. Two of the men went over to the bedside and one walked into the bathroom. Vince looked back at the doctor. "Yeah, two perps got the room key in a robbery yesterday evening. Hotel guards think they broke in sometime around two. The guys back at the precinct are still going over the security camera footage. So far nothing, though. We got the victim's possessions out before the perps got in here. Maybe when they realized there wasn't anything to take, they decided to leave a sick joke behind instead."

Simone DaQuin frowned. "Oh, it's sick alright, but believe me, Officer Cabrini, this is no joke."

Vince widened his stance and crossed his arms looking straight at Simone. In her three-inch heels, she came eye to eye to his six-foot-three height. "Not a joke? Well, why in the world would they have done this?"

Dr. DaQuin didn't answer right away. Her long pause and deep stare made him uncomfortable. Finally, she answered. "Tell me, Officer Cabrini, do you really want to know? Because I'm not here to satisfy your idle curiosity or to be made fun of at one of those parties your precinct is so famous for." She looked over at Jack who was escorting the housekeeper out the door, then she looked back at Vince.

Vince gave her a slight smile as he stared back into those icy blue eyes. He liked her no-bullshit attitude, even if she was a little scary. "I really want to know."

"You really want to know." She echoed. "Then why don't we start with the thing in the bed over there. Ever see anything like that before?"

"No, can't say that I have." Vince looked over at the bed. The two H-squad guys were masked, gowned, goggled and gloved, like Dr. Frankenstein and Igor trying to wake the dead. He looked back at Dr. DaQuin, frowning. "Why all the protective gear?"

She gave him a quick nod and a slight smile. "Officer Cabrini, how are you with blood?"

Vince shrugged his shoulders, noticing that the forensic team had already packed up and were walking out the door. "I've seen my share."

"Okay, then. Follow me." She spun on a toe and walked toward the bed. "We need protective gear because there's always the threat of toxic poison contamination in this line of work. That's why we examine everything onsite first with our mobile lab equipment. We have to make certain that it's safe to ..."

"Dr. DaQuin?" Simone stopped mid stride. Vince nearly ran into her as she turned back around to face the assistant who had gone into the bathroom. With one eyebrow raised, she stared at the man. "Yes, Raymond?"

"Ma'am, you need to see this. We've got a *Petro vève* in here."

Simone's eyes widened. "Are you sure? Which one?"

Raymond gave her a timid smile. "Looks like Erzulie Dantor."

Simone looked at Vince, a broad smile across her face. "Well, Officer Cabrini, you're about to see something rare, very rare indeed." She pushed past Vince and hurried to the bathroom. "That is if Dr. Collins here is right." Vince watched the smile on Raymond's face melt. As they entered the bathroom, Simone DaQuin froze, studying the heart drawing. "I haven't seen one of these since I was in Haiti back in 2011."

Vincent looked at the drawing and shrugged his shoulders. "It just looks like a kid's drawing to me." Both Simone and Raymond turned and stared at Vince. "Sorry, I just…well, it just looks like a heart from a Valentine's Day card only instead of an arrow, it's a knife drawn through it. I have a nephew that could've drawn it." Raymond took a small step back. Vince realized too late that maybe that was the wrong thing to say.

Simone looked back at the mirror. "I can forgive your ignorance, Officer Cabrini. The untrained eye would never see the significance of this." She stepped closer to the heart, studying it closely. She turned to Raymond. "I want pictures of every square inch of this. Samples, too."

She turned to Vince. "I don't want this touched until we get everything we need from it, understand?"

"Of course, but what is it?" Vince stepped closer to the mirror.

Simone took a deep breath. "It's part of a religious ritual in Vodou. I'm sure you've heard of Vooo-Dooo, right? Maybe you're more familiar with the word, Hooo-Dooo?" A hard edge laced her voice. "I'm not talking about the New Orleans version. I'm talking about Vodou, the Haitian religion. Following me so far?" Vince nodded. "In Vodou there is only one God but there are many manifestations of that God called Loa, sort of like saints. Each Loa has two drawings that represent their personality; one for the positive aspect and one for the negative aspect. What you're looking at is the negative aspect of one of the Loa."

Vince frowned as he looked at the drawing closely. "Vodou?" He struggled to say the word correctly.

He saw Dr. DaQuin smile through the red stripes on the mirror. "Yes, and we call the drawings *vève*, which is the Creole word for a holy drawing."

Vince turned and looked at Simone. "Yeah, but Raymond called it something else; *Petro vève?*"

Simone crossed her arms. "Well, now I am impressed, Officer Cabrini. Yes, it is a *Petro vève*. The word Petro refers to a family of Loa, but…" she turned back toward the mirror. "…I'll make this easy. This is the negative aspect of the Loa Erzulie."

Vince shook his head. "Erzulie. That's an odd name."

"She actually goes by many names, Maitresse, Freda Dahome', but the most common one is Ezilie. Her positive aspect is called Erzulie Mansur, The Blessed One. Some even worship her as a saint; Saint Ezilie. Are you Catholic, by any chance? With a name like Cabrini, I'm guessing you're Italian?"

Vincent let out a little laugh. "Catholic school all the way, though I can't say any of it stuck very well."

Simone smiled. "But you got the Virgin Mary part, right?"

Vincent laughed a little harder. "Oh yeah. Rosaries every Saturday, right after confession."

Simone nodded her head. "Erzulie Mansur is the Vodou version of the Virgin Mary; the good mother, never angry, always loving and caring for her children, just with darker skin. I've seen statues of the Black Virgin holding the child Jesus, though some scholars claim the baby that Erzulie is holding is not Jesus at all, but a girl child. Kind of a different twist to an old story, wouldn't you say?"

Vince shook his head. "The good nuns never told us about it, that's for sure."

Dr. DaQuin laughed. "Believe me, Officer Cabrini, I had to do a lot of research and a lot of travel to undo all that the church taught me. Anyway, Erzulie Mansur's *vève* is this exact same design as this; a heart and yes, it could pass for a kind of Valentine but, of course, without the knife. When you add the knife, Erzulie Mansur becomes Erzulie Dantor, the angry mother, the mother hell-bent on revenge. Ever seen your mother angry?"

Vincent smiled, rolling his eyes. "Not a pretty sight."

"Uh huh, well, keep that thought and multiply it by about a thousand. That's Erzulie Dantor. She's the one the Haitians prayed to during the slave revolution and they won their freedom!"

Vincent stepped back and looked at the entire design. "Do you have any ideas about why this would be here, though? You said you hadn't seen this since Haiti, what year did you say?"

"2011, when Baby Doc Duvalier, the deposed dictator returned to Haiti. Lots of people wanted to punish him, so it's no surprise that the Erzulie Dantor *vève* would show up." She sighed. "This symbol means someone wants revenge really badly. The fact that it was drawn on a mirror, well..." She shook her head. "...that's really powerful."

Vince turned and faced Simone. "How so?"

"Well, the mirror in Vodou is a doorway into the afterlife. When a *Petro vève* is drawn on a mirror, the message communicates a wish for a painful death. Whoever did this harbored a lot of hate. We probably need to look over the hotel staff, see if there's anybody with connections to a Vodou sect. One thing's certain: It was drawn for a specific person to see it, but I hardly think that it was meant for that little maid. Not the right nationality. No, somebody else."

Vincent's eyes widened. "Like the person who had this room?"

Dr. DaQuin turned and stared at Vince. "You mean the young woman who was robbed. This was her room, wasn't it? " Vince nodded his head. Simone's brow was wrinkled with thought. "Possibly, but a random mugging hardly fits something of this magnitude. No, this was personal, very personal." She turned to Raymond. "Did you find anything in the center of the heart?"

Raymond shook his head. "No, so I've..."

Vincent interrupted. "But there was something there, right at the tip of the knife." Simone and Raymond stared wide-eyed at Vince. "It was her picture; I think it was from her driver's license. It was stuck right at the tip."

Simone's eyes flashed. "Where is that picture now, Officer Cabrini?"

"The forensics guys have it. They left just as you got here."

Dr. DaQuin clenched her jaw and set her ice-blue eyes squarely on Vince. "Are you certain it was a picture of the young woman — the one that was robbed?"

Vince nodded. "Absolutely. Captain Brady wants me to talk to her again. He thinks she might remember something that could explain all this. After what you just told me, I think you might want to talk to her yourself. She does have an odd history with the perps."

Simone nodded thoughtfully, "Any chance she's Creole? That would explain a lot."

"No, no. She's Caucasian. I think from Baton Rouge. I can look that up back at the office."

"That would be great and can you let me know when you plan that interview? I'd like to sit in on it. When she sees the photos of all this, I'll be able to tell if she recognizes any of it. If she does, maybe she's more involved than we think."

Vince shook his head. "I doubt it. She's as straight as they come."

"Dr. DaQuin? Could you please come in here?" The muffled voice came from the bedroom, but Vince couldn't tell which one of the mad scientists had called. He followed Dr. DaQuin out of the bathroom and over to the bed. When she reached the footboard, she leaned down, opened one of the kits, put on a surgical mask and handed one to Vince. "Here, put this on."

Vince looked down at the bed. The rooster head had been removed and the body of the snake had been splayed open. On a tray nearby was a snake head, its jaw stretched out with fangs bared. Vince looked at both assistants who'd been dissecting the snake; their gloved hands striped with bright red blood. One was holding a tray like he was about to serve tea.

"What is it, Dr. Harper?" Dr. DaQuin leaned closer to the tray.

"We found this." Vince saw an odd-looking mud doll with two fang marks in its chest. "We've run an exterior tox screen and it's clean. We thought you'd want to see it before we cut it open."

Simone DaQuin drew a long breath. "I can't believe it."

Vince shook his head. "Is that what I think it is?"

She never took her eyes off the mud doll as she answered. "If you're thinking it's a Voodoo doll then you would be correct, Officer Cabrini, but let's clarify one thing before we go any further. What you're looking at is a bastardization of a sacred object in Vodou, the Nkisi. The Nkisi is a spirit doll that channels the force of the Loa and is used to ask for special favors, not dissimilar to a statue of your favorite saint. The thing that you see here has its roots strictly in New Orleans Voodoo and it's meant for only one thing: to do harm to the one it was made for. This one looks especially nasty. No pins, just fang marks." She looked straight at Dr. Harper. "Got a sample of the hair?" The young man nodded. She looked back at the doll. "The facial area looks like there might've been an identifier there. Did you find anything?"

Dr. Harper shook his head. "No. We used the x-ray over several angles. There's nothing inside the head portion or the legs and arms, either. But there is something in the chest and then a little further down in the abdomen. They're both the same size and shape, no jagged edges. Take a look."

Dr. Harper nodded his head at the computer screen. Dr. DaQuin looked closely at the x-ray photographs. "It still could be something sharp, possibly laced with poison, too." She looked back at the doll. "It's meant for a woman, breasts. There's even pubic hair here." She looked up. "There's only one thing left to do. Open it up, Dr. Harper, with great care!" Vince watched as Dr. Harper placed the tray down carefully and cut through both breasts with the scalpel. Something plastic inched forward as he pushed the mud away. He took tweezers and pulled it out, then scraped the last remnants of the mud off of the plastic. Simone DaQuin nodded to the other assistant. "Thomas, there's writing there. Get the magnifier. What does it say?"

Thomas picked up the magnifier and leaned close to the tiny piece of plastic. He frowned, "Who's Celine Dupré?"

CHAPTER 16

Sunday mornings were usually quiet at the Arnaud Gallery. The doors never opened before one p.m. Even then it was rare that anyone ever crossed the threshold until after two. That's when the Sunday strollers walked up and down Royal Street, lazily browsing through all the quaint little shops. Most of the time, they wandered in from a jazz brunch, full of rich food and fashionably tipsy. These were just the right people to be drawn into an art gallery, searching for that unique painting that they could buy and then show-off to their friends back home.

Alexandre Arnaud always loved Sundays. He'd usually lounge in his gallery apartment until the bells of St. Louis chimed 11:00. Breakfast in bed, a shower, a shave, a suit, a cigar and a Mimosa, and Alex was ready to face the onset of browsers. He relished unlocking and then opening wide the French Provincial cut-glass doors, inviting people in, but today the doors would stay locked. There was something much more important happening.

Nine a.m. found Alex sitting at the massive mahogany desk in the entrance foyer, the huge antique chandelier above him casting a thousand points of light off the mirrored wall behind him and across the highly-polished oak floor in front of him. He opened his black leather organizer and looked over the list one more time. *East Room, AIDS benefit, Derek Saxon featured, dusted. West Room, Michael's Lady of the Letters moved. Replace with New French artists - Papi Canereau featured. Adjust spotlight/ FF.* Alex looked up, searching the room for his curator. "René?"

René came out of the East Room wearing white dusting gloves. "Sir?"

"Have you adjusted the spotlight on Papi's Field of Flowers like I asked? It's causing a hideous shadow. Papi would simply die if she saw her work displayed like that. She'd never want to work with me again and that will never…" Alex stopped when he saw the distant expression on René's face. It could only mean one thing—the poor man was enduring another one of Alex's temperamental tirades. Of course, Alex preferred to call these moments 'artistic perfectionism', but he knew that he was just being ridiculously picky, at least that's what Michael always called it. "You've already done it, haven't you?"

René gave Alex a weak smile as he nodded. "I've adjusted the spotlight and dusted Derek's paintings, too. Everything's ready, sir, just like you asked."

Alex sighed and looked at his Rolex. "I'm sorry, René, but Michael's going to call as soon as they leave the hotel. That only gives us about fifteen minutes before they get here and I want everything to be perfect." He looked back at his organizer and read the list out loud to René. "Lady returned to Michael's studio?" René nodded. Alex checked it off the list. "What about the workroom? I know the supplies and the blueprints have been laid out, but what about that drafting table? You know, the really big one? I want there to be enough room for at least two people to work side by side, so…"

René nodded again. "You can check that one off, too."

Alex smiled as he neared the end of his list. "Guest bedroom prepped?"

René frowned. "I think Dora did that."

Alex drew a quick breath. "Dora's fixing brunch. I'm sure she didn't have any time! Stop what you're doing and at least go open the windows up there. It's been closed up for months. It's probably terribly musty-smelling. I don't want Miss Dupré to get sick from the dust, poor thing. That's all she needs!"

René slowly began to strip the gloves off, one finger at a time. "Mr. Arnaud, I'm sure Dora's already done it. Anyway, I thought you said Miss Dupré was staying at the St. Jeanne?"

"She is, but I've decided that she should stay here. After what happened to her yesterday, I owe it to her to make the rest of her stay as peaceful and enjoyable as I possibly can. I think we can do that better here than at the Hotel Ste. Jeanne. I don't know why I didn't think about it before. So, please, go up there and…" Alex stopped mid sentence when he heard the key turn in the lock and saw the crystal doorknob turn. He could see Michael's fragmented image through the cut-glass door. "Oh, God. They're here! Why didn't Michael call? Quick, René, go tell Dora they're here. Now!"

Alex slid from behind the desk and hurried forward as Michael opened the door. "Oh Celine, I'm so glad to see you! You look wonderful!" Alex reached out to take her hand. "A perfect picture of beauty in your white sundress. My dear, you have no idea how happy I am to see you looking so radiant."

Celine smiled as she reached out to shake Alex's hand. "Thank you. It's good to see you again, Alex! I hope we're not late. I got ready as fast as I could when Michael called with your invitation for breakfast. After missing my appointment with you last night, I didn't want to be late this morning."

Alex cocked his head, the smile disappearing from his face. He held her hand in both of his. "Late? You're not late at all. In fact you're a bit early." He turned to Michael and frowned. "Someone was supposed to call me when they left the hotel and obviously forgot."

Michael's face reddened just a little. "Sorry, Alex." He closed the door behind him. "I think we were just a little bit distracted. The lobby at the hotel was filled with police. Something must've happened."

Alex squeezed Celine's hand lightly, his face wrinkled with concern. "Not to you, I hope!"

Celine shook her head. "No, no, but Michael's right. I rode the elevator down with a policeman; I think he might've even been a detective. He had one of the housekeepers with him. The poor thing looked awful. When we got to the lobby, he escorted her out the door and into a police car."

Michael locked the door and then stood next to Celine. "Yeah, and there were several police vans parked in the street as we walked out." He smiled, looking at Celine. "So, we decided to get out of there as soon as we could."

Celine laughed. "We practically ran out of there. So, it's my fault he didn't call you. I'm really sorry."

Alex smiled, shaking his head. "Oh my dear, I can't believe that you would even think you'd need to apologize to me. This city is so full of street trash and it's only gotten worse since Katrina. No, it's me who should be apologizing to you. I should've realized that a young attractive woman walking back and forth from the hotel would be in danger, especially in the early evening hours. Heaven knows what's going on at the St. Jeanne now! I should've offered that you stay here from the very beginning. So, I have the guest bedroom all ready and waiting for you."

Celine stammered as she spoke. "Oh, but, but I didn't mean… the St. Jeanne is a beautiful hotel and you know they moved me to a different room, right? It's perfectly fine, so…"

Alex cradled her hand in his elbow as he escorted her forward. "Now, I won't take no for an answer. If I have to, I'll make it a condition of your work with me. Safety first, okay?"

Celine looked at Michael. "I'm not sure what to say."

Michael laughed as he put the set of keys in his pocket. "I wouldn't fight him on this if I were you. If you don't give him what he wants, he'll throw a little fit. You don't want to see that, I promise."

Alex walked with Celine, waving his hand at Michael as if to shoo away a gnat. "Enough! Now, let me give you a little tour as we make our way to breakfast."

Celine glanced back at Michael as she walked with Alex. Michael smiled, shrugging his shoulders. "Just do as he says. We'll all be glad you did."

Celine fell into step with Alex as he walked her to the center of the foyer. "Now, to our left is the East Room. We have Derek Saxon in there and to our right is the West Room. We have Papi Canereau in there. Are you familiar with her work? She's the hottest thing in Paris right now."

Celine looked toward the East Room. "I've heard of Papi Canereau, but I'm not familiar with Derek Saxon."

Alex smiled as he guided Celine to the first of Derek's paintings. "I'm rather proud of Derek. He's a local and another victim to this horrible AIDS epidemic. He's a very courageous young man. I'm doing all I can to help him sell his work. God knows he needs the money."

Celine walked to the first painting, an abstract portrait of a blue-haired gentleman wearing a bright fuchsia suit, a purple ascot and neon yellow fedora. She turned to Alex. "It's sort of a cross between Andy Warhol's Marilyn Monroe and George Rodrigue's Blue Dog. The colors are so vibrant."

Alex laughed. "I'll have to tell Derek you said that. Warhol is his idol."

Celine looked back at the painting, examining the detail of bright green eye shadow, mascara and scarlet red lipstick on the man in the painting. "So have you sold any of his work?"

He turned to Michael. "Michael did, just last week in fact."

Michael nodded. "Yeah, the buyer commissioned several others. I just hope Derek's up to it, though."

Celine frowned. "Is he very ill?"

Michael nodded. "Yeah. He's about like Alex was before the new meds."

Celine looked back at Alex. "Oh, that's right! You had the new treatments. I'm so sorry, I didn't even mention it. You're out of the wheelchair and really looking wonderful! How are you feeling?"

Alex smiled just as his cell phone alerted him with a text message. "Ten years younger!" He pulled his cell phone out of his coat pocket and read the message. "Oh dear." He looked at Michael. "It's Dora. We're in trouble." He turned to Celine. "Breakfast is nearly ready so we need to hurry along to the sun porch. 'Can't keep Dora waiting."

Celine looked at Michael, puzzled. "Sun porch? Guest Bedrooms? Just how big is this place? From the street it doesn't look very big."

Alex smiled as he scurried behind the mahogany desk and faced the wall of mirrors. "You'd never guess that behind these walls there's a full household, would you? He gently pushed on one of the panels. With a soft *pop*, the mirrored door opened into a hallway.

Celine looked at Michael in surprise. "A door?"

Michael placed his hand gently at Celine's back as they walked behind the desk and through the door. "This old house is filled with crazy surprises. The original house was built in 1780 but it's had lots of add-ons and extensions over the years."

As Celine walked through the hallway, she noticed a flight of stairs to the right. "1780? It's over two hundred years old? I wonder how many people have actually lived here. If these walls could talk..."

Michael laughed. "...they might say things we'd rather not hear."

As they walked into a glass-enclosed porch, Alex pointed to the circular dining room table, already set for three. The small bouquet of miniature white calla lilies in a glass bowl placed in the center of the table accentuated the pastel yellow linen tablecloth and classic white scallop-edged charger plates. Celine looked around the casually-elegant room, furnished with white rattan furniture, upholstered in lemongrass green.

"You two have a seat. I'll go tell Dora we're here."

Michael pulled the white wicker dining chair out for Celine. "I don't know exactly how many people have lived here. Probably more than a few shady characters who left skeletons in the closets. But they've all been relatives of mine, so gotta love 'em, right? Want some coffee?"

"Sure." Celine pulled the delicate bisque coffee cup closer to her as Michael walked over to the buffet and brought the silver coffee service to the table. "I hope you don't mean that literally. I might decide to stay at the Ste. Jeanne if you've got skeletons wandering around."

Michael laughed as he poured them both a cup of coffee, then sat down across from Celine. "No, I don't think you have to worry about that. Dora's such a thorough housekeeper; they wouldn't have a chance trying to hide from her!"

"She sort of sounds like my grandmother. She'd have no problem hunting down a few skeletons, especially if they were messing up her house!"

Michael laughed as Alex walked through the doors carrying a tray of three Mimosas in champagne flute glasses, garnished with a sprig of mint. "Breakfast will be ready in just a little while. In the meantime, I thought we could enjoy a refreshing mimosa or two." Alex placed a tall glass in front of Celine and Michael, picked up the last drink and placed the silver tray on the buffet. He walked back to the table and sat down with his back to the courtyard. He sipped the drink, leaning back in his chair. "Mmmm, what would Sunday brunch be without a sweet Mimosa?"

Michael gave Alex a sly little smile. "I thought you cut out drinking alcohol at meals. If Dora sees that, you know she'll fuss at you."

Alex shook his head. "This?" He looked at the drink, then back at Michael. "This is just champagne and orange juice. I left the Triple Sec out, so there's hardly any alcohol in it at all. Besides..." Alex took another sip of the drink. "Dora watched me mix them."

Michael looked back at Celine and gave her a little wink from across the table. He lowered his voice, pretending to whisper. "Now you know who's really in charge."

Alex raised an eyebrow at his nephew and gave him a mischievous little grin. "Well, I seem to remember someone from not so very long ago who needed a few of Dora's lessons in housekeeping." He turned to Celine. "When Michael first moved in, his bedroom was a total mess and his studio? Well, it's a miracle he could ever paint in there!"

"Studio?" Celine looked back at Michael. "Are you an artist, too? I thought you were Alex's business manager."

Michael's face reddened just a little. He looked back at Alex, suddenly very serious. "Oh, I am. The artist part, I'm just an amateur."

Alex took a long drink of his mimosa, set the glass down and then looked at Celine. "Michael's more than my business manager. He's my agent, my public relations man and the best I've ever had."

Celine turned to Michael. "Is there something you're working on now?" She drank the last of her coffee, not quite ready for the Mimosa in front of her.

Michael hesitated. "Um, yeah, but I haven't decided exactly which direction I want to go with it."

Alex shook his head. "Michael is just like every artist I've ever known, very private about his work. I shouldn't have said anything about the…"

"Breakfast is ready." Alex stopped mid-sentence as Dora walked into the room carrying a huge tray, the size of which dwarfed the already petite black woman. Celine wondered how someone so small could carry a tray so large. Dora walked over to the buffet and set the tray down, her hands moving fluidly as she removed the first two serving plates of food.

She walked around the table, approaching Celine from behind.

Alex turned to Celine. "Celine, this is our Dora." He looked at the serving plate Dora held. "Oh you are a delight, Dora." He looked back at Celine. "Wait until you taste this. It melts in your mouth." He reached for his linen napkin and placed it on his lap like a hungry and obedient little boy.

Celine looked up at Dora. "It's nice to meet you. I'm looking forward to trying your famous French toast." She looked at the serving plate Dora placed in front of her. She smiled broadly as she gazed at the two inch thick slice of Crème Brulée French toast delicately stenciled with a powdered sugar Fleur-de-Lys. Baked peaches and strawberries were artfully poured alongside and a twist of orange slice, drizzled with chocolate, sat on the edge of the plate. "Oh, how elegant but I'll never be able to eat all that."

Dora laughed. "Oh, all you skinny young models say that."

Celine looked at Michael across the table, puzzled. "Models?"

Dora walked behind Celine and over to Alex. "But if you just take one bite…" she put the plate in front of Alex. "…before you know it, that plate'll be clean." She walked back over to the buffet and got the last serving plate. As she walked behind Michael and served him, she stopped and looked across at Celine. "It's nice to get to meet The Lady." She patted Michael on the shoulder. "You did a very nice job, Mr. Michael. Your paintings look just like her." Celine watched Michael's face turn pale. He looked down, cutting his French toast just a little too vigorously. Dora turned and walked back over to the buffet.

Celine shook her head, smiling. "I think you may have me confused with somebody else. I'm not a model, I'm…"

Michael looked down as he spoke. "Yes, Yes, Dora's thinking of someone else." He turned to Dora. "Celine is here to help Alex with the new art addition at the School for the Blind. Alex told you, I'm sure." He turned to Alex. "Right, Alex?" Alex nodded, his mouth full of French toast. Celine noticed that Michael was cutting his toast into smaller and smaller pieces as he continued talking. "Yes, she's the Assistant Principal there and working on her Doctorate in Art Education. We're really looking forward to starting on the project as soon as possible."

Dora walked back to the table carrying three small silver bowls of fruit ambrosia. She placed the first one in front of Celine. "Oh, well, you sure look like the woman in Mr. Michael's paintings." She walked over to Alex and placed the bowl in front of him. "Don't you think so, Mr. Alex?"

Celine noticed Alex give a quick glance at Michael and then up at Dora. "Um, somewhat, yes, I guess, maybe."

She walked over to Michael and placed the last bowl in front of him. "Now, you know, Mr. Alex, there's no maybe about it. The hair and those eyes especially." She looked across the table at Celine. "You should get Mr. Michael to show you his paintings. I bet you'd see it, too."

Celine looked at Michael, his head still down. *Why is he so self-conscious about his work? This whole conversation is making him terribly uncomfortable.* "Well, of course, I'd love to see them, but I trust Michael to decide if that will ever happen." Michael looked up and gave her a little smile. She smiled back and took a bite of the French toast. "Oh my, this is delicious!"

Alex laughed. "It is quite exquisite, isn't it? That little orange zest is from the Grand Marnier she uses. Dora, my dear, you've done it again."

Dora smiled. "Thank you and I'll be right back with your pills, Mr. Alex. Best if you take them right after you eat, you know." Dora started toward the kitchen door and then stopped. "Oh, and I forgot to tell you, the electrician called. He said he'll be here first thing in the morning."

Alex sighed as she disappeared behind the door. He looked over at Michael, "Maybe we should just hire the man full-time." He popped another bite of French toast in his mouth.

Michael laughed, his face a little more relaxed. "Might be a little less expensive if we did." He turned to Celine. "That's what happens when you have a two hundred-year-old building to maintain. Something's always breaking."

Celine took another bite of the toast, scooping a few peaches onto her fork. "I can hardly imagine, but I have to say, this place is beautiful. I love this glassed-in sun porch. It's nice to be able to look out to the garden and your courtyard. You just completely forget that we're surrounded by a city."

Alex nodded. "I've tried really hard to restore the old place to its original charm. It took nearly ten years to piece together all the old plans, but I think it's as close as it'll ever be."

"You were able to get the original blueprints? Where in the world did you find them?" Celine took a bite of the coconut-laced ambrosia.

Alex laughed. "In a trunk that an old aunt of mine owned. The poor old dear was a true hoarder, but I'm very glad she had them."

Celine cut into the powdered sugar Fleur-de-Lys. "But how did she come to have them?"

"Passed down through generations. My grandmother's family was one of the first to settle New Orleans. This old place was their first home, so the plans just got stored away. They were a bit difficult to decipher at first; entirely written in French and some of the print was illegible. When I first started the renovations, the house was a total mess; tons of repairs to be made. It didn't even have a connected kitchen. Then we had to have it wired for electricity. It was bit tricky to install the central air and heat, but we did it and here we are…" Alex laughed as he drained the last of his mimosa "…still hiring people to fix everything."

"So had it been unoccupied for a long time?" Celine sipped her mimosa.

Alex looked around the room as he spoke. "Oh yes. Fifty years or so. It was used as a storage place; lots and lots of old junk that had been in our family. The first job was to clean it all out; mostly old ledgers from the sugar cane shipping company that was the original business. I donated all that to the Louisiana History Museum, well, at least the documents that hadn't fallen apart."

"And that was your grandmother's family?" Celine took one last bite of the toast, realizing that if she tried to eat anymore, she just might literally pop.

"Yes, the Beau…" The kitchen doors opened and Dora walked in, a pitcher of water in one hand and a pill dispenser in the other. Alex sighed. "Oh dear, my most unfavorite part of the day."

Michael smiled at Alex compassionately. "But Matt's pills keep you going. Just think about how much better you feel now."

Alex playfully grumbled. "Oh I know, I know. I just wish they weren't such horse-pills."

Dora poured a tall glass of water and began laying the pills out. She looked over at Celine's plate. "Miss Celine, can I get you something else? You hardly touched your food."

Celine smiled, pushing her plate away and wiping her mouth with her napkin. "Oh, no. Thank you. I am so full. I don't think I could eat another bite."

Dora looked down at Alex who was staring at the array of pills in front of him. "Now Mr. Alex, I cut them in two for you. Dr. Matt told me that I could do that. He said …"

Alex shrugged his shoulders. "…and now it'll take me twice as long to take them." He looked at Michael. "Why don't you bring Celine upstairs and show her the plans for the school. No need for the two of you to sit here and watch me agonize over these horrid things. I'll meet you in a little while."

Celine and Michael walked out of the dining room and up the flight of stairs. Michael turned to her as they reached the landing and walked down a long narrow hallway, doors on the left and windows overlooking Royal Street on the right. "The work room is just down this hall. The guest bedroom is attached to it. Really, I think Alex is right. Staying here will be better. The Quarter has gotten too dangerous at night. Here we are." Michael opened a white door in the center of the hallway. They walked into a brightly-lit room, furnished with a huge drafting table right in the center. The blueprint for the art building had been laid out in two sections. On a nearby table sat a model of the entire building. Celine smiled. "Is this it?"

Michael smiled back. "This is it."

Celine walked over and looked at the model. "Oh, this is so exciting. The kids are going to love this." She looked at the little doll house-like construction. "It's quite beautiful. So spacious."

"Yes, well, Alex has added a dance studio, too."

Celine looked at Michael, astounded. "What? You're kidding, right?"

"No, look." Michael removed the upper half of the model, revealing each room underneath. "Right here." He pointed to a large open space on one end of the model. "Maybe we should wait for him to get up here, though. He's so excited and I know he really wants to be the one to show you everything."

Celine nodded, smiling. "Absolutely. He's such a kind man and he has a very kind nephew in you, Michael. It's a rare and wonderful thing that he has you." She reached out and took his hand. "So show me this guest bedroom that has no skeletons in the closet."

Michael laughed as he led her to a door in the far right corner of the room. He opened the door and led her through it. The white lace curtains on the floor-to-ceiling windows fluttered in the breeze as they walked into the room together.

Celine stood in the middle of the room, looking at the white wrought iron, queen-sized bed covered in a white eyelet bedspread. A huge antique armoire stood against one wall. "This is beautiful."

Michael walked past her and opened another door, taking a bow and sweeping his arm in front of him. *"Les toilettes de femme, Mademoiselle."*

Celine walked past him into the bathroom, laughing. "Merci, Monsieur." When she saw the brass, claw-footed porcelain tub, she held up her hands. "This is perfect. I'd be a fool not to stay here."

Michael smiled. "Glad to hear it and Alex will be glad, too."

Celine walked through the bedroom and back into the workroom. "So, show me more of this place. It's so unique and the story behind it, well, it's like walking inside a piece of history." She turned around and saw another door. "Oh wait. Is this it?" She walked over to the door and turned the knob but it was locked.

Michael laughed. "Oh no. You can't go in there."

Celine put her back against the door, both her hands still on the doorknob. "Why? Is this where they're hiding?"

Michael arched an eyebrow and gave her a curious little smirk. "What? What's hiding?"

Celine gave him an impish little smile. "Those skeletons you were talking about."

Michael walked toward her and gave her a playful little smile in return. "No, I told you. Dora got rid of all those."

Celine felt her heart racing as he stood in front of her, his blue eyes dancing in the sunlight. "So what's behind the locked door?" She jiggled the doorknob behind her back.

Michael laughed. "Oh, no you don't!" When he reached behind her, trying to pull her hands from the doorknob, she held tight, laughing. "Oh, you want to play that way, huh? I bet you're ticklish."

Celine's eyes twinkled with playful mischief. "No!"

He brought his hands to her tiny waist. "No?" He wiggled his long fingers through the folds of her sundress until she squealed with laughter.

Celine twisted her body, letting go of the doorknob and falling into Michael's chest. "No, wait! My shoulder—you're hurting my shoulder!" She groaned and giggled at the same time. "Stop! Stop!"

His eyes grew wide as he pulled her to him, hugging her close. In a low hoarse voice, he whispered. "I'm sorry. I forgot about your bruise; those horrible people hurting you like that." She could feel his breath in her hair. Her whole body tingled with excitement as he gently put his fingertips under her chin and looked down at her, smiling. "I never want to hurt you, Celine, and I'll never do anything you don't want me to." His face grew suddenly serious as he frowned. "Uh oh…"

Celine frowned back. "What?"

He brushed her cheek. "I think you missed a little spot of powdered sugar."

Celine blushed just a little and quickly reached up, brushing any sugar that she had on her face. "Oh, lovely. You must think I'm a pig!" When she looked back up at him, she realized that he had been quietly watching her the whole time. Her stomach fluttered. *Oh God, he's so handsome.*

He reached down and took her hand. "Where did you get this beautiful ring? If you're wearing it on your left hand, it must be an engagement ring. Who's the lucky guy?"

Celine looked down at the ring and then back at Michael. "No, no. My grandmother gave it to me. It just fits better on my left hand."

He let out a little sigh as he gently stroked the sapphires with his thumb. "It's beautiful; triple Fleur-de-Lys and a fire opal." He looked back at Celine. "You really want to know what's behind those doors?"

She smiled. "Yes. Yes I do."

Michael nodded and took a small step back. He reached into his pocket and pulled out his keys. "It's my studio."

Celine stepped away from the door, surprised. "Really?"

Michael put the key in the door and turned the lock, then put his keys back in his pocket. He turned to her smiling. "Yes, really." He put his hand on the door knob. "But you have to promise me something."

Celine put her hand over his. "Of course."

Michael nodded. "After you see these paintings, you have to give me a chance to explain, okay?"

Celine pulled her hand back. "Please, don't tell me I'm going to see one of Alex's monster paintings or something like that."

Michael shook his head. "No, nothing like that, I promise. Just after you see them, I have to tell you the story behind them." He held his hand out, waiting.

Celine nodded nervously, slowly placing her hand in his. "Okay."

Michael smiled and opened the door just slightly when his phone rang. "Oh great!" He stepped back and shut the door. "It might be Alex. I'm sorry. Let me get this." Celine nodded as Michael looked at the caller ID. He frowned and then looked back at Celine. "It's Vince!"

"Hello?" Celine watched as Michael talked to the policeman. "Hey, Vince. Yeah. She's here. Want to talk to her?" He looked back at Celine, shaking his head. "Yeah, yeah sure. Now? Okay." Michael squeezed Celine's hand, smiling. "That's great, man. She'll be glad to hear it.

We'll come right over." Michael hung up and looked at Celine. "Good news. They think they've got the guy who robbed you!"

Celine stepped toward Michael, touching his arm. "Really? That's great!"

"Yeah, but they need you to ID him. We've got to get over to the station. He said he wants to talk to you about some other stuff, too; new evidence or something. He said he'll explain when we get there."

As they walked out of the workroom, Celine paused at the doorway. "Thank you, Michael. I couldn't do this without you."

"There's no way I'd ever let you go through this alone." He smiled as he shut the door behind him.

CHAPTER 17

Celine shivered in the cold room. "I should've gone to the hotel first and grabbed my sweater."

Michael put his arm around her and rubbed her bare arms, careful not to touch her badly bruised shoulder. "I could go get it for you now if you'd like."

"No, no, that's okay." She nuzzled closer to him. "With my luck lately, just about the time you leave, Officer Cabrini will walk in. I'm having a hard enough time thinking about having to identify this guy. Having to do it alone? No thanks!"

Michael smiled, happy that she needed him. He leaned a little closer to her, smelling the soft scent of roses in her hair. "I'm sure Vince is going to do everything he can to make it as easy as possible, but don't worry, I'm not leaving unless you want me to."

Celine looked around interrogation Room 3. A stainless steel table and four matching chairs sat in the middle of the twelve-by-twelve-foot space. In one corner there was a surveillance camera; a tiny red beam in the middle of the black bulb stared like an ominous eye.

Overhead was a fluorescent light that made a yellow tint reflect off the mirrored wall to her right. "I bet that's a window."

Michael looked over at the mirror. "You think someone's watching us?" He didn't wait for her to answer. Instead he looked back at Celine, his blue eyes filled with the playful mischief she liked so much and whispered, "Think we should wave?"

Celine laughed a nervous giggle, her arms breaking out in goose-flesh from the chill in the room. "No, there's probably no one there. I'm just a little paranoid, I guess. I feel like I've been sent to the principle's office. Now I know how my school kids feel when I send them to detention. I think I'll be a little more lenient from now on."

"Yeah well, I can't imagine you'd be very hard on any child. Besides, just how much trouble can a blind kid get into anyway?"

Celine laughed, shaking her head. "Oh, you would not believe the stuff I've had to…"

She was interrupted when the door opened behind them. Celine sat up a little straighter in her chair. "Hi guys, sorry for the wait." Vincent Cabrini closed the door and in two long strides was standing by the side of the table. He reached out his hand to Celine. "Miss Dupré, good to see you." His hand swallowed Celine's as he gently shook it. Cabrini turned to Michael. "Michael. Good to see you, too." Michael half raised out of the chair and shook his hand. As he sat back down, he noticed a manila folder under the officer's arm. Vincent placed the folder on the table and sat down facing them. He turned to Celine. "Michael told you the good news?"

Celine turned her body to squarely face Vincent. "You've caught the guy?"

Vincent smiled. "We certainly hope so, but we need your help. Before we start, though, I wanted to set your mind at ease. I've contacted your student's mother. Little Leah is fine. They live in a gated community, so I don't think there's any chance that these crooks can breach their security."

Celine smiled and took a deep breath. "That's great news. Thank you for calling them."

"No problem. Can I offer either of you some coffee or water?"

Celine shook her head, her stomach was already churning and her hands were trembling just a little. Coffee might warm her up a bit but the caffeine would only make everything worse. She gave him a slight smile, "No, I'm good for now."

Michael shook his head at the same time as he draped his arm over the back of Celine's chair. "I don't know how you drink that black syrup you call coffee, anyway."

Vince laughed. "Breakfast of champions!" The smile on his face gradually faded into 'policeman serious' as he folded his hands in front of him. "Okay, then, let's get started. Everything we say and do is being videotaped for verification purposes." Cabrini reached under the table. With a soft click, Celine noticed the little red light in the black bulb switch to green. Cabrini's voice shifted to a lower pitch as he continued.

"Case #14-50311, June 22, 1:35 p.m.; Case Officer, Vincent James Cabrini, Badge #2974137. First of all…" He turned to Celine. "Have you ever done a photo lineup before?"

"No. The only police station I've ever been to was for a school field trip."

Cabrini smiled. "I'm not surprised and I'm only sorry you even have to be here doing this, but your help is very valuable to us. What I'm going to do is show you six photos in this folder. They're numbered from one to six. Your perpetrator may, or may not be, in this group of photos. I want you to look at each one of them very closely and tell me if you recognize any of them, okay?"

Celine nodded, nervously looking at Michael and then back at Cabrini. "I'll try." Michael quietly reached over and took her hand as Cabrini pushed the folder in front of her and opened it. Just as Cabrini had described, the six head-shot photos were glued on the inside of the folder.

Celine took a deep breath as she looked at each one. *Number 1, no. 'Skin's too light. Number 2, not the right hair. His eyes look Asian. Number 3, maybe. He's got dread locks but no, his face is too broad. Number 4…* Celine's breath shortened when she saw the face: dark skin, gaunt hollow cheeks, pockmarked skin, decayed teeth, dread locks, sunken deep-brown eyes set in bloodshot whites. His voice still echoed in her ears, 'shut up bitch' as he shook her head violently. She looked at Cabrini. "It's number four."

"Are you sure? Look at all of them. I need you to be certain."

Celine squeezed Michael's hand as she looked back down at the pictures. Her stomach lurched as she saw the face again. She glanced over all of them once more then pushed the folder back toward the officer, trying to erase the awful memory of the man's face. "Number four."

"Okay…" Cabrini pulled out a pen from his pocket and handed it to her. "I need you to circle the picture that you've chosen and sign it; first, middle, last name, just under the photo." Cabrini placed the pen on the open folder and slowly pushed it back to her.

Celine took the pen and nervously circled the photo. With a slightly shaking hand, she wrote *Celine Bienaimée Dupré* and then put the pen down. Michael looked closely at the signature. "Bienaimée?"

Celine nodded. "Family name."

He repeated it slowly, "Bienaimée. Beautiful." He looked at Celine. Her body was trembling with the cold. He reached over and put his arm around her. "Are you alright?"

Celine nodded. "I'm just glad that's over."

Cabrini pulled out a sheet of paper with writing on it. "You're doing great, Miss Dupré. Just a few more steps and we'll be done. Now, I need to fill out some paperwork while you answer a few questions for me, alright?"

Celine nodded as he poised the pen, ready to write. "I need you to tell me what distinguishing characteristics in the photograph make you certain number four is the man that robbed you."

Celine took a deep breath. "The main thing, I think, are the scars on his face and the decayed teeth; the hollow cheeks and the dread locks, of course, and those bloodshot eyes..." Celine shivered with the memory. "I can still see his eyes."

Cabrini finished writing then read from the sheet. "On a scale from 1–10, 1 being the least and 10 being the most, how certain are you that the person you've identified in the photo is the perpetrator."

Celine sat back, thinking. "I wish I could say a 10 but I'll have to say about an 8."

Cabrini frowned. "Why an 8?"

"Well, it's hard to tell if the man in the photo is as skinny as the man who robbed me; hard to tell how tall he is, too. His clothes were hanging off of him and his hands were long and bony. I mean his face certainly looks like the man who robbed me, but without seeing his whole body, I couldn't give you 100 per cent."

Cabrini nodded as he wrote. "I understand. Actually, this picture is about a year old."

Michael leaned forward. "So, did she identify the right one?"

Cabrini shook his head. "I'm not at liberty to say just yet." He turned to Celine. "I'd like for you to do a physical ID, Miss Dupré. Could you do that?"

Celine's heart began to pound. "You mean I have to pick him out from a lineup?"

"No, no, the guy we have in custody is in a room similar to this one." He pointed to the mirror in the room. "That's an observation window. We'll seat you in the observation area while we question him. Then you can tell us if he's the guy that robbed you."

"And you're sure he won't see me?"

"Oh, absolutely. He can't see or hear you. All you need to say is yes or no and you can take as much time as you need."

She turned to Michael and put a cold hand over his warm one. "You'll be there, too, right?"

Michael turned to Cabrini. "Is that all right?"

Cabrini nodded. "Yes, as long as you don't talk to her. She can't be influenced in any way." He turned to Celine. "I'll be there, too."

Someone knocked on the door, but before Vince could get up, a police officer poked his head through the door. "Jack's got him. He's in five. Better get in there if you wanna see him."

Vince turned to Celine. "Okay?"

Celine nodded nervously. "Okay."

Vince led Celine and Michael to another room no bigger than a large closet. He pulled out a chair for her behind the observation window. She sat down. Cabrini turned to Michael, "You just stand back a bit." Michael gave Vince a small frown as he took a small step back and leaned up against the wall, reluctantly.

Through the window, Celine could see a dark-skinned man seated at the table, leaning back in a chair on two legs, and the detective sitting across from him. A police officer was standing quietly nearby in the corner, his arms crossed. Vince sat down next to Celine. The detective's hoarse voice boomed through the speaker loud and clear. "Listen, we know you were on St. Ann. We've got a witness that puts you there, so why don't you just tell me about it." The young man didn't answer. He just stared defiantly at the man across the table. "We can wait all day, you know. No rush." The detective crossed his arms and waited.

Finally, the young man blurted out. "I ain't gonna answer your questions, detective jack-ass, so jus' give it up. That's your name, ain't it? Jack-ass? Lookit, I wasn't anywhere near there. I didn't have nuthin' to do with any of it!"

"What about your mama? Was she there?"

"My mama's home, sick in bed. She's got the flu. Everybody knows that! You better leave my mama out of it, ya hear?"

"Flu, huh? Word on the street is that your mama was right there. I even heard that she held a knife up to the girl's throat."

Celine leaned over to Vince. "Wait, that's not …"

Vince smiled. "Just watch. Jack'll get him to talk."

The young man sat forward in the chair, slamming the legs of the chair down on the cement floor. "Wasn't no knife, man." The detective sat like stone, staring straight at the young man. "D'ja hear me?"

The detective nodded. "Yeah, I heard you."

The young man flinched when he realized he'd said too much. He mumbled, "I don't gotta tell you nuthin'. I'm done talkin' to you, jack-ass."

The detective grinned tauntingly. "That's all you got? Callin' me jack-ass? Hell, even my mama called me jack-ass, boy! Now, Nathaniel, what kind of name is that? Nath-an-yawl." The detective drawled it out, carefully watching the young man seethe between deep breaths. "What about it, Nath-an-yawl?" Jack turned to the policeman standing nearby.

"Hey, Bob, don't ya think his mama must've been high on crack when she named him Nath-an-yawl?"

"You honky muthafucka!" In a flash, the young man jumped up and threw the chair at the detective's head. The detective ducked and the policeman moved like lightning, grabbing the young man by the shirt. The young man screamed. "The name's Rooster, asshole!" The young man jerked away from the policeman, ripping his shirt as he lunged over the table at the detective. The policeman grabbed him, pinned his arms and slammed his body up against the window. Celine jumped back, pushing the chair as far away from the window as she could get. Her heart was pounding as the young man screeched, "Let go of me you fuckin' pig!"

Celine stood up. Michael was at her side in a heartbeat and instinctively grabbed for her hand but Cabrini turned to him. "It's okay, man. She's okay. Get back."

Celine watched, her eyes wide. The young man's face was inches away from hers. "It's him! That's where I scratched him!"

Vince looked at her and then at the young man's face. "Are you sure those are your scratch marks? Look closely, now. Make sure."

Celine reluctantly moved closer and pointed to his cheek. "Yes, right there."

Vince pressed. "So you're positive it's him? One hundred percent?"

Celine stared through the window as the police officer handcuffed him. "Yeah, I remember now. His mother called him Nate, but then she called him Rooster."

Vince beamed. "We've got him then. Sit tight. I'll be right back."

Celine collapsed in the chair burying her face in her shaking hands as she listened to Rooster scream at the detective. "Get him off me, man! I ain't done nuthin'! This is police brutality!"

Michael sat next to her and pulled her to him. "It'll all be over soon."

The detective's voice boomed through the intercom as they sat waiting for Cabrini to return. "Sure, sure. You ain't done nuthin'. I'd say we've got an attempted assault on an officer going down here. Want me to ignore the charges on that? Start talkin'!" The policeman dragged the reluctant Rooster back to the seat. Just as he handcuffed him to the table, Cabrini stepped into the interrogation room.

"Jack, I need to talk to you."

The detective stood up and walked out of the room. The interrogation room grew quiet. Celine looked up. The policeman had once again resumed his silent vigil against the wall while the now-handcuffed Rooster sat at the table, panting from the struggle, his torn shirt hanging off one shoulder. Celine sighed and looked at Michael. "I'm so glad they've caught him."

The words lit a fire of hate in Rooster's eyes. He fixed his eyes at the window, zeroing in on Celine's face and screamed. "I see you, bitch. Yeah, I see you."

Celine sat straight up, pulling back. She turned to Michael. "Did he hear me? Oh God, he looked straight at me." Just then the interrogation room door opened and the detective walked back in. The detective turned to the policeman in the room. "Stand him up, Bob. We're takin' a little trip downtown." He turned to the young man, "Nathaniel David Rousseau, you're under arrest. You have the right to remain silent…"

As the detective finished reading the Miranda rights, Cabrini walked back into the observation room with a big smile spread across his face. "Well, how's that for…" He stopped when he saw the expression on Celine's face. "What's wrong?"

Michael shook his head. "Are you sure there's no way he heard anything from this side of the window?"

Cabrini looked at the speaker on the wall. "No, man. It's only one-way. Why?"

Michael frowned. "Because he looked straight at her and said..."

Celine groaned. "I'm sure he heard me. He looked right at me." *Just like his mother did through the mirror in my dream!*

Cabrini stepped inside the observation room, closing the door quietly behind him. "I promise you, Miss Dupré, there's no way he heard or saw anything. The creep's just messing with you. This isn't the first time he's been interrogated. He knows what the window's for. Right now, he's on his way to headquarters for the arraignment. Why don't we go back down the hall to the room we were in before? There are only a couple more things to cover and then we're done. Okay?"

Celine answered in a tired voice. "Okay." Cabrini stepped out of the way as Celine and Michael walked past him and into the hallway.

"Officer Cabrini?" Vince turned around and came face to face with Simone DaQuin. "I just heard the good news. Great job."

Vince nodded his head to Celine, smiling. "All thanks to Miss Dupré here."

The doctor looked at Celine. "Yes, Miss Dupré, Simone DaQuin." She put out her long slender hand; peach nail polish matched her crepe peach suit. "Nice to meet you." In her three-inch heels she towered over Celine. She turned back to Vince. "I've got the photos."

Cabrini smiled. "We were just headed back to Room 3. Let's all sit down in there."

Celine turned to Cabrini. "More photos? I don't understand."

Cabrini nodded as they walked up to Room 3. "Dr. DaQuin is a Special Investigator. She wants to ask you a few more questions so we can wrap this up."

Celine looked at Michael anxiously as she walked through the door and sat back down at the table. As Dr. DaQuin walked into the room, Celine asked her, "Why is there a need for a special investigation?" Her chills had turned into a cold sweat.

Simone sat down across from Celine. "I'm going to let Officer Cabrini explain first. He's the case officer." She turned and looked at Cabrini as he sat down next to Simone.

Cabrini smiled at Celine as Michael settled in next to her. "Well, yesterday, this case looked like a simple robbery with aggravated assault, one like a million others we've had here in the Quarter, but sometime in the early morning hours, Miss Dupré, someone broke into your old room at Hotel Ste. Jeanne and that changed everything."

"What?" Celine drew a quick breath. She turned to Michael and then back at Cabrini.

Michael spoke up. "They really did that? I can't believe it." He reached over and took Celine's hand. "That's probably why the lobby was filled with policemen this morning."

Cabrini's brown eyes grew hard as he stared at Michael. "You were there?"

Michael nodded. "Yeah. I went to get Celine for breakfast and while I was waiting in the lobby, I was real surprised to see so many police coming back and forth from the elevators."

Tears welled in Celine's eyes. "Thank God I changed rooms last night."

Dr. DaQuin nodded, her smooth Creole face wrinkled with compassion. "Yes, it was very astute of Officer Cabrini to tell the hotel that you needed a new room."

Celine looked at Simone and then at Cabrini. "Thank you for all your help. I don't remember if I've told you that but, oh God…"

Michael squeezed Celine's hand and then looked at Cabrini. "Vince, they couldn't have gotten anything. I made sure everything of Celine's was out of that room."

Cabrini looked at Dr. DaQuin and then back at Michael. "It's not what they took. It's what they left that has us concerned." He turned to Simone. "I think Dr. DaQuin should explain."

Celine tensed, fighting back the tears. Dr. DaQuin looked at her, seeing the ashen fear in Celine's face. "Miss Dupré, you need to know that right now, you're safe. You're in the police station. Your perpetrator has been arrested…" She looked over at Michael. "…and from what I can tell, you have someone here who cares for you and supports you."

Celine looked at Michael, squeezed his hand and then looked back at the doctor. "This whole thing has just been so overwhelming."

Dr. DaQuin smiled sympathetically. "I understand, but what we need to do is show you some photos of what we found. The purpose for that is to see if you have any idea why they would have left any of these items in your room. Maybe these pictures will jog your memory of something you saw yesterday or maybe something they said."

Celine looked over at Michael. Michael smiled reassuringly. "I'm not leaving."

Celine looked back at Dr. DaQuin and took a deep breath. "Okay." She leaned forward in her seat ready to see what Simone had to show her.

"Great." Simone opened the manila folder as Cabrini leaned forward, his arms resting on the table. Dr. DaQuin pulled the first photograph out of the folder.

Celine leaned over the photo. A heart with lines drawn inside it was the first thing Celine saw. She looked closer. *Oh God! Is that what I think it is?* She sat back and pushed the photo away. "What is this?"

Dr. DaQuin pushed it gently back over to her. "Have you ever seen this symbol?"

Celine answered quickly. "No, no. I don't know what that is." *I can't say a word. I promised. Please, don't ask me anymore about it.*

Dr. DaQuin leaned closer in to Celine. "Are you sure?" Her voice was calm but stern. "Could you please look again?"

Celine looked down nervously. "No, I'm sure."

Michael looked at the photo carefully. "Yeah, yeah. I've seen it." He turned to Celine. "It's on that box that you asked me to get for you from the trunk of your car, but..." he looked closer at the photograph. "...the engraving on your box doesn't have a knife through the heart. It has that squared grid with dots, though." he turned to Celine.

Celine could feel herself shaking. *Oh Michael! Oh Jesus, why did I ask him to get it out of the car for me?* She looked back at Dr. DaQuin. "Yeah, oh that. It's just a jewelry box with a heart on it." She tapped the photo. "This isn't the same thing." Celine looked back at Michael. "Right? It's not the same thing." *Please agree with me, please!*

Michael looked at her and then back at Cabrini. "That's right. What I saw didn't have this knife through it."

Cabrini shook his head. "It was painted on the mirror in the bathroom. Miss Dupré's picture was glued right in the center of it."

Celine echoed. "My picture? On the mirror?"

Cabrini softened his voice when he saw Celine's reaction. "We're going to move through this as quickly as we can."

Dr. DaQuin collected the photos and placed them back into the folder, calmly placing her hands over the cover. "I have another set of photos here. They're quite graphic."

A bead of sweat trickled down Celine's back. "I don't know how much more of this I can do."

"I'll do my best to make it brief." She reached back into the folder and pulled out another photo. "The maid found this as she went to make up the bed first thing this morning." Simone pushed the photo in front of Celine.

When Celine saw the rooster headed snake, she sat back. "Oh, my God! I can't look at this!" *This is what the old lady did, exactly like my dream! But it wasn't a dream. It's real! She really did it!*

Michael looked at the photo. As soon as he realized what it was he looking at, he turned to Vince, horrified. "What kind of sick…?"

Dr. DaQuin kept staring at Celine, her ice blue eyes watching her closely. "Miss Dupré, is there anything about this that you recognize?" Celine shook her head. "Did either of your perpetrators mention using such an item?"

Celine kept shaking her head. "No. No." She turned her face away.

Simone reached into the folder. "Okay, the last one." She pulled out the picture of the conjure ball. "What about this one?"

Celine looked at the photo. *A black conjure ball! They want me dead!* She felt the blood drain from her face. She closed her eyes and held tightly to Michael's hand, taking deep breaths until the moment passed. When she opened her eyes, she whispered. "No, no. I don't know." Celine slumped down in her seat, looking down at the table.

Dr. DaQuin put the photos back into the folder, closed it, sat back and looked at Cabrini. "That's it." She turned back to Celine and smiled. "I know this was hard, Miss Dupré. You've done quite well and helped us immensely."

Michael bristled. "But is she safe? I mean all those pictures. These people are sick! You arrested the man, but what about that old woman? As long as she's out there, God knows what else she'll do!"

Cabrini nodded. "We're working on it. She goes by Tante Zee, but her real name is Zeneethia LeGendre. She's a piece of work, that one."

Celine looked up only to see Dr. DaQuin staring at her. She felt like a fly caught in a spider's web. Celine nervously looked at Officer Cabrini as he continued talking. "She's smart, though, I'll give her that. She gets everyone around her to do her dirty work. Of course, that's usually only petty crimes…" He looked at Celine. "…but you triggered a whole new level of nasty out of her. We've got enough on the son that he just might give her up. The hotel surveillance tape was helpful, so we'll see."

Michael shifted in his seat. "Was it the old woman who broke into the room?"

Cabrini shook his head. "We don't think so, but we're getting some interesting information from the hotel staff … a couple of things do lead back to the mother." He turned to Celine." As for your safety, Miss Dupré, I think you're fine. That old woman can't do much with her son locked up in jail and believe me, he's gonna be there a while." He put both hands on the table. "Okay, well…" He stood up. "Thanks for your time; just a few signatures out front and you're free to go." Celine breathed a sigh a relief as she stood up. Cabrini walked around the table and opened the door. "If I need you for anything else, I'll call you at the hotel."

Celine walked alongside Michael toward the door. "I won't be staying at the hotel. Not now, that's for sure. I'm staying at the gallery. You can call me there."

Cabrini nodded. "That's probably a good idea."

Dr. DaQuin called from behind them. "Oh, wait, Miss Dupré. I just thought of something else. Could I have just a minute more?" Celine turned and then looked back at Michael.

Before she could say anything, Cabrini spoke up, looking at Michael. "Tell you what. How about you and I make our way to the front? You can sign your part of the paperwork and by the time you're done, she can meet us." He turned to Celine. "Okay, Miss Dupré?"

Reluctantly Celine nodded. "Um, okay, sure."

Michael heard the hesitation in her voice. He turned and looked at her. "I can stay if you like."

Dr. DaQuin sat back down. "Really, this won't take but a minute more."

Cabrini opened the door a little wider. Celine squeezed Michael's hand, trying to give him her best reassuring smile. "It's okay; I'll be there in a little while." As soon as he followed Vince out the door, Celine's heart sank. *Why didn't I just say I was too tired or something?* The door clicked shut. *Too late.*

Celine looked nervously at Dr. DaQuin as she sat down. She glanced up at the surveillance camera. Its beady green "on" light stared back.

Dr. DaQuin smiled. "I just want to talk to you…" She hesitated. "…about your jewelry box." Celine took a deep breath and waited. "The design that Michael was talking about, the heart without the knife, the squared grid and dots, that's quite a unique description. Was the box a gift from someone?"

Celine answered, hoping to redirect the question. "Yes, my grandmother gave it to me. She's a wonderful Cajun woman, really old school. You don't find them like her anymore. I…"

Simone interrupted. "Cajun, really? Where from?"

Celine gave a little sigh of relief. "St. Maryville."

Simone's eyes widened with surprise. "St. Maryville, you're kidding. My mother's family is from New Iberia. You're so lucky! What a beautiful area. I used to stay summers with my old granny down there. She was great! She just had a way of making everything so much fun, even going to daily Mass. You're Catholic, too, I bet?"

Celine laughed. "Of course."

Simone laughed in return as she reached under the table clicking the surveillance camera off. "It sounds like we've both been blessed with some special grannies. Does yours have an altar in her house? Mine had a two-tiered thing. I was always so scared to go into that room when I was a kid; all the candles and the incense, and at the very top was a statue of our family saint…" She wrinkled her dainty café-au-lait nose, jokingly. "…watching everything I did!"

Celine laughed, relaxing a bit with the camera off and Dr. DaQuin laughing, too. "Really? Mine has that; altar, family saint, except ours is three-tiered! Family saint right at the top! It was the same for me as a kid. I was scared to death of all that… "

Simone leaned back, smiling. "Does the name Ezilie mean anything to you?"

Celine was stunned into silence. Her smile wiped clean. Her face felt feverish. *Oh God. I knew it. Why didn't I leave with Michael?*

Simone smiled. "Your grandmother told you not to tell anyone, right?"

Celine's eyes grew wide. "I…no. I mean…"

Simone nodded knowingly. "Okay, let me do the talking. My family's patron saint is Ezilie, and your jewelry box, I doubt if that's what it really is, has her symbol engraved on it. A box like that is only given to her chosen healers. Now, I know you've pledged a vow of silence and you haven't broken that vow. Okay?"

Celine shook her head. "But..."

Simone interrupted her. "No, no, really. Say nothing. Let me finish. This old woman that robbed you, she follows a darker side of Ezilie that you probably know nothing about, so I'm going to explain it to you and tell you how you can really protect yourself. I'm also going to ask you a few questions." She opened the folder and began to spread the photographs out in front of Celine like a magician with a deck of cards. "If your answer is yes, just sit there. If no, then look away, okay?" Celine stared at her, silent, trying not to look down at the photos. Simone DaQuin nodded. "Wonderful." She tapped the photo of the rooster-headed snake. "Have you seen this before?"

Thirty minutes later, Celine walked down the hall and through the door to the lobby. As soon as she walked in, she gave Michael a tired smile.

Michael bolted up from his chair, his blue eyes pleading. "I'm so sorry. Vince told me to wait out here. I really wanted to go back to meet you, but they wouldn't let me. Apparently, after you get in the lobby, the door locks behind you. Is everything okay?"

She grabbed his hand. "Yeah, yeah. I'm beat. Let's get back to the gallery, okay?"

After she signed the paperwork, they walked together out of the police station into the street. The summer heat blasted them. "What did she want to talk to you about?"

Celine squinted in the late afternoon sun. "Mostly about my safety." *Okay, I can't tell you everything, but that part really is the truth.* "What time is it anyway?"

Michael looked at his phone. "5:15. Safety? But Vince said..."

Celine kept walking, looking straight ahead. "Oh, Dr. DaQuin said I was physically safe. She's more concerned about my emotional vulnerability. She talked to me about the stages that victims go through after a trauma." *She did say that. I promise, but she also told me that Mama's herbs were the best cure. Mo-maw, Mama, we don't have as many secrets as you thought we did! Bless them, they have no idea how close they are to Voodoo. No wait, Vodou. But is Dr. DaQuin right about Ezilie's dark side? Mama and Mo-maw have never said anything about that to me. I can't believe I told her everything! So much for my promises. I don't know whether to feel guilty or relieved…*

"Celine?" Michael reached down and took Celine's hand. When she didn't answer him, he stopped walking and called her name again. "Celine?"

She turned to him when she realized that he'd been calling her. "Oh Michael. I'm so sorry. I'm just exhausted. I think I need to lie down for a while."

Michael smiled sadly. "Of course. We're almost there." They started walking again. "Would you like to eat something first? You must be starved. I could throw something together. I'm not too bad of a cook."

Celine gave him a weak smile, thinking back to the carefree brunch she had eaten with Alex and Michael. "Thank you, but I can't eat. My stomach's in knots. Would you be offended if I just went straight up to bed? Maybe I can eat later."

As they stepped in front of the gallery doors, Michael pulled out his keys. "Offended? Of course not!" He unlocked the door and they walked into the dark gallery. A rush of cool air washed over them as Michael locked the door behind them. Celine closed her eyes, happy for the silence. "Let me get you upstairs. You look like you're about to drop where you stand."

Celine nodded wearily. "I think you may be right."

They made their way to the desk and through the mirrored door, up the stairs and down the hall to the workroom. Celine smiled as they reached her bedroom door. "I love this room. It's so bright and cheerful."

"You crawl into bed. I'll go back to the hotel and get your things. I'm sorry I didn't think about doing that earlier. There's a robe in the armoire you can use for now, if you'd like, and the bathroom's fully-equipped, so make yourself at home. If you need anything, just knock on that wall."

Celine gave a soft laugh remembering the fun they had before the trip to the police station. "Why? Will the skeletons come running?"

Michael reached up and pushed a strand of hair out of her face, gently hooking it behind her ear. He smiled. "No, but I will. My bedroom's just on the other side of it." Celine nodded weakly. Michael leaned down and brushed her cheek with a soft kiss. "You sleep well, Celine Bienaimée Dupré." A shiver of delight ran through her as he turned around. She closed the door quietly and stood there for a moment. She took a deep breath, the echo of his deep voice still sounding in her ears. *I love the way he says my name.*

She faced the room, listening to Michael's footsteps as he walked away. She looked at the bed, *Yes, sleep now*, and opened the armoire. Just as Michael had said, a beautiful, fluffy white robe hung on a scented hanger. She took off her white sundress, bra and panties dropping them on the floor and put the robe on. She buried her face in the plush fabric, moaning at the luxuriant feel of the collar. *Oh, it's so soft and it smells like gardenias.* She walked over to the bed, dropped onto the feather mattress, curled up and went to sleep.

CHAPTER 18

The moonlight fell across the bed; its long silver shards lay like fingers resting on the eyelet quilt. Celine blinked once; blinked again. *Is it night already? I must've slept for hours.* She sat up slowly, her bare feet stepping quietly onto the wooden floor. She stretched, a long cat-like bend, arching her back, feeling every inch of her sinew and muscle, and that's when she heard it—a soft scratching sound. She turned and looked around the room. Nothing. She waited, listening. She heard it again, *scratch, scratch, scratch* and then two quick *tap-taps*. She pulled her robe more securely and walked around the bed, toward the sound, *scratch, scratch, scratch...tap-tap.*

She walked, unafraid but annoyed by that sound. *Maybe someone left a radio on. A TV? Wait, it's coming from out there.* She walked out of her bedroom and into the vast workroom. She looked around the moonlit room, but no one was there. Frustrated, she stood, listening. *What IS that noise? Scratch, scratch, scratch...tap-tap.* She looked to her left. *It's coming from behind that door.* She walked over to the door, turned the doorknob slowly and stepped into another room.

As she moved through the moonlight, Celine could see someone seated in a chair, a woman, dressed in an emerald green taffeta gown, her long skirts billowing into folds at her feet. She was bent over an escritoire, holding a white feather in her hand, her thick raven hair cascading down her back. *She's writing. A letter maybe? Scratch, scratch, scratch...Oh, it's a quill pen and tap, tap...of course, that's the ink well.* As Celine stepped closer to the woman she could hear quiet sobs. "Miss? Miss? Are you alright?" But the woman kept on writing at a frantic pace, *scratch, scratch, scratch...tap, tap. What is she writing?* Celine stepped closer, looking over her shoulder, gently reaching out.

As Celine touched the woman's sleeve, her fingertips stung with a shock. The woman jumped, spun around in the seat and looked straight at Celine. "*Qui se trouve present?* Who is there?" Celine stepped back into the moon shadow as the woman put the pen down and stood up. "I know you are there. Come forward and show yourself, or are you a coward, come to kill me as I write?"

Celine was panting. *How...? This woman looks just like me!*

"*Montrez-vous!* Show yourself! At least let me see you!"

Celine timidly stepped forward, completely unsure of what would happen next. When the woman saw her, she drew back and breathed a small gasp. "Bon, Dieu! What trickery is this? A phantom sent to haunt me, perhaps? What did my enemy use to conjure my twin?"

Celine shook her head. *Is she French?* "I think I'm dreaming."

The woman cocked her head. "*Que?* What did you say?"

"I must be dreaming. I'll wake up and you'll be gone." Celine nervously pushed her hair away from her face. "I'll leave you to your writing now." She turned and took a step back into the dark shadows of the room.

"Wait! Do not go!" The woman spoke with such fierceness, Celine stopped immediately. "Let me look at you." The woman picked up a silver candlestick from the desk and held it high, melting the shadows and studying Celine's face. "Tell me, phantom, what is your name?"

Celine stood mesmerized by the woman in front of her. Her face, her hair, her eyes, everything about her was like gazing into a mirror. "Celine."

The woman stepped back, looking Celine up and down by the candlelight. "You say you are in a dream, yes?"

Celine nodded. "I think so, I'm not sure."

The woman lowered the candle. "Then tell me, am I dreaming, too?" Celine smiled. "Maybe. I don't know. All I know is that I was awakened by the scratching of your pen on the paper." The woman sat wearily back down at the desk. Celine stepped closer to her. "I've told you my name. Please, tell me yours."

The woman looked up at her, tears filling her eyes. "Adele."

Celine stammered. "You...you are Adele?"

"Quite clearly you have me at a disadvantage. You recognize me, but I do not know you. You have come before perhaps?"

Celine knelt at Adele's feet. "No, but my grandmother told me about you."

"Your grandmother? Pray tell, who is this woman?"

"We all share your name."

Adele shook her head. "*Mais, je ne comprends pas*, but I do not understand."

Celine took a deep breath. "We all share the name Bienaimée."

Adele leaned back in the chair. "But that is impossible. That name is only known to two people in this world. Me and…"

"…and Etienne."

Adele's eyes grew wide when she heard the name. "You have heard of him?" She reached down and took Celine's hands in hers. "Tell me, is he alive? Has he sent word? *S'il vous plaît*, tell me now. I must know!" The woman leaned down and kissed Celine's hands. "I beg of you…" She stopped when she saw Celine's ring, an exact duplicate to her own. The two rings glistened in the candlelight. Adele's face grew dim.

She sat up, still holding Celine's hand in hers. "How is it that you have this ring?" She looked into Celine's face, waiting.

"My name is Celine Bienaimée Dupré. The name Bienaimée, as well as this ring, were given to me by my mother and grandmother, both of them Bienaimée as well. They told me the story, your story, Adele, about the love between you and Etienne; how you never heard from him again but you stayed completely devoted to him, even taking the name he gave you, Bienaimée. You had his daughter and…"

Adele's face paled. "You know of the child in my womb? I have told no one of this. Not even Etienne knows yet! How is this possible?"

Celine looked at Adele sadly. "Because from your daughter, many daughters were born through the ages, all of them Bienaimée. I'm the seventh generation of those daughters."

Adele gently stroked the ring on Celine's finger. Her shoulders sagged. "So you are a messenger from the future, come to tell me what I already know in my heart." Tears dripped down her cheeks through the faint smile on her lips. She looked into Celine's eyes, green on green. "My Etienne is dead. He died on a far away battlefield. I know that now. I have known it for a while, but did not want to believe it." Adele's voice trembled.

Celine put her hand gently on Adele's shoulder. "Please, don't despair. I don't know what's happened to him. All I know is that he never returned. It's been a mystery to our family for many, many generations."

Adele turned her beautiful tear-stained face to Celine. "But I do. I know it. When his voice faded away from me, I went in search for him. I took Zombi's Cucumber and traveled through time. I broke all the rules and poured that horrible acid down my throat, night after night, determined to find him, or die trying. When I found his poor dead body, mangled and discarded, I thought my search was ended. I had hoped that I could join him in his cold grave and we might rest in peace together, but his soul had escaped. Hopeful, I searched on.

"I found his precious soul far into the future, living as an artist, under a different name but still just as handsome as I remember him; tall with thick black hair and eyes so blue, like a brilliant cloudless sky; his hands so gentle, his voice so deep. He stood before a great canvas and breathed life into me, stroking me, painting me into existence; such joy and bliss over many long sweet nights. He knew all about me, he even read my letters, those many, many letters I wrote to my Etienne that had never been answered. It was wonderful until one night, not long ago, he put his brushes down and I was forced back here, alone. I know my sweet artist is still there, caught in his place in that future time as I am caught here in the past. I do not know why he stopped painting me so suddenly, but ..." She stopped mid-sentence and stared at Celine. 'You say you are from the seventh generation?"

Celine looked at Adele, puzzled. "Yes."

She leaned back in her chair, her thoughts racing. "How far into the future, I wonder." She looked back at Celine. "You look exactly like me." She cupped her hand underneath Celine's chin, gently turning her face left and then right. She put her hands in her lap and leaned forward again, her eyes shining brightly. "There can be only one reason that he stopped painting my image. He must've found what he's looking for in his own time."

Celine shook her head. "I'm not sure what you mean."

"You have seen him! Surely you have seen him!" She looked at Celine hopefully, taking both her hands in hers. "He comes from the same time as you."

Celine shook her head. "If I have seen him, I..."

Adele held her hand up. "Listen to me! Search deep in your heart. I know you know him. His name is Michel!"

Mee shell?" What is she trying to say? Isn't that the French pronunciation of… Celine caught her breath. "…Michael? Do you mean Michael?"

Her smile broke through the tears as she whispered his name. "Yes, as you say it." She struggled to form the sounds. "My-kul." She reached out and stroked Celine's cheek. "You are so much more than cold paints and a lifeless canvas. He has been searching for you for such a long time. His heart has been tortured, but not anymore. He has found his eternal beloved. It is not me, *non!* It is you, Celine. He has found you!"

Celine let her face lean into Adele's warm hand. "But how can I be sure that it's me he really loves? Hasn't he been with you all this time?"

Adele breathed a tired sigh. "Yes, he has been with me, but it is you he has really wanted all along." She pulled the ring from her finger. "You are his Bienaimée…" She slipped the ring on Celine's hand. "…and now he is yours, forever and a night." Celine looked down, her body shaking as she watched the two rings meld into one.

Adele closed her eyes and smiled. "I can leave now. Take good care of him." She took a deep breath. "*Merci*, Celine Bienaimée." Her image began to fade. "*Être Joyeaux*, be joyous."

Celine stood up and called out. "Adele! Wait!"

A deep voice called to her. "Celine? What are you doing in here?"

"What?" She tried to step around the voice, but hands grabbed her and pulled her to it. "Please, let me go. I have to find Adele."

"Celine, you're dreaming. Wake up. Celine…"

Celine shuddered, her eyes coming into focus. "Michael? What are you…?" She stepped back. A single shard of moonlight came in from the window, casting a silver hue on his handsome, but sad, face. His smooth, dark eyebrows carved deep arches into his creamy white skin. His thick, night-black hair was a mop of curls and a hint of a beard covered his cheeks.

Michael looked at her pleadingly; the moonlight had transformed his normally bright blue eyes into a steel blue gray. "You're dreaming, Celine." He reached out his hand to her, waiting. His bare chest heaved with deep breaths. His gray sweat pants covered his long legs as he stood there, barefoot.

Celine looked around and in the faint moonlight she could see Adele right behind him, seated at her desk, quill pen in hand. "Adele?" She blinked, trying to chase the fog of the dream from her head. She turned to Michael. "I don't understand."

Michael took a small step toward her. "You're in my studio. Are you okay?"

Celine looked around the room. Canvases, both painted and empty, were leaning along the wall. A wooden workbench filled with charcoal sketches, paints and brushes stood nearby. A slight smell of linseed oil, muslin cloth and wood hung on the air. She looked up at the life-sized portrait of Adele at her writing desk just as she had been in her dream, but she was trapped inside the canvas, propped on an easel.

Celine closed her eyes and shook her head. "I'm so sorry. I know I shouldn't be in here. I sleepwalk sometimes. Really, I didn't realize…"

Michael gently took her hand and wrapped her in his arms. "It's all right." He stroked her hair. "I heard you talking. It took me a few minutes to realize that it was you."

She looked back up at the painting. "She looks like the woman from my dream. Her name is Adele."

Michael stared at her. "I…I heard you call her name. You dreamed that?"

"Yes, and she looked just like this. It's like you stepped into my dream and painted her exactly as I saw her." Celine looked up at Michael and cocked her head, puzzled. "How could you have known that?"

Michael sighed. "Because I've dreamed of her, too, just like this, many, many nights."

Celine looked into Michael's face as bits and pieces of the dream crept back into her mind. "Oh yes, I remember now. She said you even had her letters?"

Michael took a small step back, still holding her hand. His eyes grew wide. "She did?"

Celine nodded. "Yes, that's how the dream started out. I heard her feather pen scratching on the paper. She was writing it to…" Celine stopped. *Wait, I shouldn't tell him anymore of this. It's against the rules, isn't it? I shouldn't tell him about Adele and Et…*

"Etienne. She was writing it to Etienne."

She looked up at Michael. "Michael, how could you possibly know that?"

Michael took a nervous breath. "Because I do have Adele's letters. Let me show you." He led her to the foot of his bed. "Sit here." Celine sat down as he walked over to his night table, clicked on a small bedside lamp, and pulled out a letter from the drawer. He sat down next to her on the bed. He carefully opened the aged envelope, pulled out a letter and handed it to her. Celine took the letter and began to read:

26 October, 1812

My Dearest Etienne,

On this chilly, autumn night, I sit at my desk writing you this letter, hoping beyond hope that it finds you and brings you sweet, warm memories of me. Through my window, I can see the moon shining over Bayou St. John, bright and full. For the last half hour I have watched alone in the cold silence of its glimmering light, gazing upon the ripples of the water, wondering where you are and praying that you are safe.

Everyone around me has forgotten the terrible war you are fighting so far away in Russia. No one seems to know, or even care, about the fate of Napoleon's Grand Armée. Instead these foolish people of the Vieux Carré are drunk with happiness over our new statehood. They are like a pack of starving dogs, drawn to the blood scent of American dollars, convinced that we will all be sate with wealth. They are a mindless lot! Les gens stupides!

But I remember, my love, and know your sacrifice. In visions, I see the acres of killing fields before you, blanketed with snow-covered bodies, dark and still as you await yet another vicious battle. I

remember, too, the cruelty of your father,
sending you so far away, placing you
in the hands of peril all for the sake of
keeping you away from me, all for keeping
pure the Beauvoir bloodline!

I pray constantly, your name ever on
my lips. I beg St. Ezilie as well as The Great
God BonDye and any of His children that
might be listening: Please, bring my Etienne back to me! I have even prayed to
your Je'sus Catholique, who hangs on his
cross. Surely he would hear my cries of
pain and see the suffering that you endure!
But, no matter how loud I cry, the Divine
Ones are all asleep, damning me to a
lonely, abysmal silence.

My only escape is in the night that
comes after the long days are done. I fall
into dreams and recall your face, a sweet
spectre from my happy past. You call
me; whispering, 'Bienaimée', and I know
it's you. It can only be you. No one else
knows the name that you've given me. I go
to you, gladly, but just as you stroke my
face, you disappear, wrapped in the arms
of the Ange de la Mort, that greedy angel
of death. When I awaken I can still hear
her laughing as she carries you away.
I am haunted. The void of your absence
carves a deep hole into my heart. I would
gladly give up my soul if only I could be
with you forever.

The glittering engagement ring you
have given me is the only thing that stills
my troubled mind and holds me steady. I
remember the night you slipped the golden
promise of marriage on my finger, vowing
to return, calling me your Bienaimée,
your eternal beloved. The triple Fleur-
de-Lys of sapphires soothe me with the
memory of your deep blue eyes, the eyes

that were always so filled with love for me. The fire opal burns me with sweet memories of your passion, holding me, kissing me, caressing me, making love to me. I am your eternal beloved and you are mine.

Death may come and lifetimes may pass, but I will never stop searching for you. My ghost will walk this earth, an eternity if I must, to find you and love you again. If we must wait for that some distant future in an age that we cannot foresee, I pray that it will be a warm summer's twilight just like our first blissful time together. Do you remember? I will wait for you, my love, my Etienne, my Bienaimée. Je t'aime.

Forever and a night,
Adele Bienaimée

Celine stared at the faded name long after she finished reading it. Her thoughts were racing. Adele Bienaimée? She scanned the letter again, the aged and thin paper crinkling in her trembling hand. *Etienne, Adele, Bienaimée, the ring?* She stole a glance at the ring on her finger. She looked up at Michael. "Michael, where did you get this?"

He took a deep shaky breath, his face wrinkled with worry. "This letter was found in an old trunk that belonged to my Great Aunt Chloe. Her mother, my great grandmother was a Beauvoir."

Celine was stunned. "Your great grandmother?"

Michael nodded his head as he ran his hands nervously through his hair, one black curl falling onto his forehead. "Alex was very close to her, so when she died, he inherited everything of hers. When Alex opened the trunk, he found all these letters. I think there's about fifty of them in all. At first he thought he'd donate them to the Louisiana History Museum; I mean they're like a page torn out of 1800s French Quarter life, but I think out of respect for Aunt Chloe, he decided to just keep them private. I'm very glad he did, too, because…" He stopped and looked at Celine lowering his voice. "…because these letters kept me from making a huge mistake."

Celine leaned into Michael. The agonized look on his face made him look older than his years. She could tell that whatever the mistake was, it had been eating away at him for a long time. She reached out and gently placed her hand on his arm. "A mistake? What kind of mistake?"

Michael put his hand over hers; tenderly touching it like it was a fragile bird. "Do you remember hearing in the news about that huge oil tanker that exploded out in the Gulf?" Celine nodded. "Well the whole thing was the fault of my family's company, Arnaud Oil. After that, my father decided that we needed to 'clean house', as he called it, and started firing people right and left. It was absolutely horrible. Some really good and competent people, some of them who'd been with the company for years, were gone overnight. Some of them were ruined, their lives were shattered. I couldn't stand it, so I begged my father to stop. He could've done it but all he wanted to do was cover his..." He paused and took a short breath. "He and I got into a terrible argument. I mean, we'd had arguments before, but nothing like this. He said horrible things, cruel things." He stopped and shook his head as if to shake the memory from his mind. "I told Alex what happened and he stood by me all the way. I didn't talk to my father for several weeks. Poor Alex watched me swing from total outrage over how cruel my father was to being consumed with fear that I might be just as cruel as he is. Then the guilt would set in and I'd try to rationalize all his actions.

"It was one of those nights when I had almost decided to give in and go crawling back to him that Alex pulled out these letters and explained to me that our family was made up of two types of men, cruel bastards and those that suffered because of them. He said that after I read them, I might see which type of man I was born to be. I read them, all of them, but it was this one in particular that changed everything for me. I could see this poor woman, this poor Adele, sitting at her desk, crying as she wrote it. Worse, I could see the man, my great-great whatever, Etienne Beauvoir, wanting to be with her, but unable to because his sadistic father sent him off to war just to keep the two of them apart.

"After that, it all made sense. My own father certainly had inherited the 'cruel bastard' gene. It was easy to see that his appetite for controlling and manipulating people, all for the sake of money, would never change. My decision was easy; I could never work with him again. Of course, I didn't understand the depth of his evil until the night I told him I wasn't coming back. He said he never wanted to see me again; that he would disown me. He's forbidden my mother to ever contact me. I can't even return to the house. At first, it was like he'd ripped my heart out. Alex helped me as much as he could, but he was so sick. The only one that I had was Adele. She understood.

"I picked up my brushes and started painting her, this beautiful Adele, my Lady of the Letters. Night after night, I painted her into existence and somehow, someway I was helping her find her Etienne and she was helping me heal, giving me my heart back. So, when I met you…" He sighed. "When I first saw you, you looked so much like my Adele." Michael took Celine's hand in his and looked at the ring. "And then I saw this and I wondered how you could've ended up with a ring that looked so much like the one Adele described in the letter. Then earlier today, when you said your middle name was Bienaimée, I…" He closed his eyes and took a deep breath. "Celine, is it possible that…" He stopped and squeezed her hand, trying to stay calm. "…Just now, you said her name, you called her Adele. I know it sounds crazy but after so many coincidences, well, it's got to be more than that, right? Just saying it out loud, I know you must think I've lost my mind. I don't know, maybe I have."

Celine stared at him, his eyes burning into her with a tortured, desperate hope. An overwhelming sense of *déjà vu* filled her. *I've seen him look at me like this before, but when? Where?* She took a quick breath as the memories flooded in. *Michael! Oh God, my nightmare… he was brutalized by that monster. The look that was on his face, his slight beard, his eyes, that's how he looks right now!*

Michael pulled back. "Oh, what am I saying?" He dropped her hand and looked at the floor again. "I'm sorry; I sound like a raving lunatic. I won't blame you if …Forget I said any of this. I'll…" He took the letter from her and hastily folded it, placing it back into the parched envelope. He started to stand up.

Celine reached over and took his hand in hers, pulling him back. "Shh, shh, no! No, Michael, it's not crazy, it's…" The thoughts that had been racing through her head were suddenly calm. Her eyes filled with tears. Her voice was barely above a whisper. "…Everything you've said is true. This ring did belong to Adele and it was given to her by a man named Etienne Beauvoir." She stopped. Her hands were shaking. "But he was forced to leave New Orleans by his father to fight in Napoleon's Army. She never heard from him again." Her voice began to tremble. "She had a daughter, and from that time on, adopted for herself the name Bienaimée, a name that he gave to her. The ring and the name have been handed down from generation to generation. My grandmother gave it to me to wear until it's time for me to give it to my daughter, the next Bienaimée…" She stopped and looked at Michael. "… the next eternal beloved." She could hear Adele's voice. *'You are his Bienaimée, and now he is yours, forever and a night.'*

Michael's face was flushed, his lips a deep red. He looked at Celine through tear-rimmed eyes. He pulled her to him, holding her close. She could feel her body soften with his touch. He stroked her hair as he kissed her brow. His deep husky voice rumbled as he spoke. "Do you know how long I've looked for you? Night after night, as I painted her, I was falling in love with you. She brought you to me, you know, my Lady of the Letters. I dreamed of you. I thought I was dreaming of her, but it was you all along. I knew it when I met you but I was so afraid that I was…"

Celine ran her fingers through his thick hair and whispered, "She knew. Adele knew that we were meant to be together. She told me in the dream."

He leaned down and looked at her. "My God, can this be happening?" He kissed her cheek. His deep voice filled her with desire as he whispered. "You truly are my Bienaimée." His open lips brushed her cheek.

The word seared through her as she felt his lips touch hers lightly, like the first sweet drops of a warm rain. He pressed into her, his tongue searching for hers. She opened her mouth hungrily. She moved her hands up into his soft, curly hair, then down his long, muscular back. She let herself fall gently as he pushed her softly into the pillows, her bath robe opening, revealing her naked body. He leaned over her, his smile was filled with a desire she'd never seen in any man before. He whispered as he kissed her again, "You're so beautiful, every part of you…"

Celine moved her fingertips over his sculpted chest and down to his hard, flat abdomen. She sat up and kissed his shoulder, soft groans coming from her throat. She kissed his neck, letting her lips move hungrily to this mouth.

His hands moved up her thighs, under the robe as he kissed her in return. He pulled the robe from her arms, letting it fall to the bed. He kissed her stomach, then her breasts, sucking them gently as he cupped them in his smooth hands, massaging and stroking, with slight pinches to the tips of her nipples. Celine could feel his hot breath as he kissed her throat and the nape of her neck as he laid her back gently onto the bed and followed her down.

Slowly, gently, his hands moved down her body, caressing the hair between her legs. Celine moaned with the pleasure and the pain of expectancy. She reached down, placing her hand lightly over his as she whispered in his ear, "I want you." She arched her back as he curved his fingers to fit inside her. With trembling hands, she slipped his pants off stroking his penis, now hard with desire.

He thrust his fingers into her as he brought his mouth down between her legs. He smelled her as his tongue danced lightly in and out of her. She was wet with desire. He pulled his mouth away and saw her legs wide open, ready. He moved on top of her, leaving a trail of kisses up her body as he mounted her. He let his hands leave her wetness only when he penetrated her.

Celine could feel all of him, entering, filling her. She opened her legs wider as his hard desire pressed into her from all sides. He searched for her mouth as the rhythm of his thrusting lit the fire of her orgasm from someplace deep within her. She found him and met him on the other side of pleasure. It was a long, delicious, blazing heat. She wrapped her legs around his back as he thrust, over and over, deeper and deeper. She let out a small cry as she peaked, then peaked again, then again. He held her close as she came, and then he joined her, unable to wait any longer, exploding into her. He felt every part of her and for one small moment, he knew she had opened everything to him. Everything.

She felt him as they lay together. She could still feel his fire burning, vibrating through her body. She could feel his warm, wet seed deep inside her filling her in the dry empty places that she never knew she had. She cried, cried like she hadn't cried in a very long time. Cried and he pulled her to him; cried and he rocked her, stroked her hair. When the last of the tears had fallen and they lay together quietly in each others arms, Celine looked into his smiling face and kissed him gently. "Am I still dreaming?"

He hugged her tightly and whispered. "If you are, then I am, too, and I don't want either of us to ever wake up." Michael let out a little laugh, his chest rumbling with the happy cadence. "I have to say, being in a dream with you is quite wonderful."

Celine let herself curve into Michael, the warmth of his body blanketing over her. She could smell his skin—a light scent of sandalwood and cedar. "Believe me, I'd much rather be in this dream with you than the other one I used to have."

Michael turned over on his side, propping his arm up under his head, facing her. He ran his fingertips down her cheek. "What other one?"

Celine looked into Michael's face, her hair fanned out on the pillow. "I guess while you were dreaming of Adele, I was dreaming of you."

Michael smiled. "What?"

"But I didn't know it was you, until tonight. I mean, when we first met, I wondered if the man in my dream might be you, but you didn't have this when I first met you." She reached up and playfully scratched the stubble on his face. She could still feel the tingle of his beard down the length of her body, marking the trail of kisses that he'd left.

He took her hand and rubbed his stubble in her palm and then kissed it. "You mean I was an unshaven bum in your dream? Great!"

She laughed. "No, not a bum, but..." Her smile faded as she remembered.

Michael frowned. "You look so sad. What was this dream?"

Celine sighed. "You remember Alex's monster painting?"

"Oh great, you dreamed of that thing? It would give anyone nightmares! Alex should've never shown you..."

Celine gently smoothed his wrinkles away with her fingertips. "I'd dreamed of his monster before I ever saw the painting, before I ever even met either of you."

Michael looked at her with sad eyes. "What? But that's horrible! I was in it too?" His eyes widened. "Please tell me that the monster wasn't me."

Celine touched her fingers on his lips. "No, no, far from it." She moved her fingers and kissed him gently. "Far, far from it."

Michael put his arm around her, pulling her closer into him. "Okay, now you have to tell me this dream."

Celine smiled and put her hand over his heart. She could feel the low, steady thrum of his heartbeat pulsing into her palm. "It's pretty weird. Are you sure you want to hear it?"

Michael leaned down and touched his forehead to hers, smiling. "Weird? Really? I think weird is already part of our relationship. What's a little more weird added to the mix?"

Celine turned over on her side, propping her head up with her hand, facing him. "Okay, but after you hear it, you might have second thoughts about me."

Michael reached over and tapped her nose. "Second thoughts and third thoughts and fourth thoughts and all of them good thoughts, okay?"

She took a deep breath, reached down and took his hand. "I'm in a confessional at church with a priest, and his name is Father Mauvais…"

CHAPTER **19**

Celine snuggled deeper under the covers, the delicious memories of making love to Michael the sweet night before flooding through her. She purred softly as she reached across the sheets for him, but he wasn't there. She opened her eyes. A single white rose was lying on his pillow. She smiled and picked it up. *How sweet!* She ran her hand over the surface of the pillow. It still had the indention where his head had been. She leaned over and buried her face in the soft fluff, taking a deep breath. Her body quivered with desire as she smelled his musky scent. She closed her eyes and rolled over on her back, listening to the soft patter of rain outside. *Oh, that sound is so nice. There's only one thing that could make this moment more perfect and that would be Michael right next to me. I wonder where he went.* She opened her eyes once again. Sunlight filled the room. She frowned. *Wait, I thought it was raining?* She sat up realizing that it wasn't raining at all. The sound of trickling water was coming from behind the door in the far corner of the room.

She listened. *He must be taking a shower.* She looked around the room. On a table near-by was a tray, set with buttery croissants and hot coffee. She stepped quietly out of bed and over to the tray. *When did he bring this in here? I must've been sound asleep.* Celine turned when she heard music coming from the bathroom. *Is he singing in the shower?* She smiled an impish little grin, tiptoed to the bathroom and put her ear close to the door. She could hear music and clearly he was singing with it. *What is he singing?* She knocked very softly and waited. When he didn't answer, she turned the doorknob and stepped into the bathroom. She smiled as she heard his low, soft singing coming from behind the fogged glass.

♫ *"Your precious love means more to me than any love could ever be..."* ♫

Celine stifled a delighted little laugh as she crept stealthily to the glass. *Otis Redding. Wow, he's got a great voice.*

♫ *"Your precious love means everything in the world to me…"* ♫

He'll never hear me if he keeps singing like that. Her bare feet padded soundlessly on the cool yellow travertine tile. As she crept closer, she could see that he had shampoo in his hair. *Good. He's got his eyes closed.*

♫ *I'm wanting you, keep wanting you, nobody but you…* ♫

She crept closer, admiring his handsome body. *Just how tall is he? 6'2", 6'3"? Those long muscular legs and his shoulders…* He rinsed his hair just as she got to the glass door.

♫ *I've just got to have you right here with me.* ♫

She slipped quietly inside the multi-jet stall, feeling like she'd walked into a warm waterfall. When she closed the door, it made a soft click. He stopped singing and turned around, the last of the suds running over his chest. When he saw her, he startled, laughing. "How long have you been standing there?" He stepped toward her.

"Long enough to enjoy watching you and hearing you sing. You've got a lovely voice…" She wrapped her arms around his neck and kissed him, the water pouring over them both. "…and a lovely body, too."

"Now this is a very nice Good Morning." He kissed her.

Celine smiled as she nuzzled his neck. "I wanted to thank you for the beautiful rose."

"Wow!" He laughed. "I'll make sure to get you roses every morning then!" He rubbed his soapy hands down her back and over her buttocks.

"Mmmm, that feels nice." She reached up and rubbed his smooth cheek. "This feels nice too. You shaved."

Michael looked down at her. "I couldn't get it shaved off fast enough! After that wicked dream you told me about last night, I figure if I never have a beard, both of us will be safe."

Celine laughed. "Well, I'm not sure if that's how it works, but…" She let her hands outline the contour of his shoulders and then down the curve of his back, pressing her breasts into his chest. "…a beard would only hide your handsome face. I like you like this."

"Really?" Michael's voice was a whisper. "I like you like this, too." He reached his hands into her hair and let his fingers gently comb a few strands. "You have the most beautiful hair." He reached over to the wall dispenser and pumped a little shampoo into his palm and then rubbed it into her hair, massaging her scalp.

Celine closed her eyes. "And you're a masseur, too?" The soap trickled down her breasts. "I am one lucky girl." She let out a quiet little groan as he rinsed her hair letting the warm water wash over them.

Michael rubbed the suds over Celine's naked body like a sculptor at work, his strong hands cupping her breasts. He bent down and gently kissed each nipple and traced his slightly-parted lips to her neck, into her hair and onto her mouth. He kissed her, teasing her tongue with his. Celine could feel his penis, hard, ready. She curled one leg around his back, resting it on his tight buttocks. She reached down between his legs and took him in her hand. Michael groaned, ever so slightly, as she slid her hand slowly back and forth. With one move, he picked her up, thrusting his tongue into her mouth. She put her arms around his neck as he pinned her against the cool, wet tile.

Their eyes met as he penetrated her. He pushed hard and Celine could feel every part of her pulsating with heat. The weight of her body thrust him deep inside her. Celine felt the rush of her orgasm explode between her legs, racing its way up through her. She could hear herself moaning in pleasure, but the voice didn't sound like it was hers. She felt herself close down on him, pulsating with him again and again. He pushed harder, harder until she thought she would break. He slowed, panting. The water rushed over their shaking bodies. Michael steadied himself. He let her down and pressed up against her with a deep kiss. Celine looked up and could see that he was staring down at her out of breath, the water dripping from his face like droplets of rain. He smiled. "God." His deep voice was a hoarse whisper. "I've never wanted anyone the way I want you!" He kissed her.

Celine kissed him back, holding him close. "No one has ever made me feel like this."

Michael kissed her forehead and let out a little groan of pleasure. She kissed his chest and smiled. He looked down, his face suddenly serious. "But we're going to have to be careful."

Celine frowned. "Of what?"

He gave her a playful little grin. "We could drown in here." He reached over and turned the water off then looked back at her. "Is it possible to die from too much sex?"

Celine laughed. "I don't know." She stepped back and ran her fingertips down his chest. "I've never been with anyone where that was even a remote possibility."

Michael shook his head in disbelief as he kissed her fingers. "You are kidding, right? What kind of guys have you dated?" He opened the shower door and took her hand. "They must've been brain-dead!" As they stepped out of the shower, he handed her a towel and grabbed one for himself.

She laughed as she dried herself off. "Probably. I've dated a few jerks. Maybe that was the problem. They were brain-dead and I didn't even realize it."

Michael dried himself off and wrapped the towel around his waist. "Yeah, well, I've dated a few brain-dead women, too, but uh…" He walked over to her as she dried her hair. "I'm very glad to say that all that is happily in my past."

She looked into his eyes and smiled. "Me, too."

He leaned down and gave her a gentle kiss on the lips. "I just can't believe that some guy didn't try to grab you up before now."

Celine gave him a weak smile as she wrapped the towel around her body, tucking the end in at her cleavage. "It almost happened."

Michael took her by the hand and opened the bathroom door. "Oh, and who was this very stupid guy that let you get away?"

Celine gave him a small frown as she walked into the studio. "No one who could ever compare to you." She turned around and faced Michael as he stood next to her. "Besides…" She let out a little sigh. "It's because of you that he and I broke up."

Michael gave her a puzzled look. "Okay, let's have some coffee while you explain that to me." He gently put his hand at the small of her back as they walked over to the tray. He picked it up and placed it on the bed.

They sat down as he poured a cup of coffee and handed it to her.

Celine stirred a little cream and sugar into the cup. "It was the dream that broke us up."

Michael poured himself a cup of coffee. "You mean the monster dream?" He lay on his side, propping himself up on his elbow and listened.

Celine nodded. "Yeah, I'd wake up screaming most nights and let's just say he didn't have a whole lot of patience with that."

Michael frowned. "What did he do?"

She sipped her coffee. "Mostly all the wrong stuff. 'Wanted me to take a lot of pills so it would all go away. I was even foolish enough to take them, too. Really, he just didn't want to be bothered. When that didn't work, we'd argue which only made everything worse."

Michael reached over and pushed her hair from her face. "What a jerk."

"Yeah, well ..." Celine placed her half-full cup back on the tray. "... I realize now that it just wasn't meant to be. My dream was telling me all along that you were the one I was searching for and now, here we are." Michael leaned over and kissed her on the cheek. Celine playfully pushed him away. "Now, your turn. Surely there's been a woman, or two or three, that's tried to have you all to herself?"

"Oh." Michael gave her a little side smile. "There've been a few." He grabbed a croissant from the tray. "Want one?"

She nodded, laughing. "Yeah, but don't try to change the subject. Confess!"

He handed her the croissant. "There was one. She was a sorority debutante; definitely high maintenance." He rolled his eyes. "My mother adored her. When I quit the company, the breakup was mutual. She realized that there wasn't going to be the kind of money she was used to and all I wanted was to paint Ade..." He stopped. "You. All I wanted was you."

Celine took a bite of the croissant, but then put it down. "So then my biggest rival is Adele?"

Michael put his croissant down and wiped his fingers on a napkin. "No, you have no rival. I don't want to be with anyone but you. Besides, a painting is no substitute. Not even close."

Celine sipped her coffee and gave him a teasing smile. "Yeah, right. And how many paintings have you got of Adele, anyway? I know how you suffering male artists are. A woman can never measure up to the muse in your mind, right?"

Michael stared at her, all hints of a smile gone from his face. "She may look like you, but she isn't you, not at all. And to prove that there's no one but you, I'll get rid of them."

Celine's smile faded when she realized that he was serious. "Oh wait, no! I don't want you to do that. Please, don't get rid of them. She's the reason we're together. Destroying her is destroying a part of us, isn't it?"

He paused. "I guess I hadn't looked at it like that." Michael wrinkled his brow, sat up, putting his coffee cup on the tray. "Why don't I show them to you, then you can tell me what you'd like for me to do. I'll do whatever it is you want."

"I'd love to see them."

"Okay, but…" He took her coffee cup and placed it on the tray next to his. "There's only two here in my studio." He stood up and reached out to take her hand. "The rest are in a storage room downstairs."

Celine took his hand and stood up. As she walked with him to the back of the room she saw once again the painting of Adele at the writing desk. She stopped for just a moment to admire it in the full light of day. "You really are an amazing artist, you know. She looks exactly like I saw her in the dream." She reached out and touched the ring on Adele's finger remembering that moment when the two rings melded into one. "Exactly."

Michael smiled. "That was the first one I did. It's my favorite. This other one runs a close second." He led her to a covered easel, walked over to the muslin cloth that covered the painting and pulled it down. An older Adele, dressed in a simple calico dress was looking proudly at a young and beautiful flaxen-haired, teenaged girl. The smiling girl was dressed all in white; a garland of flowers circled her head like a halo. The soft wisps of a veil fell to the ground, to her white satin slippers.

Celine stepped closer to the painting, reaching out to touch the face of the young beauty. She turned to Michael. "You really are a master at portraits. The skin looks so real." She looked back at the young girl. "This is Celeste?"

Michael nodded his head. "Yes. Adele only mentioned her daughter in two of the letters to Etienne. One said she was pregnant with a girl. I'm not sure how she knew that, other than her mother told her the baby was a girl. There's no other mention of the child until her last letter where she tells him Celeste is getting married to a Beauvoir; a fourth cousin, I believe was what she said."

Celine gave him a little laugh. "I remember when my mother told me that Celeste had married her cousin. I thought that was really gross, but she told me that was how it was done back then."

Michael gave her a little smirk. "Hmmm, could this mean we're related?"

Celine frowned. "Ewwww!" She turned and gave him a little poke in his side. "Hardly! Maybe you're like my 58th cousin or something, but uh, we're not gonna think about that!"

He laughed. "Believe me, I'm not thinking about it." He leaned down and kissed her.

She stepped back and looked at the entire painting. A massive, white-columned plantation house stood in the background, its double stairway gracefully winding from the first floor veranda to the second floor balcony. A small entry way sign had the words *BelleAnge* engraved. She turned to Michael. "My mother told me about this place. It was where the Beauvoir's lived."

"Yeah, it's still in the family and it sounds like, from one of the letters, the daughter married there. But how do you know about Celeste?"

Celine looked back at the painting, thinking. *The Bible. I could show him the genealogy in the Bible. I guess it doesn't matter anymore. I already blew it yesterday with Dr. DaQuin.* She turned and looked at Michael. "I've got something to show you. It might explain this painting a little. It's in my room." She looked down at the towel still wrapped around her body. "I'll change while I'm there and be back in a jiffy."

Michael gave her a curious smile. "Something that will explain the painting?"

"Yes, get out those two letters you were talking about, too. I'd like to see them."

She turned to walk away but Michael pulled her back, smiling. "Not without a kiss first."

Celine smiled and gave him a quick kiss. "Be back in a sec." She hurried to the bedroom door then stopped and turned around. "Were you able to get my suitcase from the hotel?"

"Yeah, I put it just outside your door. I kind of threw everything into it. I didn't want to stay at that place any longer than I had to."

Celine nodded. "Thank you for doing that." She hurried out the door and through the workroom, picking up her suitcase as she walked past it. She dropped the towel as she unzipped her bag, took the box out and set it on the bed. She slipped on a pair of panties, and rummaged around for her white capris. She looked around in her suitcase. *God, it looks like an animal's been living in here. Oh, here they are.* She put the pants on with a lemon yellow tank top, quickly brushed her hair, opened the box, took out the Bible and hurried back to Michael.

When she walked back in, Michael was dressed in jean shorts and a faded Neville Brothers T-shirt, sitting on the side of his bed, thumbing through a stack of letters, a red ribbon lying near-by. She placed the Bible on the bed and sat next to him. "Are these her letters?"

"Yeah, here's the one about the baby. It's not very long, but it's very interesting. It's dated about one month from the one you read last night." He handed the letter to Celine, leaned in and read over her shoulder.

November 28, 1812

My Dearest,

I have wonderful news! Etienne, we are to have a bébé!

Maman has seen the future and tells me that all the signs say it will be a girl, born in April. A petit femme, Etienne! Our little girl! What a wonderful joy to have some-thing of our love growing inside me. Every day I speak to her and tell her of her father who will someday return to us. Lady Beau-voir is thrilled and has sworn to me to get this news through to you.

Even she, my love, does not understand your silence. I will never stop my efforts to reach you. Please, you must return to me now. Our sweet enfant needs her papa! I wait in joy. My love is yours eternally, Père Beauvoir!

All my love,
Adele Bienaimée

Celine looked up at Michael. "This is incredible."

Michael pointed to one sentence. "What does she mean, 'Maman has seen the future'...? That part's a little confusing."

Celine handed him the letter and then reached over and pulled the Bible onto her lap. "I have something for you to see." She opened the Bible to the family genealogy.

"How old is this?" Michael leaned down looking at the faded ink inscriptions.

"I'm not sure but you can see Adele's name here." She pointed to the first name written. "And then here's Celeste's name."

Michael nodded as he studied the page. "There're birth dates and death dates but no marriage dates or even who they married. Is there a reason for that?"

Celine shrugged her shoulders. "Maybe because Adele and Etienne were never legally married? I'm not sure about that, either, but there's an oral history that's been handed down from generation to generation."

Michael looked at her, a slight frown on his face. "Oral history?"

Celine nodded. "My grandmother and mother know the story backward and forward. They told me that Adele and Etienne had a little girl and Adele named her Celeste."

"Yeah..." Michael looked back at the letters and pulled out another one. "Yeah, look right here." He opened the letter and handed it to Celine.

April 23, 1828
Belle Ange

My Dearest Etienne,

Everyone thinks I am mad to write you this letter. Fou dans la tête! Even Lady Beauvoir has said that this effort is fruitless, but they do not know the depth of our love. You may not ever read these words, but it makes no difference. Wherever you are, I know you hear me.

Celeste has just told me that she will marry. She is to marry your fourth cousin, the Marquis de Fontainebleau, Jacques Beauvoir. The wedding will be at Belle

*Ange. Your Aunt, the Lady Beauvoir, is
making all the arrangements. It is a good
union. They love each other. Maybe in
some small way they will have the love
that we once had. It is my prayer for them,
though Ezilie has been silent. Still I will let
nothing stand in their way, not even Ezilie!*

*Etienne, I am old now but I still feel the
love of my youth for you. If only you would
come back to me. To have you seated at my
side at our daughter's wedding would be
a gift eternal. I will never give up hope of
finding you.*

*Forever and a night,
Adele Bienaimée*

Celine sighed when she read the letter. "So sad. She never knew that
he was killed in battle." She turned to Michael. "How did your family
end up with these letters? You said they were in a trunk?"

Michael shrugged his shoulders. "Alex found them in Aunt Chloe's
stuff after she died. Maybe somehow this Lady Beauvoir ended up with
them." He turned and picked up the red ribbon. "They were tied with
this in a neat little stack."

Celine took the ribbon from him, turning it over in her hand. "I
think you may be right. Mo-maw told me that the Lady Beauvoir was
the only one who helped Adele and Etienne. While everyone else was
trying to keep them apart, this very nice woman did everything she
could to give them a place to meet. I guess it makes sense that she
would have saved Adele's letters."

Michael reached over and put his hand over hers, touching the
ribbon. He leaned down, kissed her hair and pointed to the empty line
on the genealogy. "Why is this line blank?" He looked closely at the
line. "It doesn't look like anything was ever written there. Just dates."
He turned and looked at Celine, waiting.

Celine took a deep breath and looked back at Michael. *It's better
that he know now, rather than later.* "That's Adele's mother."

He looked back at the Bible. "So they didn't know her name?"

Oh, what is he going to think when he hears the truth? "No, they knew her name. They just wanted to keep it a secret."

Michael frowned. "Why would they want to do that?"

Celine bit her lip as she answered. "Because she was a *voodooiene*." She closed her eyes, waiting for his reaction. When he didn't say anything, she opened her eyes. He was still looking at the Bible. Surprised, she reached out and touched his hand. He looked at her. "Did you hear me?"

"Yeah."

"And that doesn't bother you?"

Michael looked at her and shook his head. "Not really. It sort of explains the letter. You know, how Maman saw into the future. In the other one, she talks about The Great BonDye and a Saint Ezilie, I believe. I looked all that up. Those are all Voodoo references for Gods. So yeah, she practiced Voodoo."

Celine sat back. "You've really done your research."

Michael shrugged. "I had to do something when I started reading all these letters. I had so many questions. I found out that Voodoo in New Orleans was sort of commonplace in the 1800s. I've lived here all my life and well, it makes sense. I mean, it's not like her mother was Marie LaVeau, right?"

Celine felt the blood drain from her face. She swallowed hard before she answered. "Um, well, her mother was Marie LaVeau."

Michael looked at Celine and laughed, but when he saw the expressionless look on her face, he stopped. "Wait, you're serious?"

Celine nodded nervously. "I probably shouldn't have told you. I'm sorry." She closed the Bible and started to get up from the bed.

Michael put his hand over hers. "Whoa there! Stop, Celine, stop!" She stopped but looked down, waiting. "Celine, please, look at me." She looked up. "Listen, it's okay. I guess I'm not really surprised. Besides, it's kinda cool! Wow! You're related to Marie LaVeau! Wait until Alex hears this!"

Celine shook her head. "No, no. Michael, this can't be made public." *Oh Jesus, why did I show him this?* Please, promise me you won't tell anyone!"

Michael's eyes grew wide when he saw the look of desperation on her face. "Okay, sure. Look, don't worry. I won't tell anyone." He pulled her to him and gave her a warm hug. "Really, I mean it. I don't know why, but if you tell me not to tell anyone, I won't." He sat back, leaned down to look into her face and said gently, "I promise, Celine."

Celine gave him a half smile as she looked up at him. "I had the exact same reaction as you when I first learned all this. To be related to Marie LaVeau sounds pretty cool, but yeah well, it has its downside, too."

Michael hugged her again. "What could the downside be?"

Celine sighed. "Well, I might as well tell you everything." She sat up and turned her body to face Michael. "My mother and grandmother are healers. In the Cajun tradition, they're called *traiteuse*."

Michael nodded. "I read about that."

"Yeah, well, it all started with Marie's mother. She was a healer in her tribe in Africa before she was enslaved. Marie taught Adele everything she knew but there was a family rift after Marie died. That's when Adele moved to Belle Ange. After she died, Celeste took her daughter, um…" she opened the Bible again and ran her finger down the names. "Yeah, here it is, Fremanse. Celeste brought her to St. Maryville because there had been an attempt to kill Fremanse. The poor little thing was only three."

Michael's eyes grew wide. "Someone tried to kill Celeste's baby girl?"

Celine nodded. "Celeste believed it had been her mother's enemies that did it. So, to protect Fremanse, she kept everything a secret." She looked back into Michael's eyes. "It's been kept a secret ever since."

Michael reached over and squeezed Celine's hand. "But surely your family isn't worried about any danger now, right?"

Celine shrugged her shoulders. "My mother and grandmother are healers in St. Maryville. They're well-known and respected there, but it is just a little town, with little town gossip. If it were to get out that they have any connections to Voodoo, it would ruin them." She opened her hand, interlacing her fingers into his. "So that's the real reason it's still a secret." She paused. "Up until about two weeks ago, I didn't even know the whole story. That's how well-guarded they keep the family history. When they told me, they swore me to secrecy." She rolled her eyes. "And I already blew it yesterday." She turned and looked at Michael. "You remember when Dr. DaQuin kept me in the interview room?"

Michael inched closer to Celine and ran his fingers through her hair. "Yeah, it seemed like she kept you back there forever."

"Yeah, well, she's obviously well-schooled in all this stuff. She really wanted to know more about the box."

Michael kissed her hand. "You mean your jewelry box?"

Celine looked down, a little ashamed of the lie she'd told. "It's not exactly a jewelry box."

Michael leaned in to her. "Hey, you." He reached down and put his hand gently under her chin, lifting her face to his. "It's okay. You were in a tough spot. Those pictures were horrible. They shouldn't have shown them to you. I still have a bone to pick with Vince over the whole thing." He leaned down and kissed her gently on the lips. "So what did she say to you?"

She looked back at Michael. "That it's a special box given only to healers from the Vodou tradition but I don't think my mother or grandmother would ever admit that." She raised her eyebrows. "And I don't plan on trying to talk to them about it, either."

"Why not?"

Celine smiled. "Because they've done everything they can to disassociate themselves with Voodoo or anything that even comes close to it. If I ever tried to talk to them about how closely connected their healing practices are to Vodou, believe me, they'd say that I had lost my mind! It doesn't really matter, anyway. What they do is incredible! They help so many people. They're both devoutly religious women; Catholic to the core, and dedicated healers. I don't want to ever say or do anything to upset the delicate balance that they've worked so hard to create. So, when you meet them, please don't say that you know anything about this. It would break both their hearts if they found out that I've told you."

Michael smiled. "You have nothing to worry about, but..." He leaned over and kissed her on the cheek. "I get to meet them?"

Celine leaned into him. "Of course you do. I mean, if you..." she hesitated.

Michael looked at her. "If I what?"

"If all this talk of Voodoo doesn't make you want to run away from me as fast as you can."

Michael moved a few of the letters out of the way and scooped Celine into his arms, laying her back on the bed. He looked into her eyes. "Run? Yeah, I want to run, right into your arms! I can't wait to meet them! They must be wonderful people to have raised such an incredible woman."

Celine smiled as she pushed a curl of his hair away from his eyes. "They really are wonderful. When they meet you, I think they're going to be just as love-struck as I am."

Michael leaned down, smiling. "Mmmm, love-struck. That's sounds nice. I'm pretty love-struck with you, too." He kissed her then nuzzled his nose into her hair as he whispered. "But well, lots of women are love-struck with me, especially Voodoo witches."

Celine playfully pushed him away. "Hey, you! You better watch it!"

He laughed. "Oh yeah?" He gave her a little tickle in her side. "Or what? You'll turn me into a toad?"

"Hmmmm, no, I think a *loup garou* would be better. You'd make a cute little *loup garou*."

Michael laughed. "A loo-ga…what the hell is that?"

Celine tapped him on the nose, giggling at how he tried to twist his mouth around the Cajun word. "A bayou werewolf!"

Michael started making chomping noises with his mouth. "Yum, yum, I'm going to bite you!" He playfully nipped at her neck as he made growling noises.

Celine burst out laughing. "Stop it! Stop! Or I won't let you meet them after all!"

Michael stopped and looked at her smiling. "When? When can I meet them?"

"How about this weekend?"

Michael cocked his head and gave her a playful grin. "Okay!" Then he buried his face in her neck, making the growling noises again.

"You rascal!" Celine laughed pushing him away when she heard a knock at the door. "Stop! Michael, someone's at the door!"

Michael looked over at the door, listening. They both heard a soft knocking. Michael sat up, frowning. "Great! I told Alex not to bother us."

Celine sat up and ran her hands through her hair. "You did? When?"

Michael stood up, still looking at the door. "Earlier this morning when I went down to get the coffee. It must be important." He looked back at Celine. "Most likely a problem with a buyer." He walked over to the door and opened it just a crack. "Yeah?" Celine heard Alex's voice, but couldn't make out what he was saying. Michael said impatiently, "Now? Can't it wait?" Celine listened, but still couldn't make out the low, muted words. Michael turned to Celine as he shut the door behind him. "I have to go downstairs for a minute. Alex needs to talk to me about something. He's being all mysterious about it. 'Probably nothing. Just more of his drama."

Celine stood up and walked over to him. "Okay, but not without a kiss first." She stood on tiptoe to kiss his cheek. "I mean, it is Monday. We really should be working. We do have some blueprints to review."

Michael put his arms around her waist and lifted her up off the floor. "Work? I can think of better things I'd rather be doing."

Celine smiled as he put her back down. "Yeah, well, keep that thought. You better go see what Alex wants."

Michael smiled as he walked out the door.

Celine turned around and saw the painting of Adele at her desk. *I think I'll call Mama right now.* She walked over to the nightstand and picked up the bedside phone. She dialed the number and listened to it ring.

Luisah picked up. "Hello?"

"Hi, Mama. How're you doing?"

Luisah gave a delighted little laugh. "Well, I'm fine. You sure sound good, Celine. You doin' better?"

Celine smiled. "Yes, Mama. The snake tea has worked and the baths, too. My stomach's still a little queasy from time to time but it's getting better, especially now, since they caught the guy that robbed me."

Celine listened as Luisah spoke to Mo-maw in the background. "It's Celine, Mama. They caught that guy." Celine heard Mo-maw's muffled voice. "But dat's great!"

Luisah came back on the phone. "So, how's the work goin'?" Celine nodded. "Well," She laughed. "We haven't done much yet, but I'm wondering, would it would be okay if I bring someone home to meet the two of you this weekend?" Celine listened to the quiet hush over the phone. "Mama?"

"Well, of course, Celine. Who?"

Celine smiled. "His name is Michael. He's Alex's nephew. You know, the man that's funding the project for the school."

Celine heard Luisah talking to Mo-maw in the background. "She's bringing someone home this weekend."

Celine heard Mo-maw's voice. "The nephew? Is dat da one from da *cochemère* she tol' me abo't?"

Luisah spoke back into the phone. "Celine, Mo-maw wants to know…"

Celine laughed. "Tell Mo-maw, yes, he's the one and yes, he is wonderful."

Luisah turned to Mo-maw. "Did you hear that, Mama?"

There was a slight pause as Mo-maw took the phone from Luisah. "Well, chère, we can't wait to meet him. When do you t'ink you'll come? Saturday?"

The bedroom door opened and Michael walked in. Celine looked up at him and smiled but he didn't smile back. "Um, yeah, I tell you what, I'll call you back and let you know for sure. I've gotta go, okay?" Celine watched as Michael sat on the foot of the bed, staring off into space.

Mo-maw said happily. "*Mais* yeah, chère. You mama and I, we can fix some crawfish *étouffée*. How's dat sound?"

Celine kept staring at Michael. "Oh, that would be great, Mo-maw. I gotta go, okay? Tell Mama I'll call her later." Celine hung up, walked over to Michael and sat down next to him. She reached out and took his hand. "Michael? Everything okay?"

He squeezed her hand and then turned to look at her. His bright blue eyes had grown dark with sadness. "My father's dead."

CHAPTER 20

For two hundred years, the Archangels of Belle Ange graveyard stood watch. Standing back-to-back, their massive wings formed the pointed entrance to the hallowed ground. The imposing black wrought iron fence that surrounded the eternal resting place was strangled by a green blanket of thick kudzu vine, forbidding even the slightest breeze to pass through this city of the dead. No matter how hard the groundskeepers tried to fight it, the kudzu always won. On the day of the burial, the hot Louisiana sun blazed at ninety degrees, holding the blinding white cemetery in its sweltering palm while the occasional dark cloud bellowed a deep rumble, teasing a brief rain shower of relief, but the Archangels knew there would be no rain today; no relief in sight while the remains of Robert Edgar Arnaud passed under their winged gates.

Celine's high heels slowly sank into the patch of soft grass that lay in front of the Arnaud family tomb. She stood silently between Michael and Alex, shifting her weight to the balls of her feet, trying to keep herself from sinking but the effort was fruitless. *God, I can't believe how hot it is out here! Why did I wear a suit? What was I thinking?* Small beads of sweat dripped down her back, making her Ann Taylor long-sleeved black jacket damp and sticky. She straightened the jacket, feeling the stiff upraised collar move back into place, her cleavage showing ever so slightly. She squirmed as much as the back slit in her pencil skirt would allow and glanced up at Michael, standing stoically to her right.

Dressed in a slim-fitted, Dior Homme black suit, black silk shirt and tie, the sun glared fully into his face. *He must be just as miserable as I am, but he certainly doesn't show it. Is he even sweating?* She brushed the back of his hand with hers. As soon as she did, he reached out, taking her hand and pulling her a little closer to him, all the while never taking his eyes off the priest. Celine took a deep breath, but the air was stagnant.

Her head pounded with a deep, slow throb. *I wish I still had some of Mama's snake tea. I should've gone home this week and gotten some more, then come back for the funeral today. Maybe I should drive home tonight.*

The priest sprinkled holy water on the white marble crypt. With his hands outstretched and a flourish of his purple robe, he said, "Bless this grave as we bury our brother, Robert." A small cry came from the woman seated in front of Celine, her head and face covered with a black lace veil. The woman turned, reaching for Michael. He bent down, dropping Celine's hand and whispered something into the woman's ear. All Celine heard was, "Mother, it's going to be okay." He reached into his suit pocket and gave her his handkerchief.

A pale wrinkled hand adorned with blood-red nail polish and diamonds on three fingers, moved snake-like from under the black veil, wrapped around the handkerchief, letting one finger stroke Michael's wrist and disappeared back under the veil. In a muffled sobbing voice, she sputtered, "Thank you, my darling boy." She leaned over to the woman sitting next to her and whispered, "He's such a good son." She reached once again, grasped Michael's hand tightly in hers, placed it on her shoulder and held it there.

Celine looked at the two women seated in front of her; Michael's mother, Victoria Sterling Arnaud and her sister, Olivia Sterling Spaulding, the only family besides Michael and Alex to attend. The rest of the people were just a nameless, faceless sea of black standing behind them. She wiped a bead of sweat from her face, hoping her mascara hadn't melted, turning her into a black-eyed raccoon. She took a shallow breath, but the humid air sent a sharp pain to her chest. When she felt a small nudge from her left, she turned and saw Alex smiling at her. Dressed impeccably in his black Gucci suit, gray ascot and matching pocket square, he offered her his handkerchief. He leaned over and whispered.

"My dear, you look absolutely miserable. May I escort you away from this oven?"

Celine smiled back at him, grateful for the handkerchief, and dabbed under each eye. She looked over at Michael, his mother clutching his hand and leaning her head on top of it like a child hugs a sleep toy.

Celine looked back at Alex, handed his handkerchief back to him and whispered. "Thank you, but I'm okay. We probably shouldn't leave." Alex inched forward looking over at Michael's hand, grossly misshapen by his mother's tight grip. With a little twinkle in his eyes, he winked at her then looked down at his watch impatiently as the priest rambled on.

"This is the will of my Father that I should raise him up on the last day." The priest straightened his purple robe, making sure the huge gold embroidered Celtic cross was unwrinkled. He looked at the crowd, smiling. "And now we will have a reading by Miss Kelly June Ellison, a dear friend of the family."

A tall, tanned, long-haired blonde in a little black sleeveless dress, pearls and high heels came out of the crowd of mourners. Even the priest couldn't help but look down at her long legs as she walked over to the ebony casket that was shining in the sunlight like a black Cadillac. She looked up and spoke to the crowd in a high-pitched voice. "The reading is from Psalms. It's one of Miss Victoria's favorites." Kelly pushed her champagne-colored hair from her shoulders as she opened up a slip of paper that she carried in her hand. She looked at the passage and then looked straight at Michael. "Death is not the end. I come before you, calling you back to me; calling you back to my breast. *Is this Michael's ex-girlfriend?* My lips pour forth your praise. My tongue sings of your promises. I have chosen you. I long for you. *She's looking right at him.* I love you and I will never forget. *Is she trying to...* Come home to me. *At his father's funeral?* Come home. Amen." *Celine was stunned. She's still in love with him!*

Michael's mother sobbed. "Oh thank you, Kelly, my sweet Junie bean." Kelly walked over to Michael's mother and bent down from the waist, kissing her through the black lace veil, strategically exposing another few inches of thigh right in front of Michael. Victoria let go of Michael's hand, reached out and patted Kelly's face as she whispered, "You are such a dear. I miss you so much." As Kelly stood up, she reached over and placed one perfectly manicured hand on Michael's chest. She gave him a little smile and whispered, "I'm so sorry, Michael."

Michael reached over and took Celine's hand in his as he gave a slight nod to Kelly. Kelly flashed a quick glance at their clasped hands then looked back at Michael, smiling. She whispered, "I'll see you at the reception. I need to talk to you." As she walked back into the crowd of mourners, Michael looked at Celine but didn't smile. In an almost robotic move, he fixed his eyes on the priest. *Could he still have feelings for her, too? No, I'm being ridiculous. He said it was over between them.* Celine's head pounded harder. *No, not one of my headaches. Not again. Not now. Please!* She glanced down at her ring. *Please!*

The priest nodded to the two solemn-faced undertakers who had been standing on either side of the tomb. Like a well-oiled machine, they unlocked and opened the door to the space that would house Robert's body. The priest turned to the waiting crowd and said, "Would the pall bearers please come forward." Victoria's low, long cry started softly as Michael and seven other men made their way to the front and stood around the coffin as the priest prayed. "I am dust and unto dust I shall return. *Kyrie eleison, Christe eleison, Kyrie eleison.*"

Her cry grew in volume as she moaned. "No! Michael, don't let them."

As the pallbearers slowly pushed the casket into the tomb, the priest prayed, "May the heavenly hosts of angels be your defense against the wickedness and snares of the devil." Over Victoria's moans, the priest continued to pray. "Oh God, by whose mercy the souls of the faithful find rest, forgive the sins of your people, especially your son, Robert."

Victoria turned to her sister, wailing. "He was too young, Livy. What am I going to do?" Alex stepped forward and touched Victoria's shoulder. At the moment his hand touched her veil, she turned and glared at Celine, "Don't touch me! You've ruined everything!"

Startled, Celine stepped back as Alex pulled his hand away. He gave Celine a sad look and then leaned down, whispering into Victoria's ear, "Victoria, let me walk you back to the house."

Victoria looked at Alex, then over to Celine. "Get away from me!" She glared at Alex. "I want Michael!"

Celine looked up at Michael. His face was flushed with embarrassment. Their eyes met. *Poor Michael! This is awful!*

The priest whispered something in Michael's ear and then addressed the crowd again. "Lord, you know the anguish of Robert's dear widow, Victoria. Hear her cry and strengthen her in your lasting goodness."

Michael walked over to his mother and took her hand. "Come on, Mother. Let's go to the house."

Victoria stood up and leaned on Michael, clutching his arm as she cried. "I need you, Michael. Don't leave me, son. Don't leave me again."

She turned to her sister putting out a frail arm. "Livy, I need you too." Olivia stood up, taking her sister by the hand.

Celine looked nervously at Alex as the priest gave the benediction. "Should we follow them?" Alex shook his head as the priest prayed.

"Dearest Lord, let perpetual light shine upon Robert." He turned to the crowd. "Our closing hymn is the Salve Regina."

Alex whispered to Celine, "It's best we let Michael handle Victoria right now. Trust me, he knows what to do. He's done it thousands of times."

In a deep bass voice the priest began to sing. ♫ *Sal-ve Re-gi-na...* ♫

Celine's gaze followed the slow moving trio through the angel gateway as she sang in a weak voice. Her head pounded in scattered throbs. *Thousands of times? What a terrible responsibility for him.* She watched Michael holding his mother up as they disappeared around the corner of the huge white plantation house, his aunt trailing like a lost puppy dog behind them.

♫ Virgo Ma-ri-a. Alle-lu... ♫ Before Celine finished the Alleluia, Alex grabbed her hand and tucked it into his elbow. "I suggest we get out of this God-awful heat and walk to the house. I don't know about you, but I could sure use a drink about now!"

Celine leaned into him, giving him a little squeeze. "Alex..." she looked around making sure that none of the mourners were within ear-shot. "...I am so grateful that you're here. I don't know how I would've gotten through this week without you. I just hope, now that the funeral's over, things will get a little easier."

They walked under the Archangel's wings towards the house. He patted her arm. "Losing Robert was a shock for us all." He sighed. "I certainly never expected him to go before me. A heart attack..." Alex shook his head. "...I guess we never really know when the monster of death will show up."

Celine looked down as she walked along. A shiver of memory ran through her. *The monster of death from my dream. What a horrible thing to see before you die.* She tried taking a deep breath, but the muggy air made it nearly impossible. "I think it'll be a long time before you see that monster, Alex. You look fantastic. It's Michael I'm worried about. He looks like he's carrying the weight of the world on his shoulders."

Alex laughed sarcastically. "He is; the world of Arnaud Oil, and all its attachments. I should've known that Robert would have the last word. The lawyers have been very specific; Michael has to take over as CEO, or the company gets sold, which ultimately means Victoria loses her comfortable lifestyle." Alex shook his head. "Even from the grave, Robert gets the last laugh."

"But won't Victoria be okay financially? Surely she's got plenty of money, investments, you know, that kind of thing."

"Of course she does. This is more about her losing face with her country club cronies. So she's depending on Michael to come in and take care of her, as usual."

"I just wish there was something I could do to help him."

"But you have, Celine. You've been here and he knows that."

"Oh Alex, I hope you're right. I've hardly seen him and when I have, he's been exhausted. His mother's been completely unable to do anything, so the responsibilities have all fallen on Michael; the funeral arrangements, the lawyers, the company. I offered to go over to her house and be with her while he rested. That would at least have given him a little break, but he told me that wasn't a good idea. She was drinking a lot and he didn't want me to see her that way, but I think the real reason is that she just doesn't like me." Celine shook her head. "Did you hear what she said to us? I don't even know what she meant by I've ruined everything."

Alex let out a sarcastic little laugh. "Yeah, I heard. We're in the same boat. She doesn't like either of us; me, because I'm a gay artist, the exact opposite of Robert, and she's hated my relationship with Michael ever since he was born." He shrugged his shoulders. "And you, my dear, have ruined Junie bean's chances of ever being with Michael again. Victoria adores that common little bleach-blonde; sort of the daughter she never had. Kelly's just a money-hungry vulture and only wants back in the picture because Michael stands to inherit everything." He leaned down and looked at Celine, like a wise old professor. "Victoria knows there's no chance of that now. She's seen how Michael looks at you."

Celine's eyes stung with the bite of tears. "I guess that explains what she said to me at the church, too."

Alex frowned. "At the church? What did she say?"

Celine's voice began to break. "I was alone with her in the Eucharistic chapel, waiting while the pall bearers were escorting the body into the hearse. She asked me not to ride in the limo with her and

Michael to the burial. She told me that Michael was just being polite by letting me ride with the family; that I shouldn't embarrass him by giving everyone the wrong impression that we're a couple."

Alex's eyes widened in surprise. "She told you that?" Celine nodded. "Is that why you came in your car?" Celine fought back the tears as she nodded again. "Wait until Michael finds out. He's going to be furious with her."

"Oh Alex, please don't say anything to him. He's going through so much right now. I don't want to add to his list of problems."

Alex turned to look at Celine when he heard her pleading voice. "My dear, you look so sad and very pale. Let's sit down for a bit." They walked to a white wooden swing that hung from the low limb of a huge oak tree. Celine sat down and put her head back, soaking in the soft breeze and watching the Spanish moss swaying from the massive oak. As Alex sat next to her, she watched the steady stream of mourners walking along in groups of twos and threes on their way to the reception.

Alex patted her hand. "Listen, if you'd really like to get on Victoria's good side, I'll tell you how." Celine looked at Alex hopefully. "First you'll have to dye your hair blonde and then take lessons in becoming a bimbo; you know…" He flipped his hands out like a tap dancer and raised the pitch of his voice. "…talk in little-girl falsetto all the time. Victoria would love you then." Celine managed to laugh at Alex's antics. He patted her hand again. "No, Celine, no. Victoria doesn't like you because Michael's chosen you and she can't control that." He leaned into her. "Which is a wonderful thing, really."

"But doesn't she want Michael to be happy?"

"Oh now, that's the big question, isn't it? The sad answer is no, not really. Mommy's happiness comes first, always."

"That is so sad."

"Yes, it is, but I think those days are over. I've seen some wonderful changes in Michael since you've come along. The two of you are perfect together and he knows it. Michael's not stupid. He sees through all Victoria's manipulations; all the drinking and whining and crying. Yeah, he knows and I promise you, in a week or two, when the dust settles, our Michael, the one we know and love, will be back. Until then,

I just hope you can be patient. Try to ignore Victoria as much as you can, okay?"

Celine nodded. "Thank you, Alex."

"You're welcome. I know you've missed Michael this week, but I'm so glad that you and I've spent this time together. Working on the art building project has given me a chance to really get to know you. You're a wonderful young woman, Celine, and you'll always have a friend in me."

Celine's eyes teared up. "Oh, Alex. You're really like a father to me. I…"

Alex pulled out his handkerchief and handed it to her. "Now, my dear, I'm not so sure you'd want an old drag queen to be your father." Celine laughed as she dried her tears. "Please, stop crying. I'll start crying, too! It could go on for hours and hours! Believe me, you don't want that! Now dry those tears and let's go get a drink. A stiff Bushmills fixes everything!"

Celine laughed as she wiped the tears away, handed him back his handkerchief and looked around. "I think just about everyone's gone inside except you and me."

They walked around the side of the house, onto the wide veranda and up to the huge front door. As Celine stepped into the foyer, a rush of cool air washed over her. She closed her eyes briefly, grateful that she could take a deep breath again. When she opened her eyes, she saw Michael in the large room past the foyer, standing underneath an enormous crystal chandelier. His back was to her.

Alex saw him at the same time. "Oh look, there's Michael. Come on." They walked together, past a long dining room table surrounded by people filling plates with food while a harpist played soft strains of Bach.

As they got closer, Celine could hear a shrill little girl's voice. "Ohhh, Michaellll, really, I meeean it. You should come with me to Paris. It'll be good for you to get away for a while. It'll be good for both of us."

Celine rolled her eyes at Alex as she dropped his arm. Alex smiled and winked as he pointed silently to the bar just ahead and walked on. As soon as Celine walked to Michael's side, Kelly's big blue eyes widened for just a second, then she gave Celine a pasted smile. "Oh Michael, here's your little guest. Michael's been wondering where you were."

Michael leaned down and gave Celine a quick peck on the lips. "I've been looking for you. Where've you been?"

"Alex and I were just outside talking."

"Yeah?" He took Celine's hand in his and glanced around the room. "Oh, I see him. Of course, he's at the bar."

Kelly stepped closer to Michael and took his other hand. "Michael, you're being rude. Aren't you going to introduce us?" She turned to Celine. "I'm Kelly Ellison, but everybody calls me Junie." She looked up at Michael. "Well, almost everyone. You know your mother calls me Junie bean." She looked back at Celine. "It's a little embarrassing, but well, she and my mother are like, best friends." She extended her right hand as she held tightly to Michael with her left. "And you are...?" The question mark in her voice felt like fingernails screeching across a chalkboard, making Celine's headache come creeping back.

Michael wriggled his hand out of Kelly's grip. "Celine, this is Kelly."

Kelly looked at Celine's face, her brow wrinkled just a little. "You look so tired." She looked down at Celine's suit." Aren't you hot in that jacket? There's no way I would wear that in this kind of heat...." She stopped mid-sentence, reached down and grabbed Celine's left hand. "Michael, what's this?" Celine pulled her hand back but Kelly turned to Michael. "Are you en-Gaged?"

Michael reached down and took Celine's left hand in his and then looked into Celine's eyes. For the first time in days, Celine saw a little twinkle of playful mischief there. He turned to Kelly. "Oh Kel, you found us out." Kelly stood there speechless. Celine squeezed Michael's hand, surprised but determined to play along in his little game. He looked around the room as he whispered to Kelly, "You won't tell anyone, will you? We want to wait a little while before we make the announcement."

"Um, yeah, sure." Her voice dropped an octave. "But I wish you would've told me, Michael."

Celine stifled a little giggle. *Why? So you wouldn't have made such a fool of yourself falling all over him?*

"Listen, um..." Kelly awkwardly looked at her diamond watch. "I think I'd better go. Mom said something about a bridge game." She wrinkled her perky little nose. "I think she's still with your Mother, so

I'll just go get her. You take care, Michael." She turned and disappeared into the crowd.

Michael looked at Celine, a smirk curled on his lips and his eyes dancing with laughter. Celine stood on tiptoe and wrapped her arms around his neck, smiling. "It's so good to have my happy Michael back."

He laughed. "Yeah well, we might not be happy for long. If I know Kelly, we've got about two minutes before she announces to my mother and all her friends that we're getting married."

Celine stepped back. "What?"

"Yeah, look. I've got an idea." He took her by the hand, walked over to the bar and said something to the bar tender. The bar tender turned and pulled a bottle of red wine out from under the counter. He uncorked it and handed Michael the bottle with two wine glasses.

Michael turned to her. "Come on. Let's get out of here!"

Celine grabbed his elbow, pulling him back. "Are you sure we should leave? I mean all these people…"

He laughed. "I want to relax and enjoy this nice bottle of Chateau Margaux with you. Besides, there's something I want you to see." He leaned down and kissed her. "Now come on, before my mother comes out of her bedroom!"

Celine looked behind her quickly, then scurried to meet Michael. His long strides had already gotten him to the door. He tucked the wine bottle under his arm, balancing the wine glasses carefully as he opened the heavy door. He turned back, waiting for Celine. She laughed as she hurried past him onto the veranda. "Where are we going?"

Michael let the door go. "It's a one-room apartment house on the edge of the property. It's called a *garçonnière*. Here, can you carry these?" He handed her the wine glasses. "Come on, hurry up. I don't want anyone to know where we're going."

They ran down a gravel path alongside the big house, then through a manicured English garden. As they turned the corner, Celine saw a small white house with green shutters nestled amongst some trees. Panting from having to run fast enough to keep up with him, she stopped. "*Garçonnière?* Is this…?" He reached the front step of the little cottage, turned and waited for her to catch up with him. "Is this where Adele met Etienne?"

Michael paused for a moment. "I don't know." When she finally stood next to him, he opened the door. "I know Etienne lived here. That's why I wanted to show it to you." Celine handed Michael the wine glasses as she walked into a beautiful, cedar-floor bedroom; a queen-sized, four-poster, mahogany bed sat against the far wall, covered with a light blue duvet and French travesin pillow. A matching mahogany armoire with a beveled full-length mirror on the door stood against one wall while an inviting, light blue velvet chaise was against the other. Celine looked through the floor-to-ceiling windows on both sides of the bed and saw a huge field of sugar cane, the green stalks not quite ready for cutting. "Wow! I can't believe I'm standing in the exact same place..." She looked down at the ring. "...where they fell in love." She turned to Michael. "What a special place for both of us!"

She felt a nudge onto the side of her hand. "Here." Celine looked down and saw Michael offering her a full glass of red wine so dark, it almost looked black. He held his own full glass in his other hand. "Did Adele meet Etienne here? I don't remember that in any of her letters."

She smiled and took the glass from him, walked over to the chaise and sat on the end, kicking her shoes off. "Etienne was wounded in a duel, pretty badly, too. Adele took care of him here for several weeks. That's when they fell in love."

Michael walked over and sat down at the head of the chaise, kicking his shoes off next to hers. He tapped her glass with his and then took a long sip of his wine. He looked down at her, smiled and put his arm around her. "So here we are, in the place that Adele and Etienne met and fell in love." He leaned over and kissed her. She could taste the dark red wine on his lips. "The perfect place for me to tell you that I love you."

"Oh Michael, I love you, too." She kissed him, nestling closer into his shoulder draping both her legs across his lap, her skirt inching up her thigh. "I've missed you."

"And I've missed you." He put his wine glass on the floor carefully and sighed deeply as he let his hand rest on her bare leg. "At least the funeral's over. I just wish I could go back to my studio with you and hide away. I'm not sure how much more of this I can take."

Celine sipped her wine. "Lot's more to do?"

Michael reached for his black silk tie, tearing at it like it was a garotte. "Yeah, I'm afraid so." He struggled to pull it off, but it stubbornly stayed tied.

Celine put her wine glass next to his and turned. "Here, let me help." She reached over and slowly undid the knot, pulled the tie away and laid it on the chaise. "You look so handsome in your suit."

"Thank you, but I feel like I'm choking." With one hand he unbuttoned his top button and took a deep breath. "I thought I was going to die out there!"

Celine laughed. "Well, it certainly didn't show. You didn't even look like you were sweating!"

He stood up, stripped off his coat, threw it on the bed, pulled his shirttail out and picked up his wine glass again. He sat down and nestled his back into the chaise. He opened his long legs and patted the space in front of him. "Here. Sit here. I want you close to me."

Celine smiled as she picked up her wine glass, repositioned her body, curling into his arms. "Hmmmm, finally. I've missed your strong arms around me."

She could feel his long, deep breaths and the rumble of his deep voice as he said, "And I've missed holding you. Thank you so much for being here. This week has been absolute hell."

"I know, Michael. I'm not sure how much help I've been. In fact, I've wondered if I was just in the way."

Michael frowned. "In the way? Are you kidding? You have no idea how many times I've thought about you when the stress got to be too much. I know I haven't been able to show you, but I'm so happy that we're together." He shook his head. "In the way? Is that why you didn't ride with us to the burial? Cause you thought you were in the way?"

Celine looked into the deep-red wine, not sure what to say. "I wanted to ride with you, but..." She hesitated. *I need to tell him the truth.* "Your mother said it might give the wrong impression if I did."

Michael's body tensed. "She said what?"

Celine put her wine down, turned around and faced him, stroking his cheek. "Oh Michael, I'm sorry. You've got enough to worry about without me adding this."

"No, I'm glad you did. What did she say to you exactly?"

Celine looked back at Michael sadly. "It was when you were outside with the pallbearers, placing the coffin in the hearse. I was waiting with her and she said that you were just being polite by asking me to ride with the family; that I would embarrass you by giving everyone the wrong impression that we were a couple."

He took a long sip of his wine then looked at Celine. "That woman..." He shook his head. "I wondered why you were walking to your car, I almost ran to get you, but she stopped me. She told me you wanted to take your own car and that I would embarrass you by insisting that you ride with us. I knew what she said didn't make any sense, but by the time I turned around, you had already gone." His face grew stern. "I heard what she said to you at the burial, too, and I swear to you, Celine she will never talk to you like that again. Never."

"Oh dear, Alex said you'd be furious with her."

He looked into her eyes. "Is that what you and Alex were talking about outside?"

Celine nodded. "Yeah."

Michael pulled her closer to him. "Oh Celine, I'm so sorry. I'm glad you talked to Alex, though. Believe me; he knows what mother is capable of. What did he tell you?"

Celine sighed. "He certainly made me feel better. He said you and I were perfect together."

Michael's eyes brightened. "He did? Well, of course, I agree." He hugged her.

Celine smiled. "And he told me something else." Michael cocked his head, waiting. "He told me the secret to getting in your mother's good graces."

"Oh he did, did he? And what is this big secret? Tell me."

Celine drank the last of her wine and put the glass next to Michael's. "Well..." She smiled feeling relaxed from the wine. "First, I have to dye my hair blonde." Michael's mouth made a perfect O. "And then I have to take bimbo classes..."

Michael put his head back and started laughing. "Oh my God, Alex!"

Celine stood up and faced Michael, opening her eyes wide and flipping her hands out. "And then..." She raised her voice an octave. "I have to talk in a high screechy voice and say Miiiichaelllll!"

Michael stood up and threw his arms around her, laughing. "Don't you ever do that!" He picked her up off the floor and spun her around.

Celine laughed. "Don't worry."

He put her gently back on the floor and picked up his wine glass. "I'm going to get some more wine. This stuff is great. Want some?"

Celine steadied herself, not sure if she was feeling dizzy from the wine or the spinning. "No. I'd better not." She watched as he walked over to a small antique table that was in the corner of the room, picked up the wine bottle and poured more wine. "Alex also said that you're probably going to become the next CEO for Arnaud Oil."

Michael walked over to the bed and sprawled out. "Come on. Let's sit over here." Celine walked over to the bed and lay on her side, propping herself up with her elbow. Michael sipped his wine and then turned to look at her. "I have a plan that'll change all that."

Celine frowned. "Really? It sounded like your Father made sure there was no way around it."

Michael shook his head. "I've already talked to another attorney; one not with the company. If Mother is named CEO, then she won't lose a thing and I'm free of that place. Of course, that would be in name only. She'd have to agree to an acting manager handling everything. Father's Chief Financial Officer, Riva, is the best candidate. She's great! I've already talked to her about it and she's agreed to the conditions, so I'm presenting it to the Board tomorrow. It's going to take a lot of work to convince them, but I'm sure I can do it. After that, it's just a matter of waiting until the lawyers draw up the paperwork — that and staying at Mother's house all week to make sure she doesn't change her mind. But by this time next weekend, I'll be done."

Celine sighed. "I hate that you have to go through all of this."

Michael took another sip of wine then put his wine glass down. He looked at Celine, his jaw was set. "I'll be okay. It'll be a fight, but I'm going to win. Father didn't count on this little loophole, and if mother wants to keep her money, she has to say yes, because I'm NOT going to be the next CEO of Arnaud Oil."

Celine inched closer to him and gently stroked the side of his cheek. Her soft touch eased his jaw. "It's okay, I believe you and I believe in you. I'm just worried that all this is hurting you so deeply. I hate to see you in so much pain."

Michael reached over and pushed her hair away from her shoulders and gave her a gentle kiss. "Listen to me, Celine, let's not talk about this." He nuzzled her neck. "We're in the exact place that Adele and Etienne fell in love. And right now, all I can think about is making love to you. Please. I need you. I want you...now."

Celine kissed him. "Oh God, Michael. I've wanted you all week and I wasn't sure what to do."

He kissed her hungrily, reached down and unbuttoned her jacket, pulling the sleeves down her arms. As he tossed the jacket aside, he kissed her breasts and unhooked her black lace bra, pulling it off and tossing it to the floor. Celine unbuttoned his shirt then kissed his bare chest as he pulled his shirt off. She unbuckled his belt and then unzipped his pants pulling them down. Michael let out a little groan as she gently stroked his erect penis. In an instant, Michael gently pushed her back on the bed, unzipped her skirt and slipped it over her hips, pulling her black lace panties down her legs along with it.

He knelt over her and kissed her hard, his tongue reaching deep into her mouth. She pulled him to her, feeling his penis enter her. She let out a little gasp as he filled her up. He reached down and pulled one of her legs up as he urgently penetrated her more deeply. He thrust deep inside her as she arched her back. The orgasm soared its way through her, exploding as he held her, his body was hot with desire. "Oh God, Michael!" He came, hard. She could feel his penis, pulsing, deliciously filling her. With each throb, she could feel his body relax. He lay on top of her, all his energy spent, weakly holding himself up.

Celine ran her fingers through his hair. "I've ached for you every night you were away." She kissed him softly. "I've missed being with you in your studio. The bed is lonely without you."

He lay next to her and looked into her eyes. "I promise you, I won't let anything else get in the way of us being together." He nuzzled her neck again. "Even though I'm staying at Mother's this week, I'll come back to the studio in the evening and..." He laughed as he rolled over on top of her again looking into her eyes, smiling. "... we'll make mad, passionate love every night."

Celine laughed. "That sounds so wonderful, but..." she ran her fingers softly over his face. "...I need to go home for a few days. All week, I've been getting my headaches again. Today, the heat has been making them worse. My mother has this great tea that helps a lot, but I've run out of it. So, I'll go home, and let my mother and grandmother work their magic, get re-supplied with more tea and come back Tuesday or maybe Wednesday. That'll give you plenty of time to get everything done so we can make mad, passionate love every night!"

Michael stared at her, his eyes laced with sadness. He lay to her side and held her closely in his arms. "I'm so sorry. I've been so caught up in my own stuff I'd completely forgotten the hell you've been through; the robbery was bad enough. You're only just now healing from all the bruises and having to see that disgusting creep all over again at the police station, Father's death and now my mother's idiocy—all this stress. It's no wonder you've gotten those terrible headaches again. Are you all right?"

"I will be." She kissed his neck. "It helps to know that everything's okay between us. There was a moment there when I saw Kelly talking to you, inviting you to go to Paris with her…"

Michael turned his face into hers, nose to nose. "Celine! She's gone and she's gone for good! Okay?"

Celine smiled. "Okay."

He kissed her on the forehead. "My Voodoo Queen. Promise me you'll come back to me. Please, don't give up on me. I don't know what I'd do if I'd lose you."

Celine breathed a deep sigh as she closed her eyes. She could feel sleep creeping slowly over her. "I could never give up on you, Michael. I love you. Just promise me you won't give up on me, either."

His chest moved up and down in deep, long breaths like the gentle rocking of a boat on a calm sea. "Never. I love you, Bienaimée." Celine sighed, curling into Michael's arms, and gently fell asleep.

"Good morning, my love." Michael's husky deep voice pulled her out of sleep.

She nestled deeper into his shoulder and said playfully. "I'm not ready to wake up yet."

He laughed, the joyful rumble made her smile. "So is my nurse saying that I've healed enough to get up and fix her breakfast this morning?"

Celine opened her eyes. *What? Nurse?* Slowly, she sat up, turned and looked at the man lying next to her. It was Michael, but not Michael.

His entire chest and part of his left shoulder was wrapped in a gauze bandage. She pulled away. "What happened to your chest?"

He smiled as he reached out his hand and touched her arm. "But aren't we playful this morning? This?" He tapped his heart. "Nothing, save a scratch from a nasty old sword that almost killed me. But you plucked me from the clutches of death and here I am, ready to do your bidding, my Adele."

Celine pulled away, studying the man's face closely. "This isn't funny, Michael. Don't call me that."

His brow wrinkled into a quizzical frown. "Oh, you've decided to change my name? Oh, how I love these little games you play! Hmm, then I'm no longer Etienne. Very well, I don't mind being this Michael unless he is another lover." He pouted, teasingly and then smiled. "So, you want me to be Michael? That's a good, solid name. It's American, yes? So, what new name have you chosen for yourself? I like this game. Let's see, what will I call you?"

Celine jerked away as she edged herself from the bed, pulling the sheet to cover her naked body. "Stop it!" She looked around the room. The floor-to-ceiling windows were open, the warm summer's breeze wafted through the room. She could see a huge field of sugar cane, dotted with men wielding machetes, their muscular black arms swinging with the rhythm of the song they sang:

♫ *Bend yo' back, tote it to the lift.*
White boss hollers if you ain't swift.♫

"Where..." She looked back at the man lying on the bed. *What the hell...?*

Etienne frowned, struggling to sit up. "Adele, my love, you must've had another one of your dreams. You're here with me at Belle Ange, don't you remember? You and your mother saved my life. You've been staying with me ever since I was injured." He grimaced in pain as he strained to stand up. He walked over to her, leaning on the mahogany bed post. A faint tinge of blood began to seep through the white bandage. "Adele, you've just had one of your dreams. Come, let me hold you. That always helps. Come now, let me hold you."

Celine pulled back, frantically looking around the room then back at the man struggling to get to her. "No, no! Where's Michael?" Her head began to pound in rhythm with the slave song.

♫ *I be dancin' wit' da Devil,*
  I be dancin' in my head,
  I be dancin' wit' da Lawd,
  I be dancin' wit' da dead. ♫

She dropped to her knees, her heart was racing. The sheet billowed around her in a soft puff. She gasped for air as she pleaded. The room began to spin. She closed her eyes. "Please, make them stop. That song, make them stop!"

"You're dreaming again, Adele. Shh, shh, come back to me. Come back, Celine. Celine! Wake up. You're dreaming!"

Celine opened her eyes, pushing against Michael's bare chest.

"Get away. Where's Michael?" The bright afternoon sun pierced her head as the migraine drummed.

"You're here. Celine, you're with me. Look at me."

Celine looked at Michael through squinted eyes. *I'm still in bed.* She looked down at his chest. *No bandage.* She turned and looked around the room. *The window's closed and the singing's stopped.* She looked into Michael's face. "Michael?"

Michael pulled her to his chest, stroking her hair. "Oh, thank God. You were screaming in your sleep!"

Celine held him tightly. She could feel herself trembling. "I was having a nightmare."

Michael reached up and felt her forehead. "You're burning up." He pushed her gently away and looked at her. "Your face is red and…" He brushed her hair from her face looking at her neck. "Did you scratch yourself in your sleep? You have some nasty-looking marks on your neck."

She looked into Michael's eyes, those blue upon blue eyes. She could feel a hard chill crawling up her spine, the fever taking over her body. "Oh God, Michael. I need to get that tea. My headaches, my neck; it's all coming back."

He scooped her into his arms and held her, running his hand in long, even strokes down her back as she shivered. The shrill, syncopated beat of her headache dulled, merging into pace with the low deep thrum of his heartbeat. The chills ebbed away and her ragged breathing fell in sync with his. As her shivering began to subside, Michael stroked her brow. "Are you feeling any better? Would you like for me to call your mother?"

Celine nodded. "I should call them. Can I borrow your phone? I'll tell them I'm coming home tonight."

"Are you sure? You look so pale. You could stay here tonight and leave tomorrow morning."

Celine shook her head. "No, I should leave as soon as I can. Do you know where your chauffeur parked my car?"

Michael stood up, grabbed his suit pants and put them on. "Don't worry. I'll bring your car around. But, maybe I should drive you. I don't think you…"

Celine shook her head. "No, you need to stay here and be rested for the board meeting tomorrow. Look, I'll be fine. I'll take the river road up to Baton Rouge. After that it's an easy drive on I-10 all the way to St. Maryville. I've still got a few migraine pills from the emergency room. I can cut one in half. That way they won't make me sleepy. It'll ease the pain until I get there. They're in my bag in the trunk of my car."

His brow was wrinkled in deep lines. "Okay, but I'm not going to let you leave until the headache and the fever's gone. You've got to promise me you'll call when you get there. I'm going to be worried sick until I hear from you."

Celine nodded. "I will. I promise. Get my bag, okay? I need those pills."

Michael threw on his shirt and buttoned it, leaving the shirttail out. He slipped on his socks and shoes. "I'll be right back." He turned and walked out the door.

Celine stood up slowly. Naked, she walked over to the full length armoire mirror. Her eyes were bloodshot and her face was ghostly white. *When did I lose so much weight? Michael's right. Everything I've been through, I just have to get that tea again.* Without warning, her stomach cramped, buckling her nearly in two. *I should've never had that wine.* She dropped to her knees. She looked around and saw a wastepaper basket tucked alongside the armoire, grabbed it and vomited. *No, oh God, no. Please, don't let this be happening. Just get me home.* When she was done, she closed her eyes and sat back on her bare feet, trying to steady herself. *Ezilie, just hold this off till I can get home, please.* She took a deep breath, stood up and looked at herself once again in the mirror. She pushed her hair back and saw the deep red claw marks down the side of her neck. She looked back into the mirror and saw a woman, naked, seated on the side of the bed behind her, crying. *Adele?* Celine turned around and rushed to her side. *Adele?* Celine reached out to touch her trembling hand, but she vanished.

CHAPTER 21

The cursor on the computer screen blinked tauntingly from the password bar. *RE Arnaud. Locked.* Michael sighed as he leaned back in the plush, russet-brown leather chair in his father's office at Belle Ange. He spun the chair around, looking out of the picture window. The twilight shadows danced in and out of the old oaks. He pushed up his sleeve and looked at his Tag Heure watch. 7:30. He pulled his cell phone out of his pocket, looking for a message. Nothing. *Why hasn't she called?* He placed the cell phone on the walnut executive desk and looked at the computer screen again. *I need to get into those files, but the password could be anything.* He typed in a few guesses with no luck, sat back and looked at his watch again. *7:35. Where is she?*

Michael reached for the handle of the long drawer in the center of the desk. *Maybe he kept a list of his passwords in here.* He pulled on the drawer but the lock held fast. He leaned down and pulled on the smaller drawers on both sides of him. All locked. Michael looked across the camel-brown leather that stretched across the surface of the massive desk. He reached over and clicked on the brass banker's lamp that sat on the far corner. He rifled through the pen cup, his hand resting on a brass letter opener. *This might work.* He pushed the tip of the four-inch opener into the lock, turning and pulling at the same time. The lock held fast. *Damnit!* He jammed the tip of the letter opener into the lock and with one hard jerk, the drawer opened. *Yes!*

Michael leaned down and looked through the drawer, shuffling around until his hand touched something small and cold. He pulled it out and looked at it. Keys. *To a file cabinet, maybe?* He looked more closely at the key fob; a black stallion against a bright yellow background. *The Ferrari. Is it here? I thought he kept it at the house.* He put the keys in his pocket, looked deeper into the drawer, swiping his hand all the way to the back. *What's this? An envelope. I bet it's in here.* He pulled the 6x9-inch brown envelope out and realized it had an address on the front written in a very ornate script:

Robert Arnaud,
Belle Ange Plantation,
La. Hwy 1,
Vacherie, La.

Looks like a woman's handwriting. Michael looked for a return address but the space was blank. He took a deep breath and opened the flap. When he tilted the envelope, several photos came spilling out. He picked up the one on top. It was a close-up of an attractive blonde teenager tanning herself on a boat deck, topless, wearing dark sunglasses and a large pink sun hat, sipping on what looked like a lemonade. Michael sat back. *What the hell is this?* He pulled out the next one; a different girl, brunette, thirteen maybe fourteen, wearing a short plaid skirt and a white blouse, unbuttoned, exposing her young breasts. He flipped to the next one, another young girl, this one with long chestnut hair, fully naked; her hair draped across her small breasts. Her legs were open, one knee up, with a finger resting on her open red lips as she looked at the camera seductively. He shuffled through the stack, a different girl in each one, some of them barely twelve, Michael guessed, each picture more sexually explicit than the one before. *You sick bastard!* He threw the pictures across the desk. Michael spun the chair around and faced the wall behind him, breathing hard, trying to control his disgust.

"Michael?" Michael spun the chair around and saw Alex peeking through the office door. "Oh, there you are. Your mother's been asking for you."

Michael answered sharply. "Yeah? What does <u>she</u> want?"

Alex stepped inside the office, closing the door behind him. He walked across the polished oak floor toward Michael, his face wrinkled with concern. "What's wrong?" He sat down in one of the oxblood leather chairs in front of the desk.

Michael gathered the pictures from the top of the desk, reached across and handed them to Alex. "Take a look."

Alex frowned curiously as he took the pictures from Michael. His eyes grew sad as he flipped through the photos. He looked up at Michael. "But these are just children!"

Michael gave Alex a hard stare, his blue eyes almost black from the glare of the lamp. "I always knew that he cheated on Mother, but this? This is sick!" Michael placed both hands on the desk and stood up. He walked over to the bar in the corner of the room, turned over a high-ball glass and poured two fingers of scotch into the glass. He turned and looked at Alex. "Want a drink?"

"Do you have to ask? Make it a triple." Alex placed the pictures back on the desk face down. "Where did you find these disgusting things?" He wrinkled his nose in distaste.

Michael turned over another glass and poured Alex the triple scotch he requested. "In the desk drawer. They were mailed here." He capped up the Glenlivet Reserve, picked up the glass, walked over to Alex and handed him the drink.

Alex wrinkled his brow as he took the glass and watched Michael slump in the chair across from him. "Are you alright, Michael?"

Michael took a long sip of the scotch. "I'll be alright, but I sure could've done without seeing that."

Alex sipped his drink. "I'm sorry. Your father was..."

Michael interrupted him. "A greedy, womanizing pervert?"

Alex nodded. "He's dead. It's done."

Michael downed his drink, stood up and walked back to the bar. "I know. This is just another reminder of his sick bastard crap."

Alex watched Michael pour another drink and down half of it while he was standing there. "Hey, slow down. Let's talk about something more pleasant. How's Celine?"

Michael pushed up his sleeve and looked at his watch again. "7:45. She hasn't called since she left. I'm worried about her." He walked back over to the desk, picked up his cell phone and checked to make sure the ringer was on.

Alex sipped his drink. "Was she driving back to the gallery?"

"No." Michael slipped his cell phone into his pocket, walked around the desk and sat back down in the chair across from Alex. "She had a terrible headache and fever, too. She needed to go home. Her mother has some kind of special tea that gets rid of her headaches. She took a migraine pill and when she left she said the headache was gone, but I should've never let her drive. I should've at least given her my phone. She never replaced hers after the robbery. I don't know why, though."

Alex sighed. "I'm afraid it's my fault. We worked so hard on the building project, I never gave her any time to do anything else. When did she leave?"

"5:00. it only takes an hour and a half to get to St. Maryville from here. She should've gotten there and called me at least by 7:00." He looked out the window. The sun had set, covering the lawn in a deep gray evening light. "It'll be dark soon. I hope she's okay. I'd call her but I don't have..." He looked at Alex, suddenly smiling. "She called her mother with my phone. The number should be here." He scrolled through his call history. "Here it is! Luisah Dupré."

"Why don't you give her until 9:00? Chances are she's gotten there and she's eating supper with them right now. Give the poor girl a chance to relax with her mother and grandmother." Michael looked at Alex, his lips taut as he listened. "She's gone through a very rough week. I'm afraid the Arnauds have been quite a shock for her. We're hardly the warm, loving kind of family she's from, I'm sure. If I were her, I'd be getting as far away from us as I could right now."

Michael let out a sigh and put the phone back in his pocket. "You're probably right."

"She'll call you. Just wait a little while longer." Alex sat back sipping his drink. "If you try to hold on to her too tightly, you could end up being a noose around her neck, like your parents have been countless times to you, and we both know there's no good ending in that. If she doesn't phone by nine, then you can call."

Michael nodded with a frown on his face. "I know, Alex. You're right." He slipped the phone back in his pocket. "But I'm worried. She was just starting to recover from the robbery when Father died. Then she had to endure Mother. I feel awful about it all. She looked so weak and frail when she left. I just want to hear her voice and know that she's okay."

"Michael, I'm sure Celine's family is taking good care of her even as we speak. You don't need to feel bad about what's happened. She would never blame you. How could you control your father's death or your mother's reactions to it? If she were here right now, you know that's what she would say."

"Yeah, but just because I can't control it doesn't diminish the hurt that she endured, today especially. It's one thing for me to have to put up with all of Mother's manipulations. I'm practically immune to all her tricks, but the way she treated Celine, telling her that I'd be embarrassed to have her ride with us? And the way she yelled at her at the burial, I'm telling you, Alex, Mother's never going to do that to Celine again."

Alex finished his drink, cocked his head and smiled. "You know, my boy, you would've never said that six months ago."

Michael sipped his drink. "What do you mean?"

"You've grown from that quiet, brooding young man that moved in with me six months ago and become outgoing and passionate about life. I think Celine has given you a new outlook."

"She has, Alex. She certainly has." Michael leaned forward, staring into the deep-gold scotch. "This week's been absolute hell; dealing with Father's death and Mother's craziness, the lawyers and all the other crap." He sighed and looked at Alex. "But in the middle of all the chaos, I found myself running to Celine, even when we weren't together. Just thinking about her gives me so much peace." He shook his head. "The life that my parents have had, the life that they've given me, isn't what I want. I knew that six months ago, but I still questioned if I'd ever have the strength to leave it all behind. Celine has given me the courage to do what I couldn't have done myself; I don't want any part of Arnaud Oil. I want out. Completely out."

Alex frowned. "Michael, are you sure about that? Aren't you making a hasty decision?"

"No, it's not hasty at all and I know it's the right thing to do. Tomorrow at the board meeting, I'll present Mother as CEO, Riva as Acting CEO and business goes on as usual. No one loses and I'm gone."

Alex's shoulders dropped. "What are you going to do if the board doesn't approve your plan?"

"Then the company gets sold and I'm gone anyway."

"Do you realize the amount of wealth you're leaving behind? Michael, this is way past millions. Arnaud Oil has wells all over the world. We're talking billions of dollars. If the company gets sold, it's going to be like a shark feeding frenzy. It'll be a blood-fest with everyone trying to get a piece for themselves. When it's all done, all you'll have left is my little gallery. Are you certain that you'll be happy with that?"

"Your little gallery?" Michael's eyes grew wide. "Alex, I've seen your assets. I'm your business manager, remember? It's far from little. But apart from the financial part of it, I don't think you realize how happy I've been since I started working with you. All I want is to continue working at Arnaud Gallery. I'd be a fool to leave!"

"And you can, Michael, but right now might not be the best time to make such a final decision. Leaving Arnaud Oil might feel like the right thing to do right now, but maybe in six months, you'll see it all very differently. It's okay to just take a step back and let the emotional trauma pass before you make any choices."

"Alex, it's been the choices you've made in your life that's opened up the possibility of a happier life for me. You've given me my creativity back! I met Celine because of you! Now, happiness is not only possible; it's here, right now! Why would I trade that for Arnaud Oil; just so I can own my father's legacy? Greed, cruelty, infidelity and now I can add pedophilia to the list. And what about Mother's manipulation and lies? No thanks. If I go back, something inside me will die, I know it. It would kill Celine, too. She could never be part of that insanity. No, Arnaud Oil would be the end of us and that I could never live with!"

Alex smiled. "I know I'm not your biological father, but I can't imagine that any father could be more proud of you than I am right now. When do you plan on breaking the news to your mother?"

Michael looked at his watch. "It's 8:15. I'll go talk to her now. That should give me plenty of time to finish with her and then call Celine." He looked at Alex. "Did Mother tell you what she wanted?" He downed the last of his drink. "Because she always wants something."

"No, but I could tell she'd been crying. She said she'd be waiting in her bedroom for you."

Michael put the glass down and stood up. "Wonderful. One of her little bedroom talks. Let the guilt games begin. Turning on the tears even before I get there is one of her old favorites."

Alex smiled. "Yeah, but you've already made up your mind. There's no reason to fall into her trap anymore. Just tell her and get it over with."

Michael strode across the room. As he put his hand on the doorknob, he turned and looked at Alex. "Thanks, Alex. I don't know where I'd be without you."

Alex laughed as he lifted his glass in a mock toast. "You'd be either one of the richest men in the world or a just another homeless starving artist."

Michael laughed as he left the office. His footsteps echoed on the oak wood floors of the empty house. Everything was quiet except for the distant clanking of a few dishes and indistinct chatter as the house staff cleared and cleaned away the remnants of the funeral reception. As Michael ascended the stairs, dread crept into his thoughts with every step. He stood in front of his mother's bedroom door, breathing deeply. He thought of Celine, her smile, her eyes then looked at his watch. 8:20. He knocked, turned the knob and opened it just a crack. "Mother?"

The room was dark. "Michael? Is that you?"

He quietly slipped into the room. "Yeah, it's me." The scent of lilacs filled the air, the overpowering aroma of his mother's perfume that Michael knew so well. From across the room, a small tiffany lamp clicked on. He could see his mother, seated in a white velvet chair, dressed in a long baby-pink robe, the lacy ecru cuffs draping down across her wrinkled hands. She held a wine goblet, the glass half full of red wine. A nearly-empty bottle stood next to the lamp on the table at her elbow. Her freshly-brushed, long blonde hair draped down each shoulder and glistened in the light as she turned to him. He could see she had been crying. Her face looked sallow without the layers of make-up she usually wore. He walked across the room and sat down on the ottoman at her feet. "Alex said you wanted to see me?"

"Oh Michael, Michael. How could you do this to me?" She reached out her hand and began to cry. She dabbed her eyes with a lace handkerchief that she'd been holding.

Robotically, Michael reached out and took her hand in his. "What's wrong, Mother?"

She looked into his face, her hazel eyes misting golden in the lamplight. "What's wrong? What's wrong? You're marrying that girl. That's what's wrong!"

Michael frowned, confused. "What are you talking about?"

"Don't play dumb with me! Junie bean told me all about it. When were you going to tell me?" Michael dropped her hand as he remembered Kelly's face when she saw the ring. He sat back, stifling a smile. Victoria glared at him. "You have nothing to say?"

Oh brother. Here we go! "Mother, stop worrying. I…"

"Stop worrying? We just buried your father. He's not even cold in the grave and…" She took a sip of the wine and then glared at him. "We need to settle the estate before you go strutting around like some prize bull, claiming a wife!"

Michael stood up slowly. "Prize bull?"

Victoria sat back. Her face softened. "Michael, listen, I understand. All this time you've been living with Alex, you needed to have your freedom. You've needed to experiment, try out your artistic side and be with different types of women. Okay, of course I understand. It makes sense, but everything's different now. You're stepping into your father's shoes." She sat up proudly. "It's time you live up to your name, Michael Sterling Arnaud! Having the right wife at your side will be more important than you could ever imagine." She downed the last of the wine and put her glass down on the table.

Michael looked down at his watch. 8:25. He looked up and stared at his mother. *I will not get angry. I will just tell her.* "Mother, I have to talk to you about something."

Victoria shook her head putting her hand up. "No, Michael I won't listen to it." She poured more wine into her glass until the bottle was empty, picked up the glass and held it. "Don't try to tell me you love that girl. Even if you do, love is not enough to sustain the man that you will become! She'll crumble the first time you have to leave her home alone while you go abroad for months at a time. She'll never survive the devastation when you desire another pretty young woman, and that will happen."

"Mother, you've had too much to drink. Now, put the glass down."

"But it will, Michael! It will happen! The wife of a powerful man must accept these things. She must endure. Now sit down and…"

"Mother! Stop it!" Michael closed his eyes, breathing hard, his fists clenching. He looked back at Victoria. She put the wine glass on the table and sat like an obedient child. He'd seen that look in her eyes too many times before when his father had yelled at her. He lowered his voice. "Mother, just listen to me, okay?" Victoria dabbed her eyes and sat quietly. "Tomorrow, I'm announcing to the Board that I'm not going to be CEO for Arnaud Oil. I…"

"What?" Victoria's voice was shrill. "You don't mean that. You're just confused. This has all been such a shock for us. You can postpone the meeting, you know. You're in control of everything now. If you need a few days, just tell them. They have no choice but to do whatever you tell them…" Michael watched his mother rant but her words became a distant hum. *Why did I think she would ever be able to hear any of this? I'm just going to have to tell her. To hell with how she takes it.* "…so you see, Michael, if they want to keep their jobs, all you have to do is…"

Michael put his hand up and spoke very softly. "Mother, I'm keeping my job at the gallery with Alex. I'm not going back to the company." Victoria stared at Michael, wide-eyed. The room was quiet. "I plan to tell the Board tomorrow that I'm recommending you as CEO and that Riva be the acting CEO. That way you still get everything and the company stays intact. I'm hoping that you'll agree."

Victoria aimed her eyes on Michael like a gun. "She put you up to this, didn't she?"

Michael frowned at his mother. "What? Riva didn't put me up to anything. I…"

"I knew it! I knew it the minute I met her!" Victoria's voice was slowly growing in volume. "She's trying to ruin us! Who is she Michael? Who is this Celine? Do you even know?" Her thin hands shook as she screamed. "It's Alex, isn't it? You met her through Alex! They're in it together!" She stood up, throwing herself into Michael's chest. "He was always so jealous of Robert. He stole you from us and now he's going to destroy everything Robert worked for!" She grabbed the front of his shirt, pulling her to him. "Michael, don't do this! Don't marry that girl!"

Michael grabbed her hands, prying them from his collar. "Mother, STOP it!" The smell of her perfume mixed with the strong scent of the wine on her breath began to sicken him. He shook her hands as he yelled. "STOP IT! You're drunk! You need to calm down!"

She immediately stood still and lowered her voice. "I'm calm, Michael, I'm calm." She turned and walked back to the chair and sat down. She folded her hands in her lap and smiled. "See? I can be good and if I'm good, you'll be good too, right?"

Michael took a deep breath. *I am so tired of all her games! I'm so tired of all of this!*

"But Michael, Michael, be my good boy and break up with her. If it's money she wants, we can give it to her. Any amount, anything she wants. I've already talked to Kelly. She's willing to wait, Michael. I've already told her what to expect as your wife and she's already agreed."

"You did what?" Michael clenched his fists as he stood glaring at his mother.

"She'll be the perfect wife for you. I told her, I warned her about all the appetites you Arnaud men have. She was crushed when she saw that ring; such a cheap little ring she described to me. Let the girl keep it. You can get a real one for Kelly. Michael, Junie bean's willing to take you back. It's all okay now."

Michael stepped back. *This whole thing is insane. She and Father together; they're so sick. I can't do this.* He glared at Victoria, his mind screaming, but his words came out low and calm. "If you want to keep Arnaud Oil, you will go to the board meeting tomorrow. Alone. I'm done with all this, mother. I'm leaving. I'm going to be with Celine and I'm going to marry her!"

Michael turned to leave, but his mother leapt out of the chair and grabbed his arm. "No! Michael, please! They're after you and they'll take us all down if you let them! You're throwing it all away, you're throwing me away!"

He pried her fingers from his arm and pushed her. She collapsed back into the chair, crying uncontrollably. Michael turned as the bedroom door opened. "Victoria? Are you all right?" Michael stepped around his aunt and walked toward the door.

"Livy! Livy! Michael's leaving me! Robert's left and now Michael, too! Livy! Livy! Stop him! He's going to marry that little tramp!"

Olivia rushed to Victoria's side then turned and stared at Michael. "Michael, what's going on? How can you do this to your mother? After all she's done for you!"

Michael shook his head as he put his hand on the doorknob. His voice quivered in anger. "She's lost her mind, Aunt Olivia. Just take care of her. I can't do it anymore. I won't. I'm leaving."

Michael bolted from the bedroom and down the stairs, his chest heaving. He hurried through the rooms toward the front door. *I have to get out of here.* He rushed from the house onto the front lawn taking deep breaths, the cool night air filling his lungs. He looked up at the full moon, its bright silver face shining down. He took a deep breath, turned and started walking toward the *garçonnière*. He pushed back his sleeve and looked at his watch. *9:05. I need to talk to Celine. I'll tell her what happened. I don't know what she's going to say, but God, I need to see her. I've got to get out of here. I'll drive to St. Maryville. Maybe there's a hotel there.* He walked into the *garçonnière* and pulled out his cell phone. He grabbed his bag and started throwing the few things he had unpacked into it. As he dialed Luisah's number, he zipped up the bag. She picked up in the middle of the first ring.

"Hello?"

"Hello, Mrs. Dupré? This is Michael Arnaud. Is Celine th…"

"Michael, oh chère, thank God! Where's Celine? Is she all right?"

"She isn't with you?"

"No. She called at 5:00 and said she was leaving but, Michael, she's not here, chère! She never made it home!"

Michael picked up his bag. "She hasn't called you since 5:00?"

"No, Michael. Oh chère, we've been so worried. I drove down to the Interstate to see if her car was broken down, but I didn't see her. I wanted to keep going, but my car is so old, I can't go very far before it overheats. I'm so afraid that she's stranded somewhere along the Atchafalaya Bridge." Michael's thoughts turned immediately to the huge, twenty-mile-long bridge crossing over the dark, menacing swamp. No exits, only miles and miles of water. "We were just about to call our neighbor and ask him if he'd drive the Interstate from here to Baton Rouge. If she's not along there, then she's closer to New Orleans and we could call the State Police."

"But she might be on the river road. She was taking that up to Baton Rouge and then getting on Interstate-10 from there."

Luisah groaned. "She hates driving the river road. It's so dangerous and dark out there. I'm very afraid for her. We need your help. Please, could you drive up the river road and go look for her?"

Michael ran out of the *garçonnière* toward the garage. "I'll leave right now, Mrs. Dupré. I'll drive the entire route to St. Maryville and look for her. I'll call you when I find her, okay?"

"Oh, thank you, chère. Thank you! Wait. Hold on, Michael." Michael heard Luisah talking to someone else in the background, then Luisah spoke into the phone. "Celine's Mo-maw wants to talk to you."

Mo-maw came on the line. "Michael?"

Michael kept running, finding it hard to talk as he ran. "Yes, ma'am?"

"Michael, somet'ing's wrong, chère, somet'ing's very wrong. Find her, but you must be careful, too. You're the only one who can bring her home, chère. Do you understand me?"

Michael slowed down as he ran into the garage. Out of breath, he answered. "Yes, ma'am. I'll call when I find her…" He sucked for air. "…and I won't give up until I do."

"We'll be right here, chère, praying hard for her and for you."

Michael hung up and shoved his hand deep into his pocket, searching for the Ferrari keys. *Why didn't I call her earlier? Why did I let Alex talk me into waiting?* He pulled out the car keys as he hurried over to the group of chauffeurs seated at a table, who were busy with a game of poker. "Julien, where's Father's Ferrari?"

Alex's chauffeur, Julien, turned, surprised to see Michael standing there. "Mr. Michael. What can I do for you, sir?"

"The Ferrari, where is it?"

Julien frowned as he pointed to a row of limos parked in the garage, the Ferrari at the end. "Over there, sir, but the brakes need adjusting. I could drive you in the limo, sir. Where do you want to go?"

Michael didn't even answer. He hurried down the row of cars. Julien got up and followed him. "Mr. Michael, sir. The Italia, she's a bit rough. Not like your Porsche. They're similar, but her brakes need fixing again."

Michael walked up to the car. "Yeah, well, my Porsche isn't here and this is all I've got. Is the Ferrari drivable?"

Julien ran behind Michael. "Yes sir, but please, be careful. The brakes are a bit spongy. Keep your speed moderate just in case you have to jam the brakes to stop. You'll need to pump them."

Michael turned to Julien as he threw his bag in the passenger seat and slipped into the car, adjusting the seat for his long legs. "Listen, go to the house and tell Alex that I'm going to St. Maryville tonight. I don't know when I'll be back to the gallery. Got that?" Julien nodded. "Now get the garage door for me." Michael slammed the car door, turned the key and the red convertible Ferrari 458 Italia roared to life. As soon as Julien raised the door, Michael threw it in first and sped off into the night.

The tires spit gravel as he accelerated through the driveway. He barely slowed down as he pulled onto the narrow two-lane road that snaked along the Mississippi River. The car had no problem hugging the curves as Michael sped up. *Celine where are you? Oh God, please, let her be okay.* The silver moonlight helped him look far into the distance ahead; a welcome guide in the dark, unlit road. *I've got to get to the Atchafalaya Bridge. That's probably where she is.* He pressed the car for speed with each curve, the tires screaming at every turn.

He wiped tears angrily from his eyes as he pushed the car to its peak performance. *This is all my fault. I should've gone with her. I didn't even think about the bridge.* Dirt and rocks spit from the tires and he veered around a curve. Images flooded his mind; his father's body, his mother's drunk, crazed eyes. He called out. "Celine where are you?"

A voice answered from behind him. "Where do you think you're going?" Shocked, Michael looked into the rear view mirror. A beautiful black woman, her long hair flying in the wind, looked back at him, smiling. "Better keep your eyes on the road."

In an instant, the car plunged into a huge pot hole. Michael automatically hit the brakes but the car didn't slow down, plunging at full speed off the road toward the twenty-five-foot-high levee. Michael pulled the steering wheel hard, but it was too late. The car reeled out of control and skirted along the earthen embankment, screeching and ripping its way through the mud-and-grass dam. Michael pumped the brakes until finally, the svelte frame of the Ferrari came to a stop, hissing. Michael's hands shook as he reached down and turned the key off. Blood trickled down his face; a deep cut striped his forehead. He gripped the steering wheel. *I'm okay. I'll just sit here for a second. What happened? Who was that woman?* He looked back into the rear view mirror but no one was there. He reached to unbuckle his seatbelt. A sudden chill ran through him when he realized he had never put it on.

He opened the door and stepped out of the car but, his knees buckled underneath him. He knelt on the ground trying to take deep breaths. Sharp rocks cut his hands as he struggled to stand but his head was too heavy. The dizziness forced him back down. He closed his eyes. *I'll be okay. I've got to get back in the car. I've got to find Celine!* When he opened his eyes again, the woman he had seen was now sitting next to him, watching him like a cat watches a mouse. Her hair was long and flowing; her silver gown glowed in the bright moonlight. "Where do you think you're going?"

Michael shook his head, trying to shake the dizziness. "Who are you? How did you get in the car?"

The woman stood up and glared down at him. "No, no. You don't get to ask the questions. I said, where do you think you're going?"

Michael looked up at her. He wiped the blood from his eyes. "I'm going to find Celine. I've got to get back in the car." He struggled to stand, but she pushed him back down.

"It's too late. You're too late. Just like all you Beauvoir men, you're always too late."

Michael shook his head. "What are you talking about? My name's Michael Arnaud. I have to go." He struggled to stand again but the woman dug her fingers into his shoulder. Michael winced and fell back to his knees.

"Oh, you're a Beauvoir." She leaned into his neck and sniffed his skin like a hungry animal. "I can smell it in your sweat! Evil to the end. Just like all the others." The woman squatted down and put her face into Michael's. "Do you want to find her?"

Michael reached to his shoulder, trying to pry her hand away, but she held him fast. "Yes. She's in trouble out here somewhere. I have to find her."

The woman eased her grip but didn't let him go. "You want to know where she is?"

Michael stared directly into the woman's red tinted eyes. "If you know where she is, please, tell me."

The woman let go of him and laughed. "There she is…" She turned and pointed to the eastern rising moon "…exactly where you put her."

Michael followed the woman's pointed finger and watched as the silver disk swirled, changed colors, twisted then settled into an image of Celine. Michael jumped up, ran around the car. "Celine!"

The woman laughed. "She can't hear you. You let her go. She's lost to you..." Her face hardened into hate. "...and it's all your fault. All your fault!" Michael watched in horror as Celine convulsed, her body twisting. Her face was distorted and bloated. She vomited blood. Her face turned a deathly blue. "You see, I told you. You're too late."

Michael turned to the woman. "What's happening to her? Why are you doing this?" Michael took a step toward the woman. "Who are you?"

The woman put up her hand, freezing Michael's steps. "I have done nothing. It's you. You've been so selfish and blind, you couldn't even see her transformation right before your eyes. She was poisoned. That old street woman poisoned her with the white powder. Couldn't you tell that she had stopped eating? Her body was wasting away in front of your eyes and you never saw it. No, all you saw was a beautiful woman, your Lady of the Letters, right? Your muse, right? Today, she was in so much pain — her headaches, the fever. The dreams were tormenting her. She was even hallucinating. When she left you, she was in immense pain but she didn't want you to know. You were so blind, you couldn't even see the pain she was in!"

"But her fever had gone. She took that pill and her headache was gone and she was feeling better."

"Did you not hear me? Are you deaf as well as blind? She loves you, though I really don't see why. She was willing to sacrifice her own well-being so you wouldn't have to worry about her while you dealt with your sick, twisted family! That kind of love you don't understand because you're a Beauvoir, you selfish idiot! You aren't capable of thinking of anyone but yourself! Because of your selfishness, she never made it home. She was overcome with pain and was forced to take a little detour into the Atchafalaya. Poor thing, she was in so much pain, she completely forgot that there wasn't a phone at the old camp out there. Can you imagine her anguish when she was writhing in pain, knowing she was probably going to die? Here's a little secret; she collapsed screaming for you. You! You've killed her. You!"

Michael fell back to his knees. "I would never want any harm to come to her! I should've..."

"Should've what? Driven her yourself no matter what she said? Left your crazy family behind and take care of her yourself? Given her your phone? But you didn't think of any of those options, did you? No! Because you're so self-absorbed!"

"Please, there must be something I can do to help her. Please, just tell me what to do and I'll do it. Anything!" Michael buckled over in sobs.

The woman watched him crying and smiled with sadistic pleasure. "Well, well, well, I have to say you are the first of your clan to make me such an offer."

Michael looked up at her quickly. "What do you mean?"

"Would you really do anything to bring her back?"

Michael scrambled to his feet. "Anything. Just tell me."

She walked a slow circle around him. "Anything, you say? You'll live to regret those words. You have a lot to make up for, not just for what you've done tonight but for all those Beauvoirs that chose to do nothing!"

Michael pleaded. "I'm begging for your mercy. I don't know who you are, but please, help me get to Celine. She needs me. Please, tell me what to do before it's too late." Michael looked back into the moon. Celine's body was pale and lifeless. "Please, oh God, she's dying."

The woman smiled. "Call the one named Mo-maw. Tell her Celine is at the deer camp. Tell her that the old street woman gave her Zombi's Cucumber, a slow and deadly dose. Mo-maw is my child. She'll know what to do. Sweet Celine's mother and grandmother, they'll keep her from dying but she'll be in a coma. Only you can bring her back."

Michael took a deep breath. "Tell me how! I'll do it!"

She laughed. "You will take Zombi's Cucumber, an extra special dose; tell them to use the good stuff." She winked. "If you survive that, then you have my permission to enter the gate. Of course, you'll have to depend on your own wits to find the gate. It won't be easy, probably impossible, but it'll be fun watching you try, anyway. After you get inside, and if you find her, then you will stand before me and I will decide your fate. Maybe you'll get my forgiveness and a lifetime with Celine. Or maybe..." she spoke through clenched teeth. "I will slowly devour you. This is the ultimate test of love; sacrificing everything, body and soul, for the sake of another, with no expectation of reward for yourself. Can you do it? Will you? This is your last chance to change your mind!"

Michael faced her. "I'd rather die trying than live without her!"

"Oh, I'll remember you said that!" The woman stepped forward and put her face directly into his. "Look at me and remember this. I am Ezilie. I live in the shadow of the moon. I have spared your life and now you belong to me! Now go! You have very little time. Hurry!" Ezilie disappeared.

Michael looked around. He was back on his knees, just outside the car door. He slowly stood up and reached into his pocket for his cell phone. He slid into the seat and dialed Luisah's number. As it rang, he turned the key, still in the ignition. *Please, start.* The engine sputtered. *Start, damnit!* The car sprang to life.

"Hello, Michael? Did you find her? Is she okay?"

Michael snapped his seat belt on. "Miss Dupré, she's at the deer camp. You and Mo-maw have to get to her right now. I'll meet you there, but I need directions."

"Chère, why did she go there?"

He shifted the car in first. "She got too sick to drive any further. She's really sick, Mrs. Dupré. Please, get there as soon as you can."

"Michael, chère, how do you know all this? Where did she call you from? There's no phone at the deer camp."

Michael pressed the accelerator and eased back onto the river road. "Ezilie told me and you need to bring something called Zombi's Cucumber."

CHAPTER 22

Luisah's hands were shaking as she twisted the rosary beads through her fingers. She was afraid to cry and afraid not to. She knelt next to the bed watching her daughter breathe, her chest moving quietly up and down. Celine looked peaceful now, not contorted and twisted in agony the way that she and Mo-maw had found her. When they walked into the deer camp, Celine was convulsing in a pool of blood, cold and unconscious. The memory brought a fresh wave of tears for Luisah. *Oh Mother Mary, sweet, sweet, St. Ezilie, be with her in this horrible place. And please, get Michael to us safely. He's the only one who can help her now.*

Luisah gripped the rosary as she remembered holding Celine's limp body while Mo-maw poured the Black Iris down her throat, the thick inky liquid dribbling out of the sides of her mouth as she gagged. Mo-maw massaged her neck yelling her name, "CELINE! CELINE! CHÈRE! You got to drink dis!" Luisah held Celine down as Mo-maw managed to get the dark liquid down her. One more violent convulsion ravaged her body and then she was quiet. Sleep replaced the pain, but it was far from peaceful and Luisah knew it. *…now and at the hour of our death…*

There were candles everywhere. The scent of healing powders and oils filled the air. *She looks like she's only asleep.* Luisah closed her eyes, painfully aware of the war that Celine waged on forbidden ground. The Cucumber was dangerous, even taken once. But this was Celine's second time, blown into her face, inhaled and imbedded deep into her bloodstream, pulsing throughout her body. The Black Iris slowed the process down but could never stop it. Never. *Oh, sweet Ezilie. My Celine was so afraid when that horrible street woman blew the powder in her face. Why didn't I listen? This is my fault! Can she survive this a second time? Please give me the strength! I can't bear to watch her go through this again; first as a little girl and now this! To lose her would be my death!* Luisah's low mourning cries drifted on the wet, humid air.

Mo-maw put her rosary beads in her pocket when she heard Luisah's sobs coming from the bedroom. She shifted her body in the chair and looked out the living room window, searching for Michael, listening for the sound of a car. *He should be here soon.* Her eyes scanned the darkness, but all she could see were moon shadows dancing in and out of the moss-filled cypress trees. She looked out into the dark swamp waters and smiled when she saw the full shimmering moon, its silver skirt dancing on the waters below. *Oh, Ezilie, you've blessed us with a Cajun Moon tonight, the same moon that you blessed Luisah with all those years ago.* Mo-maw sighed as the memory came back. *It was a night just like this one when you unlocked Luisah's womb and opened the door so that Celine could be conceived. Here we are again. Back where you gave your permission for our Celine's beginning. Is this where her life will end?* Mo-maw closed her eyes. *Help me; show me what to do, St. Ezilie. I've honored you, given you my life. Where are you? Why can't I see you?* No answer came, only silence. Dead silence. *Please, guide Michael's way. Get him here in time and make him strong enough to do what he must do. I'd do it myself, but I am old. I could never get her out. Oh, my Sacre Cœur, make him strong!* Mo-maw opened her eyes and whispered. "But you have always answered me, Ezilie. Where are you now?"

Slowly, she stood up and shuffled toward the bedroom. She paused at the door before she entered. She had to be strong now, even though she felt so weak. She turned the doorknob with her aged hand and entered the room.

Luisah looked up anxiously. "Is he here?" Mo-maw shook her head and sat on a low stool next to her daughter. She reached out and took Luisah's hand. Luisah looked back at Celine. "How did he know, Mama? I thought only the Bienaimée women could know these secrets."

Mo-maw sighed and shook her head. "He said Ezilie tol' him." Luisah looked at her mother. "Do you believe him?"

Mo-maw frowned. "Why would he lie? When we got here, wasn't everything just as he said it would be? He said she was here at the deer camp. He said she'd be unconscious. He said that old woman gave her Zombi's Cucumber. *Mon Dieu*, Luisah! How could he know about

Zombi's Cucumber, chère, if Ezilie didn't tell him? And how could he know he was supposed to take it?"

"Do you think he'll actually drink the Cucumber for her?"

Mo-maw nodded. "I t'ink so." She looked back at Luisah. "He said he would. He loves her very much, Luisah."

"But, Mama..." She looked at Celine. "...she's deep into a coma. If he's going to reach her, he's going to have to take a strong dose." She turned back and looked at Mo-maw. "Ezilie said the 'good' stuff. You know that means the vial that we've kept in the box all these years. We've never used it. It could kill him!"

Mo-maw nodded again. "We have to go on faith, chère. Ezilie talked to Michael, tol' him what to do. Okay, now we have to do our part, too, and that means we make sure that we give him just the right amount."

"We have to tell him the risks, though. When he hears that he could die, he might decide he can't do it, then what do we do?"

Mo-maw stared at her daughter. "Luisah, listen to me, chère. Celine loves this young man. You remember when she called to tell us that his poor papa died? Luisah nodded. "You remember what she said? She called him her Bienaimée."

Luisah smiled and nodded. "Yes, Mama, I remember."

"You know what she meant, Luisah. She chose him; chose him over any other to call him her Bienaimée! So chère, we need to trust Celine. He is her eternal beloved. Ezilie talked to him. He will do dis and he will find her and bring her back. We can not lose hope, Lala, and we must be ready to act when he gets here."

Luisah squeezed her mother's hand. "She's beautiful, Mama." Luisah stood up and smoothed the sheet around Celine and stroked her long black hair. She patted her hand, adjusting the ring on her finger even though it didn't need adjusting at all. "Celine, Michael's on his way, chère. Stay with us, Celine. Stay..." Luisah fell into sobs.

Mo-maw stood up and pulled Luisah into her bosom as they both cried. Mo-maw pulled away, gently wiping her tears away. "Luisah, why don't we pray togeth..." She stopped and turned. "Wait. Do you hear that?" A motor rumbled, grew louder and then stopped. "It's him, chère." The two women rushed to the front door, just as Michael stepped onto the deep, cypress porch. Mo-maw opened the door and saw a tall, young man dressed all in black. His shirt was torn and his pants and shoes were muddy. His black hair was uncombed; a few curls falling onto his forehead. He looked tired but his eyes were bright and alert. "Michael, chère, come in."

"Thank you, ma'am. I'm sorry it took so long. I got here as fast as I could."

Mo-maw smiled, her sweet, wrinkled face looking up into the young man's blue eyes. "Mo-maw, chère, call me Mo-maw. Everybody does."

He looked anxiously at Mo-maw as he walked into the small three-room cabin. "How's Celine?"

He looked at Luisah who had stepped up to Michael and took his hand in hers. "She's been waiting for you, Michael." Luisah looked into Michael's blue eyes. "Oh, Michael, we're so glad you're here." She leaned into him and hugged him, her tears streaming down her face. "It'll be okay now. You've come to help her." Michael wrapped his arms around her, soaking in the hug. Her warmth felt so much like Celine's. She stepped back and looked at him again. She frowned when she saw a line of dried blood down the side of his cheek. "Michael, are you hurt?" She stood on tiptoe as she reached up and pushed his curls away from his forehead. When she saw the deep cut, she said, "What happened? You're bleeding!"

Michael reached up and touched the cut with his fingers. "It's okay. I, um, went off the road, but I'm all right." He looked down, noticing for the first time, the mud on his pants and shoes. "I'm sorry, I just, please, can I see her?" He looked around the living room and on into the attached kitchen. "Where is she?"

Mo-maw took both his hands in hers and looked up. "Michael, chère, Celine is very fragile right now. You're very nervous and excited. If you go in dere right now, she could have another seizure and dat would only do her more harm. So, I need you to come sit down and take some big breaths." Mo-maw led him to a chair. "Dat cut needs some help and you need to slow down for jus' a minute. I know dis sounds impossible, but you need to be calm before you see her." Michael sat down, but Mo-maw could tell he was anxious, nervous, like a race horse unable to settle. She turned to Luisah. "Lala, get him some snake tea and go get you bag." Luisah hurried into the kitchen while Mo-maw sat in a chair next to Michael.

Michael reached up to his forehead with a shaking hand and tried to wipe the dried blood away from his forehead. "I can't get what I saw out of my mind. She was in so much pain. I just really want to see her, you know?"

Mo-maw reached out and took his hand in hers. In a touch she felt his overwhelming sense of love for Celine and at the same moment a lifetime of hurt. Mo-maw let out a soft gasp as she looked into Michael's eyes. "Let's get dat cut clean, okay? You look tired, Michael. You family, they've given you a lot of pain, yeah, chère?"

Michael looked into Mo-maw's deep brown eyes. "How do you know that?"

Mo-maw patted his hand as she nodded. "It's okay, Michael. You're a strong young man and wiser dan your years. Mais yeah, chère, our Celine, she has chosen well."

Michael could feel tears welling up inside him but he fought them back. "Mo-maw, all of that doesn't matter now. All that matters is that she's alright and I do what I have to do to help her."

Mo-maw nodded just as Luisah came back with a cup of snake tea and her black bag. Luisah handed him the cup and set the bag on the floor, opened it and pulled out a bit of gauze and a brown bottle. Mo-maw nodded again. "I know you're anxious but you drink all of dis down and you let Luisah clean you cut while I talk to you, okay?" Michael nodded, then sipped the tea obediently. He let out a deep sigh. Mo-maw smiled when she saw his shoulders drop. *The snake tea will relax him and give him strength. This young man hasn't gotten much love in his short life. Lots of nice things, but very little love.* Mo-maw squinted as she studied his face; young, handsome, but his eyes held a deep sadness in them. Mo-maw could sense his love for Celine. It was alive and raw and old, very, very old. Mo-maw smiled. "You're the one. You're her Bienaimée. She tol' us you were, but I can see it for myself now."

"I love her, Mo-maw." Michael put the cup down and leaned forward just as Luisah finished cleaning the blood away. "I'll do whatever I have to do to bring her back." Michael's voice began to break. "She can't leave me. I've only just found her. Help me to bring her back. Please."

Mo-maw reached out and took his hand. "Michael, chère, we're going to do everything we can but dere's some t'ings you need to know before you go in to see her." Michael stared hard at Mo-maw. "She looks like she's asleep, but she's not. She's fighting with ever't'ing she's got against some very dark evil, the kind I haven't seen in a long time. That old woman, she gave our Celine a powerful dose, the kind that was killing her slowly, but…"

Michael looked down. His face was furrowed with deep wrinkles. His voice was laced with sadness. "This whole thing. It's my fault. I should've seen it. I should've never let her leave. I should've gone with her. I could've gotten her to you sooner."

Luisah wiped away her tears. "It's my fault too, chère. When she told us that the old woman was trying to kill her, I didn't listen."

Mo-maw shook her head. "But it does no good for us to t'ink abo't all dat now. We have to move forward and get our Celine back. You're here now and you're going to bring her home to us."

Michael nodded. "Yes, let me take whatever it is I have to take; the sooner the better."

Mo-maw looked into Michael's young and determined face. "What you're gonna drink, it's a poison, Michael. We'll do da best we can to make it taste okay, but it's bitter and it burns going down. We have to give you a strong dose but we'll mix it wit' a small bit of the antidote. Dat will stop any long-term effects. You'll pass out and after dat, we have no way of knowing how long you'll be unconscious. It could be hours, or days."

Mo-maw sighed and stared hard into his eyes. "You might not come back to us at all. Chère, you could die."

Michael nodded and looked straight into Mo-maw's eyes. "Mo-maw, I really do appreciate how you're both trying so hard to protect me, but…" He stood up and turned to Luisah. "I'm going to do it. None of what you're saying matters."

Luisah reached out and took his hand, tears streaming down her cheeks. Mo-maw nodded her head and pushed herself out of the chair wearily. She stood up and walked to the bedroom door. Quietly, she stepped inside; Luisah and Michael followed close behind her. Mo-maw whispered to Michael. "Sit beside her and talk to her. She can hear you. I know she's been waiting for you, chère."

When Michael saw Celine, he rushed to the bed and sat down next to her. Her pale face blended in with the crisp linen sheet that covered her naked body. Her long, ebony hair had been brushed and draped down one shoulder. The only signs of life Michael could see were the deep breaths that moved her chest up and down. He took her hand in his and kissed it very gently. "I'm here, Celine. I'm here." Tears streamed down his face. "I'm so, so, sorry for everything." He leaned over and kissed her forehead and suddenly, Celine took a quick, deep breath. "Celine?" Michael spoke louder. "Celine?"

Mo-maw and Luisah came to the side of the bed. Mo-maw reached out and felt Celine's forehead. She looked at Michael. "Are you ready, chère? We have to act now!"

Michael eased himself from the side of the bed. "Just tell me what I have to do."

Mo-maw turned to Luisah. "Mix up the Black Iris. Add the whisky and bring me the vial. Get the Saint Suaire. Hurry, Luisah!"

She turned back to Michael and put her hand on his arm. She looked him over quickly. "Take off your watch and belt, your shoes and socks. Empty your pockets, too. Michael stood up and did what he was told as Mo-maw talked. "Listen to me now, Michael. After you drink dis, you'll fall back so we need you to sit on da bed next to Celine, chère. Da whole time you're unconscious, we'll be praying. We won't stop until you're back. When you start to come out of it, you'll hear us. Listen for our voices, chère. Follow our voices home. Okay?"

Michael repeated. "Follow your voices home."

Mo-maw stopped, put her arms around him and hugged him tightly as Michael hugged her back. "Bring her home to us, chère..." She looked up into Michael's face with tears in her eyes. "...but not wit'out you, Michael. Celine's heart will break if she has to face dis world without you. You must be careful and come home to us, safe and sound." She wiped her tears away and motioned to the bed. Michael took a deep breath and sat down.

Luisah came back into the room holding a glass of thick black liquid in her hand. She handed the vial of Zombi's Cucumber to Mo-maw.

Michael watched as Mo-maw tapped the vial of purplish white powder once, twice, three times into the glass of black liquid. It bubbled and sizzled as Luisah stirred. Mo-maw put her hand on his head and blessed him. *"Au nom du Père, et du Fils, et du Saint Esprit. Amen."*

Luisah handed the glass to Mo-maw, who waited until Luisah picked up her black book and began to pray. "St. Michael, the Archangel, defend us in battle; be our defense against the wickedness and snares of the devil and protect your good son, Michael Arnaud, as he journeys into the abyss of Hell. *Pour Honorer Le Saint Suaire de Notre Seigneur Jesus Christ...*"

Luisah recited the Saint Suaire as Mo-maw handed Michael the glass. "Drink, chère. We're here. We're not leaving and we'll be here to welcome you both home."

Michael looked into the glass, took a deep breath, then as quickly as he could, he began to drink. One gulp. It burnt going down. Another. His stomach lurched. He forced his throat open for yet one more swallow but everything inside him blazed with the fire of acid. He could feel the flesh of his insides being eaten away. He dropped the glass, clutching his throat. He fell back, the breath taken from him. He gasped, opening his eyes wide. *Mo-maw! Help me.* He reached for her, but she was fading away from him as he slipped deeper and deeper into nothing.

His skull throbbed with a hideous pounding that ripped its way through his body. He convulsed, the seizures taking total control. The driving, possessing agony engulfed him as he felt himself being split in two. He twisted, clawing at the air, trying to get free. Far away, he could hear screams, chants, words. "Oh my God, Mama! What have we done?"

It was Mo-maw's voice that saved him. "*Leg-ba, nous pra allé, Papa, si n'a passé.* Papa Legba let him pass. Grant him entrance. Ezilie, St. Ezilie, grant him entrance." Her droning, never ceasing, chanting voice lifted him and pulled him away. His soul was finally free, away from the painful eternity of suffering and what came in its place was emptiness, darkness, a shroud of nothing.

The abyss was cool and refreshing. He felt no pain. There was no sound, only silence and for one sweet moment, there was no memory, no attachment to anything; floating, flying, dreamless sleep. There was no time, no judgment, only oblivion. Then he heard a voice from far away, a whispered word, "Michael". The sound filled him with a body-crushing pain. Every part of him was in agony as he came crashing down onto a rock surface.

Face down, he moaned then opened his eyes to a deep, dark, swallowing black night. He slowly moved his fingers and felt the sharp prickling of gravel beneath his hands. He pushed down, trying to lift himself, but his strength had been drained. *I'll lie here for a while and then try again.* He closed his eyes. "Michael!" Michael heard a man's voice, loud and urgent. He reached out into the darkness with a trembling, unsteady hand. "Michael! Get up! He's coming!" Michael felt hot breath on the side of his face and an ice-cold hand on his shoulder. "Michael! God-damnit! Didn't you hear me?" The man pushed Michael onto his back and jerked his arm trying to get him to stand up.

Michael looked up through blurry eyes at the naked man standing over him. The man's eyes were darting back and forth and his face was pale, taut with absolute fear. He was breathing hard and his chest was heaving like he'd been running. "Father?"

"Stand up, Michael! Now! He's coming!"

Michael struggled to stand up. He coughed and sputtered as he did his best to regain his strength. He looked down at his father, blinking, trying to focus. "I don't understand. Why are you here?"

Robert grabbed his son's arm. "We've got to run. That thing is coming. Come on!"

Michael looked around doing his best to see where he was. Old and crumbling crypts covered every inch of ground as far as he could see. Michael stumbled as his father pulled him along. "Hurry, Michael."

Michael looked at his father, realizing that the man was terrified at whatever was chasing him. Both his legs were covered in blood and long claw marks ran from his neck and down his back. There was a large gaping wound on the back of his head and what looked like bite marks down each of his arms. "What's happened to you? Why are you…?"

Robert stopped running and took a step away from Michael. He dropped to his knees, closed his eyes, put his hands over his ears and screamed. "Don't you hear it? God, make the screeching stop!"

Michael squatted to the ground next to his father and listened for a sound but all he heard was a stillborn silence. "I don't…" Robert stood up, reached out and grabbed Michael's wrist, pulling him deeper into the cemetery. "Come on, son. Over here!" Michael looked behind him and saw a huge wrought iron gate. *Wait. I should get to that gate.* He looked up and saw a full moon, dipping low in the sky. A deep sadness fell over him and his heart filled with longing. He felt a sharp pain in his chest as he mourned the loss of something precious, something he could never replace. *What have I lost? Not what. Who?* Michael pulled his hand back and turned around toward the gate. *The gate; I'll find whatever I've lost at the gate.* Robert reached back and grabbed his arm. "No! Not that way. That's the wrong way!" Robert pulled Michael behind one of the crypts, crouching down. "We can't go near that gate. We can hide here!"

Michael looked hard at his father. *Am I feeling this sadness at the loss of Father?* Michael shook his head, leaned up against the crypt wall, drew his legs to his chest and placed his hands on the ground. He looked up into the sky. The moonlight cast shadows around the tombstones. *But I'm here with him. Does that mean I'm dead?* He turned to Robert who was sitting next to him, panting. "Father, where is this place?"

Robert put his hands over his ears again. His entire body shook with fear as he cried like a child. Michael felt a warm trickle of water run over his hand. He looked down realizing that his father had wet himself. Disgusted, Michael pulled his hand away and wiped the urine off his hands into the grass. Robert began to rock back and forth crying quietly, "Makeitstopmakeitstopmakeitstop!"

Michael reached out and touched Robert's arm. "Father, there's nothing here. It's just you and me. You're alright!"

Robert dropped his hands from his ears and looked at Michael. A strange smile began to etch across his face. "Why are you here, Michael? You shouldn't have come. I wouldn't have had to give you to him if you just would've stayed away."

Michael shook his head. "What are you talking about?"

Robert stood up and called to someone in the distance. "He's here and I kept him away from the gate just like you told me!"

He looked back down at Michael. "You'll be okay. Really, you should thank me. I talked him into going easy on you. It's going to hurt at first, but then it'll be alright. Just don't fight it. The more you fight, the worse it'll be."

A wave of terror washed over Michael as he stood up. "What? Who are you talking about?"

A voice, deep and rumbling came from behind Michael. "Yes. He'll do nicely."

A clawed hand pierced Michael's shoulder, its long razor-sharp fingernails digging into his collarbone. The pain engulfed him, forcing Michael to his knees. He screamed as he pried at the claw, but the more he pulled, the deeper it imbedded into his shoulder. Michael cried out as the pain drained him of his strength. "Father, help me!"

Robert backed up, his face expressionless. "You really shouldn't have come here, Michael! This is all your fault!"

Michael twisted his body, straining to see what had him, but all he could make out was the yellow, oozing skin and one flesh-covered wing. The monster stepped closer to Michael. He could feel its hot spittle burning his neck and the overpowering reek of its sulfur-smelling breath blowing into his face. In a low deep voice it whispered, "Don't you remember me?"

Michael panted, trying to stave off the pain. "No. Let me go!"

The monster snorted as it traced one claw through his hair, hooked onto the collar of his shirt and began slowly ripping the fabric down the length of his back. "Oh, but I remember you. Celine introduced us. Don't you remember? Oh well, maybe not. 'Her dream, not yours. But now it's your turn. Such a sweet and tender young man and so..." The monster laughed. "...virginal. First times are always the best."

Michael could feel the weight of the monster pushing him further to the ground, bending him over onto all fours, forcing his legs apart. He looked up at Robert. "Father, please!" The monster hooked its claw in the waist of his pants.

Robert stepped forward, a smile curled on his lips as he squatted down, staring hungrily into Michael's face. The monster let out a low, grinding laughter. "He's not going to help you. Don't you know he likes to watch?"

Michael shrieked at Robert, his voice filled with hate. "You sick bastard! Watch? Oh, you've done more than watch! All those little girls! Did it stop there? What about little boys?"

The monster stopped and craned its serpentine head, looking at Robert. "Really? Is this true?" The monster slowly unhooked its claw from Michael's pants, took a step away from Michael and set its eyeless skull onto Robert.

When Michael felt the monster lean back, he screamed. "Yes, it's true! I found photos in his desk drawer. All of them little girls, some of them barely twelve, maybe younger."

Robert stood up. "He's lying! You want him! Not me! He's ripe! Ready for plucking! I never touched him, I swear. There were others, yes; only a few little boys, but not him. Take him!"

The monster eased its grip on Michael's shoulder as it leered at Robert. "So, you're saying that your son is lying? Oh, let me check." The monster pushed its putrid face into Michael's neck and licked the bleeding gash on Michael's shoulder. Michael screamed as the rough, cat-like tongue scraped the raw wound. The beast pulled back and spit into the ground. "No, Robert! Lies taste sweet. He's telling the truth." The monster stepped to Michael's side and smiled wickedly at Robert. "You're my kind of guy, Daddy. Why didn't you tell me you were into kids?"

Robert backed up. "No! No! I don't do kids! Michael, tell him! I never touched you! There were times I wanted to. I'd go in your bedroom at night and watch you sleeping. You were so innocent. I thought about it, of course I did, but I never touched you. Tell him!"

The monster ran at Robert. "Shut up! Stop whining and take it like a man!" Robert turned to run but fell against one of the crypts. The monster's long claws grabbed Robert's chest, flipped him over and pushed him faced down onto the hard ground. It plunged its long whip-like penis into him, lifting his body up off the ground as it pounded into him. Robert screamed as the thing cackled. "An eternity of this; what could be more fun?"

Michael pulled back into the shadow of the crypt, horrified. He turned his face into the cold stone. *I've got to get out of here!* As he crept around the crypt, he looked up and read the inscription on the headstone. *Michael Sterling Arnaud.* It can't be! No! He jumped up, pulled his torn shirt off and ran toward the gate. He shook the wrought iron bars but it was bolted shut. He looked up into the moon, screaming. "Help me!" He turned and saw the monster still pounding into his father. He shook the gate again and looked up. *I'll climb over it!* He tried to scale the cold, thin poles but his hands kept slipping. Michael pressed his face between the bars and in the distance could see someone hurrying up the path.

"I'm coming! I'm coming!"

Michael screamed. "Hurry! Please, let me in!"

As the figure drew nearer, Michael looked behind him and saw the hideous predator look at him, its mouth open and bloody. It screeched. "I'm done with Daddy. Time for you, now!"

Michael turned and shook the gate again. "Hurry! Please!"

"I said I'm coming!" An old black man drew nearer, frowning at Michael. "What's the big hurry?" He looked beyond Michael and over to the monster. "Oh, damnit, he's at it again! Mauvais!" The old man's deep voice came bellowing out. "Mauvais! Cut that shit out!" The monster averted his gaze from Michael and looked at the old man. When Michael heard the name Mauvais, a chord of memory struck from deep inside him. *Celine. Oh God, Celine! No! NO!!*

"Mauvais! I said cut it out. Go back to that hole where you belong!" The monster snarled, flipped Robert over, bit into his stomach and carried him off. Michael dropped to his knees as he heard his father screaming in agony. *Is she dead, too?* Tears fell onto his bare chest. *She dreamed this. She dreamed her end and mine, too.*

"Come on, now. Get up!" Michael looked up. The old black man was gray-haired, carried a burlap shoulder bag across his chest and held a walking cane. He stood behind the wrought iron gate. "Come on, now. I can't keep that wicked Mauvais away from you all day." Michael tried to pull himself up, but the loss of Celine overwhelmed him. The old man pulled a huge set of keys out of his bag and began to unlock the gate. "Michael, I said get your ass up! If you want to ever see your little lady again, you'll move it, now!"

Michael looked up and pulled himself to standing. "She's alive?" The keys clanked as he opened the huge gate, its hinges screeching with age.

"Of course she's alive! She's got better sense than to come this way..." He shook his head. "...unlike you, I see."

Michael breathed a sigh of relief. "You know where she is? Can you take me..."

As he tried to step through the gate, the old man took his cane and put it squarely into his chest looking him up and down. "Look at you! You're a mess! You don't even have a shirt on!" Michael looked down at his pants, his hands and feet were cut and bleeding and his chest had lines of blood streaming down from the gaping wound on his shoulder. He looked up at the old man who was looking at Michael's neck. "Hmmm, Mauvais nearly got you there, but…" He stepped back and pushed his cane into Michael's chest. "…you gotta pay me b'fore you can come in here!"

Michael frowned. "What? Pay you? I don't have anything." Michael reached for his wallet, hoping it was there. "Look I don't have time for this! I have to get to Celine."

The old man laughed. "Oh, you've got lots of time and I heard your family has lots of money, too. Give me some!" He reached down and patted Michael's pockets. When he didn't feel anything there, he thumped Michael's chest with his cane. "You ain't gettin' in unless you pay me!"

Michael began to panic. "I don't have anything. No money, nothing. Maybe when I get home I could…"

"Get home?" The old man threw his head back and laughed. "Buddy, for all I know you ain't gettin' home! So you give me somethin' now!"

Michael grabbed the old man's cane and pushed it away from his chest. "Look, old man, nothing, and I mean nothing, is going to keep me from getting inside. You said Celine is in there and I'm here to bring her home. Now, if you know where she is, take me to her. I promise you I'll pay you when I can."

A slow smile crept across the old man's face. "So you're payin' me with a promise, huh? Whatever I want, huh?"

"Yes! Now please, take me to Celine!"

The old man nodded. "Okay, but I won't forget what you said. I never forget nuthin!" He stepped aside and Michael rushed passed him. The old man locked the gate, placed the huge ring of keys into his tattered shoulder bag and toddled alongside Michael. "Come on, now. You're late!" The old man stabbed his cane into the ground with a thump and began to walk.

"Where are we going?" Michael looked around, noticing through the growing gray light that they were walking through an open field filled with waist-high grass.

The old man shook his head. "Didn't nobody tell you nuthin'?"

Michael shook his head as the memories came crashing back. He'd only been with Mo-maw and Luisah about an hour before he drank that horrible stuff. "There wasn't any time."

Legba stopped walking. "You don't even know where you are, do you?"

Michael stopped reluctantly and looked at the old man. "Look, all I know is that I have to get Celine out of here. She's dying! Please, I need your help."

Legba shook his head, leaning on his cane. "I can't believe this. Even the smartest ones, you know, the ones who've studied this place all their lives, some of them never even make it past Mauvais' little cemetery. The poor cats that get trapped in there, they spend the rest of eternity playing all his little games. I don't know how you did it, but you made it. You're either just plain stupid or one lucky mother-fucker!"

Michael closed his eyes trying to hold back his frustration. "Listen. All I know is I have to get her…"

Legba nodded his head. "Yeah, yeah, blah, blah, blah, you got to get Celine out. No, you're not stupid, you're not lucky, it's worse. You're in love, which makes you blind and blind ain't gonna do you no good with all you're about to face! Look, why don't you make it a lot easier on yourself, huh? Turn around right now and go back. I'll even help you get past old Mauvais. Just tell everyone you tried. Your sweet lady'll be fine. There's plenty of guys up in here that'd take her in a heartbeat." Legba straightened up. "I'll take her, man, if it makes you feel better. Then we're even. I get the girl and you don't owe me nuthin'!"

Michael grabbed the old man's cane from him and yelled. "You don't touch her! Get me to her, now!"

Legba teetered on his feet for a second then turned his choco-late-brown eyes onto Michael. "Okay, okay, I heard you. Just don't you be cryin' at me later that I didn't give you no chance. Now give me back my cane and we'll go."

Michael breathed hard, his nostrils flaring. He handed the cane back. "Hurry!"

The old man stabbed the cane into the ground again and started walking. "Since you're fool-headed enough to do this, you need to know some stuff, so listen up and don't ask me any God-damned questions. I hate it when they ask me questions! And, answer me right away when I ask you somethin'. Got it?" Michael nodded. "Okay, Einstein, you're at the gateway of the African Powers. Have you heard of them?" Michael shook his head no. "So, then I guess you haven't heard of the Loa? You know Vodoun Gods and Goddesses? Michael shook his head again. "Danbhalah?" He kept going. "Aida-wedo? Ogou? Michael kept shaking his head. The old man yawned. "Legba? Ezilie?"

Michael's eyes lit up. "Wait, yes, Ezilie."

The old man shook his head. "I shoulda known the only one you'd know is Ezilie. Everybody knows her. Everybody loves her. They don't know the whole story, though. She can fool you. Man, she fooled me! Got me in bed with her and she did things that every man wishes a woman would do. 'Got me to marry her. That sweet little bitch got me to marry her mean little ass!"

"You're Ezilie's husband?"

"That's a question but I'll let it slide. Yeah, I'm Legba, Papa Legba and Ezilie is my wife. But wait..." he stopped walking and looked at Michael. "That little lady of yours, Celine, she's one of Ezilie's special girls, right?" Legba's mouth curled slowly into a smile. "Oh yeah, but you know what I'm talkin' about don't you? She's really good in bed, am I right? Ezilie's girls always are!"

Michael stood next to Legba and took a deep breath. "Keep walking."

Legba laughed. "Now I get it! I know why you want her back! You find a good piece like that, you'd fight anything, right? Hell, you'd even kill to keep that sweet thing in your bed!"

Michael shook his head trying to ignore Legba. "Keep walking!"

Legba leaned into him, laughing. "I bet you ain't never cum the way you cum with her. She knows how to grip that cock of yours in her sweet pussy, am I right, man?"

Michael lunged at Legba, grabbing him by his clothes and yelling. "Get me to Celine and stop playing these games with me!"

With an unexpected strength, Legba punched Michael in the gut with his cane, sending him falling backwards, flat on his back, hitting the ground hard. Michael gasped, the wind knocked out of him. As he struggled to get up, Legba put the tip of his cane into Michael's chest, pushing him back down. "Don't you ever touch me like that again, you dig? Only reason you're alive is 'cause Ezilie told me that you're gonna be put on trial and I have to get you there. I shoulda just let Mauvais have you! Now get up!"

Legba took his cane from Michael's chest, turned and began to walk faster. Michael scrambled to his feet and followed along. Legba looked up into the sky and then shook his head. "Man, you are late. If you would've gotten here a little sooner, Ezilie Mansur would've been presiding over your trial. She would've forgiven you in a heartbeat and you could've taken your sweet little Celine out of there without an ounce of trouble. But in a few minutes, Mansur's gonna be gone and Ezilie Dantur will be sittin' on the bench. Now she is one wicked-ass judge and oh, she is gonna have some kind of fun with you!"

Michael shook his head, confused. "Are there two Ezilies? I don't understand. Isn't there just one St. Ezilie?"

Legba stopped as they reached a gravel path. He rolled his eyes at Michael. "I didn't think you could get any dumber! Shit, man, the two of them are the same bitch, she's just moody! One minute she be all sweet and cuddly, that's Ezilie Mansur. She's the one I like the best. But then there's the mean one, the one you get. That's the one called Ezilie Dantur. Only way I can stay married to her is if I change myself from the handsome creature you see before you into something really hot and sexy. Dantur likes me hot and sexy." He looked into the sky. "Too late. Dantur is sitting now!" He looked back at Michael, "She's really pissed at you for some shit your family did, so don't do anything that'll make her any madder. Just do everything she tells you and you might get to live."

A warm glow in the distance was burning away the gray haze, turning the sky a deep scarlet red. Legba looked at the orange fireball rising rapidly over the horizon. Michael could feel its intense heat already burning his skin, making his bloody wound on his shoulder prickle. Legba shook his head. "See how the sun's chasing the moon? Oh, those two. Always wantin' to make some long, mad sweet love! We gotta hurry. When that old man sun catches his lady moon, they're gonna start at each other 'til there's nothing left of either one of them! We can't stay here much longer. It ain't safe!" He picked up his cane and pointed it into the sizzling sun. "Now, Celine is at the end of this path. There's a hut…"

Michael didn't wait for him to finish and ran as fast as he could down the path. He could hear Legba yelling behind him, "You can't face Dantur without Kalfou!"

The old man's words faded as Michael ran. In the distance he saw a circular, black mud hut. He slapped at mosquitoes and biting flies as he approached the crude structure, slowing his pace and walking to it cautiously. He called out, "Celine!", but there was no answer. He walked around the hut, tracing his hand along the slimy, wet surface looking for an entrance. As he came around the other side of it, he saw the sun blazing in the sky, rising to meet the full silver moon.

It was getting hotter by the second. Beads of sweat dripped down Michael's face. He turned back to the hut, knowing that he needed desperately to find the entrance. The long fingers of daybreak were creeping up the side of the hut and that's when Michael saw it: the man-sized cross drawn inside a circle. *Is this the way in?* He reached out to touch it when he heard panting and wheezing and the sound of shuffling feet hurrying up the path.

Michael looked back and saw Legba hobbling as fast as his legs could move. Out of breath, Legba looked up. "Almost time!" He toddled to the circle and picked up his cane, knocking loudly three times on the center of the cross. His voice startled Michael with its deep bass volume when he began to chant: "I am Kalfou, here to bless my children!" A multitude of voices returned from the depths of the hut: "Kalfou, your children await!"

The chanting grew louder and Michael watched as the circle gave way to a wide, gaping doorway. The sound of drums boomed and cracked from the depths of the hut. Hot air belched forth; the smell of sweat and everything human, alive and dead, washed over Michael. Confused, he looked back at Legba, but instead of the old man, a tall, handsome, young, Creole man with long flowing night-black hair and beautiful green eyes, dressed in red pants and a red shirt, took his place.

Michael frowned at the young man. "Who are you? Where's Legba?"

He grinned at Michael through perfect white teeth, picked up his cane and propped it on his shoulder. "The name's Kalfou! Only way I can stay married to Ezilie Dantur is if I'm hot and sexy, remember?" He threw his head back and laughed then looked at Michael with a wide grin. "Come on, man. The fun's just about to begin."

CHAPTER 23

Drums echoed from inside the hut, their syncopated, dissonant beat screaming: *kat-atatack-at-ak kat!* Kalfou looked back over his shoulder at Michael. He winked then stepped through the doorway and disappeared into a chasm of black. People cried in ecstasy, "Kalfou! Kalfou!" Michael hurried through the door after him and was immediately thrown into an ocean of dancers, gyrating and screaming wildly to the frenetic drum beats. Dressed all in red, the men ripped open their shirts while the women hoisted their skirts as an invitation, their hands grabbing at Michael as he pushed his way through the mob.

He looked around, searching for Kalfou but he was lost in the sea of crimson. The rattle of gourds and the crack of a whip forced Michael to look behind him, but all he could see were wide-eyed faces in hues of brown, marked with red, green and yellow stripes. Torches hung from the walls of the cramped hut, illuminating the crude ornate paintings sketched there. Crosses, snakes, hearts and skulls of all shapes and sizes shimmered as if they were alive.

Along the wall, four bare-chested men pounded on long, thin drums, chopping and slapping with their bare hands; the rapid 6/8 rhythm propelling the dancers into frenzy. Rapping on cowbells with sticks, chanting and singing praises to Ezilie; the cacophony was deafening. The fluid motion of the dancers swirled across the room in a swath of red. The raw, earth scent of human sweat poured from body to body, baptizing Michael as his chest smeared against theirs. Open sensual hands stretched out, reaching and stroking over every part of his body; pulling, pushing, caressing and slapping. Voices sang out in perfect-pitch praises, while others cursed in sharp minor keys. Engulfed by the stifling heat, all of it washed over Michael, deluging his senses.

He fought against it, but the more he fought, the more the dancers pushed back, surrounding him. A woman, tall and beautiful, blew a white powder into his face. He coughed, unable to catch his breath. He felt himself slipping away, growing dizzy, his legs weak. *The powder; is it the same...?* The faces, the voices, the drums, the smells all melted into liquid shades of blue and black, disjointing into a surrealistic painting. Michael's eyes rolled back. His body felt numb, but he was still moving forward. A naked woman threw herself into him, pressing her breasts against his chest and stroked his face; a man grabbed his arm, pulling him away; a high-pitched laugh pierced his head; a gourd rattle shook in his face; the crack of a whip snapped at his heels, echoes and then a sense of calm. Euphoria.

The pulsing, mindless crowd moved Michael to the front of the hut toward a huge, stair-stepped, triangular altar, draped in bright yellow and royal blue homespun cloth overflowing with baked breads, yams, dishes of rice and beans and bottles of rum. The still-twitching bodies of black hens and bleeding pigs were adorned with yellow orchids and flowering blue nightshade. White, yellow and blue candles burned, transforming into long wisps of black smoke and wax dripping in rivulets down the length of the altar. Old faded photographs, some framed, some torn and wrinkled, were placed on the steps in homage to ancestors long gone, draped with rosaries made of red clay or glittering glass.

Seated on a golden throne in the center of the altar was a life-sized statue of Ezilie. Her flawless ebony skin glistened in the candlelight. She was dressed in a long gossamer robe, the rainbow of colors changing in the torchlight, like the iridescent wings of a dragonfly. The robe was loosely tied at her waist, the long center slit exposing both of her full, supple breasts. She sat with her long legs open, each bare foot adorned with silver anklets. She sat proudly, her long neck draped with a multitude of silver necklaces and from each ear, a huge silver loop hung down to her shoulders. Her long, ink-black hair had been braided into perfectly straight corn rows and twisted into a crown on top of her head. On one cheek, a crystal tear fell from her beautiful yellow-green eyes. Michael stared, mesmerized by her perfect, motionless beauty, unable to look away. *Ezilie! She's here! I've got to get to her.*

He pushed his way forward, the dancers smiling as they moved aside and made a path for him to walk through. He looked into the queen's face. The statue's beauty drew him in, one step after another, until he came to the base of the altar and dropped to his knees. Everything fell into silence as he stared into her eyes in adoration, unable to move, frozen in time. Her yellow-green eyes flickered, then softened in the candlelight. Her lips relaxed into a gentle, warm and loving smile. A sudden breath expanded her chest as she lowered her chin and smiled. Michael reached out. *I've got to touch her.* She outstretched her arms and opened her robe wide, revealing the soft hair between her legs. "Be with me Michael. Come."

Michael began to crawl up the altar, his heart overjoyed, forgetting everything and everyone. No sounds, his senses filled with only her, he pushed food and offerings aside. His gaze locked into Ezilie's sultry eyes until a voice rang out from behind, "Michael! NO!" *That voice.* He sat back on his heels, closed his eyes and exhaled a long, deep breath. *That voice!* Michael looked up just as Ezilie's head snapped up, staring angrily across the hall, her eyes turning blood red. Michael turned, following the line of her gaze and saw Celine through the crowd, fighting to make her way to him but getting tossed aimlessly like a twig caught in a current. Michael drew a quick breath suddenly remembering where he was. He stood up, the sights, sounds and smells rushing into him like a tidal wave, throwing him back into the ecstatic dancers.

Ezilie screamed, "Kalfou! How did she get out?"

Michael struggled to stand up, looking into the crowd, trying desperately to find Celine, but the dancers pressed him from all sides, their bodies slamming into him as he fought his way through them. Their eyes were rolled back; their bare feet were moving swiftly and violently as they stomped, pounded and slapped the rough-hewn wooden floor.

"Michael!" He turned and saw Celine just inches away from him; dressed all in white, she stood out from the crowd. He reached for her, but she was pulled back. Michael lunged forward, but just as he did, a woman jumped on his back, forcing him to his knees, sending him face down onto the floor. An ocean of undulating bodies folded over him, holding him down like a drowning tide. He closed his eyes and rolled into a ball, trying to keep himself from being crushed.

"Michael!" He opened his eyes and felt Celine's hand on his arm, trying to pull him up from the floor. Michael took her hand and pulled himself up. He threw his arms around her as the dancers grabbed at them, trying to pull them apart. Michael held her tightly, his arms like a shield against the scratching and clawing. He yelled over the din. "We've got to get out of here!"

Celine shook her head and screamed over the drums. "What are we going to do? There's no way out!"

"Kalfou!" Michael and Celine turned when they heard Ezilie's voice boom across the hall. "Where is she? They can not escape!"

Michael looked back toward the door, the vague outline of a cross inside a circle flickering faintly. He looked back at the altar and saw Kalfou, his face wrinkled in fury, making his way through the dancers toward them, using his cane to push the people aside.

Michael crouched down out of view, pulling Celine with him. "I think I can see the door. Come on!" They held onto each other tightly and fought their way back towards the door, crouching low and hoping that neither Ezilie nor Kalfou would see them. Just as Michael touched the wall, the drums stopped, a shrill whistle sounded and a bull whip cracked.

"Enough!" Everything fell into silence as Kalfou's command rumbled through the hall. He stood tall and erect, his long, silky hair falling down to his waist as he pounded his cane three times onto the floor. The sound echoed through the hut and the dancers bowed low, backing up against the walls, dropping to their knees and lowering their heads in a reverent silence.

Ezilie's voice was low as she narrowed her eyes at Kalfou. "Find them now!"

Celine grabbed Michael's hand and whispered, "Stay still. Say nothing." They joined the dancers, kneeling and bowing their heads. Michael knelt in front of Celine, hoping that he could hide the bright white of her dress. He wedged himself behind the people, hoping to camouflage both of them inside the throng. Michael squeezed Celine's hand, doing his best to calm his ragged breathing.

Kalfou surveyed the room like radar on watch, narrowing his bright green eyes. His gaze stopped when he caught a glimpse of Michael. He smiled. "Come and bring your woman with you."

Michael looked over at Celine. Her eyes were wide with fear. Michael whispered into her ear, "Stay down." Michael dropped Celine's hand stood up and took a step forward. "Just me, Kalfou, or whatever your name is. I don't know where…"

Celine stepped out of the crowd, taking Michael's hand. "No, Michael. I won't let you face them alone."

Kalfou laughed as he walked toward the two of them. "Well, now, isn't this sweet?" His face lost all traces of a smile as he stood before them. "Come on!" He grabbed Celine's arm and jerked her away from Michael. "How did you escape? Wasn't your little black box comfortable?"

Michael jumped at Kalfou, grabbing at his cane, but he missed. Kalfou's movements were swift and graceful. Kalfou laughed. "I'm not that old man you met outside!"

"Let go of her, Kalfou. If you've hurt her, I'll…"

"You'll what? Ezilie's huge booming voice came from the throne. The dancers bowed low to the floor, whispering in awe, "Our Queen has come!" Ezilie, tall and slender walked regally down the steps of the altar, her eyes glaring at Michael. "You'll what?" Ezilie laughed. "You'll do nothing. You're powerless. Both of you! She turned to Kalfou. "Bring them to the *vève!*"

Kalfou took his cane and prodded Michael in the back, then turned to Celine. "You, too, Missy!" He herded the two of them to the middle of the hall. He looked at Celine, tapping his cane on the floor. "Recognize this?"

Celine looked down. The floor was etched with white paint; a huge heart, marked off with a grid of blocks, a dot in each one. "Ezilie's *vève!*"

Kalfou stood behind them shaking his head. "Look again!"

Michael squeezed Celine's hand when he saw a machete piercing the center of the heart. A shiver ran down his spine as he pulled Celine closer to him. "It's me she wants, not you."

"Quiet!" Ezilie stepped forward, honing her stare at Michael. "Well, well, well, you made it, I see. I'm a little surprised. I thought if the Cucumber didn't kill you, Mauvais surely would."

Celine squeezed Michael's arm. "Mauvais?" She looked at Michael, noticing the open bleeding wound on his shoulder for the first time. "Oh, Michael, what did he do to you?" He winced, dropping his shoulder when she touched his collarbone.

Ezilie stood in front of them, staring hard at Celine then looked back at Michael, a sneer curling her lips. "From the looks of it, he nearly

did. Too bad, you know. He had such a nice family reunion planned."
She leaned in closer to Michael's face. "But we still have plenty of time
for that."

Celine stepped toward Ezilie. "You're evil! Why would you do that
to him?" Kalfou grabbed Celine's shoulder with an iron fist and jerked
her back, giving her a sharp jab with his cane.

Ezilie reached out and gently touched Celine's chin with a long
bony finger. "Oh my dear, don't you see how special you are to me?"

Celine pulled away from Kalfou, her anger propelling her forward.
"If I'm so special, why did you let that old woman give me Zombi's
Cucumber? You knew she wanted to kill me. Is that what you want?
For me to die?"

Kalfou raised his cane to strike Celine again, but Ezilie raised her
hand, stopping him in mid-air. She looked back at Celine, a smile
painted on her face. "Oh, but my dear, I had to silence you somehow."
She stepped closer to Celine, her face within inches of hers. "You've
broken too many rules." Ezilie's eyes flickered red. "This is all your
grandmother's fault. You can thank her. She broke the vow of silence by
telling you the secrets too soon. You weren't ready!" She reached down
and grabbed Celine's hand, but Celine jerked back. "She gave you that
ring, even told you about Zombi's Cucumber. Too much, too soon!
I thought a little breath of my special powder would slow you down,
but you didn't stop there, oh no! You broke your promise of silence by
telling that police woman everything!"

Celine narrowed her eyes, staring at Ezilie. "Yes, and Simone
DaQuin told me things I needed to know; things that..."

Ezilie screamed. "Things that she should NEVER have told you! I
will deal with her AND that grandmother of yours all in good time,
but for now YOU will answer for all of the crimes: your grandmother's,
Simone's AND yours!" She shrugged her shoulders, the silver necklaces jingling as she moved. "It didn't have to be this way. If you just
would've left well enough alone, that little bit of Cucumber would've
never hurt you; maybe a little headache, a stomach ache. It would've
passed, but you just couldn't keep your mouth shut, could you? You
just had to keep asking questions and telling secrets so, you left me no
choice. I let the Cucumber burn its way through your body and eat
into your soul." Ezilie smiled. "You've been a very bad girl, Celine, and

you'll have to be punished for it. Don't worry. I'll forgive you when I'm done. When I'm satisfied that you've learned your lesson, I'll send you back..." She looked at Michael. "...without him of course." She looked back at Celine. "You see, it's not just that you told my secrets, it's that you told HIM!"

She turned to Michael, the pupils of her eyes becoming narrow slits. "You! The seed of the Beauvoir family, she told YOU those secrets! How long did you think I would let your little love affair last? One of MY children? With a Beauvoir? A family filled with hate for my people? How long would it take for you to start using those secrets against her? Did you think I would just hand over all my power to you through her?" Ezilie laughed. "I knew that you would follow her." She laughed. "All I had to do was show you her dying face in the moon and you went racing off to save her. You fool! You swallowed one of the most potent doses of the Cucumber ever given! I got you here, and now I'm done with you." She flicked the back of her hand at Michael and turned to Kalfou. "Take him back to Mauvais!" She looked at his shoulder, then down between his legs. "Let him finish what he started!"

Celine's face fell. "No! Ezilie, please!" She dropped to her knees, and buried her face in the hem of Ezilie's robe, crying. "Please, I'm begging you. Don't do this! I'll do anything you want, just please don't send him back there!"

Michael knelt next to Celine, gently pulling her into his chest. "Ezilie, I've done everything you told me to do, so please let Celine go home and I'll..."

Ezilie threw her head back and laughed. "...You'll what? Do you really think that YOU can decide what YOU'LL do?" She turned to Celine. "Both of you are pathetic! Neither of you will dictate anything to me! You are in my courtroom and I am your judge." Ezilie pointed at the circle of panting, sweaty dancers kneeling along the wall. "These are my people, my faithful, loyal children who have suffered because of the Beauvoir family." She turned back to Michael, her eyes filled with hate. "These are the souls of the people your family enslaved, tortured, and then discarded like trash!" She turned to Celine. "These people are your tribe; your sisters and brothers. How can you turn your back on them? How can you betray them by revealing their ancient mysteries to a man who carries such hatred in his blood for them?"

Celine looked up, tears streaming down her cheeks. "Please, Ezilie. I plead for mercy from you. Punish me! You're right; I did share those secrets. I broke the rule, but Michael has done nothing wrong. He's done everything he can to leave his family's cruelty behind and start a new life for himself. He's not like the others! If he didn't love me, would he have come here? Risked his life to save mine? He's..."

"Silence, you traitor! You've admitted your fault and you dare to speak? Kalfou will be your voice! Stand up and listen!" Celine and Michael stood up as Ezilie turned to Kalfou. "We begin!" Ezilie held her head high and began to walk around the circle of dancers.

In low whispers, the people reached out to touch the hem of her robe chanting, *"Pa pavoa metres Ezilie Dantur!"*

Kalfou leaned in to Celine whispering. "If you want him to live, keep your mouth shut!" Kalfou raised his cane over his head and chanted in a loud baritone voice: *"N'a remercie, n'a remercie*, we give thanks!"

The drummers pounded out the cadence as the people stood up and chanted back, *"To Our Great God we give thanks, Après BonDye's remercie, yo!"*

Ezilie smiled seductively. Then in a low resounding voice, she began. "This is Hall of the Great BonDye, our one God, the Great God over all the Gods, who called order out of chaos and danced all things to life. When the cosmic drama was finally set into place, BonDye grew tired and named Mawu, the wet and seductive moon Goddess, as guardian of the night and Lissa, the erect and powerful sun God, as guardian of the day. BonDye yawned, knowing that all was right with the world and fell into a forever and peaceful sleep.

"Ah, but my children, all was not right with the world. While BonDye slept, Lissa burned with desire for the cool and flirtatious Mawu. One day Lissa's burning desire roared into lust and he raced across the sky into the night, catching the beautiful Mawu in his hot fingers. Mawu, who had secretly desired him all along, welcomed him into her and they made long and delicious love. So great was their love that they tore a great black hole in the sky, giving birth to their children; seven pairs of twins, the African Powers. Fulfilled and happy, Mawu and Lissa returned to their sky and left their children to rule the Earth."

Ezilie stopped and pointed to the ceiling and spoke in a loud, commanding voice. "I, Ezilie Dantor, royal child of Mawu and Lissa, equal sister to Ezilie Mansur, claim my right to judge all those who have broken my laws and hurt my Earthly children." Michael and Celine looked up into a burst of flames eating away at the ceiling like a huge hungry mouth. Michael threw his arms around Celine pulling her down to the floor as flames and ash fell at their feet.

Kalfou laughed and prodded them with his cane. "Stand up! Now!" Celine looked up into a pitch black starless night, took Michael's hand and together they stood up.

Ezilie spoke majestically. "Behold my parents! Mawu and Lissa are one again!" Celine whimpered with fear, tears streaming down her cheeks. The sun and the moon had disappeared, leaving a huge black orb, its swollen pupil surrounded by fine wisps of silver light and copper-colored dust. "Tonight justice will be served, swift and merciless; I deliver judgment on these two!"

Michael pulled Celine to him, holding her tightly. He whispered softly into her ear, his voice trembling, "No matter what happens, please remember, I will always love you."

Kalfou thrust his cane in between them, forcing them apart. "Kneel, both of you!" Celine kneeled but Michael glared at Kalfou defiantly. Kalfou stepped to Michael and growled. "Kneel or I'll hurt her, hurt her bad!" Celine reached up and gently touched Michael's hand. He kneeled reluctantly, getting as close to Celine as he dared.

Ezilie turned and walked slowly toward them. She pointed a long and accusing finger at Michael. "We have before us this man, a descendant of the family Beauvoir, a murderous and sadistic people who have a long history of slavery and torture and continue even to this day to use their power and influence to destroy." She lowered her finger and trained her icy stare on Celine. "He has claimed this woman as his own, one of our tribe, and she has given him everything; fallen in love with him and has told him many of the great secrets of our tribe. Together, they pose a deadly threat to future generations of our people! By tribal law they both should be put to death. What say you, my people?"

Screams of hate rose from the crowd, their voices screeching. Crying and cursing belched forth. Ezilie stood motionless, a smug smile across her face, as the dancers wailed and tore their clothes, raging and spitting at Michael and Celine. "He killed my baby! I was beat to death with his whip!" Michael dropped his head, filled with shame. "She's a traitor! Kill them both!" Celine sobbed.

Ezilie turned to Kalfou slyly. "What say you in defense of these two before I pass judgment?"

Kalfou tossed his long hair back and looked at Celine. "Ezilie, my Queen and my wife, you are correct in your accusation. This woman has indeed revealed tribal secrets, but it was her grandmother that broke the law. Her grandmother revealed the secrets to her before she was ready and just as any child would, she told those secrets in innocence."

Ezilie stared at Celine icily but nodded. "Yes, I can see what you are saying is true, but..."

Kalfou rushed without allowing Ezilie to say anything more. "Your child Simone Daquin, you know that she is a habitual law-breaker, one that you have tried for years to capture inside this great Hall. Shrewd is that one, She has victimized many, many of your children."

Ezilie looked at Kalfou, her eyes red with anger. "I will get her here. Someday she won't be expecting me and I WILL get her here!"

Kalfou nodded. "Oh yes, my Queen, I have no doubt that someday soon that one will feel your wrath, but see the child that kneels before you? She is your child, beautiful, bright, innocent, and a descendant of great teachers and healers; from your lineage, Ezilie, from your seed. As I can see, she has only broken one law and that is to have fallen in love with your enemy, a Beauvoir.

"I do remember another time when one of your children fell in love with a Beauvoir; Adele who had her child by him. In your great benevolence, did you not forgive her? And did you not love the child that she had? Oh, great and generous Queen, you loved her sweet Celeste as you have loved each of the descendants of Adele. The last of those descendents kneels before you now, asking for your forgiveness and mercy."

Kalfou turned and looked at Michael. "Ezilie, my Queen and my life, the Beauvoirs are a wicked and evil clan, just as you have proclaimed, responsible for the deaths and destruction of many of your children, but there is one small fact that you have overlooked with regard to this one. This man is also the direct descendant of your family line, a descendent of Adele's. Even though he carries the Beauvoir name, he also carries the blood of Adele. She has visited him in dreams, blessed him, loved him. He has even painted her portrait, Ezilie. No Beauvoir would ever do that! How can you harm him? To destroy him is to destroy a part of Adele. Surely, my great Queen, you see that?"

Ezilie glared at Kalfou, her eyes flashing red. "My love for Adele, that was long ago, all of it long ago; it was a mistake for me to love her so dearly. I should've listened to her mother, my favorite child, Marie LaVeau. I should've destroyed Adele's bloodline. It's done nothing but brought me great pain. It's time to start over. I will destroy both of these and start anew!"

Kalfou shook his head. "Oh, but my sweet Ezilie, I can see the pain that you feel for your people! It increases my love for you! The sword that pierces your heart is heavy and we are grateful for the burden that you carry, but in your ardent love you have once again forgotten." Ezilie's eyes softened as Kalfou continued. "You've tried to start over before. The child's name was Fremanse, Adele's grandchild. You tortured her with snakes. Their venomous bites were slow and painful, but at the very point of death, you were overcome with love for the child and let her go. Do you not remember?" He turned and nodded to Celine. "You even tried to prevent this one from ever being born. You blocked her mother's womb, but in the end you relented. And then again when she was just a sweet baby, you called her into the swamp. Do you remember? You nearly drowned her amongst the reeds in the undercurrent, but at the last moment, you couldn't do it; your love for her was so great. You've tried to destroy Adele's bloodline before, but you could not do it. My Queen, the love you have for your children is strong and everlasting. You are a great and generous mother and could never allow their destruction."

Ezilie turned her red eyes onto Michael. "Then I will destroy every one who carries the Beauvoir name; the name that reminds me of all the hate and evil that has tortured and hurt my people; the name that stole my Adele from me! There is no good that comes out of that name. Even the Lady Beauvoir deceived my Adele in the end. Not one letter did she ever send to Adele's lover. She kept them hidden, all the while lying to Adele that the letters had been sent. She lied! Lied because she was afraid that her family would disown her! Lied, because in the end money is always more important to a Beauvoir than love! Adele, my poor sweet Adele, died, never knowing that her dear friend, the Lady

Beauvoir, was a deceitful, greedy witch! No, the Beauvoir name should be erased for all time!"

Kalfou nodded his head again. "You are right, my great Queen, the Beauvoirs are a wicked, selfish people and deserving of an eternity with Mauvais, but this one…" Kalfou walked around and faced Michael. "…this one is different. This woman speaks the truth when she claims that he has taken great steps to leave his vicious family. Maybe, my sweet one, the power of Adele's bloodline has finally taken root in this one. I must painfully remind you that if you destroy him, a part of you will be destroyed as well. Your people can not have you weakened. We need your strength, we need your…"

Ezilie screeched at Kalfou. "How dare you even suggest that I would be weakened by the loss of this vermin? Long ago, when Queen Marie LaVeau was on her deathbed, she begged me for vengeance for her daughter, Adele; that the Beauvoirs be rooted out and destroyed. Queen Marie and I made a pact, sealed in blood. I promised her the destruction of the Beauvoirs and she promised me a long line of healers from her family. You are right. I did fail in all of my attempts to destroy them, but this one…" She looked down at Michael. "He is the last of his line. If I kill him, there will be no children and that promise will be fulfilled…" She turned to Celine. "…and she will follow me forever!"

Celine screamed at Ezilie from her knees. "NO!" She stood up, her eyes leveling at Ezilie. "I WILL NOT!" She walked slowly toward Ezilie, her hands clenched in rage. "I denounce you! You are not the Queen I serve! My family since Adele has only served St. Ezilie, Ezilie Mansur, the good and kind mother, the ONLY mother!"

Celine's anger surprised Ezilie and pushed her backward. "What?" She screamed in a panic. "Kalfou, stop her!"

Celine screamed as she charged forward. "You tried to prevent me from ever being born? You tried to kill me as a child? What are you? You're no mother! You're a monster!" She stood directly in front of Ezilie, pulled her hand back and clawed at her face, leaving a scratch on her perfect cheek. "I will never follow you! Never! If you kill him, I will do everything I can to destroy you in return! Just as we struck Marie LaVeau's name from our family, I strike you out now!"

Ezilie fell back onto the floor, gasping for breath, holding her cheek. Two of the dancers ran to her side helping her up from the floor. She wailed like a wounded animal, her howls vibrating throughout the hall. Kalfou stepped in front of Celine. With his back to Ezilie he grabbed both Celine's arms, shaking her violently. "You dare to touch the Queen?" He pulled her roughly into his chest and whispered into her ear with a little laugh. "No one has ever dared do that!" He pushed her hard into Michael. When Celine looked back at Kalfou, she saw a sly smile curling the edge of his mouth. The smile disappeared from his face as he turned and rushed to Ezilie's side. "Oh, my Queen, my Queen!"

Ezilie screamed as tears of blood dripped from her eyes. "Kill them, my love. Kill them now!"

Kalfou laughed and Ezilie looked up into his face, her eyes transforming from red into yellow-green. "There's another way, my Queen; a way that will end this once and for all!"

Ezilie's wailing diminished as she turned slowly to face Celine. She spoke through gritted teeth. "Make them pay for what they've done! I will watch! All my people will watch and she goes first!"

Kalfou stepped in front of Celine. "Yes, she goes first!"

Celine took a step back as Michael grabbed at Kalfou's arm. Kalfou kicked Michael away, sending him down to the floor. He turned to Celine, grabbing her arm. "Give me your hand!"

Celine screamed as she struggled against him. Kalfou grabbed her left hand, wrestling the ring from her finger in one fluid motion. Michael stood up and grabbed for it, but Kalfou punched him hard into his chest with his cane and then pushed Celine down next to him. Kalfou turned and knelt in front of Ezilie. He quickly slipped the ring on her left hand. "My Queen, she will never touch you again. You now control the love that exists between these two from this day and forevermore. And, as long as you control that love, you control her!"

Ezilie looked down at the ring, a smile curling her lips. She looked down at Kalfou. "Oh you are wise, my sweet Kalfou. This will be much more fun!" She looked at Celine. "Kneel before me!" Like a puppet, Celine knelt before Ezilie, her body no longer her own. Celine whimpered, her head down, unable to say anything. Ezilie lifted her chin, glaring into her face. "You are now MY eternal beloved! You will do WHATEVER I want, WHENEVER I want it!" Ezilie looked up and frowned as she glared at Michael. "But what about him?"

Kalfou walked over to Michael and jerked him up to his knees. He held him there, his fingers digging into Michael's wounded shoulder. "My sweet Queen, this one owes you everything, but there is only one thing he has that is worthy of your greatness." Kalfou swiftly reached down and wrapped both of Michael's hands inside his, slowly squeezing down like a vise as he talked. "He is an artist. What better gift to give you…" Kalfou bore down with all his strength, breaking Michael's wrists and fingers. "…than his hands!" Michael screamed as Kalfou snapped Michael's palms in half, leaving him with deformed and mangled claws.

Celine, frozen on her knees was powerless to do anything as she heard Michael's bones crack. She fought with every muscle to scream when finally her voice rang out. "Stop! Please stop! Ezilie!" Ezilie laughed with delight as Kalfou stood up, leaving Michael buckled over, writhing in pain. He turned to Ezilie. "This punishment is better than death. She is your slave now and can never betray you again! He's been robbed of her love and robbed of his art. No woman would have this broken man, so there will be no children! Send them back and see if they can love each other now."

Ezilie smiled and walked over to Celine. "Oh, but I will have one more gift from her." Ezilie stood over Celine, her eyes boring into her. She drew her hand back and slapped Celine hard across the face, sending her sprawling across the floor. Celine gasped in pain, her face cut with three long gashes in her cheek. Ezilie laughed. "Something for you to remember me by! You will marry who I command! Your children will be mine and you will never, EVER disobey me again!" She looked at the ring on her left hand then turned to Kalfou smiling broadly. "Oh yes, I am at peace now. Kalfou…" She turned and touched his arm. "… you are my favorite, always my favorite."

He threw his arms around her and kissed her hard. "I would do anything for you, my Queen!"

Ezilie gave him a quick smile. "Later. Come to me and I will reward you with everything you desire." She looked at Michael and Celine and snarled. "Get them out of here!" She turned to the dancers. "We have defeated the evil amongst us. Let the celebration begin!" The drums pounded and the dancers poured onto the floor, screaming praises to

Ezilie and Kalfou. Ezilie ascended the altar and sat down on her throne, smiling as she watched her people dance.

Kalfou picked Michael up by his wounded shoulder then turned and grabbed Celine by her hair and walked across the hall, dragging them both. Michael stumbled forward, groaning in pain holding both his hands close to his chest. Celine screamed at Kalfou, grabbing at his feet. "Leave us alone! You're wicked and evil, just like her!"

Kalfou let go of her hair, spun her around and screamed into her face. "You want me to leave you alone? You're still alive only because of me! Now shut up and help me get him out of here!" Michael fainted as Kalfou angrily propped Michael's arm behind his neck.

Celine ran to Michael's side and gently eased her shoulder up under his other arm. Tears ran down her cheeks as she whispered softly to Michael. "Stay with me, Michael. Please, stay with me." Michael moaned as they made their way through the dancers and toward the door.

When they reached the door, Kalfou looked back at Ezilie and nodded. "You're in luck. She's not watching." He turned to Celine. "We can go another way." He pointed to a large metal grate in the wall. "Hurry, before she sees us!"

Celine shook her head as she studied the grate. "Where does that go?"

Kalfou dragged Michael along. "Come on! It'll get you out of here!" When they reached the grate, Kalfou and Celine eased Michael to the floor. When Kalfou pulled the grate from the wall, he turned to Celine. "You first."

Celine shook her head. "No! Why should I trust you?"

Kalfou sneered. He reached over and grabbed Celine behind her neck and jerked her face into his. "Because you have to! You want to stay here? Do you have any idea what she'll do to you? She's a master at torture! Snakes? Drowning? The Cucumber? Sweetie, that's nothing!" Kalfou's face broke into a grin as he eased his grip only slightly. "Besides, I'm fascinated with you. No one's ever done what you did to that bitch!" He ran his lips down her neck then looked back into her eyes.

Celine struggled but he tightened his grip. "I want you to live..." He looked over at Michael. "...him too. It'll be great fun to watch the two of you go through the shitstorm she has planned for you. Maybe when it's all over, you'll beg for me instead of him." He pulled her to him and kissed her, forcing his tongue deep into her mouth. Celine fought against him until he finally let her go. He laughed as he prodded her forward. "Now go!" Celine squatted down and inched her way through the hole. "When you get in there, you're gonna have to pull him while I push him through." Kalfou turned to the nearly-unconscious Michael. "Okay, now you."

Michael sputtered between waves of pain. "You bastard! How could you do this to us?"

Kalfou pushed him through the hole as Celine pulled. "Shut up, man. She'll hear you!" Kalfou looked behind him as he crawled into the hole after them, pulling the grate closed as he disappeared into the tunnel.

Celine and Kalfou carefully put Michael's arms around their shoulders again and dragged him, nearly-unconscious, through the long dark tunnel. The narrow cave grew in height as they inched along. Slowly, they were able to stand up. A soft light cast shadows on the tunnel walls, making it easier to see the way. Celine noticed that Kalfou was beginning to pant; his steps becoming slower. She looked over at him. His smooth face was becoming wrinkled and tired. After what seemed like hours, they came to a mud pool. Kalfou turned to Celine. His voice rattled as he said, "Put him down and soak his hands in there. It'll help with the pain." He stood up slowly, straightening his back. "Just stay here. I'll be right back."

Celine looked at Kalfou, his smooth face suddenly older. Streaks of gray ran through his long hair. "Where are you going?"

Kalfou stepped away from them. "If you hear anything, don't move! Got it?"

Celine shook her head. "I knew you'd leave us! What's in this tunnel?" But it was too late Kalfou had already disappeared into the darkness.

Celine fought back tears as she helped Michael place his hands in the cool mud. "Oh Michael, I'm so sorry! So sorry for all of this! I love you Michael, no matter what she says!"

Michael shook his head as he looked up into Celine's face, her cheek cut, bleeding and bruised. He whispered through waves of pain. "I should've never let you leave."

Celine cried. "Shh, we're here together now." She lowered his hands into the cool mud.

As soon as it touched his skin, he could feel the fire in his bones begin to wash away. He took a deep breath. "We have to…" He panted. "…

get out of here. We can't trust Kalfou. He's probably…" Michael paused, taking a breath. "…going to give us to Mauvais anyway. Can you see another way out?"

Celine looked around. "Not really. The light gets brighter up ahead but I don't know where it leads."

Michael managed to sit up, the pain in his hands growing less. "Maybe if we go now before he gets back we could find a way to…"

The two of them heard a low, repetitive thud coming toward them. Celine reached over and grabbed Michael as they looked back into the dark tunnel. A deep rasping voice echoed from the darkness "Not without me, you don't!"

Celine frowned and looked back at Michael. "Who is that?" An old hunched over black man, his white hair cropped close to his head, came hobbling toward them. He wore a shoulder bag and leaned on a gnarled walking cane as he toddled along.

"Papa Legba at your service." He knelt next to her, took her hand in his and turned it palm up. "Here's a little gift for you!" He stuck out his tongue and dropped the ring into her hand.

When Celine saw the ring, she gasped, letting out a little laugh. "Is this really it? Is this my ring?" She turned and stared at him then picked up the ring to make sure it was the same one. The sapphires of the triple Fleur-de-Lys glittered, giving off a blue light of its own. The fire opal glowed as she slipped the ring back onto her finger.

Legba laughed. "I need payment for that. A kiss would do!"

Celine kissed his bristly, unshaven cheek then threw her arms around him, hugging him tightly. Legba hummed a pleasurable moan as he rubbed his hands up and down her back. "Oh, if only I were a younger man and if only we had the time."

Michael reached out with his elbow and pushed Legba away from Celine. "Hands off, Legba!"

Legba laughed as he sat back. "Hey, every woman needs her man to have good hands." He looked at Michael's muddy dripping misshapen claws. "All you got is stubs, brother. I'm just helping you out!"

Celine sat back, staring at Legba. "How did you get the ring back?"

"Never you mind about that, pretty lady. Right now, I've gotta work on him!" He turned to Michael. "Give me your hands."

Michael pulled away. "No! The mud is helping. Why should I trust you, anyway? How do I know you're not really Kalfou?"

"Cause I ain't, that's why. I ain't like my lying shit of a brother, Kalfou!" Legba reached into his side bag and pulled out a small stick. "I think your little lady here is gonna appreciate what I'm about to do. Here…" He shoved the stick to Michael's lips. "…bite down on this."

Michael's eyes grew wide as Legba quickly forced the stick between his teeth. He turned to Celine. "Hold him down." Legba pulled from his bag a handful of herbs and ashes. He spit on the mix, took Michael's hands forcing them open. Michael panted as Legba stared into his eyes. "This might hurt a little." Michael bit down hard as Legba drove his thumb straight into Michael's palms. Popping and cracking sounds echoed through the tunnel as Michael whimpered and then screamed. He threw his head back. Tears ran down his cheeks as the pain riveted through his body. Legba stopped and looked at Michael's hands closely. "Okay, let me see you move 'em."

Michael took a deep breath as he did his best to move his fingers. Celine laughed. "Michael, they're straightening out!"

"Shh! You're too loud!" Legba turned and looked behind him. "Stand up. You gotta go."

Exhausted, Michael struggled to stand. He wiggled his fingers and although his hands still ached, he knew that Legba had healed them. He looked at Legba, amazed. "Why? I don't understand…"

Legba smiled. "You'll pay me later…" He paused, turning a sly smile back at Celine. "…unless you want to pay me now." He looked back at Michael. "Tell you what, you give me the girl and we'll call it even."

Both Michael and Celine yelled at Legba, "NO!"

Legba's eyes grew wide. "Shh! Okay! Okay!" He looked back over his shoulder and then turned to Michael. "Listen man, you can't blame a guy for trying. I'll collect from you later. In the meantime, you take good care of her and don't ever be taking no Zombi Cucumber shit! I don't want to see you up in this place again, you dig?"

Michael smiled, reaching out his weak mangled hand out to Legba. "Thank you, Legba."

Legba looked at his empty hand then back at Michael. "I don't shake a man's hand unless there's something in it for me. Now hurry and get on outta here!" He pointed with his cane. "When you get to the end there, you'll see a hole through the ceiling. Crawl through it. After that you're on your own!" A hideous screech echoed down the length of the tunnel. Legba turned. "Shit! She must've realized the ring is gone. Go now, hurry!"

Michael and Celine stood up and ran to the end of the tunnel. Just as Legba described they came to a hole in the low ceiling. They helped each other up and over, collapsing on the hard, flat ground above. Celine stood up but Michael pulled her back down. "Wait! We have to watch out for any open graves." Breathless, Michael looked around in the dark, starless night. Celine reached for Michael through the abyss. Her voice began to break as she whispered. "Michael, what do we do now?"

Michael pulled her close to him and kissed her forehead. "Shh, we have to listen for their voices!"

Celine held him tight. "What? Whose voices?"

Michael whispered. "Listen." In the distance, Michael heard a woman crying and a prayer being said. *Oh Mary, I give you my heart. Please give it to your son while we wait for our children to return. Michael and Celine, hear our voices, chère. Hear our voices and come home.*

Michael laughed, turning to Celine. "Do you hear them?"

Celine began to cry and laugh at the same time. "Is that...?"

Michael stood up and grabbed Celine's hand, still feeling the remnants of pain. "Come on. This way!" Celine stood up and together they staggered toward the voices.

CHAPTER 24

It rained. The soft tapping of water on the tin roof settled into Mo-maw's soul and gave her a deep sense of peace. It was over now. The ordeal had passed. Now the rain brought a new beginning, a new life. The vast spread of the Atchafalaya Swamp echoed distant thunder. The sound billowed across the waters and came to the old woman's ears as a far away rumble. The raindrops skimmed across the swamp's surface like a thousand small pebbles dancing a ballet. Mo-maw took a deep breath. The smell was wonderful. The Earth was alive all around her and she could feel her part in it. She pushed the porch swing with her tiptoes, content, happy, relieved. She smiled. She knew the rain was a blessing from God, washing away the past.

Celine and Michael returned to her, safe but not unharmed. The old woman shuddered as the memory of that night came creeping back. Michael gasped as he dropped the glass and clutched his throat; the horrific gurgling sounds were unlike any that she'd ever heard. Tears welled in Mo-maw's eyes. *He sounded like he was drowning and dere was nothing I could do. Then he fell back, motionless, breathless, dead.* Luisah's screams still echoed in Mo-maw's ears as he lay there. *'Michael? Michael!'* Mo-maw closed her eyes as she remembered the waiting and praying, frozen as she counted away the seconds; ten, thirty, nearly a minute. Relief washed over her when he drew a long, life-giving breath and then fell into a deep coma. Luisah and Mo-maw worked quickly, positioning his body next to Celine's, making sure they kept his body cool, but not cold.

They waited. How many hours had she and Luisah knelt and prayed, the Saint Suaire constantly on their lips? How many hours had they waited and worried, anointing Michael and Celine with oils, wiping their fevered brows? Mo-maw wasn't sure how long their vigil lasted, but the night seemed endless in that dark and humid bedroom, watching the two of them breathing, sometimes in long deep breaths, sometimes in short broken gasps.

Then the long, painful moans started. Michael's shoulder dropped, his body twisting grotesquely, his legs thrashing like he was running as he lay on the bed. Luisah rushed to his side, calling his name, praying directly over him but then everything was quiet again. How long? How many hours? Then it was Celine's turn; another seizure and Mo-maw ran to her side trying to pour more Black Iris down her throat, but she fought, slapping the liquid across the room, her ring flying off her hand when she did. Luisah heard it hit something but didn't see where it landed. She ran to look for it but it was gone. Mo-maw closed her eyes, remembering the clock ticking away, praying in time with each beat. Tick, tick…*Now…*tick… *and at the hour… tick… of our death…*

Michael's screams pierced the cold, isolated silence; screams that weren't from fear, but from intense pain brought by something inhuman; something that was sadistic enough to inflict torture. She and Luisah ran to his side. *His hands, Oh Mon Dieu, his hands! What did dat to him?* Mo-maw fought back the tears. There had never been a time when she felt so helpless to ease someone's suffering; never until that night. *Our poor, poor Michael. I thought somet'ing horrible was killing him.*

Mo-maw opened her eyes and sighed, breathing in the fresh scent of the rain, remembering that moment when Luisah found the ring. When Luisah put it back on her hand, Celine laughed even though her eyes were still closed, trapped in that horrible world! *Oh, what a wonderful sound! And den Michael's hands began to relax and he smiled. Dat's when I knew then they were coming home!* Mo-maw and Luisah prayed loudly, calling to Michael and Celine, massaging their arms and legs. *Celine! Michael!* They yelled as loud as they could. It was Celine who came back first. She sat up as if something had forced her back upright. Almost immediately, Michael sat up as well. Both were panting like they'd been running a long way and air couldn't get into their lungs fast enough.

The pain for both of them was excruciating. Celine's face was bruised and three deep scratches were etched across her cheek. She was pale and weak; crying uncontrollably, checking to make sure the ring was on her finger. Michael suffered the most, though. A horrible gash emerged on his shoulder and although his hands weren't broken, they were crippled. Anytime something touched them he winced in pain.

That was over a week ago. All the physical scars were gone. The scratches on Celine's face had healed and Michael's hands, although they were still stiff, had relaxed. Mo-maw looked down, giving the swing a little push. *They still suffer, though. All their injuries are in spirit now. Who ever knew that dere were really two Ezilies? But it explains a lot; all her long silences, all dose times I thought my prayers fell on deaf ears. And who is dis Kal foo dey keep talking about?* Mo-maw shook her head. *So much I don't know, St. Ezilie. You and me, we've been together for so long. Maybe it's time for me to step down and let the young ones take over.*

Celine and Michael had told them most of what had happened, but Mo-maw knew a lot of the details had been too horrible for either one of them to share. That was easy to see when she watched the two of them whispering to each other when they thought she wasn't looking; tears, pain, sadness and love, lots of love. *Dat's all dey really need now. The love dey share will heal dem better than anyt'ing either Luisah or I can do for dem.*

The rain continued in a steady stream, slowing down only at intervals. Mo-maw smiled as she pushed the swing, knowing that her young patients would heal faster with this peaceful rain that blessed them all. In a few days, they would return to St. Maryville. Celine and Michael could finish their healing there. Luisah had called Michael's uncle, inviting him to stay with them for a few days. *Such a nice man, dis Uncle Alex. Yeah, it's a good idea to get home. Dere'll be people needing our help; always people needing help.*

Mo-maw was snapped out of her reverie when she heard laughter coming from inside the deer camp. As her aged body slowly turned in the swing, she saw Luisah, Celine and Michael coming through the door and onto the porch. "Well, you two iz up early! It's good to see you both laughing, chère!"

Celine walked over to her grandmother and kissed her on the forehead. "It feels good to be able to laugh, Mo-maw." Celine reached back and gently took Michael's hand. Michael smiled at Celine as the two sat on the front steps. Celine sat in front of him nestled into his chest; Michael wrapped his arms around her. He reached out and caught a few raindrops in his open flat palm; the cool healing waters dripping down his arm.

Mo-maw looked at Luisah, curious why she was smiling so broadly. "Well, what's got you so happy? I haven't seen you dis happy in a long time, Lala!"

"Oh Mama, it's the most wonderful thing, but I can't believe you don't sense it!"

Mo-maw gave a playful but suspicious look at her daughter. Then she turned and looked at Celine and Michael, both of them smiling at her as well. She looked back at Luisah. "Okay, what's goin' on?"

Luisah looked at Celine, her chocolate-brown eyes sparkling. "Celine, walk up the porch a ways and then walk back. Let's see if your Mo-maw can guess."

Celine did what she was told, walking slowly. Mo-maw squinted as she studied her granddaughter. All of a sudden, Mo-maw's eyes opened wide. "But Celine, chère! You iz pregnant!"

The other three laughed as Mo-maw quickly moved off the swing to hug Celine. "*Ça c'est bon!* Me, I can't believe it. Here, turn around. Let me see."

Luisah spoke up." I think it's still too soon to tell how long, but she already has a small belly."

Mo-maw wrinkled her brow as she walked around Celine. "Did you give her the blackberry root? We need to make sure that the Cucumber hasn't hurt the *bébé.*"

Luisah nodded. "Yeah, her tongue turned a bright pink, so I think it's all okay."

Mo-maw looked at Luisah. "Bright pink?" Luisah nodded. She looked at Celine. "You chewed it all?"

Celine nodded, wrinkling up her face in a look of disgust. "It tasted awful; nothing at all like blackberries."

Mo-maw nodded. "So it didn't taste sweet?" Celine shook her head.

Michael let out a little laugh. "It tasted sweet to me but when Celine tried it, her face looked like she'd bitten straight into a lemon!"

Mo-maw looked at Luisah and chuckled, "You let Michael try it?"

Luisah nodded. "Yeah, he wanted to taste it." Luisah turned to Michael. "You're not like most of the men I know, at least the ones from around here, that's for sure! They usually run as fast as they can when it comes to 'women' things. But then, not too many of them would've taken the Cucumber, either!"

Mo-maw shook her head smiling. "Well, I'm glad you're not pregnant, Michael. If it tasted sour and your tongue turned pink, we'd have a big problem, chère!" Mo-maw turned back to Celine. "Open your mouth, Celine, and show me your tongue." Celine opened her mouth and stuck out her tongue. Mo-maw blinked, tilting her head to get a closer look. "But Luisah, it's not just bright pink. It's strip-ed too!" Mo-maw began to giggle. Her giggling became louder and nearly uncontrollable.

Luisah smiled cautiously and walked to her mother's side. "What? Where?" She looked back at Celine. "Let me see?" Luisah looked at Celine's tongue. "Mama, I don't see any stripes." Luisah looked back at Mo-maw. She'd never heard her mother laugh so much like a young girl. Her laughter matched the rain's cheerful patter, like she and the swamp were together in some playful secret. Luisah couldn't wait any longer. "Mama, what's so funny?"

Mo-maw tried to control herself. She took her glasses off as she wiped the tears of joy from her face. "Oh, they're there, Luisah, bright pink stripes—lots of dem!" She let out another little giggle as she placed her glasses back on her face. She looked at all three of them and then she looked back at Celine.

Celine frowned at Mo-maw. "Is everything all right, Mo-maw? I mean, did the Zombi's Cucumber do something? You're starting to worry me. If Mama doesn't see them, does that mean something?"

Michael stood up and walked over to Celine's side, squeezing her hand, all traces of a smile gone. "Mo-maw, if there's something we need to know..."

Mo-maw shook her head. "No, no..." She looked down and put her hand gently on Celine's belly. "Chère, you iz havin' twin girls!"

Celine's green eyes grew wide as she looked down at her flat stomach. She looked at Michael as he put his arm around her. Her voice was quivering as she asked, "Twins?"

Michael looked at her stomach, stunned, his eyebrows arched. "Alex and my father. I guess..."

She turned to her mother. "Mama?"

Luisah smiled back. "Well, your Mo-maw Aurelia did predict that someday Mo-maw's arms would overflow with great grandchildren, but I sure never dreamed that she meant twins!"

Celine looked back at her grandmother. "But Mo-maw, are you sure? I mean, how can you tell?" There was just a moment's hesitation. Mo-maw answered with another giggle. Celine smiled and then they all began to giggle. It grew into uproarious laughter that echoed through the swamp. The joy resounded as the rain fell.

"Come on. Let's have some breakfast." Luisah walked toward the door as she turned to Celine. "I'll show you how to save da grease." Luisah went into the house and Celine obediently followed, but Michael slipped his arms around her waist and gently pulled her back.

His face beamed with absolute joy. "I love you, Celine." He kissed her deeply when Mo-maw walked up behind the two of them.

Still in a playful mood, Mo-maw tapped Michael on the head, interrupting the kiss. She feigned a serious expression. "Chère Michael, we need to talk." Michael gave her a puzzled look. Her smile brought more wrinkles across the old woman's face. "Wedding plans. Celine will be showing soon an' I won't be having any granddaughter of mine walking up to da altar wit a fat belly." As the door slammed behind them, no one saw the quiet eyes of the Atchafalaya crying tears of joy. Still, it rained.

"Follow your dreams. They know the way."
—Celine Bienaimée Dupré

Now that you've read *Cajun Moon*, have you been dreaming?
Tell me about it!
Find *Cajun Moon* on Facebook

www.ingramcontent.com/pod-product-compliance
Lightning Source LLC
Chambersburg PA
CBHW070217260626
47160CB00002B/580